Loves & Deaths

NOVELISTS' TALES
OF THE
NINETEENTH CENTURY:
FROM SCOTT TO HARDY

Selected and introduced
by
PETER BAYLEY

OXFORD UNIVERSITY PRESS
1972

Oxford University Press, Ely House, London W. 1

GLASGOW NEW YORK TORONTO MELBOURNE WELLINGTON
CAPE TOWN IBADAN NAIROBI DAR ES SALAAM LUSAKA ADDIS ABABA
DELHI BOMBAY CALCUTTA MADRAS KARACHI LAHORE DACCA
KUALA LUMPUR SINGAPORE HONG KONG TOKYO

PRINTED IN GREAT BRITAIN
AT THE UNIVERSITY PRESS, OXFORD
BY VIVIAN RIDLER
PRINTER TO THE UNIVERSITY

CONTENTS

Introduction vii

Sir Walter Scott

The Highland Widow 1

The Two Drovers 58

Charles Dickens

The Tuggses at Ramsgate 87

The Signal-man 108

William Makepeace Thackeray

Mr. and Mrs. Frank Berry 122

Dennis Haggarty's Wife 140

Anthony Trollope

La Mère Bauche 161

Malachi's Cove 192

George Meredith

The Case of General Ople and Lady Camper 213

Thomas Hardy

The Withered Arm 266

On the Western Circuit 295

INTRODUCTION

THIS collection of short stories of the nineteenth century is unusual and will, I hope, prove interesting. The tales have been chosen not to illustrate the history or development of the form but simply because they are by great novelists. For this reason none of the classic short stories of the period, by Hawthorne, Poe, Mrs. Gaskell, Wilkie Collins, Mark Rutherford, Bret Harte, and R. L. Stevenson, are included.

All of them reveal the characteristics of their authors in style, subject-matter, preoccupations, and attitudes. The two stories by Sir Walter Scott economically isolate two attitudes which lie behind most of his Scottish novels: his nostalgic affection for the dying romance and heroism of the Highlands and his balancing respect for English discipline, authority, and law. The conflict between them is in both cases the cause of the tragedy. The deep-seated national pride, the individualism and heroic spirit of the Highlander inevitably fall to the disciplined power of England. Scott's power of building up scene, character, and atmosphere is the more telling for the concentration he here imposed upon himself. They are at once genuinely epic and genuinely tragic tales, in their doom-laden steady movement to clearly forseen disaster. Scott gives grandeur to the tales by elevated language, especially in 'The Highland Widow' in which the enriched speech of the widow and her doomed son admirably suggests the old Gaelic tongue, and contributes also to the epic feel of the tale. The stories are given a further grandeur by their unimpassioned leisurely telling, noble passages of description, and by the summing-up, as it were, by which the tragedy is objectively scrutinized and assessed—in the one by the minister of Glenorchy, in the other by the judge in his charge to the jury. We are persuaded into forgetting that these heroic narratives concern a Highland deserter and a murdering drover.

Dickens's short stories are mostly frivolous sketches, absurd melodramas, or sickly-sweet anecdotes full of moral platitude.

He thought it 'a troublesome form', and that it was 'an arbitrary custom' that prescribed 'that a story should have a conclusion in addition to a commencement'. He was not good at the compression required for a short story, obviously thought it a slight and limited form, and took little trouble with it, although in the course of his writing he turned out scores of sketches and anecdotes for the periodicals he edited. But I could not omit the greatest creator of the century, and 'The Tuggses at Ramsgate' (in which the quoted remarks about the short story form appeared) and 'The Signal-man'—the latter a genuine short story—both have a conclusion. The former is early. Its jaunty fluency, exaggeration of idiosyncrasies of speech and character into high comic caricature, its veracity of detail and understanding of English life, together with its amused exposure of snobbery, class-consciousness, and pretentiousness, mark it as being of the same period as *Pickwick Papers*. It shares with that comic masterpiece inventive absurdity and tremendous energy and vivacity. The other tale, 'The Signal-man', shows quite another Dickens, as detailed in description but here sober and factual, to make convincing a macabre tale of supernatural warning.

We are always conscious of the personality of the author in reading Dickens: of his excessiveness, his exaggeration, his quirkish vision, and his involvement in his characters and their situations. We are equally conscious, but in quite different ways, of the author in the work of Thackeray. He is always adjusting our sympathies and controlling our response, forcing us to share his implied judgements. In both the stories I have chosen the narrator is closely in touch with the characters; indeed he is an old friend of the protagonists. He coolly observes the comic subjugation of Frank Berry and the pathetic humiliation of Dennis Haggarty by their wives. The world of these stories is a part of the world of *Vanity Fair*. It has some of the agonies and wickedness of that world, and also some of its virtues and simplicities—here, as so often, outraged. The vision is ironic, not tragic. If the bad are clever, they are helped by the stupidity or gullibility of the good. Although what happens in 'Dennis Haggarty's Wife' is dreadful—morbid enough for Strindberg to admire it—Thackeray keeps always at a cool distance, not requiring of his reader any intense involvement. These two stories show his professionalism as a comic writer and as a precise anatomizer of human snobbery and pretensions. He can set a scene or create a character in two sentences. Look at the description of the Berrys' apartment in Versailles with the 'eternal simper' of the plaster statues of Venus and Cupid (p. 125), of Mrs. Berry's 'small mouth with no lips—a sort of feeble pucker in the face' (p. 126) or of Mrs. Haggarty in glory (p. 142) and in dereliction (p. 149). And Thackeray's ear for dialogue, accent, and intonation is perfect: notice, for example, the immaculate differentiation of Captain Goff's Ulster speech in 'Mr. and Mrs. Frank Berry' from the accents of the Irish in 'Dennis Haggarty's Wife', and, in the former also, the contrast of Mrs. Berry's French with that of M. le Vicomte. Dickens's world, comic or tragic, is a poetic world of fantasy, and there is usually a feeling of obsession. In contrast, Thackeray generates, if not exactly a realistic world—because it has its element of fancy and exaggeration—a believable and palpable one in extremely efficient prose; but it *is* a prose world he presents.

Trollope's work is much more sober: straightforward, unassertive, and precise. It carries conviction of a serious and concerned understanding of human behaviour without either the *brio* of Dickens or Thackeray, or their respective fantasy and cynicism. Neutral—or unheightened rather—as his world is, Trollope acutely investigates some large areas of human feeling, and his work provides a good example of the art that conceals art. In 'La Mère Bauche', for example, the reader is drawn unsuspectingly through the light and casual tones of the opening into an enclosed world of growing tragedy. Gradually, unemphatically, the portrait of the stern, unyielding mother, who will destroy her son's beloved, is established. The style is plain. When the first clear simile comes—half-way through the story—its suggestive impact is the stronger: on the day of the return of the lover who has written to break off their understanding, Marie, unlike all the other inhabitants of Mme Bauche's hotel, 'now that the world was on the move lay hidden like a hare in its form'[1] (p. 174). And the Frenchness of the setting and characters is

[1] Lair.

conveyed by rather formal un-English dialogue, not exactly imitating French idiom but subtly suggesting it. Trollope's strength here, as in the novels, is in his authenticity. The very different world of 'Malachi's Cove' is as convincingly established. One of the reasons for my choice of these two stories was because of the complementary contrasts between them: the stormy north Cornish coast and inland southern France; a lonely girl who moves from rejecting to loving, another who moves from love to rejection to suicide; one story proceeding lightly into tragedy, the other set from the beginning for tragedy but drawing back from it. Trollope may be plain, but he is not unsubtle. La Mère Bauche comes to feel deep guilt for thwarting Marie, though she thinks to commute it by prayer and by material generosity. And in 'Malachi's Cove' Trollope shows a clear understanding of the petty miseries of peasant possessiveness and hatred between neighbours. 'I'm afraid it's no good anyone telling me that Thackeray is a better novelist than Trollope', wrote Walter Raleigh. 'It's not true. Trollope starts off with ordinary people, that bore you in life and in books, and makes an epic of them because he understands affection, which the others take for granted or are superior about.'

I would have liked to include a comic tale, say 'The Chateau of Prince Polignac', to show another aspect of Trollope's art: an amused irony, not bitter or cynical like Thackeray's. George Meredith, however, far outshone him in social comedy, with a dazzle and fancy that transform his mannered prose into a kind of poetry. 'The Case of General Ople and Lady Camper' brilliantly illustrates many of the powers of a prolific, indeed a verbose, author who, like Scott, seems at present to be acceptable—if at all—only in small doses. Meredith's stylishness and wit, his sense of the often charming ridiculousness of man the social animal, his imaginative verbal humour, and his flickering loving playfulness, make this story perhaps the most enjoyable of the whole collection. Its plot is a simple one, of confused purposes in a middle-aged courtship, but it is enriched by Meredith's mischievous powers of observation and glittering sense of fun. Both may be observed in the way he extends military metaphors through the whole length of the story, using it for all General

Ople's embarrassments, set-backs and aspirations. Yet Meredith's shrewd understanding of human beings informs the whole story, mannered though it is, making it also a serious discussion of love and self-love, and of compatibility and comradeship in marriage. Indeed, it is a moral tale: Lady Ople educates the love-struck general in true understanding by a series of comic humiliating tests.

Meredith's long story is set in upper-class London society in the eighteen-seventies when it was written. Hardy deals with a remote provincial world considerably earlier in the century. Although in one story given here a young London barrister appears, Hardy's stories chiefly concern labouring or farming folk of Wessex. His tales are unsophisticated in comparison with Meredith's: they have melodramatic plots of betrayed girls, unwanted pregnancies, and illegitimate offspring, and depend on coincidence or chance for their *dénouements.* Such a description applies equally well to Hardy's greatest novels. He is a great writer despite these crudities. His short stories tend to be either fairly primitive anecdotes—like Trollope's 'Malachi's Cove'—or as it were full-length novels compressed into eight or nine thousand words. Those I have chosen were originally written for magazines, and the titles of the collections in which they later appeared—*Wessex Tales* and *Life's Little Ironies*—suggest useful identifications of them. 'The Withered Arm' is a macabre tale, drawn from real life—though Hardy himself said that the real details were 'in some respects more gruesome' than in the story as he told it. It is a harrowing story, in which Hardy's concern for the wronged and his understanding of unhappiness are clearly expressed. And it is very characteristic of Hardy, almost an epitome of a Wessex novel, with its tragic outcome, its accurate and loving detail of country life and its use of landscape for symbolic as well as narrative purpose—here, Egdon Heath, as in *The Return of the Native.* Its detached tone, that of a dispassionate recorder of known events, makes an improbable tale of bewitchment and coincidence convincing and more affecting. It is a beautifully balanced story. Notice how, gradually, our concern shifts from the wronged Rhoda Brook, now 'a thin fading woman of thirty', to the wronged wife Gertude Lodge, and finally back again; and how the story ends, as it began, with Rhoda on her own, her head pressing against a cow's side, and the sound of the alternating 'purr of the milk streams' in Farmer Lodge's eighty-cow dairy.

Hardy's second wife thought 'On the Western Circuit' the best of all his stories. It is certainly the most subtle, and its irony is more controlled so that, but for the misery of the ending, it might almost have been a Meredith plot. Hardy succeeds surprisingly well here—better than in his novels—in depicting middle-class people. Who could guess that the words 'Anna is really very forward—and he very wicked and nice' were words spoken by a Hardy character: a young married woman just beginning to be impelled towards a young man by whom her maid is about to be infatuated and very soon seduced? The story, of a 'man who played the disturbing part in two quiet feminine lives', begins quietly, as it continues. From a comedy of mistake—the prolonged correspondence which links a London barrister, an illiterate Wiltshire maid, and her affectionate mistress—quietly emerges the certain unhappiness of yet another tragically mistaken marriage. The inevitability of events, once they are in train, is as strong here as in the novels, but the urbane setting and tone, the potentially comic plot of the letter-writing, and the conclusion—of acceptance not actual disaster—forbid the use of the word tragic. It is another of life's little ironies, but it quite powerfully suggests that world of mistaken decisions, irrevocable actions, and nullified hopes which Hardy characters frequent and which is not always a gross distortion of life.

I am sorry I could not include stories by Jane Austen, the Brontës, or George Eliot. The *juvenilia* of the first two would not do, and any stories of George Eliot brief enough to include—such as 'Brother Jacob'—are unworthy of her name. Apart from them the selection represents all the outstanding novelists of the nineteenth century, except Conrad and Henry James at the very end, who really belong to another era. The range is wide in all respects; from farce to sophisticated comedy of manners, from melodrama to tragedy; from Scotland of the days of the claymore, to Dublin and Paris of the post-Napoleonic period, to railway England; from rural Wessex to suburban London, from the

Cornish coast to the Pyrenees; from shepherds and drovers, grocers and signalmen, to barristers and generals and ladies of the (suburban) *haute-monde*. There is, too, a fair balance of subjects. Honour, racial pride, love, loyalty, snobbery, class-consciousness, faithlessness, and the tragedy of sexual infatuation and rebuff are among the themes discussed. I believe they are discussed so well that they are perfectly relevant today, although the last of the stories was written 80 and the first 150 years ago. All the kinds of short stories of the nineteenth century are represented, and so are all the great novelists of the period (with the unfortunate exception of the three women novelists). They offer an intriguing taste of their great writers, which, it is hoped, may induce a desire for further replenishment.

I have added some necessary notes and glossed unusual dialect words.

I am very grateful to Colin Dexter for his help and advice.

For permission to include the two stories by Thomas Hardy the publishers and I wish to thank the Trustees of the Hardy Estate and Macmillan & Co., London and Basingstoke.

University College, Oxford *Collingwood College, Durham*
March 1971

SIR WALTER SCOTT
(1771–1832)

'The Highland Widow' and 'The Two Drovers' both appear in *Chronicles of the Canongate* (1827), which Scott worked on after the death of his wife (on 14 May 1826). On 27 May of that year he wrote in his Journal: 'It is time that I should be up and doing . . . the necessity of exertion becomes apparent.' Shortly afterwards he wrote: 'I must try an *hors d'œuvre* . . . Mrs. Murray Keith's Tale of the Deserter, with her interview with the lad's mother, may be most affecting, but will hardly endure expansion.' In fact it had to endure expansion, and it is undeniably too long. Scott later wrote that the story was given 'very much as the excellent old lady used to tell the story' but that 'I cannot but suspect myself of having marred its simplicity by some of those interpolations which, at the time when I penned them, no doubt passed with myself for embellishments.' I have shortened it a little by removing the first half-dozen pages, which introduce Mrs. Bethune Balliol (who is based on Mrs. Murray Keith) and her 'Memorandum' about the short Highland tour which she undertook 'to relieve the dejection of spirits occasioned by a great family loss sustained two or three months before'. As the account of her meeting with the old Highland Widow unfolds, Mrs. Bethune Balliol drops out of the story until the very end, and from Chapter II onwards the story is direct narrative. In order to make room for this splendid tale in the volume, I have made some other cuts which I have indicated. They are 'embellishments' and I do not think I have excised anything of significance.

Chronicles of the Canongate purports to be a miscellany of stories collected by a Mr. Chrystal Croftangry, who lives in the Canongate, a part of old Edinburgh near Holyrood, and who tells of his life in the first five introductory chapters, introduces and describes Mrs. Bethune Balliol in Chapters VI and VII, and then sets down her tale of the deserter.

It is followed by 'The Two Drovers' which Scott tells us he heard from another old friend, George Constable (who was the original of Jonathan Oldbuck of Monkbarns, the Antiquary in the novel of that name). Constable, Scott thought, had been present at the trial at Carlisle of the original of Robin Oig.

The Highland Widow

CHAPTER I

Mrs. Bethune Balliol on her short Highland tour observed in the bare wilderness under Ben Cruachan in Argyll one large oak 'of extraordinary magnitude and picturesque beauty' growing some distance away under a great rock by a waterfall. She wished to go nearer to draw it, but the coachman Donald MacLeish was strangely reluctant. But she insisted, they drew nearer and she saw that there was 'a human habitation' there.

It was a hut of the least dimensions and most miserable description that I ever saw even in the Highlands. The walls of sod, or *divot,* as the Scotch call it, were not four feet high—the roof was of turf, repaired with reeds and sedges—the chimney was composed of clay, bound round by straw ropes—and the whole walls, roof and chimney, were alike covered with the vegetation of house-leek, ryegrass, and moss common to decayed cottages formed of such materials. There was not the slightest vestige of a kale-yard,[1] the usual accompaniment of the very worst huts; and of living things we saw nothing, save a kid which was browsing on the roof of the hut, and a goat, its mother, at some distance, feeding betwixt the oak and the river Awe.

'What man,' I could not help exclaiming, 'can have committed sin deep enough to deserve such a miserable dwelling!'

'Sin enough,' said Donald MacLeish, with a half-suppressed groan; 'and God he knoweth misery enough too;—and it is no man's dwelling neither, but a woman's.'

'A woman's!' I repeated, 'and in so lonely a place—What sort of a woman can she be?'

'Come this way, my leddy, and you may judge that for yourself,' said Donald. And by advancing a few steps, and making a sharp turn to the left, we gained a sight of the side of the great broad-breasted oak, in the direction opposed to that in which we had hitherto seen it.

'If she keeps her old wont, she will be there at this hour of the day,' said Donald, but immediately became silent, and pointed

[1] Vegetable-garden.

with his finger, as one afraid of being overheard. I looked, and beheld, not without some sense of awe, a female form seated by the stem of the oak, with her head drooping, her hands clasped, and a dark-coloured mantle drawn over her head, exactly as Judah is represented in the Syrian medals as seated under her palm-tree. I was infected with the fear and reverence which my guide seemed to entertain towards this solitary being, nor did I think of advancing towards her to obtain a nearer view until I had cast an inquiring look on Donald; to which he replied in a half-whisper—'She has been a fearfu' bad woman, my leddy.'

'Mad woman, said you,' replied I, hearing him imperfectly; 'then she is perhaps dangerous?'

'No—she is not mad,' replied Donald; 'for then it may be she would be happier than she is; though when she thinks on what she has done, and caused to be done, rather than yield up a hair-breadth of her ain wicked will, it is not likely she can be very well settled. But she neither is mad nor mischievous; and yet, my leddy, I think you had best not go nearer to her.' And then, in a few hurried words, he made me acquainted with the story which I am now to tell more in detail. I heard the narrative with a mixture of horror and sympathy, which at once impelled me to approach the sufferer and speak to her the words of comfort, or rather of pity, and at the same time made me afraid to do so.

This indeed was the feeling with which she was regarded by the Highlanders in the neighbourhood, who looked upon Elspat MacTavish, or the Woman of the Tree, as they called her, as the Greeks considered those who were pursued by the Furies,[2] and endured the mental torment consequent on great criminal actions. They regarded such unhappy beings as Orestes and Œdipus[3] as being less the voluntary perpetrators of their crimes than as the passive instruments by which the terrible decrees of Destiny had been accomplished; and the fear with which they beheld them was not unmingled with veneration.

I also learned further from Donald MacLeish that there was some apprehension of ill luck attending those who had the

[2] The avenging deities of Greek mythology.

[3] Greek tragic characters, both of whom killed a parent: Orestes his mother and Oedipus his father, as a consequence of which a long period of doom hung over their families. (See the plays by Sophocles and Æschylus.)

boldness to approach too near or disturb the awful solitude of a being so unutterably miserable; that it was supposed that whosoever approached her must experience in some respect the contagion of her wretchedness.

It was therefore with some reluctance that Donald saw me prepare to obtain a nearer view of the sufferer, and that he himself followed to assist me in the descent down a very rough path. I believe his regard for me conquered some ominous feelings in his own breast, which connected his duty on this occasion with the presaging fear of lame horses, lost linch-pins, overturns, and other perilous chances of the postillion's life.

I am not sure if my own courage would have carried me so close to Elspat, had he not followed. There was in her countenance the stern abstraction of hopeless and overpowering sorrow, mixed with the contending feelings of remorse, and of the pride which struggled to conceal it. She guessed, perhaps, that it was curiosity, arising out of her uncommon story, which induced me to intrude on her solitude—and she could not be pleased that a fate like hers had been the theme of a traveller's amusement. Yet the look with which she regarded me was one of scorn instead of embarrassment. The opinion of the world and all its children could not add or take an iota from her load of misery; and, save from the half-smile that seemed to intimate the contempt of a being rapt by the very intensity of her affliction above the sphere of ordinary humanities, she seemed as indifferent to my gaze as if she had been a dead corpse or a marble statue.

Elspat was above the middle stature; her hair, now grizzled, was still profuse, and it had been of the most decided black. So were her eyes, in which, contradicting the stern and rigid features of her countenance, there shone the wild and troubled light that indicates an unsettled mind. Her hair was wrapped round a silver bodkin with some attention to neatness, and her dark mantle was disposed around her with a degree of taste, though the materials were of the most ordinary sort.

After gazing on this victim of guilt and calamity till I was ashamed to remain silent, though uncertain how I ought to address her, I began to express my surprise at her choosing such a desert and deplorable dwelling. She cut short these expressions of sympathy by answering in a stern voice, without the least change of countenance or posture, 'Daughter of the stranger, he has told you my story.' I was silenced at once, and felt how little all earthly accommodation must seem to the mind which had such subjects as hers for rumination. Without again attempting to open the conversation, I took a piece of gold from my purse (for Donald had intimated she lived on alms), expecting she would at least stretch her hand to receive it. But she neither accepted nor rejected the gift—she did not even seem to notice it, though twenty times as valuable, probably, as was usually offered. I was obliged to place it on her knee, saying involuntarily, as I did so, 'May God pardon you, and relieve you!' I shall never forget the look which she cast up to heaven, nor the tone in which she exclaimed, in the very words of my old friend, John Home—[4]

'My beautiful—my brave!'

It was the language of nature, and arose from the heart of the deprived mother, as it did from that gifted imaginative poet while furnishing with appropriate expressions the ideal grief of Lady Randolph.[5]

[4] 1722–1808, author of *Douglas*, a romantic tragedy based on a Scottish ballad.
[5] In the play, in which her son is slain.

CHAPTER II

ELSPAT had enjoyed happy days, though her age had sunk into hopeless and inconsolable sorrow and distress. She was once the beautiful and happy wife of Hamish MacTavish, for whom his strength and feats of prowess had gained the title of MacTavish Mhor.[1] His life was turbulent and dangerous, his habits being of the old Highland stamp, which esteemed it shame to want anything that could be had for the taking. Those in the Lowland line who lay near him, and desired to enjoy their lives and property in quiet, were contented to pay him a small composition, in name of protection money, and comforted themselves with the old proverb that it was better to 'fleech[2] the de'il than fight him.' Others, who accounted such composition dishonourable, were often surprised

[1] Great. [2] Flatter.

by MacTavish Mhor and his associates and followers, who usually inflicted an adequate penalty, either in person or property, or both. The creagh[3] is yet remembered in which he swept one hundred and fifty cows from Monteith in one drove; and how he placed the Laird of Ballybught naked in a slough, for having threatened to send for a party of the Highland Watch to protect his property.

Whatever were occasionally the triumphs of this daring cateran,[4] they were often exchanged for reverses; and his narrow escapes, rapid flights, and the ingenious stratagems with which he extricated himself from imminent danger, were no less remembered and admired than the exploits in which he had been successful. In weal or woe, through every species of fatigue, difficulty, and danger, Elspat was his faithful companion. She enjoyed with him the fits of occasional prosperity; and when adversity pressed them hard, her strength of mind, readiness of wit, and courageous endurance of danger and toil are said often to have stimulated the exertions of her husband.

Their morality was of the old Highland cast, faithful friends and fierce enemies: the Lowland herds and harvests they accounted their own, whenever they had the means of driving off the one or of seizing upon the other; nor did the least scruple on the right of property interfere on such occasions. . . .

. . . But those days of perilous though frequently successful depredation began to be abridged, after the failure of the expedition of Prince Charles Edward.[5] MacTavish Mhor had not sat still on that occasion, and he was outlawed, both as a traitor to the State and as a robber and cateran. Garrisons were now settled in many places where a redcoat had never before been seen, and the Saxon war-drum resounded among the most hidden recesses of the Highland mountains. The fate of MacTavish became every day more inevitable; and it was the more difficult for him to make his exertions for defence or escape, that Elspat, amid his evil days, had increased his family with an infant child, which was a considerable incumbrance upon the necessary rapidity of their motions.

At length the fatal day arrived. In a strong pass on the skirts

[3] Cattle-stealing raid. [4] Cattle-thief, free-booter. [5] In 1745.

of Ben Cruachan, the celebrated MacTavish Mhor was surprised by a detachment of the Sidier Roy.[6] His wife assisted him heroically, charging his piece from time to time; and, as they were in possession of a post that was nearly unassailable, he might have perhaps escaped if his ammunition had lasted. But at length his balls were expended, although it was not until he had fired off most of the silver buttons from his waistcoat, and the soldiers, no longer deterred by fear of the unerring marksman, who had slain three, and wounded more of their number, approached his stronghold, and, unable to take him alive, slew him, after a most desperate resistance.

All this Elspat witnessed and survived, for she had, in the child which relied on her for support, a motive for strength and exertion. In what manner she maintained herself it is not easy to say. Her only ostensible means of support were a flock of three or four goats, which she fed wherever she pleased on the mountain pastures, no one challenging the intrusion. In the general distress of the country, her ancient acquaintances had little to bestow; but what they could part with from their own necessities they willingly devoted to the relief of others. From Lowlanders she sometimes demanded tribute rather than requested alms. She had not forgotten she was the widow of MacTavish Mhor, or that the child who trotted by her knee might, such were her imaginations, emulate one day the fame of his father, and command the same influence which he had once exerted without control. She associated so little with others, went so seldom and so unwillingly from the wildest recesses of the mountains, where she usually dwelt with her goats, that she was quite unconscious of the great change which had taken place in the country around her, the substitution of civil order for military violence, and the strength gained by the law and its adherents over those who were called in Gaelic song 'the stormy sons of the sword.' Her own diminished consequence and straitened circumstances she indeed felt, but for this the death of MacTavish Mhor was, in her apprehension, a sufficing reason; and she doubted not that she should rise to her former state of importance, when Hamish Bean (or Fair-haired James) should be able to wield the arms of his father. If, then,

[6] The Red Soldier, redcoats, i.e. English soldiery.

Elspat was repelled rudely when she demanded anything necessary for her wants, or the accommodation of her little flock, by a churlish farmer, her threats of vengeance, obscurely expressed, yet terrible in their tenor, used frequently to extort, through fear of her maledictions, the relief which was denied to her necessities; and the trembling goodwife who gave meal or money to the widow of MacTavish Mhor wished in her heart that the stern old carline[7] had been burnt on the day her husband had his due.

Years thus ran on, and Hamish Bean grew up, not indeed to be of his father's size or strength, but to become an active, high-spirited, fair-haired youth, with a ruddy cheek, an eye like an eagle, and all the agility, if not all the strength, of his formidable father, upon whose history and achievements his mother dwelt, in order to form her son's mind to a similar course of adventures. But the young see the present state of this changeful world more keenly than the old. Much attached to his mother, and disposed to do all in his power for her support, Hamish yet perceived, when he mixed with the world, that the trade of the cateran was now alike dangerous and discreditable, and that if he were to emulate his father's prowess it must be in some other line of warfare more consonant to the opinions of the present day.

As the faculties of mind and body began to expand, he became more sensible of the precarious nature of his situation, of the erroneous views of his mother, and her ignorance respecting the changes of the society with which she mingled so little. In visiting friends and neighbours he became aware of the extremely reduced scale to which his parent was limited, and learned that she possessed little or nothing more than the absolute necessaries of life, and that these were sometimes on the point of failing. At times his success in fishing and the chase was able to add something to her subsistence; but he saw no regular means of contributing to her support, unless by stooping to servile labour, which, if he himself could have endured it, would, he knew, have been like a death's-wound to the pride of his mother.

Elspat, meanwhile, saw with surprise that Hamish Bean, although now tall and fit for the field, showed no disposition to enter on his father's scene of action. There was something of the

[7] Hag.

mother at her heart which prevented her from urging him in plain terms to take the field as a cateran, for the fear occurred of the perils into which the trade must conduct him; and, when she would have spoken to him on the subject, it seemed to her heated imagination as if the ghost of her husband arose between them in his bloody tartans, and, laying his finger on his lips, appeared to prohibit the topic. Yet she wondered at what seemed his want of spirit, sighed as she saw him from day to day lounging about in the long-skirted Lowland coat which the legislature had imposed upon the Gael instead of their own romantic garb, and thought how much nearer he would have resembled her husband had he been clad in the belted plaid and short hose, with his polished arms gleaming at his side.

Besides these subjects for anxiety, Elspat had others arising from the engrossing impetuosity of her temper. Her love of MacTavish Mhor had been qualified by respect and sometimes even by fear; for the cateran was not the species of man who submits to female government; but over his son she had exerted, at first during childhood, and afterwards in early youth, an imperious authority, which gave her maternal love a character of jealousy. She could not bear, when Hamish, with advancing life, made repeated steps towards independence, absented himself from her cottage at such season and for such length of time as he chose, and seemed to consider, although maintaining towards her every possible degree of respect and kindness, that the control and responsibility of his actions rested on himself alone. This would have been of little consequence, could she have concealed her feelings within her own bosom; but the ardour and impatience of her passions made her frequently show her son that she conceived herself neglected and ill used. When he was absent for any length of time from her cottage, without giving intimation of his purpose, her resentment on his return used to be so unreasonable that it naturally suggested to a young man fond of independence, and desirous to amend his situation in the world, to leave her, even for the very purpose of enabling him to provide for the parent whose egotistical demands on his filial attention tended to confine him to a desert in which both were starving in hopeless and helpless indigence.

Upon one occasion, the son having been guilty of some independent excursion, by which the mother felt herself affronted and disobliged, she had been more than usually violent on his return, and awakened in Hamish a sense of displeasure, which clouded his brow and cheek. At length, as she persevered in her unreasonable resentment, his patience became exhausted, and taking his gun from the chimney corner, and muttering to himself the reply which his respect for his mother prevented him from speaking aloud, he was about to leave the hut which he had but barely entered.

'Hamish,' said his mother, 'are you again about to leave me?' But Hamish only replied by looking at and rubbing the lock of his gun.

'Ay, rub the lock of your gun,' said his parent, bitterly. 'I am glad you have courage enough to fire it, though it be but at a roe-deer.' Hamish started at this undeserved taunt, and cast a look of anger at her in reply. She saw that she had found the means of giving him pain.

'Yes,' she said, 'look fierce as you will at an old woman, and your mother; it would be long ere you bent your brow on the angry countenance of a bearded man.'

'Be silent, mother, or speak of what you understand,' said Hamish, much irritated, 'and that is of the distaff and the spindle.'

'And was it of spindle and distaff that I was thinking when I bore you away on my back through the fire of six of the Saxon[8] soldiers, and you a wailing child? I tell you, Hamish, I know a hundredfold more of swords and guns than ever you will; and you will never learn so much of noble war by yourself as you have seen when you were wrapped up in my plaid.'

'You are determined at least to allow me no peace at home, mother; but this shall have an end,' said Hamish, as, resuming his purpose of leaving the hut, he rose and went towards the door.

'Stay, I command you,' said his mother; 'stay! or may the gun you carry be the means of your ruin—may the road you are going be the track to your funeral!'

'What makes you use such words, mother?' said the young man, turning a little back. 'They are not good, and good cannot come

[8] i.e. English.

of them. Farewell just now, we are too angry to speak together—farewell; it will be long ere you see me again.' And he departed, his mother, in the first burst of her impatience, showering after him her maledictions, and in the next invoking them on her own head, so that they might spare her son's. She passed that day and the next in all the vehemence of impotent and yet unrestrained passion, now entreating Heaven, and such powers as were familiar to her by rude tradition, to restore her dear son, 'the calf of her heart'; now in impatient resentment, meditating with what bitter terms she should rebuke his filial disobedience upon his return, and now studying the most tender language to attach him to the cottage, which, when her boy was present, she would not, in the rapture of her affection, have exchanged for the apartments of Taymouth Castle.[9]

Two days passed, during which, neglecting even the slender means of supporting nature which her situation afforded, nothing but the strength of a frame accustomed to hardships and privations of every kind could have kept her in existence, notwithstanding the anguish of her mind prevented her being sensible of her personal weakness. Her dwelling, at this period, was the same cottage near which I had found her, but then more habitable by the exertions of Hamish, by whom it had been in a great measure built and repaired.

It was on the third day after her son had disappeared, as she sat at the door rocking herself, after the fashion of her countrywomen when in distress or in pain, that the then unwonted circumstance occurred of a passenger being seen on the high-road above the cottage. She cast but one glance at him—he was on horseback, so that it could not be Hamish, and Elspat cared not enough for any other being on earth, to make her turn her eyes towards him a second time. The stranger, however, paused opposite to her cottage, and, dismounting from his pony, led it down the steep and broken path which conducted to her door.

'God bless you, Elspat MacTavish!'—She looked at the man as he addressed her in her native language, with the displeased air of one whose reverie is interrupted; but the traveller went on to say, 'I bring you tidings of your son Hamish.' At once, from

[9] Near Dundee.

being the most uninteresting object, in respect to Elspat, that could exist, the form of the stranger became awful in her eyes, as that of a messenger descended from Heaven, expressly to pronounce upon her death or life. She started from her seat, and with hands convulsively clasped together, and held up to heaven, eyes fixed on the stranger's countenance, and person stooping forward to him, she looked those inquiries which her faltering tongue could not articulate. 'Your son sends you his dutiful remembrance, and this,' said the messenger, putting into Elspat's hand a small purse containing four or five dollars.[10]

'He is gone, he is gone!' exclaimed Elspat. 'He has sold himself to be the servant of the Saxons, and I shall never more behold him! Tell me, Miles MacPhadraick, for now I know you, is it the price of the son's blood that you have put into the mother's hand?'

'Now, God forbid!' answered MacPhadraick, who was a tacksman,[11] and had possession of a considerable tract of ground under his chief, a proprietor who lived about twenty miles off—'God forbid I should do wrong, or say wrong, to you, or to the son of MacTavish Mhor! I swear to you by the hand of my chief that your son is well, and will soon see you; and the rest he will tell you himself.' So saying, MacPhadraick hastened back up the pathway, gained the road, mounted his pony, and rode upon his way.

[10] Equivalent to the English 'crown'—five shillings.

[11] An important tenant of a large area of land, some of which he sublet in small farms. Dr. Johnson wrote: 'Next in dignity to the laird is the tacksman.'

CHAPTER III

ELSPAT MACTAVISH remained gazing on the money, as if the impress of the coin could have conveyed information how it was procured.

'I love not this MacPhadraick,' she said to herself; 'it was his race of whom the Bard hath spoken, saying, Fear them not when their words are loud as the winter's wind, but fear them when they fall on you like the sound of the thrush's song. And yet this riddle can be read but one way: My son hath taken the sword, to win that with strength like a man which churls would keep him from with the words that frighten children.' This idea, when once it occurred to her, seemed the more reasonable, that MacPhadraick, as she well knew, himself a cautious man, had so far encouraged her husband's practices as occasionally to buy cattle of MacTavish, although he must have well known how they were come by, taking care, however, that the transaction was so made as to be accompanied with great profit and absolute safety. Who so likely as MacPhadraick to indicate to a young cateran the glen in which he could commence his perilous trade with most prospect of success, who so likely to convert his booty into money? The feelings which another might have experienced on believing that an only son had rushed forward on the same path in which his father had perished were scarce known to the Highland mothers of that day. She thought of the death of MacTavish Mhor as that of a hero who had fallen in his proper trade of war, and who had not fallen unavenged. She feared less for her son's life than for his dishonour. She dreaded on his account the subjection to strangers, and the death-sleep of the soul which is brought on by what she regarded as slavery.

The moral principle which so naturally and so justly occurs to the mind of those who have been educated under a settled government of laws, that protect the property of the weak against the incursions of the strong, was to poor Elspat a book sealed and a fountain closed. She had been taught to consider those whom they called Saxons as a race with whom the Gael were constantly at war, and she regarded every settlement of theirs within the reach of Highland incursion as affording a legitimate object of attack and plunder. Her feelings on this point had been strengthened and confirmed, not only by the desire of revenge for the death of her husband, but by the sense of general indignation entertained, not unjustly, through the Highlands of Scotland, on account of the barbarous and violent conduct of the victors after the battle of Culloden.[1] Other Highland clans, too, she regarded as the fair objects of plunder when that was possible, upon the score of ancient enmities and deadly feuds.

[1] 1746, when the Young Pretender was defeated by the Duke of Cumberland near Inverness. This marked the end of the 'Forty-Five'—the second and final uprising of the clans to reinstate the Stuart line.

The prudence that might have weighed the slender means which the times afforded for resisting the efforts of a combined government, which had, in its less compact and established authority, been unable to put down the ravages of such lawless caterans as MacTavish Mhor, was unknown to a solitary woman, whose ideas still dwelt upon her own early times. She imagined that her son had only to proclaim himself his father's successor in adventure and enterprise, and that a force of men as gallant as those who had followed his father's banner would crowd around to support it when again displayed. To her, Hamish was the eagle who had only to soar aloft and resume his native place in the skies, without her being able to comprehend how many additional eyes would have watched his flight, how many additional bullets would have been directed at his bosom. To be brief, Elspat was one who viewed the present state of society with the same feelings with which she regarded the times that had passed away. She had been indigent, neglected, oppressed, since the days that her husband had no longer been feared and powerful, and she thought that the term of her ascendence would return when her son had determined to play the part of his father. If she permitted her eye to glance farther into futurity, it was but to anticipate that she must be for many a day cold in the grave, with the coronach[2] of her tribe cried duly over her, before her fair-haired Hamish could, according to her calculation, die with his hand on the basket-hilt of the red claymore.[3] His father's hair was grey, ere, after a hundred dangers, he had fallen with his arms in his hands—That she should have seen and survived the sight was a natural consequence of the manners of that age. And better it was—such was her proud thought—that she had seen him so die, than to have witnessed his departure from life in a smoky hovel —on a bed of rotten straw, like an over-worn hound or a bullock which died of disease. But the hour of her young, her brave Hamish was yet far distant. He must succeed—he must conquer, like his father. And when he fell at length—for she anticipated for him no bloodless death—Elspat would ere then have lain long in the grave, and could neither see his death-struggle nor mourn over his grave-sod.

[2] Dirge, funeral-song. [3] Great sword.

With such wild notions working in her brain, the spirit of Elspat rose to its usual pitch, or rather to one which seemed higher. In the emphatic language of Scripture, which in that idiom does not greatly differ from her own, she arose, she washed and changed her apparel, and ate bread, and was refreshed.

She longed eagerly for the return of her son, but she now longed not with the bitter anxiety of doubt and apprehension. She said to herself, that much must be done ere he could in these times arise to be an eminent and dreaded leader. Yet when she saw him again, she almost expected him at the head of a daring band, with pipes playing and banners flying, the noble tartans fluttering free in the wind, in despite of the laws which had suppressed, under severe penalties, the use of the national garb, and all the appurtenances of Highland chivalry. For all this, her eager imagination was content only to allow the interval of some days.

From the moment this opinion had taken deep and serious possession of her mind, her thoughts were bent upon receiving her son at the head of his adherents in the manner in which she used to adorn her hut for the return of his father.

The substantial means of subsistence she had not the power of providing, nor did she consider that of importance. The successful caterans would bring with them herds and flocks. But the interior of her hut was arranged for their reception—the usquebaugh[4] was brewed or distilled in a larger quantity than it could have been supposed one lone woman could have made ready. Her hut was put into such order as might, in some degree, give it the appearance of a day of rejoicing. It was swept and decorated with boughs of various kinds, like the house of a Jewess upon what is termed the Feast of the Tabernacles. The produce of the milk of her little flock was prepared in as great variety of forms as her skill admitted, to entertain her son and his associates whom she expected to receive along with him.

But the principal decoration, which she sought with the greatest toil, was the cloud-berry, a scarlet fruit, which is only found on very high hills, and there only in small quantities. Her husband, or perhaps one of his forefathers, had chosen this as the emblem

[4] Whisky.

of his family, because it seemed at once to imply by its scarcity the smallness of their clan, and by the places in which it was found the ambitious height of their pretensions.

For the time that these simple preparations of welcome endured, Elspat was in a state of troubled happiness. In fact, her only anxiety was that she might be able to complete all that she could do to welcome Hamish and the friends who she supposed must have attached themselves to his band before they should arrive, and find her unprovided for their reception.

But when such efforts as she could make had been accomplished, she once more had nothing left to engage her save the trifling care of her goats; and when these had been attended to, she had only to review her little preparations, renew such as were of a transitory nature, replace decayed branches and fading boughs, and then to sit down at her cottage door and watch the road, as it ascended on the one side from the banks of the Awe, and on the other wound round the heights of the mountain, with such a degree of accommodation to hill and level as the plan of the military engineer permitted. While so occupied, her imagination, anticipating the future from recollections of the past, formed out of the morning mist or the evening cloud the wild forms of an advancing band, which were then called 'Sidier Dhu'—dark soldiers—dressed in their native tartan, and so named to distinguish them from the scarlet ranks of the British army. In this occupation she spent many hours of each morning and evening.

CHAPTER IV

It was in vain that Elspat's eyes surveyed the distant path, by the earliest light of the dawn and the latest glimmer of the twilight. No rising dust awakened the expectation of nodding plumes or flashing arms—the solitary traveller trudged listlessly along in his brown Lowland greatcoat, his tartans dyed black or purple, to comply with or evade the law which prohibited their being worn in their variegated hues. The spirit of the Gael, sunk and broken by the severe though perhaps necessary laws that proscribed the dress and arms which he considered as his birthright, was intimated by his drooping head and dejected appearance. Not in such depressed wanderers did Elspat recognise the light and free step of her son, now, as she concluded, regenerated from every sign of Saxon thraldom. Night by night, as darkness came, she removed from her unclosed door to throw herself on her restless pallet,[1] not to sleep, but to watch. The brave and the terrible, she said, walk by night—their steps are heard in darkness, when all is silent save the whirlwind and the cataract—the timid deer comes only forth when the sun is upon the mountain's peak; but the bold wolf walks in the red light of the harvest-moon. She reasoned in vain—her son's expected summons did not call her from the lowly couch, where she lay dreaming of his approach. Hamish came not.

'Hope deferred,' saith the royal sage, 'maketh the heart sick;' and, strong as was Elspat's constitution, she began to experience that it was unequal to the toils to which her anxious and immoderate affection subjected her, when early one morning the appearance of a traveller on the lonely mountain-road revived hopes which had begun to sink into listless despair. There was no sign of Saxon subjugation about the stranger. At a distance she could see the flutter of the belted plaid, that drooped in graceful folds behind him, and the plume that, placed in the bonnet, showed rank and gentle birth. He carried a gun over his shoulder, the claymore was swinging by his side, with its usual appendages, the dirk,[2] the pistol, and the *sporran mollach*.[3] Ere yet her eye had scanned all these particulars, the light step of the traveller was hastened, his arm was waved in token of recognition—a moment more, and Elspat held in her arms her darling son, dressed in the garb of his ancestors, and looking, in her maternal eyes, the fairest among ten thousand.

The first outpouring of affection it would be impossible to describe. Blessings mingled with the most endearing epithets which her energetic language affords, in striving to express the wild rapture of Elspat's joy. Her board was heaped hastily with all she had to offer; and the mother watched the young soldier, as he partook of the refreshment, with feelings how similar to, yet

[1] Bed. [2] Dagger.
[3] Goat-skin pouch worn by Highlanders round their waist.

how different from, those with which she had seen him draw his first sustenance from her bosom!

When the tumult of joy was appeased, Elspat became anxious to know her son's adventures since they parted, and could not help greatly censuring his rashness for traversing the hills in the Highland dress in the broad sunshine, when the penalty was so heavy, and so many red soldiers were abroad in the country.

'Fear not for me, mother,' said Hamish, in a tone designed to relieve her anxiety, and yet somewhat embarrassed; 'I may wear the *breacan*[4] at the gate of Fort Augustus,[5] if I like it.'

'Oh, be not too daring, my beloved Hamish, though it be the fault which best becomes thy father's son—yet be not too daring! Alas, they fight not now as in former days, with fair weapons and on equal terms, but take odds of numbers and of arms, so that the feeble and the strong are alike levelled by the shot of a boy. And do not think me unworthy to be called your father's widow, and your mother, because I speak thus; for God knoweth that, man to man, I would peril thee against the best in Breadalbane, and broad Lorn besides.'

'I assure you, my dearest mother,' replied Hamish, 'that I am in no danger. But have you seen MacPhadraick, mother, and what has he said to you on my account?'

'Silver he left me in plenty, Hamish; but the best of his comfort was, that you were well, and would see me soon. But beware of MacPhadraick, my son; for when he called himself the friend of your father, he better loved the most worthless stirk[6] in his herd than he did the life-blood of MacTavish Mhor. Use his services, therefore, and pay him for them—for it is thus we should deal with the unworthy; but take my counsel, and trust him not.'

Hamish could not suppress a sigh, which seemed to Elspat to intimate that the caution came too late. 'What have you done with him?' she continued, eager and alarmed. 'I had money of him, and he gives not that without value—he is none of those who exchange barley for chaff. Oh, if you repent you of your

[4] The tartan.

[5] In Inverness-shire. Built in 1716 to check the Highlanders after the 1715 uprising, it was captured by the Jacobites in the 'Forty-Five' but recaptured after their defeat at Culloden, and named after the victorious Duke of Cumberland.

[6] Young bullock or heifer.

bargain, and if it be one which you may break off without disgrace to your truth or your manhood, take back his silver, and trust not to his fair words.'

'It may not be, mother,' said Hamish; 'I do not repent my engagement, unless that it must make me leave you soon.'

'Leave me! how leave me? Silly boy, think you I know not what duty belongs to the wife or mother of a daring man? Thou art but a boy yet; and when thy father had been the dread of the country for twenty years, he did not despise my company and assistance, but often said my help was worth that of two strong gillies.'[7]

'It is not on that score, mother; but since I must leave the country'——

'Leave the country!' replied his mother, interrupting him. 'And think you that I am like a bush, that is rooted to the soil where it grows, and must die if carried elsewhere? I have breathed other winds than these of Ben Cruachan—I have followed your father to the wilds of Ross, and the impenetrable deserts of Y Mac Y Mhor—Tush, man, my limbs, old as they are, will bear me as far as your young feet can trace the way.'

'Alas, mother,' said the young man, with a faltering accent, 'but to cross the sea'——

'The sea! who am I that I should fear the sea? Have I never been in a birling[8] in my life—never known the Sound of Mull, the Isles of Treshornish, and the rough rocks of Harris?'

'Alas, mother, I go far, far from all of these—I am enlisted in one of the new regiments, and we go against the French in America.'

'Enlisted!' uttered the astonished mother—'against *my* will—without *my* consent—You could not—you would not'—then rising up and assuming a posture of almost imperial command, 'Hamish, you DARED not!'

'Despair, mother, dares everything,' answered Hamish, in a tone of melancholy resolution. 'What should I do here, where I can scarce get bread for myself and you, and when the times are growing daily worse? Would you but sit down and listen, I would convince you I have acted for the best.'

[7] Highland servants. [8] Large rowing boat.

With a bitter smile Elspat sat down, and the same severe ironical expression was on her features as, with her lips firmly closed, she listened to his vindication.

Hamish went on, without being disconcerted by her expected displeasure. 'When I left you, dearest mother, it was to go to MacPhadraick's house, for although I knew he is crafty and worldly, after the fashion of the Sassenach,[9] yet he is wise, and I thought how he would teach me, as it would cost him nothing, in which way I could mend our estate in the world.'

'Our estate in the world!' said Elspat, losing patience at the word. 'And went you to a base fellow, with a soul no better than that of a cow-herd, to ask counsel about your conduct? Your father asked none, save of his courage and his sword.'

'Dearest mother,' answered Hamish, 'how shall I convince you that you live in this land of our fathers as if our fathers were yet living? You walk as it were in a dream, surrounded by the phantoms of those who have been long with the dead. When my father lived and fought, the great respected the man of the strong right hand, and the rich feared him. He had protection from MacCallum More, and from Caberfae,[10] and tribute from meaner men. That is ended, and his son would only earn a disgraceful and unpitied death, by the practices which gave his father credit and power among those who wear the breacan. The land is conquered—its lights are quenched—Glengarry, Lochiel, Perth, Lord Lewis, all the high chiefs are dead or in exile—We may mourn for it, but we cannot help it. Bonnet, broadsword, and sporran—power, strength, and wealth, were all lost on Drummossie Muir.'[11]

'It is false!' said Elspat, fiercely. 'You, and such like dastardly spirits, are quelled by your own faint hearts, not by the strength of the enemy; you are like the fearful waterfowl, to whom the least cloud in the sky seems the shadow of the eagle.'

'Mother,' said Hamish, proudly, 'lay not faint heart to my charge. I go where men are wanted who have strong arms and bold hearts too. I leave a desert for a land where I may gather fame.'

[9] Gaelic for 'Saxon', that is English.

[10] Caberfae—the stag's head, the Celtic designation for the arms of the family of the high Chief of Seaforth.

[11] Highland name for Culloden which formed a part of the big moor of Drummossie near Inverness.

'And you leave your mother to perish in want, age, and solitude,' said Elspat, essaying successively every means of moving a resolution which she began to see was more deeply rooted than she had at first thought.

'Not so, neither,' he answered; 'I leave you to comfort and certainty, which you have yet never known. Barcaldine's son is made a leader, and with him I have enrolled myself; MacPhadraick acts for him, and raises men, and finds his own in it.'

'That is the truest word of the tale, were all the rest as false as hell,' said the old woman, bitterly.

'But we are to find our good in it also,' continued Hamish; 'for Barcaldine is to give you a shieling[12] in his wood of Letterfindreight, with grass for your goats, and a cow, when you please to have one, on the common; and my own pay, dearest mother, though I am far away, will do more than provide you with meal, and with all else you can want. Do not fear for me. I enter a private gentleman; but I will return, if hard fighting and regular duty can deserve it, an officer, and with half a dollar a day.'

'Poor child!' replied Elspat, in a tone of pity mingled with contempt. 'And you trust MacPhadraick?'

'I might, mother,' said Hamish, the dark red colour of his race crossing his forehead and cheeks, 'for MacPhadraick knows the blood which flows in my veins, and is aware that, should he break trust with you, he might count the days which could bring Hamish back to Breadalbane, and number those of his life within three suns more. I would kill him at his own hearth, did he break his word with me—I would, by the great Being who made us both!'

The look and attitude of the young soldier for a moment overawed Elspat; she was unused to see him express a deep and bitter mood, which reminded her so strongly of his father, but she resumed her remonstrances in the same taunting manner in which she had commenced them.

'Poor boy!' she said. 'And you think that at the distance of half the world your threats will be heard or thought of! But, go—go—place your neck under him of Hanover's yoke, against whom every true Gael fought to the death—Go, disown the royal Stuart,

[12] Piece of pasture (also used for hut near such land).

for whom your father, and his fathers, and your mother's fathers have crimsoned many a field with their blood.—Go, put your head under the belt of one of the race of Dermid, whose children murdered—Yes,' she added, with a wild shriek, 'murdered your mother's fathers in their peaceful dwellings in Glencoe!—Yes,' she again exclaimed, with a wilder and shriller scream, 'I was then unborn, but my mother has told me—and I attended to the voice of *my* mother—well I remember her words!—They came in peace, and were received in friendship, and blood and fire arose, and screams and murder!'[13]

'Mother,' answered Hamish, mournfully, but with a decided tone, 'all that I have thought over—there is not a drop of the blood of Glencoe on the noble hand of Barcaldine—with the unhappy house of Glenlyon the curse remains, and on them God hath avenged it.'

'You speak like the Saxon priest already,' replied his mother. 'Will you not better stay, and ask a kirk from MacCallum More, that you may preach forgiveness to the race of Dermid?'

'Yesterday was yesterday,' answered Hamish, 'and to-day is to-day. When the clans are crushed and confounded together, it is well and wise that their hatreds and their feuds should not survive their independence and their power. He that cannot execute vengeance like a man should not harbour useless enmity like a craven. Mother, young Barcaldine is true and brave; I know that MacPhadraick counselled him that he should not let me take leave of you, lest you dissuaded me from my purpose; but he said, "Hamish MacTavish is the son of a brave man, and he will not break his word." Mother, Barcaldine leads a hundred of the bravest of the sons of the Gael in their native dress, and with their fathers' arms—heart to heart—shoulder to shoulder. I have sworn to go with him—He has trusted me, and I will trust him.'

At this reply, so firmly and resolvedly pronounced, Elspat remained like one thunderstruck, and sunk in despair. The arguments which she had considered so irresistibly conclusive had

[13] Massacre of Glencoe, 1692, when MacDonald of Glencoe and his followers were treacherously massacred by Campbell of Glenlyon after he had received them in friendship. MacDonald had by accident been delayed from taking the oath of allegiance to William III and therefore from being indemnified in time, and his execution had been ordered.

recoiled like a wave from a rock. After a long pause, she filled her son's quaigh,[14] and presented it to him with an air of dejected deference and submission.

'Drink,' she said, 'to thy father's roof-tree, ere you leave it for ever; and tell me—since the chains of a new king and of a new chief, whom your fathers knew not save as mortal enemies, are fastened upon the limbs of your father's son—tell me how many links you count upon them?'

Hamish took the cup, but looked at her as if uncertain of her meaning. She proceeded in a raised voice. 'Tell me,' she said, 'for I have a right to know, for how many days the will of those you have made your masters permits me to look upon you?—In other words, how many are the days of my life—for when you leave me the earth has naught besides worth living for!'

'Mother,' replied Hamish MacTavish, 'for six days I may remain with you, and, if you will set out with me on the fifth, I will conduct you in safety to your new dwelling. But if you remain here, then I will depart on the seventh by daybreak—then, as at the last moment, I MUST set out for Dumbarton, for if I appear not on the eighth day I am subject to punishment as a deserter, and am dishonoured as a soldier and a gentleman.'

'Your father's foot,' she answered, 'was free as the wind on the heath—it were as vain to say to him where goest thou, as to ask that viewless driver of the clouds, Wherefore blowest thou? Tell me under what penalty thou must—since go thou must, and go thou wilt—return to thy thraldom?'

'Call it not thraldom, mother, it is the service of an honourable soldier—the only service which is now open to the son of MacTavish Mhor.'

'Yet say what is the penalty if thou shouldst not return?' replied Elspat.

'Military punishment as a deserter,' answered Hamish; writhing, however, as his mother failed not to observe, under some internal feelings, which she resolved to probe to the uttermost.

'And that,' she said, with assumed calmness, which her glancing eye disowned, 'is the punishment of a disobedient hound, is it not?'

[14] Drinking-cup.

'Ask me no more, mother,' said Hamish; 'the punishment is nothing to one who will never deserve it.'

'To me it is something,' replied Elspat, 'since I know better than thou that where there is power to inflict there is often the will to do so without cause. I would pray for thee, Hamish, and I must know against what evils I should beseech Him who leaves none unguarded to protect thy youth and simplicity.'

'Mother,' said Hamish, 'it signifies little to what a criminal may be exposed, if a man is determined not to be such. Our Highland chiefs used also to punish their vassals, and, as I have heard, severely. Was it not Lachlan MacIan, whom we remember of old, whose head was struck off by order of his chieftain for shooting at the stag before him?'

'Ay,' said Elspat, 'and right he had to lose it, since he dishonoured the father of the people even in the face of the assembled clan. But the chiefs were noble in their ire—they punished with the sharp blade, and not with the baton. Their punishments drew blood, but they did not infer dishonour. Canst thou say the same for the laws under whose yoke thou hast placed thy freeborn neck?'

'I cannot—mother—I cannot,' said Hamish, mournfully. 'I saw them punish a Sassenach for deserting, as they called it, his banner. He was scourged—I own it—scourged like a hound who has offended an imperious master. I was sick at the sight—I confess it. But the punishment of dogs is only for those worse than dogs, who know not how to keep their faith.'

'To this infamy, however, thou hast subjected thyself, Hamish,' replied Elspat, 'if thou shouldst give, or thy officers take, measure of offence against thee.—I speak no more to thee on thy purpose.—Were the sixth day from this morning's sun my dying day, and thou wert to stay to close mine eyes, thou wouldst run the risk of being lashed like a dog at a post—yes! unless thou hadst the gallant heart to leave me to die alone, and upon my desolate hearth, the last spark of thy father's fire, and of thy forsaken mother's life, to be extinguished together!'—Hamish traversed the hut with an impatient and angry pace.

'Mother,' he said at length, 'concern not yourself about such things. I cannot be subjected to such infamy, for never will I deserve it; and were I threatened with it, I should know how to die before I was so far dishonoured.'

'There spoke the son of the husband of my heart!' replied Elspat; and she changed the discourse, and seemed to listen in melancholy acquiescence, when her son reminded her how short the time was which they were permitted to pass in each other's society, and entreated that it might be spent without useless and unpleasant recollections respecting the circumstances under which they must soon be separated.

Elspat was now satisfied that her son, with some of his father's other properties, preserved the haughty masculine spirit which rendered it impossible to divert him from a resolution which he had deliberately adopted. She assumed, therefore, an exterior of apparent submission to their inevitable separation; and if she now and then broke out into complaints and murmurs, it was either that she could not altogether suppress the natural impetuosity of her temper, or because she had the wit to consider that a total and unreserved acquiescence might have seemed to her son constrained and suspicious, and induced him to watch and defeat the means by which she still hoped to prevent his leaving her. Her ardent though selfish affection for her son, incapable of being qualified by a regard for the true interests of the unfortunate object of her attachment, resembled the instinctive fondness of the animal race for their offspring; and, diving little further into futurity than one of the inferior creatures, she only felt that to be separated from Hamish was to die.

In the brief interval permitted them, Elspat exhausted every art which affection could devise to render agreeable to him the space which they were apparently to spend with each other. Her memory carried her far back into former days, and her stores of legendary history, which furnish at all times a principal amusement of the Highlander in his moments of repose, were augmented by an unusual acquaintance with the songs of ancient bards, and traditions of the most approved seannachies[15] and tellers of tales. Her officious attentions to her son's accommodation, indeed, were so unremitted as almost to give him pain; and he endeavoured quietly to prevent her from taking so much

[15] Chroniclers.

personal toil in selecting the blooming heath for his bed, or preparing the meal for his refreshment. 'Let me alone, Hamish,' she would reply on such occasions; 'you follow your own will in departing from your mother, let your mother have hers in doing what gives her pleasure while you remain.'

So much she seemed to be reconciled to the arrangements which he had made in her behalf, that she could hear him speak to her of her removing to the lands of Green Colin, as the gentleman was called, on whose estate he had provided her an asylum. In truth, however, nothing could be further from her thoughts. From what he had said during their first violent dispute, Elspat had gathered that, if Hamish returned not by the appointed time permitted by his furlough, he would incur the hazard of corporal punishment. Were he placed within the risk of being thus dishonoured, she was well aware that he would never submit to the disgrace, by a return to the regiment where it might be inflicted. Whether she looked to any further probable consequences of her unhappy scheme cannot be known; but the partner of MacTavish Mhor in all his perils and wanderings was familiar with a hundred instances of resistance or escape, by which one brave man, amidst a land of rocks, lakes, and mountains, dangerous passes, and dark forests, might baffle the pursuit of hundreds. For the future, therefore, she feared nothing: her sole engrossing object was to prevent her son from keeping his word with his commanding officer.

With this secret purpose, she evaded the proposal which Hamish repeatedly made, that they should set out together to take possession of her new abode; and she resisted it upon grounds apparently so natural to her character, that her son was neither alarmed nor displeased. 'Let me not,' she said, 'in the same short week, bid farewell to my only son, and to the glen in which I have so long dwelt. Let my eye, when dimmed with weeping for thee, still look around, for a while at least, upon Lock Awe and on Ben Cruachan.'

Hamish yielded the more willingly to his mother's humour in this particular, that one or two persons who resided in a neighbouring glen, and had given their sons to Barcaldine's levy, were also to be provided for on the estate of the chieftain, and it was apparently settled that Elspat was to take her journey along with them when they should remove to their new residence. Thus, Hamish believed that he had at once indulged his mother's humour and insured her safety and accommodation. But she nourished in her mind very different thoughts and projects!

The period of Hamish's leave of absence was fast approaching, and more than once he proposed to depart, in such time as to insure his gaining easily and early Dumbarton, the town where were the headquarters of his regiment. But still his mother's entreaties, his own natural disposition to linger among scenes long dear to him, and, above all, his firm reliance in his speed and activity, induced him to protract his departure till the sixth day, being the very last which he could possibly afford to spend with his mother, if indeed he meant to comply with the conditions of his furlough.

CHAPTER V

On the evening which preceded his proposed departure Hamish walked down to the river with his fishing-rod, to practise in the Awe, for the last time, a sport in which he excelled, and to find, at the same time, the means for making one social meal with his mother on something better than their ordinary cheer. He was as successful as usual, and soon killed a fine salmon. On his return homeward an incident befell him which he afterwards related as ominous, though probably his heated imagination, joined to the universal turn of his countrymen for the marvellous, exaggerated into superstitious importance some very ordinary and accidental circumstance.

In the path which he pursued homeward he was surprised to observe a person who, like himself, was dressed and armed after the old Highland fashion. The first idea that struck him was that the passenger belonged to his own corps, who, levied by government, and bearing arms under royal authority, were not amenable for breach of the statutes against the use of the Highland garb or weapons. But he was struck on perceiving, as he mended his pace to make up to his supposed comrade, meaning to request his company for the next day's journey, that the stranger wore a white cockade,[1] the fatal badge which was proscribed in the Highlands. The stature of the man was tall, and there was something shadowy in the outline which added to his size; and his mode of motion, which rather resembled gliding than walking, impressed Hamish with superstitious fears concerning the character of the being which thus passed before him in the twilight. He no longer strove to make up to the stranger, but contented himself with keeping him in view, under the superstition common to the Highlanders, that you ought neither to intrude yourself on such supernatural apparitions as you may witness, nor avoid their presence, but leave it to themselves to withhold or extend their communication, as their power may permit, or the purpose of their commission require.

Upon an elevated knoll by the side of the road, just where the pathway turned down to Elspat's hut, the stranger made a pause, and seemed to await Hamish's coming up. Hamish, on his part, seeing it was necessary he should pass the object of his suspicion, mustered up his courage, and approached the spot where the stranger had placed himself; who first pointed to Elspat's hut, and made, with arm and head, a gesture prohibiting Hamish to approach it, then stretched his hand to the road which led to the southward, with a motion which seemed to enjoin his instant departure in that direction. In a moment afterwards the plaided form was gone—Hamish did not exactly say vanished, because there were rocks and stunted trees enough to have concealed him; but it was his own opinion that he had seen the spirit of MacTavish Mhor, warning him to commence his instant journey to Dumbarton, without waiting till morning, or again visiting his mother's hut.

In fact, so many accidents might arise to delay his journey, especially where there were many ferries, that it became his settled purpose, though he could not depart without bidding his mother adieu, that he neither could nor would abide longer than for that object; and that the first glimpse of next day's sun should see him many miles advanced towards Dumbarton. He descended the path, therefore, and entering the cottage, he communicated, in a hasty and troubled voice, which indicated mental agitation,

[1] Emblem of the Stuart royal family.

his determination to take his instant departure. Somewhat to his surprise, Elspat appeared not to combat his purpose, but she urged him to take some refreshment ere he left her for ever. He did so hastily, and in silence, thinking on the approaching separation, and scarce yet believing it would take place without a final struggle with his mother's fondness. To his surprise, she filled the quaigh with liquor for his parting cup.

'Go,' she said, 'my son, since such is thy settled purpose; but first stand once more on thy mother's hearth, the flame on which will be extinguished long ere thy foot shall again be placed there.'

'To your health, mother!' said Hamish, 'and may we meet again in happincss, in spite of your ominous words.'

'It were better not to part,' said his mother, watching him as he quaffed the liquor, of which he would have held it ominous to have left a drop.

'And now,' she said, muttering the words to herself, 'go—if thou canst go.'

'Mother,' said Hamish, as he replaced on the table the empty quaigh, 'thy drink is pleasant to the taste, but it takes away the strength which it ought to give.'

'Such is its first effect, my son,' replied Elspat; 'but lie down upon that soft heather couch, shut your eyes but for a moment, and, in the sleep of an hour, you shall have more refreshment than in the ordinary repose of three whole nights, could they be blended into one.'

'Mother,' said Hamish, upon whose brain the potion was now taking rapid effect, 'give me my bonnet—I must kiss you and begone—yet it seems as if my feet were nailed to the floor.'

'Indeed,' said his mother, 'you will be instantly well, if you will sit down for half an hour—but half an hour, it is eight hours to dawn, and dawn were time enough for your father's son to begin such a journey.'

'I must obey you, mother—I feel I must,' said Hamish, inarticulately; 'but call me when the moon rises.'

He sat down on the bed—reclined back, and almost instantly was fast asleep. With the throbbing glee of one who has brought to an end a difficult and troublesome enterprise, Elspat proceeded tenderly to arrange the plaid of the unconscious slumberer, to whom her extravagant affection was doomed to be so fatal, expressing, while busied in her office, her delight, in tones of mingled tenderness and triumph. 'Yes,' she said, 'calf of my heart, the moon shall arise and set to thee, and so shall the sun; but not to light thee from the land of thy fathers, or tempt thee to serve the foreign prince or the feudal enemy! . . .'

While the misjudging mother thus exulted in the success of her stratagem, we may mention to the reader that it was founded on the acquaintance with drugs and simples, which Elspat, accomplished in all things belonging to the wild life which she had led, possessed in an uncommon degree, and which she exercised for various purposes. With the herbs, which she knew how to select as well as how to distil, she could relieve more diseases than a regular medical person could easily believe. She applied some to dye the bright colours of the tartan—from others she compounded draughts of various powers, and unhappily possessed the secret of one which was strongly soporific. Upon the effects of this last concoction, as the reader doubtless has anticipated, she reckoned with security on delaying Hamish beyond the period for which his return was appointed; and she trusted to his horror for the apprehended punishment to which he was thus rendered liable, to prevent him from returning at all.

Sound and deep, beyond natural rest, was the sleep of Hamish MacTavish on that eventful evening, but not such the repose of his mother. Scarce did she close her eyes from time to time, but she awakened again with a start, in the terror that her son had arisen and departed; and it was only on approaching his couch, and hearing his deep-drawn and regular breathing, that she reassured herself of the security of the repose in which he was plunged.

Still, dawning, she feared, might awaken him, notwithstanding the unusual strength of the potion with which she had drugged his cup. If there remained a hope of mortal man accomplishing the journey, she was aware that Hamish would attempt it, though he were to die from fatigue upon the road. Animated by this new fear, she studied to exclude the light, by stopping all the crannies and crevices through which, rather than through any regular entrance, the morning beams might find access to her miserable dwelling; and this in order to detain amid its wants and wretchedness the being on whom, if the world itself had been at her disposal, she would have joyfully conferred it.

Her pains were bestowed unnecessarily. The sun rose high above the heavens, and not the fleetest stag in Breadalbane, were the hounds at his heels, could have sped, to save his life, so fast as would have been necessary to keep Hamish's appointment. Her purpose was fully attained—her son's return within the period assigned was impossible. She deemed it equally impossible that he would ever dream of returning, standing, as he must now do, in the danger of an infamous punishment. By degrees, and at different times, she had gained from him a full acquaintance with the predicament in which he would be placed by failing to appear on the day appointed, and the very small hope he could entertain of being treated with lenity.

It is well known that the great and wise Earl of Chatham prided himself on the scheme by which he drew together for the defence of the colonies those hardy Highlanders who, until his time, had been the objects of doubt, fear, and suspicion, on the part of each successive administration. But some obstacles occurred, from the peculiar habits and temper of this people, to the execution of his patriotic project. By nature and habit, every Highlander was accustomed to the use of arms, but at the same time totally unaccustomed to, and impatient of, the restraints imposed by discipline upon regular troops. They were a species of militia, who had no conception of a camp as their only home. If a battle was lost, they dispersed to save themselves, and look out for the safety of their families; if won, they went back to their glens to hoard up their booty, and attend to their cattle and their farms. This privilege of going and coming at pleasure they would not be deprived of even by their chiefs, whose authority was in most other respects so despotic. It followed, as a matter of course, that the new-levied Highland recruits could scarce be made to comprehend the nature of a military engagement, which compelled a man to serve in the army longer than he pleased; and perhaps, in many instances, sufficient care was not taken at enlisting to explain to them the permanency of the engagement which they came under, lest such a disclosure should induce them to change their mind. Desertions were therefore become numerous from the newly raised regiment, and the veteran general who commanded at Dumbarton saw no better way of checking them than by causing an unusually severe example to be made of a deserter from an English corps. The young Highland regiment was obliged to attend upon the punishment, which struck a people, peculiarly jealous of personal honour, with equal horror and disgust, and not unnaturally indisposed some of them to the service. The old general, however, who had been regularly bred in the German wars, stuck to his own opinion, and gave out in orders that the first Highlander who might either desert, or fail to appear at the expiry of his furlough, should be brought to the halberds, and punished like the culprit whom they had seen in that condition. No man doubted that General —— would keep his word rigorously whenever severity was required, and Elspat, therefore, knew that her son, when he perceived that due compliance with his orders was impossible, must at the same time consider the degrading punishment denounced against his defection as inevitable, should he place himself within the general's power. . . .

It was near evening when Hamish first awoke, and then he was far from being in the full possession either of his mental or bodily powers. From his vague expressions and disordered pulse, Elspat at first experienced much apprehension; but she used such expedients as her medical knowledge suggested; and in the course of the night she had the satisfaction to see him sink once more into a deep sleep, which probably carried off the greater part of the effects of the drug, for about sun-rising she heard him arise and call to her for his bonnet. This she had purposely removed, from a fear that he might awaken and depart in the night-time without her knowledge.

'My bonnet—my bonnet,' cried Hamish, 'it is time to take farewell. Mother, your drink was too strong—the sun is up—but with the next morning I will still see the double summit of the ancient Dun.[2] My bonnet—my bonnet! mother, I must be instant in my departure.' These expressions made it plain that poor

[2] The Dun (rock) of Dumbarton is a twin-peaked hill.

Hamish was unconscious that two nights and a day had passed since he had drained the fatal quaigh, and Elspat had now to venture on what she felt as the almost perilous as well as painful task of explaining her machinations.

'Forgive me, my son,' she said, approaching Hamish, and taking him by the hand with an air of deferential awe, which perhaps she had not always used to his father, even when in his moody fits.

'Forgive you, mother—for what?' said Hamish, laughing; 'for giving me a dram that was too strong, and which my head still feels this morning, or for hiding my bonnet to keep me an instant longer! Nay, do *you* forgive *me*. Give me the bonnet, and let that be done which now must be done. Give me my bonnet, or I go without it; surely I am not to be delayed by so trifling a want as that—I, who have gone for years with only a strap of deer's hide to tie back my hair. Trifle not, but give it me, or I must go bareheaded, since to stay is impossible.'

'My son,' said Elspat, keeping fast hold of his hand, 'what is done cannot be recalled; could you borrow the wings of yonder eagle, you would arrive at the Dun too late for what you purpose —too soon for what awaits you there. You believe you see the sun rising for the first time since you have seen him set, but yesterday beheld him climb Ben Cruachan, though your eyes were closed to his light.'

Hamish cast upon his mother a wild glance of extreme terror, then, instantly recovering himself, said—'I am no child to be cheated out of my purpose by such tricks as these—Farewell, mother, each moment is worth a lifetime.'

'Stay,' she said, 'my dear—my deceived son! Rush not on infamy and ruin—Yonder I see the priest upon the high-road on his white horse—ask him the day of the month and week—let him decide between us.'

With the speed of an eagle Hamish darted up the acclivity, and stood by the minister of Glenorchy, who was pacing out thus early to administer consolation to a distressed family near Bunawe.

The good man was somewhat startled to behold an armed Highlander, then so unusual a sight, and apparently much agitated, stop his horse by the bridle, and ask him with a faltering voice the day of the week and month. 'Had you been where you should have been yesterday, young man,' replied the clergyman, 'you would have known that it was God's Sabbath; and that this is Monday, the second day of the week, and twenty-first of the month.'

'And this is true?' said Hamish.

'As true,' answered the surprised minister, 'as that I yesterday preached the word of God to this parish.—What ails you, young man? Are you sick? Are you in your right mind?'

Hamish made no answer, only repeated to himself the first expression of the clergyman—'Had you been where you should have been yesterday;' and, so saying, he let go the bridle, turned from the road, and descended the path towards the hut, with the look and pace of one who was going to execution. The minister looked after him with surprise; but although he knew the inhabitant of the hovel, the character of Elspat had not invited him to open any communication with her, because she was generally reputed a Papist, or rather one indifferent to all religion, except some superstitious observances which had been handed down from her parents. On Hamish the Reverend Mr. Tyrie had bestowed instructions when he was occasionally thrown in his way, and, if the seed fell among the brambles and thorns of a wild and uncultivated disposition, it had not yet been entirely checked or destroyed. There was something so ghastly in the present expression of the youth's features, that the good man was tempted to go down to the hovel and inquire whether any distress had befallen the inhabitants, in which his presence might be consoling and his ministry useful. Unhappily he did not persevere in this resolution, which might have saved a great misfortune, as he would have probably become a mediator for the unfortunate young man; but a recollection of the wild moods of such Highlanders as had been educated after the old fashion of the country prevented his interesting himself in the widow and son of the far-dreaded robber MacTavish Mhor; and he thus missed an opportunity, which he afterwards sorely repented, of doing much good.

When Hamish MacTavish entered his mother's hut, it was

only to throw himself on the bed he had left, and, exclaiming, 'Undone, undone!' to give vent, in cries of grief and anger, to his deep sense of the deceit which had been practised on him, and of the cruel predicament to which he was reduced. . . .

. . . She suffered his complaints and his reproaches, which were, even in the midst of his agony, respectful and affectionate, to die away without returning any answer; and when, at length, having exhausted all the exclamations of sorrow which his language, copious in expressing the feelings of the heart, affords to the sufferer, he sank into a gloomy silence, she suffered the interval to continue near an hour ere she approached her son's couch.

'And now,' she said at length, with a voice in which the authority of the mother was qualified by her tenderness, 'have you exhausted your idle sorrows, and are you able to place what you have gained against what you have lost? Is the false son of Dermid your brother, or the father of your tribe, that you weep because you cannot bind yourself to his belt, and become one of those who must do his bidding? Could you find in yonder distant country the lakes and the mountains that you leave behind you here? Can you hunt the deer of Breadalbane in the forests of America, or will the ocean afford you the silver-scaled salmon of the Awe? Consider, then, what is your loss, and, like a wise man, set it against what you have won.'

'I have lost all, mother,' replied Hamish, 'since I have broken my word, and lost my honour. I might tell my tale, but who—oh, who would believe me?' The unfortunate young man again clasped his hands together, and, pressing them to his forehead, hid his face upon the bed.

Elspat was now really alarmed, and perhaps wished the fatal deceit had been left unattempted. She had no hope or refuge saving in the eloquence of persuasion, of which she possessed no small share, though her total ignorance of the world as it actually existed rendered its energy unavailing. She urged her son, by every tender epithet which a parent could bestow, to take care for his own safety.

'Leave me,' she said, 'to baffle your pursuers. I will save your life—I will save your honour—I will tell them that my fair-haired Hamish fell from the Corri dhu [black precipice] into the gulf, of which human eye never beheld the bottom. I will tell them this, and I will fling your plaid on the thorns which grow on the brink of the precipice, that they may believe my words. They will believe, and they will return to the Dun of the double-crest; for though the Saxon drum can call the living to die, it cannot recall the dead to their slavish standard. Then will we travel together far northward to the salt lakes of Kintail and place glens and mountains betwixt us and the sons of Dermid. We will visit the shores of the dark lake, and my kinsmen—(for was not my mother of the children of Kenneth, and will they not remember us with the old love?)—my kinsmen will receive us with the affection of the olden time, which lives in those distant glens, where the Gael still dwell in their nobleness, unmingled with the churl Saxons, or with the base brood that are their tools and their slaves.' . . .

On the mind of Hamish her eloquence made no impression. He knew far better than she did the actual situation of the country, and was sensible, that, though it might be possible to hide himself as a fugitive among more distant mountains, there was now no corner in the Highlands in which his father's profession could be practised, even if he had not adopted, from the improved ideas of the time when he lived, the opinion that the trade of the cateran was no longer the road to honour and distinction. Her words were therefore poured into regardless ears, and she exhausted herself in vain in the attempt to paint the regions of her mother's kinsmen in such terms as might tempt Hamish to accompany her thither. She spoke for hours, but she spoke in vain. She could extort no answer, save groans, and sighs, and ejaculations, expressing the extremity of despair.

At length, starting on her feet, and changing the monotonous tone in which she had chanted, as it were, the praises of the province of refuge, into the short, stern language of eager passion —'I am a fool,' she said, 'to spend my words upon an idle, poor-spirited, unintelligent boy, who crouches like a hound to the lash. Wait here, and receive your taskmasters, and abide your chastisement at their hands; but do not think your mother's eyes will behold it. I could not see it and live. My eyes have looked often upon death, but never upon dishonour. Farewell, Hamish!—We never meet again.'

She dashed from the hut like a lapwing, and perhaps for the moment actually entertained the purpose which she expressed, of parting with her son for ever. A fearful sight she would have been that evening to any who might have met her wandering through the wilderness like a restless spirit, and speaking to herself in language which will endure no translation. She rambled for hours, seeking rather than shunning the most dangerous paths. The precarious track through the morass, the dizzy path along the edge of the precipice, or by the banks of the gulfing river, were the roads which, far from avoiding, she sought with eagerness, and traversed with reckless haste. But the courage arising from despair was the means of saving the life which (though deliberate suicide was rarely practised in the Highlands) she was perhaps desirous of terminating. Her step on the verge of the precipice was firm as that of the wild goat. Her eye, in that state of excitation, was so keen as to discern, even amid darkness, the perils which noon would not have enabled a stranger to avoid.

Elspat's course was not directly forward, else she had soon been far from the bothy[3] in which she had left her son. It was circuitous, for that hut was the centre to which her heartstrings were chained, and, though she wandered around it, she felt it impossible to leave the vicinity. With the first beams of morning she returned to the hut. A while she paused at the wattled[4] door, as if ashamed that lingering fondness should have brought her back to the spot which she had left with the purpose of never returning; but there was yet more of fear and anxiety in her hesitation—of anxiety lest her fair-haired son had suffered from the effects of her potion—of fear lest his enemies had come upon him in the night. She opened the door of the hut gently, and entered with noiseless step. Exhausted with his sorrow and anxiety, and not entirely relieved perhaps from the influence of the powerful opiate, Hamish Bean again slept the stern sound sleep by which the Indians are said to be overcome during the interval of their torments. His mother was scarcely sure that she actually discerned his form on the bed, scarce certain that her ear caught the sound of his breathing. With a throbbing heart Elspat went to the fireplace in the centre of the hut, where

[3] Cottage. [4] Of wicker, i.e. of interlaced twigs.

slumbered, covered with a piece of turf, the glimmering embers of the fire, never extinguished on a Scottish hearth until the indwellers leave the mansion for ever.

'Feeble greishogh,'[5] she said, as she lighted, by the help of a match, a splinter of bog pine which was to serve the place of a candle; 'weak greishogh, soon shalt thou be put out for ever, and may Heaven grant that the life of Elspat MacTavish have no longer duration than thine!'

While she spoke she raised the blazing light towards the bed, on which still lay the prostrate limbs of her son, in a posture that left it doubtful whether he slept or swooned. As she advanced towards him the light flashed upon his eyes—he started up in an instant, made a stride forward with his naked dirk in his hand, like a man armed to meet a mortal enemy, and exclaimed, 'Stand off!—on thy life, stand off!'

'It is the word and the action of my husband,' answered Elspat; 'and I know by his speech and his step the son of MacTavish Mhor.'

'Mother,' said Hamish, relapsing from his tone of desperate firmness into one of melancholy expostulation—'oh, dearest mother, wherefore have you returned hither?'

'Ask why the hind comes back to the fawn,' said Elspat; 'why the cat of the mountain returns to her lodge and her young. Know you, Hamish, that the heart of the mother only lives in the bosom of the child.'

'Then will it soon cease to throb,' said Hamish, 'unless it can beat within a bosom that lies beneath the turf.—Mother, do not blame me; if I weep, it is not for myself but for you, for my sufferings will soon be over; but yours——Oh, who but Heaven shall set a boundary to them!'

Elspat shuddered and stepped backward, but almost instantly resumed her firm and upright position and her dauntless bearing.

'I thought thou wert a man but even now,' she said, 'and thou art again a child. Hearken to me yet, and let us leave this place together. Have I done thee wrong or injury? If so, yet do not avenge it so cruelly—See, Elspat MacTavish, who never kneeled before even to a priest, falls prostrate before her own son, and

[5] A glowing ember.

craves his forgiveness.' And at once she threw herself on her knees before the young man, seized on his hand, and, kissing it a hundred times, repeated as often, in heartbreaking accents, the most earnest entreaties for forgiveness. 'Pardon,' she exclaimed, 'pardon, for the sake of your father's ashes—pardon, for the sake of the pain with which I bore thee, the care with which I nurtured thee!—Hear it, Heaven, and behold it, Earth—the mother asks pardon of her child, and she is refused!'

It was in vain that Hamish endeavoured to stem this tide of passion, by assuring his mother, with the most solemn asseverations, that he forgave entirely the fatal deceit which she had practised upon him.

'Empty words,' she said; 'idle protestations, which are but used to hide the obduracy of your resentment. Would you have me believe you, then leave the hut this instant, and retire from a country which every hour renders more dangerous.—Do this, and I may think you have forgiven me—refuse it, and again I call on moon and stars, heaven and earth, to witness the unrelenting resentment with which you prosecute your mother for a fault which, if it be one, arose out of love to you.'

'Mother,' said Hamish, 'on this subject you move me not. I will fly before no man. . . . Here I will abide my fate; nor is there in Scotland a voice of power enough to bid me stir from hence, and be obeyed.'

'Here, then, I also stay,' said Elspat, rising up and speaking with assumed composure. 'I have seen my husband's death—my eyelids shall not grieve to look on the fall of my son. But MacTavish Mhor died as became the brave, with his good sword in his right hand; my son will perish like the bullock that is driven to the shambles by the Saxon owner who has bought him for a price.'

'Mother,' said the unhappy young man, 'you have taken my life; to that you have a right, for you gave it; but touch not my honour! It came to me from a brave train of ancestors, and should be sullied neither by man's deed nor woman's speech. What I shall do, perhaps I myself yet know not; but tempt me no further by reproachful words; you have already made wounds more than you can ever heal.'

'It is well, my son,' said Elspat, in reply. 'Expect neither further complaint nor remonstrance from me; but let us be silent, and wait the chance which Heaven shall send us.'

The sun arose on the next morning, and found the bothy silent as the grave. The mother and son had arisen, and were engaged each in their separate task—Hamish in preparing and cleaning his arms with the greatest accuracy, but with an air of deep dejection. Elspat, more restless in her agony of spirit, employed herself in making ready the food which the distress of yesterday had induced them both to dispense with for an unusual number of hours. She placed it on the board before her son so soon as it was prepared . . .

. . . When his mother saw that he had eaten what sufficed him, she again filled the fatal quaigh, and proffered it as the conclusion of the repast. But he started aside with a convulsive gesture, expressive at once of fear and abhorrence.

'Nay, my son,' she said, 'this time, surely, thou hast no cause of fear.'

'Urge me not, mother,' answered Hamish; 'or put the leprous toad into a flagon, and I will drink; but from that accursed cup, and of that mind-destroying potion, never will I taste more!'

'At your pleasure, my son,' said Elspat, haughtily, and began, with much apparent assiduity, the various domestic tasks which had been interrupted during the preceding day. Whatever was at her heart, all anxiety seemed banished from her looks and demeanour. It was but from an over-activity of bustling exertion that it might have been perceived, by a close observer, that her actions were spurred by some internal cause of painful excitement; and such a spectator, too, might also have observed how often she broke off the snatches of songs or tunes which she hummed, apparently without knowing what she was doing, in order to cast a hasty glance from the door of the hut. Whatever might be in the mind of Hamish, his demeanour was directly the reverse of that adopted by his mother. Having finished the task of cleaning and preparing his arms, which he arranged within the hut, he sat himself down before the door of the bothy, and watched the opposite hill, like the fixed sentinel who expects the approach of an enemy. Noon found him in the same unchanged posture, and it was an hour after that period, when his mother, standing beside him, laid her hand on his shoulder, and said, in a tone indifferent, as if she had been talking of some friendly visit, 'When dost thou expect them?'

'They cannot be here till the shadows fall long to the eastward,' replied Hamish; 'that is, even supposing the nearest party, commanded by Sergeant Allan Breack Cameron, has been commanded hither by express from Dumbarton, as it is most likely they will.'

'Then enter beneath your mother's roof once more; partake the last time of the food which she has prepared; after this, let them come, and thou shalt see if thy mother is a useless incumbrance in the day of strife. Thy hand, practised as it is, cannot fire these arms so fast as I can load them; nay, if it is necessary, I do not myself fear the flash or the report, and my aim has been held fatal.'

'In the name of Heaven, mother, meddle not with this matter!' said Hamish. 'Allan Breack is a wise man and a kind one, and comes of a good stem. It may be, he can promise for our officers, that they will touch me with no infamous punishment; and if they offer me confinement in the dungeon, or death by the musket, to that I may not object.'

'Alas, and wilt thou trust to their word, my foolish child? Remember the race of Dermid were ever fair and false, and no sooner shall they have gyves[6] on thy hands than they will strip thy shoulders for the scourge.'

'Save your advice, mother,' said Hamish, sternly; 'for me, my mind is made up.'

But though he spoke thus, to escape the almost persecuting urgency of his mother, Hamish would have found it, at that moment, impossible to say upon what course of conduct he had thus fixed. On one point alone he was determined—namely, to abide his destiny, be what it might, and not to add to the breach of his word, of which he had been involuntarily rendered guilty, by attempting to escape from punishment. This act of self-devotion he conceived to be due to his own honour, and that of his countrymen. Which of his comrades would in future be

[6] Shackles.

trusted, if he should be considered as having broken his word, and betrayed the confidence of his officers? and whom but Hamish Bean MacTavish would the Gael accuse, for having verified and confirmed the suspicions which the Saxon general was well known to entertain against the good faith of the Highlanders? He was, therefore, bent firmly to abide his fate. But whether his intention was to yield himself peaceably into the hands of the party who should come to apprehend him, or whether he purposed, by a show of resistance, to provoke them to kill him on the spot, was a question which he could not himself have answered. His desire to see Barcaldine, and explain the cause of his absence at the appointed time, urged him to the one course; his fear of the degrading punishment, and of his mother's bitter upbraidings, strongly instigated the latter and the more dangerous purpose. He left it to chance to decide when the crisis should arrive; nor did he tarry long in expectation of the catastrophe.

Evening approached, the gigantic shadows of the mountains streamed in darkness towards the east, while their western peaks were still glowing with crimson and gold. The road which winds round Ben Cruachan was fully visible from the door of the bothy, when a party of five Highland soldiers, whose arms glanced in the sun, wheeled suddenly into sight from the most distant extremity, where the highway is hidden behind the mountain. One of the party walked a little before the other four, who marched regularly and in files, according to the rules of military discipline. There was no dispute, from the firelocks which they carried, and the plaids and bonnets which they wore, that they were a party of Hamish's regiment, under a non-commissioned officer; and there could be as little doubt of the purpose of their appearance on the banks of Loch Awe.

'They come briskly forward,' said the widow of MacTavish Mhor. 'I wonder how fast or how slow some of them will return again! But they are five, and it is too much odds for a fair field. Step back within the hut, my son, and shoot from the loophole beside the door. Two you may bring down ere they quit the highroad for the foot-path—there will remain but three; and your father, with my aid, has often stood against that number.'

Hamish Bean took the gun which his mother offered, but did

not stir from the door of the hut. He was soon visible to the party on the high-road, as was evident from their increasing their pace to a run; the files, however, still keeping together like coupled greyhounds, and advancing with great rapidity. In far less time than would have been accomplished by men less accustomed to the mountains, they had left the high-road, traversed the narrow path, and approached within pistol-shot of the bothy, at the door of which stood Hamish, fixed like a statue of stone, with his firelock in his hand, while his mother, placed behind him, and almost driven to frenzy by the violence of her passions, reproached him, in the strongest terms which despair could invent, for his want of resolution and faintness of heart. Her words increased the bitter gall which was arising in the young man's own spirit, as he observed the unfriendly speed with which his late comrades were eagerly making towards him, like hounds towards the stag when he is at bay. The untamed and angry passions which he inherited from father and mother were awakened by the supposed hostility of those who pursued him; and the restraint under which these passions had been hitherto held by his sober judgment began gradually to give way. The sergeant now called to him, 'Hamish Bean MacTavish, lay down your arms and surrender.'

'Do *you* stand, Allan Breack Cameron, and command your men to stand, or it will be the worse for us all.'

'Halt, men!' said the sergeant, but continuing himself to advance. 'Hamish, think what you do, and give up your gun; you may spill blood, but you cannot escape punishment.'

'The scourge—the scourge—my son, beware the scourge!' whispered his mother.

'Take heed, Allan Breack,' said Hamish. 'I would not hurt you willingly, but I will not be taken unless you can assure me against the Saxon lash.'

'Fool!' answered Cameron, 'you know I cannot. Yet I will do all I can. I will say I met you on your return, and the punishment will be light—but give up your musket—Come on, men.'

Instantly he rushed forward, extending his arm as if to push aside the young man's levelled firelock. Elspat exclaimed, 'Now, spare not your father's blood to defend your father's hearth!'

Hamish fired his piece, and Cameron dropped dead.—All these things happened, it might be said, in the same moment of time. The soldiers rushed forward and seized Hamish, who, seeming petrified with what he had done, offered not the least resistance. Not so his mother, who, seeing the men about to put handcuffs on her son, threw herself on the soldiers with such fury that it required two of them to hold her, while the rest secured the prisoner.

'Are you not an accursed creature,' said one of the men to Hamish, 'to have slain your best friend, who was contriving, during the whole march, how he could find some way of getting you off without punishment for your desertion?'

'Do you hear *that*, mother?' said Hamish turning himself as much towards her as his bonds would permit—but the mother heard nothing, and saw nothing. She had fainted on the floor of her hut. Without waiting for her recovery, the party almost immediately began their homeward march towards Dumbarton, leading along with them their prisoner. They thought it necessary, however, to stay for a little space at the village of Dalmally, from which they despatched a party of the inhabitants to bring away the body of their unfortunate leader, while they themselves repaired to a magistrate to state what had happened, and require his instructions as to the further course to be pursued. The crime being of a military character, they were instructed to march the prisoner to Dumbarton without delay.

The swoon of the mother of Hamish lasted for a length of time; the longer perhaps that her constitution, strong as it was, must have been much exhausted by her previous agitation of three days' endurance. She was roused from her stupor at length by female voices, which cried the coronach, or lament for the dead, with clapping of hands and loud exclamations; while the melancholy note of a lament, appropriate to the clan Cameron, played on the bagpipe, was heard from time to time.

Elspat started up like one awakened from the dead, and without any accurate recollection of the scene which had passed before her eyes. There were females in the hut who were swathing the corpse in its bloody plaid before carrying it from the fatal spot. 'Women,' she said, starting up and interrupting their chant at once and their labour—'Tell me, women, why sing you the dirge of MacDhonuil Dhu in the house of MacTavish Mhor?'

'She-wolf, be silent with thine ill-omened yell,' answered one of the females, a relation of the deceased, 'and let us do our duty to our beloved kinsman! There shall never be coronach cried, or dirge played, for thee or thy bloody wolf-burd.[7] The ravens shall eat him from the gibbet, and the foxes and wild-cats shall tear thy corpse upon the hill. Cursed be he that would sain[8] your bones, or add a stone to your cairn!'

'Daughter of a foolish mother,' answered the widow of MacTavish Mhor, 'know that the gibbet with which you threaten us is no portion of our inheritance. For thirty years the Black Tree of the Law, whose apples are dead men's bodies, hungered after the beloved husband of my heart; but he died like a brave man, with the sword in his hand, and defrauded it of its hopes and its fruit.'

'So shall it not be with thy child, bloody sorceress,' replied the female mourner, whose passions were as violent as those of Elspat herself. 'The ravens shall tear his fair hair to line their nests, before the sun sinks beneath the Treshornish islands.'

These words recalled to Elspat's mind the whole history of the last three dreadful days. At first she stood fixed as if the extremity of distress had converted her into stone; but in a minute the pride and violence of her temper, outbraved as she thought herself on her own threshold, enabled her to reply—'Yes, insulting hag, my fair-haired boy may die, but it will not be with a white hand—it has been dyed in the blood of his enemy, in the best blood of a Cameron—remember that; and when you lay your dead in his grave, let it be his best epitaph, that he was killed by Hamish Bean for essaying to lay hands on the son of MacTavish Mhor on his own threshold. Farewell—the shame of defeat, loss, and slaughter remain with the clan that has endured it!'

The relative of the slaughtered Cameron raised her voice in reply; but Elspat, disdaining to continue the objurgation, or perhaps feeling her grief likely to overmaster her power of expressing her resentment, had left the hut, and was walking forth in the bright moonshine.

[7] Wolf-brood, i.e. wolf-cub. [8] Bless.

The females who were arranging the corpse of the slaughtered man hurried from their melancholy labour to look after her tall figure as it glided away among the cliffs. 'I am glad she is gone,' said one of the younger persons who assisted. 'I would as soon dress a corpse when the great fiend himself—God sain us—stood visibly before us, as when Elspat of the Tree is amongst us.—Ay—ay, even overmuch intercourse hath she had with the Enemy in her day.'

'Silly woman,' answered the female who had maintained the dialogue with the departed Elspat, 'thinkest thou that there is a worse fiend on earth, or beneath it, than the pride and fury of an offended woman, like yonder bloody-minded hag. Know that blood has been as familiar to her as the dew to the mountain-daisy. Many and many a brave man has she caused to breathe their last for little wrong they had done to her or theirs. But her hough-sinews[9] are cut, now that her wolf-burd must, like a murderer as he is, make a murderer's end.'

Whilst the women thus discoursed together, as they watched the corpse of Allan Breack Cameron, the unhappy cause of his death pursued her lonely way across the mountain. While she remained within sight of the bothy, she put a strong constraint on herself, that by no alteration of pace or gesture she might afford to her enemies the triumph of calculating the excess of her mental agitation, nay, despair. She stalked, therefore, with a slow rather than a swift step, and, holding herself upright, seemed at once to endure with firmness that woe which was passed, and bid defiance to that which was about to come. But when she was beyond the sight of those who remained in the hut, she could no longer suppress the extremity of her agitation. Drawing her mantle wildly round her, she stopped at the first knoll, and, climbing to its summit, extended her arms up to the bright moon, as if accusing heaven and earth for her misfortunes, and uttered scream on scream, like those of an eagle whose nest has been plundered of her brood. A while she vented her grief in these inarticulate cries, then rushed on her way with a hasty and unequal step, in the vain hope of overtaking the party which was conveying her son a prisoner to Dumbarton. But her

[9] Hip or thigh sinews.

strength, super-human as it seemed, failed her in the trial, nor was it possible for her, with her utmost efforts, to accomplish her purpose.

Yet she pressed onward, with all the speed which her exhausted frame could exert. When food became indispensable, she entered the first cottage: 'Give me to eat,' she said; 'I am the widow of MacTavish Mhor—I am the mother of Hamish MacTavish Bean—give me to eat, that I may once more see my fair-haired son.' Her demand was never refused, though granted in many cases with a kind of struggle between compassion and aversion in some of those to whom she applied, which was in others qualified by fear. The share she had had in occasioning the death of Allan Breack Cameron, which must probably involve that of her own son, was not accurately known; but, from a knowledge of her violent passions and former habits of life, no one doubted that in one way or other she had been the cause of the catastrophe; and Hamish Bean was considered, in the slaughter which he had committed, rather as the instrument than as the accomplice of his mother.

This general opinion of his countrymen was of little service to the unfortunate Hamish. As his captain, Green Colin, understood the manners and habits of his country, he had no difficulty in collecting from Hamish the particulars accompanying his supposed desertion, and the subsequent death of the non-commissioned officer. He felt the utmost compassion for a youth who had thus fallen a victim to the extravagant and fatal fondness of a parent. But he had no excuse to plead which could rescue his unhappy recruit from the doom which military discipline and the award of a court-martial denounced against him for the crime he had committed.

No time had been lost in their proceedings, and as little was interposed betwixt sentence and execution. General —— had determined to make a severe example of the first deserter who should fall into his power, and here was one who had defended himself by main force, and slain in the affray the officer sent to take him into custody. A fitter subject for punishment could not have occurred, and Hamish was sentenced to immediate execution. All which the interference of his captain in his favour could procure was that he should die a soldier's death; for there had been a purpose of executing him upon the gibbet.

The worthy clergyman of Glenorchy chanced to be at Dumbarton, in attendance upon some church courts, at the time of this catastrophe. He visited his unfortunate parishioner in his dungeon, found him ignorant indeed, but not obstinate, and the answers which he received from him, when conversing on religious topics, were such as induced him doubly to regret that a mind naturally pure and noble should have remained unhappily so wild and uncultivated.

When he ascertained the real character and disposition of the young man, the worthy pastor made deep and painful reflections on his own shyness and timidity, which, arising out of the evil fame that attached to the lineage of Hamish, had restrained him from charitably endeavouring to bring this strayed sheep within the great fold. While the good minister blamed his cowardice in times past, which had deterred him from risking his person, to save, perhaps, an immortal soul, he resolved no longer to be governed by such timid counsels, but to endeavour, by application to his officers, to obtain a reprieve, at least, if not a pardon, for the criminal, in whom he felt so unusually interested, at once from his docility of temper and his generosity of disposition.

Accordingly the divine sought out Captain Campbell at the barracks within the garrison. There was a gloomy melancholy on the brow of Green Colin, which was not lessened, but increased, when the clergyman stated his name, quality, and errand. 'You cannot tell me better of the young man than I am disposed to believe,' answered the Highland officer; 'you cannot ask me to do more in his behalf than I am of myself inclined, and have already endeavoured to do. But it is all in vain. General —— is half a Lowlander, half an Englishman. He has no idea of the high and enthusiastic character which in these mountains often brings exalted virtues in contact with great crimes, which, however, are less offences of the heart than errors of the understanding. I have gone so far as to tell him that in this young man he was putting to death the best and the bravest of my company, where all, or almost all, are good and brave. I explained to him by what strange delusion the culprit's apparent desertion was occasioned, and how little his heart was accessory to the crime which his hand unhappily committed. His answer was, "These are Highland visions, Captain Campbell, as unsatisfactory and vain as those of the second sight. An act of gross desertion may, in any case, be palliated under the plea of intoxication; the murder of an officer may be as easily coloured over with that of temporary insanity. The example must be made, and, if it has fallen on a man otherwise a good recruit, it will have the greater effect."—Such being the General's unalterable purpose,' continued Captain Campbell, with a sigh, 'be it your care, reverend sir, that your penitent prepare by break of day tomorrow for that great change which we shall all one day be subjected to.'

'And for which,' said the clergyman, 'may God prepare us all, as I in my duty will not be wanting to this poor youth.'

Next morning, as the very earliest beams of sunrise saluted the grey towers which crown the summit of that singular and tremendous rock, the soldiers of the new Highland regiment appeared on the parade, within the Castle of Dumbarton, and, having fallen into order, began to move downward by steep staircases and narrow passages towards the external barrier-gate, which is at the very bottom of the rock. The wild wailings of the pibroch[10] were heard at times, interchanged with the drums and fifes, which beat the Dead March.

The unhappy criminal's fate did not, at first, excite that general sympathy in the regiment which would probably have arisen had he been executed for desertion alone. The slaughter of the unfortunate Allan Breack had given a different colour to Hamish's offence; for the deceased was much beloved, and, besides, belonged to a numerous and powerful clan, of whom there were many in the ranks. The unfortunate criminal, on the contrary, was little known to, and scarcely connected with, any of his regimental companions. His father had been, indeed, distinguished for his strength and manhood; but he was of a broken clan, as those names were called who had no chief to lead them to battle.

It would have been almost impossible in another case to have turned out of the ranks of the regiment the party necessary for

[10] Highland (bag-pipe) music.

execution of the sentence; but the six individuals selected for that purpose were friends of the deceased, descended, like him, from the race of MacDhonuil Dhu; and while they prepared for the dismal task which their duty imposed, it was not without a stern feeling of gratified revenge. The leading company of the regiment began now to defile from the barrier-gate, and was followed by the others, each successively moving and halting according to the orders of the adjutant, so as to form three sides of an oblong square, with the ranks faced inwards. The fourth or blank side of the square was closed up by the huge and lofty precipice on which the castle rises. About the centre of the procession, bareheaded, disarmed, and with his hands bound, came the unfortunate victim of military law. He was deadly pale, but his step was firm and his eye as bright as ever. The clergyman walked by his side—the coffin which was to receive his mortal remains was borne before him. The looks of his comrades were still, composed, and solemn. They felt for the youth, whose handsome form and manly yet submissive deportment had, as soon as he was distinctly visible to them, softened the hearts of many, even of some who had been actuated by vindictive feelings.

The coffin destined for the yet living body of Hamish Bean was placed at the bottom of the hollow square, about two yards distant from the foot of the precipice, which rises in that place as steep as a stone wall to the height of three or four hundred feet. Thither the prisoner was also led, the clergyman still continuing by his side, pouring forth exhortations of courage and consolation, to which the youth appeared to listen with respectful devotion. With slow and, it seemed, almost unwilling steps, the firing party entered the square, and were drawn up facing the prisoner, about ten yards distant. The clergyman was now about to retire—'Think, my son,' he said, 'on what I have told you, and let your hope be rested on the anchor which I have given. You will then exchange a short and miserable existence here for a life in which you will experience neither sorrow nor pain.—Is there aught else which you can intrust to me to execute for you?'

The youth looked at his sleeve-buttons. They were of gold, booty perhaps which his father had taken from some English officer during the civil wars. The clergyman disengaged them from his sleeves.

'My mother!' he said with some effort, 'give them to my poor mother?—See her, good father, and teach her what she should think of all this. Tell her Hamish Bean is more glad to die than ever he was to rest after the longest day's hunting. Farewell, sir—farewell!'

The good man could scarce retire from the fatal spot. An officer afforded him the support of his arm. At his last look towards Hamish, he beheld him alive and kneeling on the coffin; the few that were around him had all withdrawn. The fatal word was given, the rock rang sharp to the sound of the discharge, and Hamish, falling forward with a groan, died, it may be supposed, without almost a sense of the passing agony.

Ten or twelve of his own company then came forward, and laid with solemn reverence the remains of their comrade in the coffin, while the Dead March was again struck up, and the several companies, marching in single files, passed the coffin one by one, in order that all might receive from the awful spectacle the warning which it was peculiarly intended to afford. The regiment was then marched off the ground, and reascended the ancient cliff, their music, as usual on such occasions, striking lively strains, as if sorrow, or even deep thought, should as short a while as possible be the tenant of the soldier's bosom.

At the same time the small party which we before mentioned bore the bier of the ill-fated Hamish to his humble grave, in a corner of the churchyard of Dumbarton usually assigned to criminals. Here, amongst the dust of the guilty, lies a youth whose name, had he survived the ruin of the fatal events by which he was hurried into crime, might have adorned the annals of the brave.

The minister of Glenorchy left Dumbarton immediately after he had witnessed the last scene of this melancholy catastrophe. His reason acquiesced in the justice of the sentence, which required blood for blood, and he acknowledged that the vindictive character of his countrymen required to be powerfully restrained by the strong curb of social law. But still he mourned over the individual victim. . . . Musing on these melancholy

9110212 C

events, noon found him engaged in the mountain passes, by which he was to return to his still distant home.

Confident in his knowledge of the country, the clergyman had left the main road, to seek one of those shorter paths which are only used by pedestrians, or by men, like the minister, mounted on the small but sure-footed, hardy, and sagacious horses of the country. The place which he now traversed was in itself gloomy and desolate, and tradition had added to it the terror of superstition, by affirming it was haunted by an evil spirit, termed *Cloght-dearg*, that is, Redmantle, who at all times, but especially at noon and at midnight, traversed the glen, in enmity both to man and the inferior creation, did such evil as her power was permitted to extend to, and afflicted with ghastly terrors those whom she had not licence otherwise to hurt. . . .

These legends came across the mind of the clergyman; and, solitary as he was, a melancholy smile shaded his cheek, as he thought of the inconsistency of human nature, and reflected how many brave men, whom the yell of the pibroch would have sent headlong against fixed bayonets, as the wild bull rushes on his enemy, might have yet feared to encounter those visionary terrors, which he himself, a man of peace, and in ordinary perils no way remarkable for the firmness of his nerves, was now risking without hesitation.

As he looked around the scene of desolation, he could not but acknowledge, in his own mind, that it was not ill chosen for the haunt of those spirits which are said to delight in solitude and desolation. The glen was so steep and narrow that there was but just room for the meridian sun to dart a few scattered rays upon the gloomy and precarious stream which stole through its recesses, for the most part in silence, but occasionally murmuring sullenly against the rocks and large stones which seemed determined to bar its farther progress. In winter or in the rainy season this small stream was a foaming torrent of the most formidable magnitude, and it was at such periods that it had torn open and laid bare the broad-faced and huge fragments of rock which, at the season of which we speak, hid its course from the eye, and seemed disposed totally to interrupt its course. 'Undoubtedly,' thought the clergyman, 'this mountain rivulet, suddenly swelled by a water-spout or thunder-storm, has often been the cause of those accidents which, happening in the glen called by her name, have been ascribed to the agency of the Cloght-dearg.'

Just as this idea crossed his mind, he heard a female voice exclaim, in a wild and thrilling accent, 'Michael Tyrie—Michael Tyrie!' He looked round in astonishment, and not without some fear. It seemed for an instant as if the Evil Being, whose existence he had disowned, was about to appear for the punishment of his incredulity. This alarm did not hold him more than an instant, nor did it prevent his replying in a firm voice, 'Who calls—and where are you?'

'One who journeys in wretchedness, between life and death,' answered the voice; and the speaker, a tall female, appeared from among the fragments of rocks which had concealed her from view.

As she approached more closely, her mantle of bright tartan, in which the red colour much predominated, her stature, the long stride with which she advanced, and the writhen features and wild eyes which were visible from under her curch, would have made her no inadequate representative of the spirit which gave name to the valley. But Mr. Tyrie instantly knew her as the Woman of the Tree, the widow of MacTavish Mhor, the now childless mother of Hamish Bean. I am not sure whether the minister would not have endured the visitation of the Cloght-dearg herself, rather than the shock of Elspat's presence, considering her crime and her misery. He drew up his horse instinctively, and stood endeavouring to collect his ideas, while a few paces brought her up to his horse's head.

'Michael Tyrie,' said she, 'the foolish women of the Clachan[11] hold thee as a god—be one to me, and say that my son lives. Say this, and I too will be of thy worship—I will bend my knees on the seventh day in thy house of worship, and thy God shall be my God.'

'Unhappy woman,' replied the clergyman, 'man forms not pactions[12] with his Maker as with a creature of clay like himself. Thinkest thou to chaffer[13] with Him who formed the earth and

[11] Village, literally 'the stones'. [12] Contracts.
[13] Barter or bargain.

spread out the heavens, or that thou canst offer aught of homage or devotion that can be worth acceptance in his eyes? He hath asked obedience, not sacrifice; patience under the trials with which he afflicts us, instead of vain bribes, such as man offers to his changeful brother of clay, that he may be moved from his purpose.'

'Be silent, priest!' answered the desperate woman; 'speak not to me the words of thy white book. Elspat's kindred were of those who crossed themselves and knelt when the sacring bell was rung;[14] and she knows that atonement can be made on the altar for deeds done in the field. Elspat had once flocks and herds, goats upon the cliffs, and cattle in the strath. She wore gold around her neck and on her hair—thick twists as those worn by the heroes of old. All these would she have resigned to the priest—all these; and if he wished for the ornaments of a gentle lady, or the sporran of a high chief, though they had been great as MacCallum More himself, MacTavish Mhor would have procured them if Elspat had promised them. Elspat is now poor, and has nothing to give. But the Black Abbot of Inchaffray would have bidden her scourge her shoulders and macerate her feet by pilgrimage, and he would have granted his pardon to her when he saw that her blood had flowed, and that her flesh had been torn. These were the priests who had indeed power even with the most powerful—they threatened the great men of the earth with the word of their mouth, the sentence of their book, the blaze of their torch, the sound of their sacring bell. The mighty bent to their will, and unloosed at the word of the priests those whom they had bound in their wrath, and set at liberty, unharmed, him whom they had sentenced to death, and for whose blood they had thirsted. These were a powerful race, and might well ask the poor to kneel, since their power could humble the proud. But you!—against whom are ye strong, but against women who have been guilty of folly, and men who never wore sword? The priests of old were like the winter torrent which fills this hollow valley, and rolls these massive rocks against each other as easily as the boy plays with the ball which he casts before him—But you! you do but resemble the summer-stricken stream, which is turned aside by

[14] i.e. Catholics.

the rushes, and stemmed by a bush of sedges—Woe worth you, for there is no help in you!'

The clergyman was at no loss to conceive that Elspat had lost the Roman Catholic faith without gaining any other, and that she still retained a vague and confused idea of the composition with the priesthood, by confessions, alms, and penance, and of their extensive power, which, according to her notion, was adequate, if duly propitiated, even to effecting her son's safety. Compassionating her situation, and allowing for her errors and ignorance, he answered her with mildness.

'Alas, unhappy woman! Would to God I could convince thee as easily where thou oughtest to seek, and art sure to find, consolation, as I can assure you with a single word that were Rome and all her priesthood once more in the plenitude of their power, they could not, for largesse or penance, afford to thy misery an atom of aid or comfort.—Elspat MacTavish, I grieve to tell you the news.'

'I know them without thy speech,' said the unhappy woman—'My son is doomed to die.'

'Elspat,' resumed the clergyman, 'he *was* doomed, and the sentence has been executed.' The hapless mother threw her eyes up to heaven, and uttered a shriek so unlike the voice of a human being, that the eagle which soared in middle air answered it as she would have done the call of her mate.

'It is impossible!' she exclaimed, 'it is impossible! Men do not condemn and kill on the same day! Thou art deceiving me. The people call thee holy—hast thou the heart to tell a mother she has murdered her only child?'

'God knows,' said the priest, the tears falling fast from his eyes, 'that were it in my power I would gladly tell better tidings—But these which I bear are as certain as they are fatal—My own ears heard the death-shot, my own eyes beheld thy son's death—thy son's funeral.—My tongue bears witness to what my ears heard and my eyes saw.'

The wretched female clasped her hands close together, and held them up towards heaven like a sibyl announcing war and desolation, while, in impotent yet frightful rage, she poured forth a tide of the deepest imprecations.—'Base Saxon churl!' she exclaimed, 'vile hypocritical juggler! May the eyes that looked tamely on the death of my fair-haired boy be melted in their sockets with ceaseless tears, shed for those that are nearest and most dear to thee! May the ears that heard his death-knell be dead hereafter to all other sounds save the screech of the raven and the hissing of the adder! May the tongue that tells me of his death and of my own crime be withered in thy mouth—or, better, when thou wouldst pray with thy people, may the Evil One guide it, and give voice to blasphemies instead of blessings, until men shall fly in terror from thy presence, and the thunder of heaven be launched against thy head, and stop for ever thy cursing and accursed voice! Begone, with this malison![15]—Elspat will never, never again bestow so many words upon living man.'

She kept her word—from that day the world was to her a wilderness, in which she remained without thought, care, or interest, absorbed in her own grief, indifferent to everything else. . . .

Every attempt to place any person in her hut to take charge of her miscarried, through the extreme resentment with which she regarded all intrusion on her solitude, or by the timidity of those who had been pitched upon to be inmates with the terrible Woman of the Tree. At length, when Elspat became totally unable (in appearance at least) to turn herself on the wretched settle which served her for a couch, the humanity of Mr. Tyrie's successor sent two women to attend upon the last moments of the solitary, which could not, it was judged, be far distant, and to avert the possibility that she might perish for want of assistance or food, before she sank under the effects of extreme age or mortal malady.

It was on a November evening that the two women appointed for this melancholy purpose arrived at the miserable cottage which we have already described. Its wretched inmate lay stretched upon the bed, and seemed almost already a lifeless corpse, save for the wandering of the fierce dark eyes, which rolled in their sockets in a manner terrible to look upon, and seemed to watch with surprise and indignation the motions of the strangers, as persons whose presence was alike unexpected

[15] Curse.

and unwelcome. They were frightened at her looks; but, assured in each other's company, they kindled a fire, lighted a candle, prepared food, and made other arrangements for the discharge of the duty assigned them.

The assistants agreed they should watch the bedside of the sick person by turns; but about midnight, overcome by fatigue (for they had walked far that morning), both of them fell fast asleep. When they awoke, which was not till after the interval of some hours, the hut was empty, and the patient gone. They rose in terror, and went to the door of the cottage, which was latched as it had been at night. They looked out into the darkness, and called upon their charge by her name. The night-raven screamed from the old oak-tree, the fox howled on the hill, the hoarse waterfall replied with its echoes, but there was no human answer. The terrified women did not dare to make further search till morning should appear; for the sudden disappearance of a creature so frail as Elspat, together with the wild tenor of her history, intimidated them from stirring from the hut. They remained, therefore, in dreadful terror, sometimes thinking they heard her voice without, and, at other times, that sounds of a different description were mingled with the mournful sigh of the night-breeze, or the dash of the cascade. Sometimes, too, the latch rattled, as if some frail and impotent hand were in vain attempting to lift it, and ever and anon they expected the entrance of their terrible patient, animated by supernatural strength, and in the company, perhaps, of some being more dreadful than herself. Morning came at length. They sought brake, rock, and thicket in vain. Two hours after daylight, the minister himself appeared, and, on the report of the watchers, caused the country to be alarmed, and a general and exact search to be made through the whole neighbourhood of the cottage and the oak-tree. But it was all in vain. Elspat MacTavish was never found, whether dead or alive; nor could there ever be traced the slightest circumstance to indicate her fate.

The neighbourhood was divided concerning the cause of her disappearance. The credulous thought that the evil spirit under whose influence she seemed to have acted had carried her away in the body; and there are many who are still unwilling at untimely hours, to pass the oak-tree, beneath which, as they allege, she may still be seen seated according to her wont. Others less superstitious supposed that had it been possible to search the gulf of the Corrie Dhu, the profound deeps of the lake, or the whelming eddies of the river, the remains of Elspat MacTavish might have been discovered; as nothing was more natural, considering her state of body and mind, than that she should have fallen in by accident, or precipitated herself intentionally into one or other of those places of sure destruction. The clergyman entertained an opinion of his own. He thought that, impatient of the watch which was placed over her, this unhappy woman's instinct had taught her, as it directs various domestic animals, to withdraw herself from the sight of her own race, that the death-struggle might take place in some secret den, where, in all probability, her mortal relics would never meet the eyes of mortals. This species of instinctive feeling seemed to him of a tenor with the whole course of her unhappy life, and most likely to influence her, when it drew to a conclusion.

The Two Drovers

CHAPTER I

It was the day after Doune Fair when my story commences. It had been a brisk market; several dealers had attended from the northern and midland counties in England, and English money had flown so merrily about as to gladden the hearts of the Highland farmers. Many large droves were about to set off for England, under the protection of their owners, or of the topsmen[1] whom they employed in the tedious, laborious, and responsible office of driving the cattle for many hundred miles, from the market where they had been purchased, to the fields or farm-yards where they were to be fattened for the shambles.

The Highlanders, in particular, are masters of this difficult trade of driving, which seems to suit them as well as the trade of

[1] Head drovers.

war. It affords exercise for all their habits of patient endurance and active exertion. They are required to know perfectly the drove-roads, which lie over the wildest tracts of the country, and to avoid as much as possible the highways, which distress the feet of the bullocks, and the turnpikes, which annoy the spirit of the drover; whereas, on the broad green or grey track, which leads across the pathless moor, the herd not only move at ease and without taxation, but, if they mind their business, may pick up a mouthful of food by the way. At night, the drovers usually sleep along with their cattle, let the weather be what it will; and many of these hardy men do not once rest under a roof during a journey on foot from Lochaber to Lincolnshire. They are paid very highly, for the trust reposed is of the last importance, as it depends on their prudence, vigilance, and honesty, whether the cattle reach the final market in good order, and afford a profit to the grazier. But as they maintain themselves at their own expense, they are especially economical in that particular. At the period we speak of, a Highland drover was victualled for his long and toilsome journey with a few handfuls of oatmeal, and two or three onions, renewed from time to time, and a ram's horn filled with whisky, which he used regularly, but sparingly, every night and morning. His dirk, or *skene-dhu* (i.e. black-knife), so worn as to be concealed beneath the arm, or by the folds of the plaid, was his only weapon, excepting the cudgel with which he directed the movements of the cattle. A Highlander was never so happy as on these occasions. There was a variety in the whole journey, which exercised the Celt's natural curiosity and love of motion; there were the constant change of place and scene, the petty adventures incidental to the traffic, and the intercourse with the various farmers, graziers, and traders, intermingled with occasional merry-makings, not the less acceptable to Donald[2] that they were void of expense;—and there was the consciousness of superior skill; for the Highlander, a child amongst flocks, is a prince amongst herds, and his natural habits induce him to disdain the shepherd's slothful life, so that he feels himself nowhere more at home than when following a gallant drove of his country cattle in the character of their guardian.

[2] Standing for 'the typical Highland drover'.

Of the number who left Doune in the morning, and with the purpose we described, not a *Glunamie*[3] of them all cocked his bonnet more briskly, or gartered his tartan hose under knee over a pair of more promising *spiogs* (legs) than did Robin Oig M'Combich, called familiarly Robin Oig, that is, Young, or the Lesser, Robin. Though small of stature, as the epithet Oig implies, and not very strongly limbed, he was as light and alert as one of the deer of his mountains. He had an elasticity of step which, in the course of a long march, made many a stout fellow envy him; and the manner in which he busked[4] his plaid and adjusted his bonnet, argued a consciousness that so smart a John Highlandman as himself would not pass unnoticed among the Lowland lasses. The ruddy cheek, red lips, and white teeth, set off a countenance which had gained by exposure to the weather a healthful and hardy rather than a rugged hue. If Robin Oig did not laugh, or even smile frequently, as indeed is not the practice among his countrymen, his bright eyes usually gleamed from under his bonnet with an expression of cheerfulness ready to be turned into mirth.

The departure of Robin Oig was an incident in the little town, in and near which he had many friends, male and female. He was a topping person in his way, transacted considerable business on his own behalf, and was entrusted by the best farmers in the Highlands, in preference to any other drover in that district. He might have increased his business to any extent had he condescended to manage it by deputy; but except a lad or two, sister's sons of his own, Robin rejected the idea of assistance, conscious, perhaps, how much his reputation depended upon his attending in person to the practical discharge of his duty in every instance. He remained, therefore, contented with the highest premium given to persons of his description, and comforted himself with the hopes that a few journeys to England might enable him to conduct business on his own account, in a manner becoming his birth. For Robin Oig's father, Lachlan M'Combich (or *son of my friend,* his actual clan-surname being M'Gregor), had been so called by the celebrated Rob Roy, because of the particular friendship which had subsisted between the grandsire of Robin

[3] Rough Highlander. [4] Arranged.

and that renowned cateran.[5] Some people even say that Robin Oig derived his Christian name from one as renowned in the wilds of Loch Lomond as ever was his namesake Robin Hood, in the precincts of merry Sherwood. 'Of such ancestry,' as James Boswell says, 'who would not be proud?' Robin Oig was proud accordingly; but his frequent visits to England and to the Lowlands had given him tact enough to know that pretensions, which still gave him a little right to distinction in his own lonely glen, might be both obnoxious and ridiculous if preferred elsewhere. The pride of birth, therefore, was like the miser's treasure, the secret subject of his contemplation, but never exhibited to strangers as a subject of boasting.

Many were the words of gratulation and good luck which were bestowed on Robin Oig. The judges commended his drove, especially Robin's own property, which were the best of them. Some thrust out their snuff-mulls for the parting pinch—others tendered the *doch-an-dorrach,* or parting cup. All cried—'Good luck travel out with you and come home with you.—Give you luck in the Saxon market—brave notes in the *leabhar-dhu*' (black pocket-book), 'and plenty of English gold in the *sporran*' (pouch of goatskin).

The bonny lasses made their adieus more modestly, and more than one, it was said, would have given her best brooch to be certain that it was upon her that his eye last rested as he turned towards the road.

Robin Oig had just given the preliminary '*Hoo-hoo!*' to urge forward the loiterers of the drove, when there was a cry behind him.

'Stay, Robin—bide a blink. Here is Janet of Tomahourich—auld Janet, your father's sister.'

'Plague on her, for an auld Highland witch and spaewife,'[6] said a farmer from the Carse of Stirling; 'she'll cast some of her cantrips[7] on the cattle.'

'She canna do that,' said another sapient of the same profession —'Robin Oig is no the lad to leave any of them, without tying

[5] Cattle-thief, free-booter. [6] Fortune-telling crone.
[7] Spells.

St. Mungo's[8] knot on their tails,[9] and that will put to her speed the best witch that ever flew over Dimayet[10] upon a broomstick.'

It may not be indifferent to the reader to know, that the Highland cattle are peculiarly liable to be *taken*, or infected, by spells and witchcraft; which judicious people guard against by knitting knots of peculiar complexity on the tuft of hair which terminates the animal's tail.

But the old woman who was the object of the farmer's suspicion, seemed only busied about the drover, without paying any attention to the drove. Robin, on the contrary, appeared rather impatient of her presence.

'What auld-world fancy,' he said, 'has brought you so early from the ingle-side this morning, Muhme?[11] I am sure I bid you good-even, and had your God-speed, last night.'

'And left me more siller than the useless old woman will use till you come back again, bird of my bosom,' said the sibyl. 'But it is little I would care for the food that nourishes me, or the fire that warms me, or for God's blessed sun itself, if aught but weel should happen to the grandson of my father. So let me walk the *deasil* round you, that you may go safe out into the foreign land, and come safe home.'

Robin Oig stopped, half embarrassed, half laughing, and signing to those near that he only complied with the old woman to soothe her humour. In the meantime, she traced around him, with wavering steps, the propitiation, which some have thought has been derived from the Druidical mythology. It consists, as is well known, in the person who makes the *deasil* walking three times round the person who is the object of the ceremony, taking care to move according to the course of the sun. At once, however, she stopped short, and exclaimed, in a voice of alarm and horror, 'Grandson of my father, there is blood on your hand.'

'Hush, for God's sake, aunt,' said Robin Oig; 'you will bring more trouble on yourself with this *taishataragh*' (second sight) 'than you will be able to get out of for many a day.'

[8] A Scottish saint of the sixth century, also known as Kentigern.

[9] i.e. in order to avert witchcraft.

[10] Dumyat, a prominent hill to the east of Stirling, one of the peaks of the Ochils.

[11] From the Gaelic *muime*, a stepmother or nurse.

The old woman only repeated, with a ghastly look, 'There is blood on your hand, and it is English blood. The blood of the Gael is richer and redder. Let us see—let us'——

Ere Robin Oig could prevent her, which, indeed, could only have been done by positive violence, so hasty and peremptory were her proceedings, she had drawn from his side the dirk[12] which lodged in the folds of his plaid, and held it up, exclaiming, although the weapon gleamed clear and bright in the sun, 'Blood, blood—Saxon blood again. Robin Oig M'Combich, go not this day to England!'

'Prutt trutt,' answered Robin Oig, 'that will never do neither—it would be next thing to running the country. For shame, Muhme—give me the dirk. You cannot tell by the colour the difference betwixt the blood of a black bullock and a white one, and you speak of knowing Saxon from Gaelic blood. All men have their blood from Adam, Muhme. Give me my skene-dhu, and let me go on my road. I should have been half-way to Stirling Brig by this time.—Give me my dirk, and let me go.'

'Never will I give it to you,' said the old woman—'Never will I quit my hold on your plaid, unless you promise me not to wear that unhappy weapon.'

The women around him urged him also, saying few of his aunt's words fell to the ground; and as the Lowland farmers continued to look moodily on the scene, Robin Oig determined to close it at any sacrifice.

'Well, then,' said the young drover, giving the scabbard of the weapon to Hugh Morrison, 'you Lowlanders care nothing for these freats.[13] Keep my dirk for me. I cannot give it to you, because it was my father's; but your drove follows ours, and I am content it should be in your keeping, not in mine.—Will this do, Muhme?'

'It must,' said the old woman—'that is, if the Lowlander is mad enough to carry the knife.'

The strong westlandman laughed aloud.

'Goodwife,' said he, 'I am Hugh Morrison from Glenae, come of the Manly Morrisons of auld langsyne, that never took short weapon against a man in their lives. And neither needed they.

[12] Dagger. [13] Superstitious notions.

They had their broadswords, and I have this bit supple,' showing a formidable cudgel—'for dirking[14] ower the board, I leave that to John Highlandman—Ye needna snort, none of you Highlanders, and you in especial, Robin. I'll keep the bit knife, if you are feared for the auld spaewife's tale, and give it back to you whenever you want it.'

Robin was not particularly pleased with some part of Hugh Morrison's speech; but he had learned in his travels more patience than belonged to his Highland constitution originally, and he accepted the service of the descendant of the Manly Morrisons without finding fault with the rather depreciating manner in which it was offered.

'If he had not had his morning in his head, and been but a Dumfriesshire hog into the boot, he would have spoken more like a gentleman. But you cannot have more of a sow than a grumph. It's shame my father's knife should ever slash a haggis for the like of him.'

Thus saying (but saying it in Gaelic), Robin drove on his cattle, and waved farewell to all behind him. He was in the greater haste, because he expected to join at Falkirk a comrade and brother in profession, with whom he proposed to travel in company.

Robin Oig's chosen friend was a young Englishman, Harry Wakefield by name, well known at every northern market, and in his way as much famed and honoured as our Highland driver of bullocks. He was nearly six feet high, gallantly formed to keep the rounds at Smithfield, or maintain the ring at a wrestling match; and although he might have been overmatched, perhaps, among the regular professors of the Fancy, yet, as a yokel, or rustic, or a chance customer, he was able to give a bellyful to any amateur of the pugilistic art. Doncaster races saw him in his glory, betting his guinea, and generally successfully; nor was there a main[15] fought in Yorkshire, the feeders being persons of celebrity, at which he was not to be seen, if business permitted. But though a *sprack*[16] lad, and fond of pleasure and its haunts, Harry Wakefield was steady, and not the cautious Robin Oig M'Combich himself was more attentive to the main chance. His holidays

[14] Stabbing (with a dirk). [15] Cockfight. [16] Lively.

were holidays indeed; but his days of work were dedicated to steady and persevering labour. In countenance and temper, Wakefield was the model of old England's merry yeomen, whose clothyard shafts, in so many hundred battles, asserted her superiority over the nations, and whose good sabres, in our own time, are her cheapest and most assured defence. His mirth was readily excited; for, strong in limb and constitution, and fortunate in circumstances, he was disposed to be pleased with everything about him; and such difficulties as he might occasionally encounter were, to a man of his energy, rather matter of amusement than serious annoyance. With all the merits of a sanguine temper, our young English drover was not without his defects. He was irascible, sometimes to the verge of being quarrelsome; and perhaps not the less inclined to bring his disputes to a pugilistic decision, because he found few antagonists able to stand up to him in the boxing ring.

It is difficult to say how Harry Wakefield and Robin Oig first became intimates; but it is certain a close acquaintance had taken place betwixt them, although they had apparently few common subjects of conversation or of interest, so soon as their talk ceased to be of bullocks. Robin Oig, indeed, spoke the English language rather imperfectly upon any other topics but stots[17] and kyloes,[18] and Harry Wakefield could never bring his broad Yorkshire tongue to utter a single word of Gaelic. It was in vain Robin spent a whole morning, during a walk over Minch Moor, in attempting to teach his companion to utter, with true precision, the shibboleth *Llhu*, which is the Gaelic for a calf. From Traquair to Murder-cairn, the hill rang with the discordant attempts of the Saxon upon the unmanageable monosyllable, and the heartfelt laugh which followed every failure. They had, however, better modes of awakening the echoes; for Wakefield could sing many a ditty to the praise of Moll, Susan, and Cicely, and Robin Oig had a particular gift at whistling interminable pibrochs[19] through all their involutions, and what was more agreeable to his companion's southern ear, knew many of the northern airs, both lively and pathetic, to which Wakefield learned to pipe a bass. Thus, though Robin could hardly have comprehended his companion's

[17] Bulls. [18] Highland cattle. [19] Highland airs.

stories about horse-racing, and cock-fighting or fox-hunting, and although his own legends of clan-fights and *creaghs*,[20] varied with talk of Highland goblins and fairy folk, would have been caviare to his companion, they contrived nevertheless to find a degree of pleasure in each other's company, which had for three years back induced them to join company and travel together, when the direction of their journey permitted. Each, indeed, found his advantage in this companionship; for where could the Englishman have found a guide through the Western Highlands like Robin Oig M'Combich? and when they were on what Harry called the *right* side of the Border, his patronage, which was extensive, and his purse, which was heavy, were at all times at the service of his Highland friend, and on many occasion his liberality did him genuine yeoman's service.

[20] Cattle-stealing raids.

CHAPTER II

THE pair of friends had traversed with their usual cordiality the grassy wilds of Liddesdale, and crossed the opposite part of Cumberland, emphatically called The Waste. In these solitary regions, the cattle under the charge of our drovers derived their subsistence chiefly by picking their food as they went along the drove-road, or sometimes by the tempting opportunity of a *start and owerloup*, or invasion of the neighbouring pasture, where an occasion presented itself. But now the scene changed before them; they were descending towards a fertile and enclosed country, where no such liberties could be taken with impunity, or without a previous arrangement and bargain with the possessors of the ground. This was more especially the case, as a great northern fair was upon the eve of taking place, where both the Scotch and English drover expected to dispose of a part of their cattle, which it was desirable to produce in the market, rested and in good order. Fields were therefore difficult to be obtained, and only upon high terms. This necessity occasioned a temporary separation betwixt the two friends, who went to bargain, each as he could, for the separate accommodation of his herd. Unhappily it chanced that both of them, unknown to each other, thought of bargaining for the ground they wanted on the property of a country gentleman of some fortune, whose estate lay in the neighbourhood. The English drover applied to the bailiff on the property, who was known to him. It chanced that the Cumbrian squire, who had entertained some suspicions of his manager's honesty, was taking occasional measures to ascertain how far they were well founded, and had desired that any inquiries about his enclosures, with a view to occupy them for a temporary purpose, should be referred to himself. As, however, Mr. Ireby had gone the day before upon a journey of some miles' distance to the northward, the bailiff chose to consider the check upon his full powers as for the time removed, and concluded that he should best consult his master's interest, and perhaps his own, in making an agreement with Harry Wakefield. Meanwhile, ignorant of what his comrade was doing, Robin Oig, on his side, chanced to be overtaken by a good-looking smart little man upon a pony, most knowingly[1] hogged[2] and cropped, as was then the fashion, the rider wearing tight leather breeches and long-necked bright spurs. This cavalier asked one or two pertinent questions about markets and the price of stock. So Robin, seeing him a well-judging civil gentleman, took the freedom to ask him whether he could let him know if there was any grassland to be let in that neighbourhood, for the temporary accommodation of his drove. He could not have put the question to more willing ears. The gentleman of the buckskin was the proprieter with whose bailiff Harry Wakefield had dealt or was in the act of dealing.

'Thou art in good luck, my canny Scot,' said Mr. Ireby, 'to have spoken to me, for I see thy cattle have done their day's work, and I have at my disposal the only field within three miles that is to be let in these parts.'

'The drove can pe gang two, three, four miles very pratty weel indeed,' said the cautious Highlander; 'put what would his honour be axing for the peasts pe the head, if she was to tak the park for twa or three days?'

'We won't differ, Sawney,[3] if you let me have six stots for winterers, in the way of reason.'

[1] Fashionably. [2] Clipped.
[3] 'Sandy' (Englishman's name for a Scotsman).

'And which peasts wad your honour pe for having?'

'Why—let me see—the two black—the dun one—yon doddy[4]—him with the twisted horn—the brocket[5]—How much by the head?'

'Ah,' said Robin, 'your honour is a shudge—a real shudge—I couldna have set off the pest six peasts petter mysell, me that ken them as if they were my pairns, puir things.'

'Well, how much per head, Sawney?' continued Mr. Ireby.

'It was high markets at Doune and Falkirk,' answered Robin.

And thus the conversation proceeded, until they had agreed on the *prix juste* for the bullocks, the squire throwing in the temporary accommodation of the enclosure for the cattle into the boot, and Robin making, as he thought, a very good bargain, provided the grass was but tolerable. The squire walked his pony alongside of the drove, partly to show him the way, and see him put into possession of the field, and partly to learn the latest news of the northern markets.

They arrived at the field, and the pasture seemed excellent. But what was their surprise when they saw the bailiff quietly inducting the cattle of Harry Wakefield into the grassy Goshen[6] which had just been assigned to those of Robin Oig M'Combich by the proprietor himself! Squire Ireby set spurs to his horse, dashed up to his servant, and learning what had passed between the parties, briefly informed the English drover that his bailiff had let the ground without his authority, and that he might seek grass for his cattle wherever he would, since he was to get none there. At the same time he rebuked his servant severely for having transgressed his commands, and ordered him instantly to assist in ejecting the hungry and weary cattle of Harry Wakefield, which were just beginning to enjoy a meal of unusual plenty, and to introduce those of his comrade, whom the English drover now began to consider as a rival.

The feelings which arose in Wakefield's mind would have induced him to resist Mr. Ireby's decision; but every Englishman has a tolerably accurate sense of law and justice, and John Fleecebumpkin, the bailiff, having acknowledged that he had exceeded

[4] Without horns. [5] Black and white or parti-coloured.
[6] (Biblical)—fertile land.

his commission, Wakefield saw nothing else for it than to collect his hungry and disappointed charge, and drive them on to seek quarters elsewhere. Robin Oig saw what had happened with regret, and hastened to offer to his English friend to share with him the disputed possession. But Wakefield's pride was severely hurt, and he answered disdainfully, 'Take it all, man—take it all—never make two bites of a cherry—thou canst talk over the gentry, and blear a plain man's eye—Out upon you, man—I would not kiss any man's dirty latchets[7] for leave to bake in his oven.'

Robin Oig, sorry but not surprised at his comrade's displeasure, hastened to entreat his friend to wait but an hour till he had gone to the squire's house to receive payment for the cattle he had sold, and he would come back and help him to drive the cattle into some convenient place of rest, and explain to him the whole mistake they had both of them fallen into. But the Englishman continued indignant: 'Thou hast been selling, hast thou? Aye, aye,—thou is a cunning lad for kenning the hours of bargaining. Go to the devil with thyself, for I will ne'er see thy fause loon's visage again—thou should be ashamed to look me in the face.'

'I am ashamed to look no man in the face,' said Robin Oig, something moved; 'and, moreover, I will look you in the face this blessed day, if you will bide at the clachan[8] down yonder.'

'Mayhap you had as well keep away,' said his comrade; and turning his back on his former friend, he collected his unwilling associates, assisted by the bailiff, who took some real and some affected interest in seeing Wakefield accommodated.

After spending some time in negotiating with more than one of the neighbouring farmers, who could not, or would not, afford the accommodation desired, Henry Wakefield at last, and in his necessity, accomplished his point by means of the landlord of the alehouse at which Robin Oig and he had agreed to pass the night, when they first separated from each other. Mine host was content to let him turn his cattle on a piece of barren moor, at a price little less than the bailiff had asked for the disputed enclosure; and the wretchedness of the pasture, as well as the price paid for

[7] Shoe-strings. [8] Hamlet.

it, were set down as exaggerations of the breach of faith and friendship of his Scottish crony. This turn of Wakefield's passions was encouraged by the bailiff (who had his own reasons for being offended against poor Robin, as having been the unwitting cause of his falling into disgrace with his master), as well as by the innkeeper, and two or three chance guests, who stimulated the drover in his resentment against his quondam associate,—some from the ancient grudge against the Scots which, when it exists anywhere, is to be found lurking in the Border counties, and some from the general love of mischief, which characterizes mankind in all ranks of life, to the honour of Adam's children be it spoken. Good John Barleycorn[9] also, who always heightens and exaggerates the prevailing passions, be they angry or kindly, was not wanting in his offices on this occasion; and confusion to false friends and hard masters was pledged in more than one tankard.

In the meanwhile Mr. Ireby found some amusement in detaining the northern drover at his ancient hall. He caused a cold round of beef to be placed before the Scot in the butler's pantry, together with a foaming tankard of home-brewed, and took pleasure in seeing the hearty appetite with which these unwonted edibles were discussed by Robin Oig M'Combich. The squire himself lighting his pipe, compounded between his patrician dignity and his love of agricultural gossip, by walking up and down while he conversed with his guest.

'I passed another drove,' said the squire, 'with one of your countrymen behind them—they were something less beasts than your drove, doddies most of them—a big man was with them—none of your kilts though, but a decent pair of breeches—D'ye know who he may be?'

'Hout aye—that might, could, and would be Hughie Morrison—I didna think he could hae peen sae weel up. He had made a day on us; but his Argyleshires will have wearied shanks. How far was he pehind?'

'I think about six or seven miles,' answered the squire, 'for I passed them at the Christenbury Crag, and I overtook you at the Hollan Bush. If his beasts be leg-weary, he will be maybe selling bargains.'

[9] Meaning 'drink'; malt liquors made from barley.

'Na, na, Hughie Morrison is no the man for pargains—ye maun come to some Highland body like Robin Oig hersell for the like of these—put I maun pe wishing you goot night, and twenty of them let alane ane, and I maun down to the Clachan to see if the lad Harry Waakfelt is out of his humdudgeons yet.'

The party at the ale-house were still in full talk, and the treachery of Robin Oig still the theme of conversation, when the supposed culprit entered the apartment. His arrival, as usually happens in such a case, put an instant stop to the discussion of which he had furnished the subject, and he was received by the company assembled with that chilling silence which, more than a thousand exclamations, tells an intruder that he is unwelcome. Surprised and offended, but not appalled by the reception which he experienced, Robin entered with an undaunted and even a haughty air, attempted no greeting as he saw he was received with none, and placed himself by the side of the fire, a little apart from a table at which Harry Wakefield, the bailiff, and two or three other persons, were seated. The ample Cumbrian kitchen would have afforded plenty of room, even for a larger separation.

Robin, thus seated, proceeded to light his pipe, and call for a pint of twopenny.

'We have no twopence ale,' answered Ralph Heskett, the landlord; 'but as thou find'st thy own tobacco, it's like thou may'st find thy own liquor too—it's the wont of thy country, I wot.'

'Shame, goodman,' said the landlady, a blithe bustling housewife, hastening herself to supply the guest with liquor—'Thou knowest well enow what the strange man wants, and it's thy trade to be civil, man. Thou shouldst know, that if the Scot likes a small pot, he pays a sure penny.'

Without taking any notice of this nuptial dialogue, the Highlander took the flagon in his hand, and addressing the company generally, drank the interesting toast of 'Good markets', to the party assembled.

'The better that the wind blew fewer dealers from the north,' said one of the farmers, 'and fewer Highland runts[10] to eat up the English meadows.'

'Saul of my pody, put you are wrang there, my friend,'

[10] Cows.

answered Robin, with composure; 'it is your fat Englishmen that eat up our Scots cattle, puir things.'

'I wish there was a summat to eat up their drovers,' said another; 'a plain Englishman canna make bread within a kenning of them.'[11]

'Or an honest servant keep his master's favour, but they will come sliding in between him and the sunshine,' said the bailiff.

'If these pe jokes,' said Robin Oig, with the same composure, 'there is ower mony jokes upon one man.'

'It is no joke, but downright earnest,' said the bailiff. 'Harkye, Mr. Robin Ogg, or whatever is your name, it's right we should tell you that we are all of one opinion, and that is, that you, Mr. Robin Ogg, have behaved to our friend Mr. Harry Wakefield here, like a raff[12] and a blackguard.'

'Nae doubt, nae doubt,' answered Robin, with great composure; 'and you are a set of very pretty judges, for whose prains or pe-haviour I wad not gie a pinch of sneeshing.[13] If Mr. Harry Waak-felt kens where he is wranged, he kens where he may be righted.'

'He speaks truth,' said Wakefield, who had listened to what passed, divided between the offence which he had taken at Robin's late behaviour, and the revival of his habitual feelings of regard.

He now arose, and went towards Robin, who got up from his seat as he approached, and held out his hand.

'That's right, Harry—go it—serve him out,' resounded on all sides—'tip him the nailer—show him the mill.'

'Hold your peace all of you, and be——,' said Wakefield; and then addressing his comrade, he took him by the extended hand, with something alike of respect and defiance. 'Robin,' he said, 'thou hast used me ill enough this day; but if you mean, like a frank fellow, to shake hands, and make a tussle for love on the sod, why I'll forgie thee, man, and we shall be better friends than ever.'

'And would it not pe petter to pe cood friends without more of the matter?' said Robin; 'we will be much petter friendships with our panes hale than proken.'

[11] Without them knowing.
[12] Worthless fellow.
[13] Snuff.

Harry Wakefield dropped the hand of his friend, or rather threw it from him.

'I did not think I had been keeping company for three years with a coward.'

'Coward pelongs to none of my name,' said Robin, whose eyes began to kindle, but keeping the command of his temper. 'It was no coward's legs or hands, Harry Waakfelt, that drew you out of the fords of Frew, when you was drifting ower the plack rock, and every eel in the river expected his share of you.'

'And that is true enough, too,' said the Englishman, struck by the appeal.

'Adzooks!' exclaimed the bailiff—'sure Harry Wakefield, the nattiest lad at Whitson Tryste, Wooler Fair, Carlisle Sands, or Stagshaw Bank, is not going to show white feather? Ah, this comes of living so long with kilts and bonnets—men forget the use of their daddles.'[14]

'I may teach you, Master Fleecebumpkin, that I have not lost the use of mine,' said Wakefield, and then went on. 'This will never do, Robin. We must have a turn-up, or we shall be the talk of the country-side. I'll be d——d if I hurt thee—I'll put on the gloves gin thou like. Comc, stand forward like a man.'

'To pe peaten like a dog,' said Robin; 'is there any reason in that? If you think I have done you wrong, I'll go before your shudge, though I neither know his law nor his language.'

A general cry of 'No, no—no law, no lawyer! a bellyful and be friends,' was echoed by the bystanders.

'But,' continued Robin, 'if I am to fight, I've no skill to fight like a jackanapes, with hands and nails.'

'How would you fight, then,' said his antagonist; 'though I am thinking it would be hard to bring you to the scratch anyhow.'

'I would fight with proadswords, and sink point on the first plood drawn—like a gentlemans.'

A loud shout of laughter followed the proposal, which indeed had rather escaped from poor Robin's swelling heart, than been the dictate of his sober judgement.

'Gentleman, quotha!' was echoed on all sides, with a shout of unextinguishable laughter; 'a very pretty gentleman, God wot—

[14] Fists.

Canst get two swords for the gentlemen to fight with, Ralph Heskett?'

'No, but I can send to the armoury at Carlisle, and lend them two forks, to be making shift with in the meantime.'

'Tush, man,' said another, 'the bonny Scots come into the world with the blue bonnet on their heads, and dirk and pistol at their belt.'

'Best send post,' said Mr. Fleecebumpkin, 'to the squire of Corby Castle, to come and stand second to the *gentleman*.'

In the midst of this torrent of general ridicule, the Highlander instinctively griped beneath the folds of his plaid.

'But it's better not,' he said in his own language. 'A hundred curses on the swine-eaters, who know neither decency nor civility!'

'Make room, the pack of you,' he said, advancing to the door.

But his former friend interposed his sturdy bulk, and opposed his leaving the house; and when Robin Oig attempted to make his way by force, he hit him down on the floor, with as much ease as a boy bowls down a nine-pin.

'A ring, a ring!' was now shouted, until the dark rafters, and the hams that hung on them, trembled again, and the very platters on the *bink*[15] clattered against each other. 'Well done, Harry,'—'Give it him home, Harry,'—'Take care of him now,—he sees his own blood!'

Such were the exclamations, while the Highlander, starting from the ground, all his coldness and caution lost in frantic rage, sprang at his antagonist with the fury, the activity, and the vindictive purpose, of an incensed tiger-cat. But when could rage encounter science and temper? Robin Oig again went down in the unequal contest; and as the blow was necessarily a severe one, he lay motionless on the floor of the kitchen. The landlady ran to offer some aid, but Mr. Fleecebumpkin would not permit her to approach.

'Let him alone,' he said, 'he will come to within time, and come up to the scratch again. He has not got half his broth yet.'

'He has got all I mean to give him, though,' said his antagonist, whose heart began to relent towards his old associate; 'and I would rather by half give the rest to yourself, Mr. Fleecebumpkin,

[15] Rack, bench

for you pretend to know a thing or two, and Robin had not art enough even to peel before setting to, but fought with his plaid dangling about him.—Stand up, Robin, my man! all friends now; and let me hear the man that will speak a word against you, or your country, for your sake.'

Robin Oig was still under the dominion of his passion, and eager to renew the onset; but being withheld on the one side by the peace-making Dame Heskett, and on the other, aware that Wakefield no longer meant to renew the combat, his fury sank into gloomy sullenness.

'Come, come, never grudge so much at it, man,' said the brave-spirited Englishman, with the placability of his country, 'shake hands, and we will be better friends than ever.'

'Friends!' exclaimed Robin Oig, with strong emphasis—'friends! Never. Look to yourself, Harry Waakfelt.'

'Then the curse of Cromwell on your proud Scots stomach, as the man says in the play, and you may do your worst, and be d——d; for one man can say nothing more to another after a tussle, than that he is sorry for it.'

On these terms the friends parted; Robin Oig drew out, in silence, a piece of money, threw it on the table, and then left the ale-house. But turning at the door, he shook his hand at Wakefield, pointing with his forefinger upwards, in a manner which might imply either a threat or a caution. He then disappeared in the moonlight.

Some words passed after his departure, between the bailiff, who piqued himself on being a little of a bully, and Harry Wakefield, who, with generous inconsistency, was now not indisposed to begin a new combat in defence of Robin Oig's reputation, 'although he could not use his daddles like an Englishman, as it did not come natural to him.' But Dame Heskett prevented this second quarrel from coming to a head by her peremptory interference. 'There should be no more fighting in her house,' she said; 'there had been too much already.—And you, Mr. Wakefield, may live to learn,' she added, 'what it is to make a deadly enemy out of a good friend.'

'Pshaw, dame! Robin Oig is an honest fellow, and will never keep malice.'

'Do not trust to that—you do not know the dour temper of the Scots, though you have dealt with them so often. I have a right to know them, my mother being a Scot.'

'And so is well seen on her daughter,' said Ralph Heskett.

This nuptial sarcasm gave the discourse another turn; fresh customers entered the tap-room or kitchen, and others left it. The conversation turned on the expected markets, and the report of prices from different parts both of Scotland and England—treaties were commenced, and Harry Wakefield was lucky enough to find a chap for a part of his drove, and at a very considerable profit; an event of consequence more than sufficient to blot out all remembrances of the unpleasant scuffle in the earlier part of the day. But there remained one party from whose mind that recollection could not have been wiped away by the possession of every head of cattle betwixt Esk and Eden.

This was Robin Oig M'Combich.—'That I should have had no weapon,' he said, 'and for the first time in my life!—Blighted be the tongue that bids the Highlander part with the dirk—the dirk—ha! the English blood!—My Muhme's word—when did her word fall to the ground?'

The recollection of the fatal prophecy confirmed the deadly intention which instantly sprang up in his mind.

'Ha! Morrison cannot be many miles behind; and if it were a hundred, what then?'

His impetuous spirit had now a fixed purpose and motive of action, and he turned the light foot of his country towards the wilds, through which he knew, by Mr. Ireby's report, that Morrison was advancing. His mind was wholly engrossed by the sense of injury—injury sustained from a friend; and by the desire of vengeance on one whom he now accounted his most bitter enemy. The treasured ideas of self-importance and self-opinion—of ideal birth and quality, had become more precious to him, like the hoard to the miser, because he could only enjoy them in secret. But that hoard was pillaged, the idols which he had secretly worshipped had been desecrated and profaned. Insulted, abused, and beaten, he was no longer worthy, in his own opinion, of the name he bore, or the lineage which he belonged to—nothing was left to him—nothing but revenge; and, as the reflection added a galling spur to every step, he determined it should be as sudden and signal as the offence.

When Robin Oig left the door of the ale-house, seven or eight English miles at least lay betwixt Morrison and him. The advance of the former was slow, limited by the sluggish pace of his cattle; the last left behind him stubble-field and hedge-row, crag and dark heath, all glittering with frost-rime in the broad November moonlight, at the rate of six miles an hour. And now the distant lowing of Morrison's cattle is heard; and now they are seen creeping like moles in size and slowness of motion on the broad face of the moor; and now he meets them—passes them, and stops their conductor.

'May good betide us,' said the Southlander—'Is this you, Robin M'Combich, or your wraith?'

'It is Robin Oig M'Combich,' answered the Highlander, 'and it is not.—But never mind that, put pe giving me the skene-dhu.'

'What! you are for back to the Highlands—The devil!—Have you selt all off before the fair? This beats all for quick markets!'

'I have not sold—I am not going north—May pe I will never go north again.—Give me pack my dirk, Hugh Morrison, or there will pe words petween us.'

'Indeed, Robin, I'll be better advised before I gie it back to you —it is a wanchancy[16] weapon in a Highlandman's hand, and I am thinking you will be about some barns-breaking.'[17]

'Prutt, trutt! let me have my weapon,' said Robin Oig, impatiently.

'Hooly, and fairly,' said his well-meaning friend. 'I'll tell you what will do better than these dirking doings—Ye ken Highlander, and Lowlander, and Border-men, are a' ae man's bairns when you are over the Scots dyke. See, the Eskdale callants, and fighting Charlie of Liddesdale, and the Lockerby lads, and the four Dandies of Lustruther, and a wheen mair grey plaids, are coming up behind, and if you are wranged, there is the hand of a Manly Morrison, we'll see you righted, if Carlisle and Stanwix baith took up the feud.'

'To tell you the truth,' said Robin Oig, desirous of eluding the

[16] Unlucky.
[17] Escapade.

suspicions of his friend, 'I have enlisted with a party of the Black Watch,[18] and must march off to-morrow morning.'

'Enlisted! Were you mad or drunk?—You must buy yourself off—I can lend you twenty notes, and twenty to that, if the drove sell.'

'I thank you—thank ye, Hughie; but I go with good will the gate that I am going,—so the dirk—the dirk!'

'There it is for you then, since less wunna serve. But think on what I was saying.—Waes me, it will be sair news in the braes of Balquidder, that Robin Oig M'Combich should have run an ill gate, and ta'en on.'

'Ill news in Balquidder, indeed!' echoed poor Robin. 'But Cot speed you, Hughie, and send you good marcats. Ye winna meet with Robin Oig again, either at tryste or fair.'

So saying, he shook hastily the hand of his acquaintance, and set out in the direction from which he had advanced, with the spirit of his former pace.

'There is something wrang with the lad,' muttered the Morrison to himself, 'but we'll maybe see better into it the morn's morning.'

But long ere the morning dawned, the catastrophe of our tale had taken place. It was two hours after the affray had happened, and it was totally forgotten by almost every one, when Robin Oig returned to Heskett's inn. The place was filled at once by various sorts of men, and with noises corresponding to their character. There were the grave low sounds of men engaged in busy traffic, with the laugh, the song, and the riotous jest of those who had nothing to do but to enjoy themselves. Among the last was Harry Wakefield, who, amidst a grinning group of smock-frocks, hob-nailed shoes, and jolly English physiognomies, was trolling forth the old ditty,

> What though my name be Roger,
> Who drives the plough and cart—

when he was interrupted by a well-known voice saying in a high and stern tone, marked by the sharp Highland accent, 'Harry Waakfelt—if you be a man, stand up!'

[18] The first regiment of Highlanders raised for the royal service.

'What is the matter?—what is it?' the guests demanded of each other.

'It is only a d——d Scotsman,' said Fleecebumpkin, who was by this time very drunk, 'whom Harry Wakefield helped to his broth the day, who is now come to have *his cauld kail* het[19] again.'

'Harry Waakfelt,' repeated the same ominous summons, 'stand up, if you be a man!'

There is something in the tone of deep and concentrated passion, which attracts attention and imposes awe, even by the very sound. The guests shrank back on every side, and gazed at the Highlander as he stood in the middle of them, his brows bent, and his features rigid with resolution.

'I will stand up with all my heart, Robin, my boy, but it shall be to shake hands with you, and drink down all unkindness. It is not the fault of your heart, man, that you don't know how to clench your hands.'

But this time he stood opposite to his antagonist; his open and unsuspecting look strangely contrasted with the stern purpose, which gleamed wild, dark, and vindictive in the eyes of the Highlander.

''Tis not thy fault, man, that, not having the luck to be an Englishman, thou canst not fight more than a schoolgirl.'

'I *can* fight,' answered Robin Oig sternly, but calmly, 'and you shall know it. You, Harry Waakfelt, showed me to-day how the Saxon churls fight—I show you now how the Highland Dunniè-wassel[20] fights.'

He seconded the word with the action, and plunged the dagger, which he suddenly displayed, into the broad breast of the English yeoman, with such fatal certainty and force, that the hilt made a hollow sound against the breast-bone, and the double-edged point split the very heart of his victim. Harry Wakefield fell and expired with a single groan. His assassin next seized the bailiff by the collar, and offered the bloody poniard to his throat, whilst dread and surprise rendered the man incapable of defence.

'It were very just to lay you beside him,' he said, 'but the blood of a base pickthank shall never mix on my father's dirk with that of a brave man.'

[19] Cold cabbage heated. [20] Gentleman.

As he spoke, he cast the man from him with so much force that he fell on the floor, while Robin, with his other hand, threw the fatal weapon into the blazing turf-fire.

'There,' he said, 'take me who likes—and let fire cleanse blood if it can.'

The pause of astonishment still continuing, Robin Oig asked for a peace-officer, and a constable having stepped out, he surrendered himself to his custody.

'A bloody night's work you have made of it,' said the constable.

'Your own fault,' said the Highlander. 'Had you kept his hands off me twa hours since, he would have been now as well and merry as he was twa minutes since.'

'It must be sorely answered,' said the peace-officer.

'Never you mind that—death pays all debts; it will pay that too.'

The horror of the bystanders began now to give way to indignation; and the sight of a favourite companion murdered in the midst of them, the provocation being, in their opinion, so utterly inadequate to the excess of vengeance, might have induced them to kill the perpetrator of the deed even upon the very spot. The constable, however, did his duty on this occasion, and with the assistance of some of the more reasonable persons present, procured horses to guard the prisoner to Carlisle, to abide his doom at the next assizes. While the escort was preparing, the prisoner neither expressed the least interest nor attempted the slightest reply. Only, before he was carried from the fatal apartment, he desired to look at the dead body, which, raised from the floor, had been deposited upon the large table (at the head of which Harry Wakefield had presided but a few minutes before, full of life, vigour, and animation) until the surgeons should examine the mortal wound. The face of the corpse was decently covered with a napkin. To the surprise and horror of the bystanders, which displayed itself in a general *Ah!* drawn through clenched teeth and half-shut lips, Robin Oig removed the cloth, and gazed with a mournful but steady eye on the lifeless visage, which had been so lately animated, that the smile of good-humoured confidence in his own strength, of conciliation at once and contempt towards his enemy, still curled his lip. While those present expected that the wound, which had so lately flooded the apartment with gore, would send forth fresh streams at the touch of the homicide, Robin Oig replaced the covering with the brief exclamation—'He was a pretty man!'

My story is nearly ended. The unfortunate Highlander stood his trial at Carlisle. I was myself present, and as a young Scottish lawyer, or barrister at least, and reputed a man of some quality, the politeness of the Sheriff of Cumberland offered me a place on the bench. The facts of the case were proved in the manner I have related them; and whatever might be at first the prejudice of the audience against a crime so un-English as that of assassination from revenge, yet when the rooted national prejudices of the prisoner had been explained, which made him consider himself as stained with indelible dishonour when subjected to personal violence; when his previous patience, moderation, and endurance, were considered, the generosity of the English audience was inclined to regard his crime as the wayward aberration of a false idea of honour rather than as flowing from a heart naturally savage, or perverted by habitual vice. I shall never forget the charge of the venerable judge to the jury, although not at that time liable to be much affected either by that which was eloquent or pathetic.

'We have had,' he said, 'in the previous part of our duty' (alluding to some former trials) 'to discuss crimes which infer disgust and abhorrence, while they call down the well-merited vengeance of the law. It is now our still more melancholy task to apply its salutary though severe enactments to a case of a very singular character, in which the crime (for a crime it is, and a deep one) arose less out of the malevolence of the heart, than the error of the understanding—less from any idea of committing wrong, than from an unhappily perverted notion of that which is right. Here we have two men, highly esteemed, it has been stated, in their rank of life, and attached, it seems, to each other as friends, one of whose lives has been already sacrificed to a punctilio, and the other is about to prove the vengeance of the offended laws; and yet both may claim our commiseration at least, as men acting in ignorance of each other's national prejudices, and unhappily misguided rather than voluntarily erring from the path of right conduct.

'In the original cause of the misunderstanding, we must in justice give the right to the prisoner at the bar. He had acquired possession of the enclosure, which was the object of competition, by a legal contract with the proprietor, Mr. Ireby; and yet, when accosted with reproaches undeserved in themselves, and galling doubtless to a temper at least sufficiently susceptible of passion, he offered nothwithstanding to yield up half his acquisition for the sake of peace and good neighbourhood, and his amicable proposal was rejected with scorn. Then follows the scene at Mr. Heskett the publican's, and you will observe how the stranger was treated by the deceased, and, I am sorry to observe, by those around, who seem to have urged him in a manner which was aggravating in the highest degree. While he asked for peace and for composition, and offered submission to a magistrate, or to a mutual arbiter, the prisoner was insulted by a whole company, who seem on this occasion to have forgotten the national maxim of "fair play"; and while attempting to escape from the place in peace, he was intercepted, struck down, and beaten to the effusion of his blood.

'Gentlemen of the jury, it was with some impatience that I heard my learned brother, who opened the case for the crown, give an unfavourable turn to the prisoner's conduct on this occasion. He said the prisoner was afraid to encounter his antagonist in fair fight, or to submit to the laws of the ring; and that therefore, like a cowardly Italian, he had recourse to his fatal stiletto, to murder the man whom he dared not meet in manly encounter. I observed the prisoner shrink from this part of the accusation with the abhorrence natural to a brave man; and as I would wish to make my words impressive when I point his real crime, I must secure his opinion of my impartiality, by rebutting everything that seems to me a false accusation. There can be no doubt that the prisoner is a man of resolution—too much resolution—I wish to Heaven that he had less, or rather that he had had a better education to regulate it.

'Gentlemen, as to the laws my brother talks of, they may be known in the bull-ring, or the bear-garden, or the cockpit, but they are not known here. Or, if they should be so far admitted as furnishing a species of proof that no malice was intended in this sort of combat, from which fatal accidents do sometimes arise, it can only be so admitted when both parties are *in pari casu*,[21] equally acquainted with, and equally willing to refer themselves to, that species of arbitrement. But will it be contended that a man of superior rank and education is to be subjected, or is obliged to subject himself, to this coarse and brutal strife, perhaps in opposition to a younger, stronger, or more skilful opponent? Certainly even the pugilistic code, if founded upon the fair play of Merry Old England, as my brother alleges it to be, can contain nothing so preposterous. And, gentlemen of the jury, if the laws would support an English gentleman, wearing, we will suppose, his sword, in defending himself, by force against a violent personal aggression of the nature offered to this prisoner, they will not less protect a foreigner and a stranger, involved in the same unpleasing circumstances. If, therefore, gentlemen of the jury, when thus pressed by a *vis major*,[22] the object of obloquy to a whole company, and of direct violence from one at least, and, as he might reasonably apprehend, from more, the panel had produced the weapon which his countrymen, as we are informed, generally carry about their persons, and the same unhappy circumstance had ensued which you have heard detailed in evidence, I could not in my conscience have asked from you a verdict of murder. The prisoner's personal defence might, indeed, even in that case, have gone more or less beyond the *Moderamen inculpatae tutelae*,[23] spoken of by lawyers, but the punishment incurred would have been that of manslaughter, not of murder. I beg leave to add that I should have thought this milder species of charge was demanded in the case supposed, notwithstanding the statute of James I, cap. 8, which takes the case of slaughter by stabbing, with a short weapon, even without malice prepense,[24] out of the benefit of clergy.[25] For this statute of stabbing, as it is

[21] On the same footing. [22] Greater force.

[23] In law the regulation of justifiable defence. It expresses that degree of force in defence of person or property which a person might safely use, even though it should cause the death of the aggressor.

[24] Aforethought or previous intention.

[25] Exemption from capital punishment, accorded to *clerks*, those who could read. The privilege came to be abused, and Parliament took to enacting that certain crimes should be without benefit of clergy, and finally it was altogether abolished—in fact in 1827, the year in which this story was written.

9110212 D

termed, arose out of a temporary cause; and as the real guilt is the same, whether the slaughter be committed by the dagger, or by sword or pistol, the benignity of the modern law places them all on the same, or nearly the same footing.

'But, gentlemen of the jury, the pinch of the case lies in the interval of two hours interposed betwixt the reception of the injury and the fatal retaliation. In the heat of affray and *chaude mêlée*,[26] law, compassionating the infirmities of humanity, makes allowance for the passions which rule such a stormy moment—for the sense of present pain, for the apprehension of further injury, for the difficulty of ascertaining with due accuracy the precise degree of violence which is necessary to protect the person of the individual, without annoying or injuring the assailant more than is absolutely requisite. But the time necessary to walk twelve miles, however speedily performed, was an interval sufficient for the prisoner to have recollected himself; and the violence with which he carried his purpose into effect, with so many circumstances of deliberate determination, could neither be induced by the passion of anger, nor that of fear. It was the purpose and the act of predetermined revenge, for which law neither can, will, nor ought to have sympathy or allowance.

'It is true, we may repeat to ourselves, in alleviation of this poor man's unhappy action, that his case is a very peculiar one. The country which he inhabits, was, in the days of many now alive, inaccessible to the laws, not only of England, which have not even yet penetrated thither, but to those to which our neighbours of Scotland are subjected, and which must be supposed to be, and no doubt actually are, founded upon the general principles of justice and equity which pervade every civilized country. Amongst their mountains, as among the North American Indians, the various tribes were wont to make war upon each other, so that each man was obliged to go armed for his own protection. These men, from the ideas which they entertained of their own descent and of their own consequence, regarded themselves as so many cavaliers or men-at-arms, rather than as the peasantry of a peaceful country. Those laws of the ring, as my

[26] In the heat of an affray, a homicide committed under the influence of passion. (I am grateful to John Finnis for legal definitions.)

brother terms them, were unknown to the race of warlike mountaineers; that decision of quarrels by no other weapons than those which nature has given every man, must to them have seemed as vulgar and as preposterous as to the noblesse of France. Revenge, on the other hand, must have been as familiar to their habits of society as to those of the Cherokees or Mohawks. It is indeed, as described by Bacon, at bottom a kind of wild untutored justice; for the fear of retaliation must withhold the hands of the oppressor where there is no regular law to check daring violence. But though all this may be granted, and though we may allow that, such having been the case of the Highlands in the days of the prisoner's fathers, many of the opinions and sentiments must still continue to influence the present generation, it cannot, and ought not, even in this most painful case, to alter the administration of the law, either in your hands, gentlemen of the jury, or in mine. The first object of civilization is to place the general protection of the law, equally administered, in the room of that wild justice, which every man cut and carved for himself, according to the length of his sword and the strength of his arm. The law says to the subjects, with a voice only inferior to that of the Deity, 'Vengeance is mine.' The instant that there is time for passion to cool, and reason to interpose, an injured party must become aware that the law assumes the exclusive cognizance of the right and wrong betwixt the parties, and opposes her inviolable buckler to every attempt of the private party to right himself. I repeat, that this unhappy man ought personally to be the object rather of our pity than our abhorrence, for he failed in his ignorance, and from mistaken notions of honour. But his crime is not the less that of murder, gentlemen, and, in your high and important office, it is your duty so to find. Englishmen have their angry passions as well as Scots; and should this man's action remain unpunished, you may unsheath, under various pretences, a thousand daggers betwixt the Land's-end and the Orkneys.'

The venerable judge thus ended what, to judge by his apparent emotion, and by the tears which filled his eyes, was really a painful task. The jury, according to his instructions, brought in a verdict of Guilty; and Robin Oig M'Combich, *alias* M'Gregor, was sentenced to death and left for execution, which took place accordingly. He met his fate with great firmness, and acknowledged the justice of his sentence. But he repelled indignantly the observations of those who accused him of attacking an unarmed man. 'I give a life for the life I took,' he said, 'and what can I do more?'

CHARLES DICKENS
(1812–1870)

'The Tuggses at Ramsgate' was written for Chapman and Hall's *Library of Fiction*, appearing in 1836. In October 1837 Dickens put it in the third volume of his collection *Sketches by Boz, Illustrative of Everyday Life and Everyday People*, his first published work.

'The Signal-man' was Chapter IV of *Mugby Junction* which appeared in four chapters in 1866 as the special Christmas number issued with the weekly magazine *All the Year Round* which Dickens founded in 1859 and edited until his death. He sometimes included *Mugby Junction*, which has a long sentimental story as well as vivid description of the life and work of a railway junction (based on Rugby), in his public readings.

The Tuggses at Ramsgate

ONCE upon a time there dwelt, in a narrow street on the Surrey side of the water, within three minutes' walk of old London Bridge, Mr. Joseph Tuggs—a little dark-faced man, with shiny hair, twinkling eyes, short legs, and a body of very considerable thickness, measuring from the centre button of his waistcoat in front, to the ornamental buttons of his coat behind. The figure of the amiable Mrs. Tuggs, if not perfectly symmetrical, was decidedly comfortable; and the form of her only daughter, the accomplished Miss Charlotte Tuggs, was fast ripening into that state of luxuriant plumpness which had enchanted the eyes, and captivated the heart, of Mr. Joseph Tuggs in his earlier days. Mr. Simon Tuggs, his only son, and Miss Charlotte Tuggs's only brother, was as differently formed in body, as he was differently constituted in mind, from the remainder of his family. There was that elongation in his thoughtful face, and that tendency to weakness in his interesting legs, which tell so forcibly of a great mind and romantic disposition. The slightest traits of character in such a being, possess no mean interest to speculative minds. He usually appeared in public, in capacious shoes with black cotton stockings; and was observed to be particularly attached to a black glazed stock, without tie or ornament of any description.

There is perhaps no profession, however useful; no pursuit, however meritorious; which can escape the petty attacks of vulgar minds. Mr. Joseph Tuggs was a grocer. It might be supposed that a grocer was beyond the breath of calumny; but no—the neighbours stigmatised him as a chandler; and the poisonous voice of envy distinctly asserted that he dispensed tea and coffee by the quartern, retailed sugar by the ounce, cheese by the slice, tobacco by the screw, and butter by the pat. These taunts, however, were lost upon the Tuggses. Mr. Tuggs attended to the grocery department; Mrs. Tuggs to the cheesemongery; and Miss Tuggs to her education. Mr. Simon Tuggs kept his father's books, and his own counsel.

One fine spring afternoon, the latter gentleman was seated on a tub of weekly Dorset,[1] behind the little red desk with a wooden rail, which ornamented a corner of the counter; when a stranger dismounted from a cab, and hastily entered the shop. He was habited in black cloth, and bore with him a green umbrella and a blue bag.

'Mr. Tuggs?' said the stranger, inquiringly.

'*My* name is Tuggs,' replied Mr. Simon.

'It's the other Mr. Tuggs,' said the stranger, looking towards the glass door which led into the parlour behind the shop, and on the inside of which, the round face of Mr. Tuggs, senior, was distinctly visible, peeping over the curtain.

Mr. Simon gracefully waved his pen, as if in intimation of his wish that his father would advance. Mr. Joseph Tuggs, with considerable celerity, removed his face from the curtain and placed it before the stranger.

'I come from the Temple,'[2] said the man with the bag.

'From the Temple!' said Mrs. Tuggs, flinging open the door of the little parlour and disclosing Miss Tuggs in perspective.

[1] Blue Dorset (or blue 'vinny') cheese sent up once a week to London(?).

[2] The district of the City of London, called after the Knights Templars who owned it in the twelfth and thirteenth centuries, where the Inns of Court became established; so, the legal quarter of London.

'From the Temple!' said Miss Tuggs and Mr. Simon Tuggs at the same moment.

'From the Temple!' said Mr. Joseph Tuggs, turning as pale as a Dutch cheese.

'From the Temple,' repeated the man with the bag; 'from Mr. Cower's, the solicitor's. Mr. Tuggs, I congratulate you, sir. Ladies, I wish you joy of your prosperity! We have been successful.' And the man with the bag leisurely divested himself of his umbrella and glove, as a preliminary to shaking hands with Mr. Joseph Tuggs.

Now the words 'we have been successful,' had no sooner issued from the mouth of the man with the bag, than Mr. Simon Tuggs rose from the tub of weekly Dorset, opened his eyes very wide, gasped for breath, made figures of eight in the air with his pen, and finally fell into the arms of his anxious mother, and fainted away without the slightest ostensible cause or pretence.

'Water!' screamed Mrs. Tuggs.

'Look up, my son,' exclaimed Mr. Tuggs.

'Simon! dear Simon!' shrieked Miss Tuggs.

'I'm better now,' said Mr. Simon Tuggs. 'What! successful!' And then, as corroborative evidence of his being better, he fainted away again, and was borne into the little parlour by the united efforts of the remainder of the family, and the man with the bag.

To a casual spectator, or to any one unacquainted with the position of the family, this fainting would have been unaccountable. To those who understood the mission of the man with the bag, and were moreover acquainted with the excitability of the nerves of Mr. Simon Tuggs, it was quite comprehensible. A long-pending law-suit respecting the validity of a will, had been unexpectedly decided; and Mr. Joseph Tuggs was the possessor of twenty thousand pounds.

A prolonged consultation took place, that night, in the little parlour—a consultation that was to settle the future destinies of the Tuggses. The shop was shut up, at an unusually early hour; and many were the unavailing kicks bestowed upon the closed door by applicants for quarterns of sugar, or half-quarterns of bread, or penn'orths of pepper, which were to have been 'left till

Saturday,' but which fortune had decreed were to be left alone altogether.

'We must certainly give up business,' said Miss Tuggs.

'Oh, decidedly,' said Mrs. Tuggs.

'Simon shall go to the bar,' said Mr. Joseph Tuggs.

'And I shall always sign myself "Cymon"[3] in future,' said his son.

'And I shall call myself Charlotta,' said Miss Tuggs.

'And you must always call *me* "Ma," and father "Pa,"' said Mrs. Tuggs.

'Yes, and Pa must leave off all his vulgar habits,' interposed Miss Tuggs.

'I'll take care of all that,' responded Mr. Joseph Tuggs, complacently. He was, at that very moment, eating pickled salmon with a pocket-knife.

'We must leave town immediately,' said Mr. Cymon Tuggs.

Everybody concurred that this was an indispensable preliminary to being genteel. The question then arose, Where should they go?

'Gravesend?' mildly suggested Mr. Joseph Tuggs. The idea was unanimously scouted. Gravesend was *low*.

'Margate?' insinuated Mrs. Tuggs. Worse and worse—nobody there, but tradespeople.

'Brighton?' Mr. Cymon Tuggs opposed an insurmountable objection. All the coaches had been upset, in turn, within the last three weeks; each coach had averaged two passengers killed, and six wounded; and, in every case, the newspapers had distinctly understood that 'no blame whatever was attributable to the coachman.'

'Ramsgate?' ejaculated Mr. Cymon, thoughtfully. To be sure; how stupid they must have been, not to have thought of that before! Ramsgate was just the place of all others.

Two months after this conversation, the City of London Ramsgate steamer was running gaily down the river. Her flag was flying, her band was playing, her passengers were conversing; everything about her seemed gay and lively.—No wonder—the Tuggses were on board.

[3] Dickens must be thinking ironically of the clownish Cimon, son of a very wealthy man, who was transformed into a man of noble valour by his love for Iphigenia (in Boccaccio's *Decameron*: Story One of the Fifth Day).

'Charming, ain't it?' said Mr. Joseph Tuggs, in a bottle-green great-coat, with a velvet collar of the same; and a blue travelling-cap with a gold band.

'Soul-inspiring,' replied Mr. Cymon Tuggs—he was entered at the bar. 'Soul-inspiring!'

'Delightful morning, sir!' said a stoutish, military-looking gentleman in a blue surtout buttoned up to his chin, and white trousers chained down to the soles of his boots.

Mr. Cymon Tuggs took upon himself the responsibility of answering the observation. 'Heavenly!' he replied.

'You are an enthusiastic admirer of the beauties of Nature, sir?' said the military gentleman.

'I am, sir,' replied Mr. Cymon Tuggs.

'Travelled much, sir?' inquired the military gentleman.

'Not much,' replied Mr. Cymon Tuggs.

'You've been on the continent, of course?' inquired the military gentleman.

'Not exactly,' replied Mr. Cymon Tuggs—in a qualified tone, as if he wished it to be implied that he had gone half-way and come back again.

'You of course intend your son to make the grand tour, sir?' said the military gentleman, addressing Mr. Joseph Tuggs.

As Mr. Joseph Tuggs did not precisely understand what the grand tour was, or how such an article was manufactured, he replied, 'Of course.' Just as he said the word, there came tripping up, from her seat at the stern of the vessel, a young lady in a puce-coloured silk cloak, and boots of the same; with long black ringlets, large black eyes, brief petticoats, and unexceptionable ankles.

'Walter, my dear,' said the young lady to the military gentleman.

'Yes, Belinda, my love,' responded the military gentleman to the black-eyed young lady.

'What have you left me alone so long for?' said the young lady. 'I have been stared out of countenance by those rude young men.'

'What! stared at?' exclaimed the military gentleman, with an emphasis which made Mr. Cymon Tuggs withdraw his eyes from the young lady's face with inconceivable rapidity. 'Which young men—where?' and the military gentleman clenched his fist, and glared fearfully on the cigar-smokers around.

'Be calm, Walter, I entreat,' said the young lady.

'I won't,' said the military gentleman.

'Do, sir,' interposed Mr. Cymon Tuggs. 'They ain't worth your notice.'

'No—no—they are not, indeed,' urged the young lady.

'I *will* be calm,' said the military gentleman. 'You speak truly, sir. I thank you for a timely remonstrance, which may have spared me the guilt of manslaughter.' Calming his wrath, the military gentleman wrung Mr. Cymon Tuggs by the hand.

'My sister, sir!' said Mr. Cymon Tuggs; seeing that the military gentleman was casting an admiring look towards Miss Charlotta.

'My wife, ma'am—Mrs. Captain Waters,' said the military gentleman, presenting the black-eyed young lady.

'My mother, ma'am—Mrs. Tuggs,' said Mr. Cymon. The military gentleman and his wife murmured enchanting courtesies; and the Tuggses looked as unembarrassed as they could.

'Walter, my dear,' said the black-eyed young lady, after they had sat chatting with the Tuggses some half-hour.

'Yes, my love', said the military gentleman.

'Don't you think this gentleman (with an inclination of the head towards Mr. Cymon Tuggs) is very much like the Marquis Carriwini?'

'Lord bless me, very!' said the military gentleman.

'It struck me the moment I saw him,' said the young lady, gazing intently, and with a melancholy air, on the scarlet countenance of Mr. Cymon Tuggs. Mr. Cymon Tuggs looked at everybody; and finding that everybody was looking at him, appeared to feel some temporary difficulty in disposing of his eyesight.

'So exactly the air of the marquis,' said the military gentleman.

'Quite extraordinary!' sighed the military gentleman's lady.

'You don't know the marquis, sir?' inquired the military gentleman.

Mr. Cymon Tuggs stammered a negative.

'If you did,' continued Captain Walter Waters, 'you would feel how much reason you have to be proud of the resemblance—a most elegant man, with a most prepossessing appearance.'

'He is—he is indeed!' exclaimed Belinda Waters energetically. As her eye caught that of Mr. Cymon Tuggs, she withdrew it from his features in bashful confusion.

All this was highly gratifying to the feelings of the Tuggses; and when, in the course of farther conversation, it was discovered that Miss Charlotta Tuggs was the *facsimile* of a titled relative of Mrs. Belinda Walters, and that Mrs. Tuggs herself was the very picture of the Dowager Duchess of Dobbleton, their delight in the acquisition of so genteel and friendly an acquaintance knew no bounds. Even the dignity of Captain Walter Waters relaxed to that degree, that he suffered himself to be prevailed upon by Mr. Joseph Tuggs to partake of cold pigeon-pie and sherry, on deck; and a most delightful conversation, aided by these agreeable stimulants, was prolonged until they ran alongside Ramsgate Pier.

'Good by'e, dear!' said Mrs. Captain Waters to Miss Charlotta Tuggs, just before the bustle of landing commenced; 'we shall see you on the sands in the morning; and, as we are sure to have found lodgings before then, I hope we shall be inseparables for many weeks to come.'

'Oh! I hope so,' said Miss Charlotta Tuggs, emphatically.

'Tickets, ladies and gen'lm'n,' said the man on the paddle-box.

'Want a porter, sir?' inquired a dozen men in smock-frocks.

'Now, my dear!' said Captain Waters.

'Good by'e!' said Mrs. Captain Waters—'good by'e, Mr. Cymon!' and with a pressure of the hand which threw the amiable young man's nerves into a state of considerable derangement, Mrs. Captain Waters disappeared among the crowd. A pair of puce-coloured boots were seen ascending the steps, a white handkerchief fluttered, a black eye gleamed. The Waterses were gone, and Mr. Cymon Tuggs was alone in a heartless world.

Silently and abstractedly did that too sensitive youth follow his revered parents, and a train of smock-frocks and wheelbarrows, along the pier, until the bustle of the scene around recalled him to himself. The sun was shining brightly; the sea, dancing to its own music, rolled merrily in; crowds of people promenaded to and fro; young ladies tittered; old ladies talked; nursemaids displayed their charms to the greatest possible advantage; and their little charges ran up and down, and to and fro, and in and out, under the feet, and between the legs, of the assembled concourse, in the most playful and exhilarating manner. There were old gentlemen, trying to make out objects through long telescopes; and young ones, making objects of themselves in open shirt-collars; ladies, carrying about portable chairs, and portable chairs carrying about invalids; parties, waiting on the pier for parties who had come by the steam-boat; and nothing was to be heard but talking, laughing, welcoming, and merriment.

'Fly,[4] sir?' exclaimed a chorus of fourteen men and six boys, the moment Mr. Joseph Tuggs, at the head of his little party, set foot in the street.

'Here's the gen'lm'n at last!' said one, touching his hat with mock politeness. 'Werry glad to see you, sir,—been a-waitin' for you these six weeks. Jump in, if you please, sir!'

'Nice little fly and a fast trotter, sir,' said another: 'fourteen mile a hour, and surroundin' objects rendered inwisible by ex-treme welocity!'

'Large fly for your luggage, sir,' cried a third. 'Werry large fly here, sir—reg'lar bluebottle!'

'Here's *your* fly, sir!' shouted another aspiring charioteer, mounting the box, and inducing an old grey horse to indulge in some imperfect reminiscences of a canter. 'Look at him, sir!—temper of a lamb and haction of a steam-ingein!'

Resisting even the temptation of securing the services of so valuable a quadruped as the last named, Mr. Joseph Tuggs beckoned to the proprietor of a dingy conveyance of a greenish hue, lined with faded striped calico; and, the luggage and the family having been deposited therein, the animal in the shafts, after describing circles in the road for a quarter of an hour, at last consented to depart in quest of lodgings.

'How many beds have you got?' screamed Mrs. Tuggs out of the fly, to the woman who opened the door of the first house which displayed a bill intimating that apartments were to be let within.

'How many did you want, ma'am?' was, of course, the reply.

'Three.'

[4] A one-horse light hackney carriage.

'Will you step in, ma'am?' Down got Mrs. Tuggs. The family were delighted. Splendid view of the sea from the front windows—charming! A short pause. Back came Mrs. Tuggs again.—One parlour and a mattress.

'Why the devil didn't they say so at first?' inquired Mr. Joseph Tuggs, rather pettishly.

'Don't know,' said Mrs. Tuggs.

'Wretches!' exclaimed the nervous Cymon. Another bill—another stoppage. Same question—same answer—similar result.

'What do they mean by this?' inquired Mr. Joseph Tuggs, thoroughly out of temper.

'Don't know,' said the placid Mrs. Tuggs.

'Orvis the vay here, sir,' said the driver, by way of accounting for the circumstance in a satisfactory manner; and off they went again, to make fresh inquiries, and encounter fresh disappointments.

It had grown dusk when the 'fly'—the rate of whose progress greatly belied its name—after climbing up four or five perpendicular hills, stopped before the door of a dusty house, with a bay window, from which you could obtain a beautiful glimpse of the sea—if you thrust half of your body out of it, at the imminent peril of falling into the area. Mrs. Tuggs alighted. One ground-floor sitting-room, and three cells with beds in them up-stairs. A double house. Family on the opposite side. Five children milk-and-watering in the parlour, and one little boy, expelled for bad behaviour, screaming on his back in the passage.

'What's the terms?' said Mrs. Tuggs. The mistress of the house was considering the expediency of putting on an extra guinea; so she coughed slightly, and affected not to hear the question.

'What's the terms?' said Mrs. Tuggs, in a louder key.

'Five guineas a week, ma'am, *with* attendance,' replied the lodging-house keeper. (Attendance means the privilege of ringing the bell as often as you like, for your own amusement.)

'Rather dear,' said Mrs. Tuggs.

'Oh dear, no, ma'am!' replied the mistress of the house, with a benign smile of pity at the ignorance of manners and customs which the observation betrayed, 'Very cheap!'

Such an authority was indisputable. Mrs. Tuggs paid a week's rent in advance, and took the lodgings for a month. In an hour's time, the family were seated at tea in their new abode.

'Capital srimps!' said Mr. Joseph Tuggs.

Mr. Cymon eyed his father with a rebellious scowl, as he emphatically said '*Shrimps.*'

'Well then, shrimps,' said Mr. Joseph Tuggs. 'Srimps or shrimps, don't much matter.'

There was pity, blended with malignity, in Mr. Cymon's eye, as he replied, 'Don't matter, father! What would Captain Waters say, if he heard such vulgarity?'

'Or what would dear Mrs. Captain Waters say,' added Charlotta, 'if she saw mother—ma, I mean—eating them whole, heads and all!'

'It won't bear thinking of!' ejaculated Mr. Cymon, with a shudder. 'How different,' he thought, 'from the Dowager Duchess of Dobbleton!'

'Very pretty woman, Mrs. Captain Waters, is she not, Cymon?' inquired Miss Charlotta.

A glow of nervous excitement passed over the countenance of Mr. Cymon Tuggs, as he replied, 'An angel of beauty!'

'Hallo!' said Mr. Joseph Tuggs. 'Hallo, Cymon, my boy, take care. Married lady, you know;' and he winked one of his twinkling eyes knowingly.

'Why,' exclaimed Cymon, starting up with an ebullition of fury, as unexpected as alarming, 'why am I to be reminded of that blight of my happiness, and ruin of my hopes? Why am I to be taunted with the miseries which are heaped upon my head? Is it not enough to—to—to—' and the orator paused; but whether for want of words, or lack of breath, was never distinctly ascertained.

There was an impressive solemnity in the tone of this address, and in the air with which the romantic Cymon, at its conclusion, rang the bell, and demanded a flat candlestick, which effectually forbade a reply. He stalked dramatically to bed, and the Tuggses went to bed too, half an hour afterwards, in a state of considerable mystification and perplexity.

If the pier had presented a scene of life and bustle to the Tuggses on their first landing at Ramsgate, it was far surpassed by the appearance of the sands on the morning after their arrival. It was a fine, bright, clear day, with a light breeze from the sea. There were the same ladies and gentlemen, the same children, the same nursemaids, the same telescopes, the same portable chairs. The ladies were employed in needlework, or watch-guard making, or knitting, or reading novels; the gentlemen were reading newspapers and magazines; the children were digging holes in the sand with wooden spades, and collecting water therein; the nursemaids, with their youngest charges in their arms, were running in after the waves, and then running back with the waves after them; and, now and then, a little sailing-boat either departed with a gay and talkative cargo of passengers, or returned with a very silent and particularly uncomfortable-looking one.

'Well, I never!' exclaimed Mrs. Tuggs, as she and Mr. Joseph Tuggs, and Miss Charlotta Tuggs, and Mr. Cymon Tuggs, with their eight feet in a corresponding number of yellow shoes, seated themselves on four rush-bottomed chairs, which, being placed in a soft part of the sand, forthwith sunk down some two feet and a half—'Well, I never!'

Mr. Cymon, by an exertion of great personal strength, uprooted the chairs, and removed them further back.

'Why, I'm blessed if there ain't some ladies a-going in!' exclaimed Mr. Joseph Tuggs, with intense astonishment.

'Lor, pa!' exclaimed Miss Charlotta.

'There *is*, my dear,' said Mr. Joseph Tuggs. And, sure enough, four young ladies, each furnished with a towel, tripped up the steps of a bathing-machine. In went the horse, floundering about in the water; round turned the machine; down sat the driver; and presently out burst the young ladies aforesaid, with four distinct splashes.

'Well, that's sing'ler, too!' ejaculated Mr. Joseph Tuggs, after an awkward pause. Mr. Cymon coughed slightly.

'Why, here's some gentlemen a-going in on this side!' exclaimed Mrs. Tuggs, in a tone of horror.

Three machines—three horses—three flounderings—three turnings round—three splashes—three gentlemen, disporting themselves in the water like so many dolphins.

'Well, *that's* sing'ler!' said Mr. Joseph Tuggs again. Miss Charlotta coughed this time, and another pause ensued. It was agreeably broken.

'How d'ye do, dear?' We have been looking for you all the morning,' said a voice to Miss Charlotta Tuggs. Mrs. Captain Waters was the owner of it.

'How d'ye do?' said Captain Walter Waters, all suavity; and a most cordial interchange of greetings ensued.

'Belinda, my love,' said Captain Walter Waters, applying his glass to his eye, and looking in the direction of the sea.

'Yes, my dear,' replied Mrs. Captain Waters.

'There's Harry Thompson!'

'Where?' said Belinda, applying her glass to her eye.

'Bathing.'

'Lor, so it is! He don't see us, does he?'

'No, I don't think he does,' replied the captain. 'Bless my soul, how very singular!'

'What?' inquired Belinda.

'There's Mary Golding, too.'

'Lor!—where?' (Up went the glass again.)

'There!' said the captain, pointing to one of the young ladies before noticed, who, in her bathing costume, looked as if she was enveloped in a patent Mackintosh, of scanty dimensions.

'So it is, I declare!' exclaimed Mrs. Captain Waters. 'How very curious we should see them both!'

'Very,' said the captain, with perfect coolness.

'It's the reg'lar thing here, you see,' whispered Mr. Cymon Tuggs to his father.

'I see it is,' whispered Mr. Joseph Tuggs in reply. 'Queer, though ain't it?' Mr. Cymon Tuggs nodded assent.

'What do you think of doing with yourself this morning?' inquired the captain. 'Shall we lunch at Pegwell?'

'I should like that very much indeed,' interposed Mrs. Tuggs. She had never heard of Pegwell; but the word 'lunch' had reached her ears, and it sounded very agreeably.

'How shall we go?' inquired the captain; 'it's too warm to walk.'

'A shay?' suggested Mr. Joseph Tuggs.

'Chaise,'[5] whispered Mr. Cymon.

'I should think one would be enough,' said Mr. Joseph Tuggs aloud, quite unconscious of the meaning of the correction. 'However, two shays if you like.'

'I should like a donkey *so* much,' said Belinda.

'Oh, so should I!' echoed Charlotta Tuggs.

'Well, we can have a fly,' suggested the captain, 'and you can have a couple of donkeys.'

A fresh difficulty arose. Mrs. Captain Waters declared it would be decidedly improper for two ladies to ride alone. The remedy was obvious. Perhaps young Mr. Tuggs would be gallant enough to accompany them.

Mr. Cymon Tuggs blushed, smiled, looked vacant, and faintly protested that he was no horseman. The objection was at once overruled. A fly was speedily found; and three donkeys—which the proprietor declared on his solemn asseveration to be 'three parts blood, and the other corn'—were engaged in the service.

'Kim up!' shouted one of the two boys who followed behind, to propel the donkeys, when Belinda Waters and Charlotta Tuggs had been hoisted, and pushed, and pulled, into their respective saddles.

'Hi—hi—hi!' groaned the other boy behind Mr. Cymon Tuggs. Away went the donkey, with the stirrups jingling against the heels of Cymon's boots, and Cymon's boots nearly scraping the ground.

'Way—way! Wo—o—o—o—!' cried Mr. Cymon Tuggs as well as he could, in the midst of the jolting.

'Don't make it gallop!' screamed Mrs. Captain Waters, behind.

'My donkey *will* go into the public-house!' shrieked Miss Tuggs in the rear.

'Hi—hi—hi!' groaned both the boys together; and on went the donkeys as if nothing would ever stop them.

Everything has an end, however; even the galloping of donkeys will cease in time. The animal which Mr. Cymon Tuggs bestrode, feeling sundry uncomfortable tugs at the bit, the intent of which he could by no means divine, abruptly sidled against a brick

[5] A four-wheeled-open carriage.

wall, and expressed his uneasiness by grinding Mr. Cymon Tuggs's leg on the rough surface. Mrs. Captain Waters's donkey, apparently under the influence of some playfulness of spirit, rushed suddenly, head first, into a hedge, and declined to come out again: and the quadruped on which Miss Tuggs was mounted, expressed his delight at this humorous proceeding by firmly planting his fore-feet against the ground, and kicking up his hind-legs in a very agile, but somewhat alarming manner.

This abrupt termination to the rapidity of the ride naturally occasioned some confusion. Both the ladies indulged in vehement screaming for several minutes; and Mr. Cymon Tuggs, besides sustaining intense bodily pain, had the additional mental anguish of witnessing their distressing situation, without having the power to rescue them, by reason of his leg being firmly screwed in between the animal and the wall. The efforts of the boys, however, assisted by the ingenious expedient of twisting the tail of the most rebellious donkey, restored order in a much shorter time than could have reasonably been expected, and the little party jogged slowly on together.

'Now let 'em walk,' said Mr. Cymon Tuggs. 'It's cruel to overdrive 'em.'

'Werry well, sir,' replied the boy, with a grin at his companion, as if he understood Mr. Cymon to mean that the cruelty applied less to the animals than to their riders.

'What a lovely day, dear!' said Charlotta.

'Charming; enchanting, dear!' responded Mrs. Captain Waters. 'What a beautiful prospect, Mr. Tuggs!'

Cymon looked full in Belinda's face, as he responded—'Beautiful, indeed!' The lady cast down her eyes, and suffered the animal she was riding to fall a little back. Cymon Tuggs instinctively did the same.

There was a brief silence, broken only by a sigh from Mr. Cymon Tuggs.

'Mr. Cymon,' said the lady suddenly, in a low tone, 'Mr. Cymon—I am another's.'

Mr. Cymon expressed his perfect concurrence in a statement which it was impossible to controvert.

'If I had not been——' resumed Belinda; and there she stopped.

'What—what?' said Mr. Cymon earnestly. 'Do not torture me. What would you say?'

'If I had not been'—continued Mrs. Captain Waters—'if, in earlier life, it had been my fate to have known, and been beloved by, a noble youth—a kindred soul—a congenial spirit—one capable of feeling and appreciating the sentiments which——'

'Heavens! what do I hear?' exclaimed Mr. Cymon Tuggs. 'Is it possible! can I believe my—Come up!' (This last unsentimental parenthesis was addressed to the donkey, who, with his head between his forelegs, appeared to be examining the state of his shoes with great anxiety.)

'Hi—hi—hi,' said the boys behind. 'Come up,' expostulated Cymon Tuggs again. 'Hi—hi—hi,' repeated the boys. And whether it was that the animal felt indignant at the tone of Mr. Tuggs's command, or felt alarmed by the noise of the deputy proprietor's boots running behind him; or whether he burned with a noble emulation to outstrip the other donkeys; certain it is that he no sooner heard the second series of 'hi—hi's,' than he started away, with a celerity of pace which jerked Mr. Cymon's hat off instantaneously, and carried him to the Pegwell Bay hotel in no time, where he deposited his rider without giving him the trouble of dismounting, by sagaciously pitching him over his head into the very doorway of the tavern.

Great was the confusion of Mr. Cymon Tuggs, when he was put right end uppermost by two waiters; considerable was the alarm of Mrs. Tuggs in behalf of her son; agonizing were the apprehensions of Mrs. Captain Waters on his account. It was speedily discovered, however, that he had not sustained much more injury than the donkey—he was grazed, and the animal was grazing—and then it *was* a delightful party to be sure! Mr. and Mrs. Tuggs, and the captain, had ordered lunch in the little garden behind:—small saucers of large shrimps, dabs of butter, crusty loaves, and bottled ale. The sky was without a cloud; there were flower-pots and turf before them; the sea, from the foot of the cliff, stretching away as far as the eye could discern anything at all; vessels in the distance with sails as white, and as small, as nicely-got-up cambric handkerchiefs. The shrimps were delightful, the ale better, and the captain even more pleasant than either. Mrs. Captain Waters was in *such* spirits after lunch!—chasing, first the captain across the turf, and among the flower-pots; and then Mr. Cymon Tuggs; and then Miss Tuggs; and laughing, too, quite boisterously. But as the captain said, it didn't matter; who knew what they were, there? For all the people of the house knew, they might be common people. To which Mr. Joseph Tuggs responded, 'To be sure.' And then they went down the steep wooden steps a little further on, which led to the bottom of the cliff; and looked at the crabs, and the seaweed, and the eels, till it was more than fully time to go back to Ramsgate again. Finally, Mr. Cymon Tuggs ascended the steps last, and Mrs. Captain Waters last but one; and Mr. Cymon Tuggs discovered that the foot and ankle of Mrs. Captain Waters were even more unexceptionable than he had at first supposed.

Taking a donkey towards his ordinary place of residence is a very different thing, and a feat much more easily to be accomplished, than taking him from it. It requires a great deal of foresight and presence of mind in the one case, to anticipate the numerous flights of his discursive imagination; whereas, in the other, all you have to do is to hold on, and place a blind confidence in the animal. Mr. Cymon Tuggs adopted the latter expedient on his return; and his nerves were so little discomposed by the journey, that he distinctly understood they were all to meet again at the library in the evening.

The library was crowded. There were the same ladies, and the same gentlemen, who had been on the sands in the morning, and on the pier the day before. There were young ladies, in maroon-coloured gowns and black velvet bracelets, dispensing fancy articles in the shop, and presiding over games of chance in the concert-room. There were marriageable daughters, and marriage-making mammas, gaming and promenading, and turning over music, and flirting. There were some male beaux doing the sentimental in whispers, and others doing the ferocious in moustache. There were Mrs. Tuggs in amber, Miss Tuggs in sky-blue, Mrs. Captain Waters in pink. There was Captain Waters in a braided surtout; there was Mr. Cymon Tuggs in pumps and a gilt waistcoat; there was Mr. Joseph Tuggs in a blue coat and a shirt-frill.

'Numbers three, eight, and eleven!' cried one of the young ladies in the maroon-coloured gowns.

'Numbers three, eight, and eleven!' echoed another young lady in the same uniform.

'Number three's gone,' said the first young lady. 'Numbers eight and eleven!'

'Numbers eight and eleven!' echoed the second young lady.

'Number eight's gone, Mary Ann,' said the first young lady.

'Number eleven!' screamed the second.

'The numbers are all taken now, ladies, if you please,' said the first. The representatives of numbers three, eight, and eleven, and the rest of the numbers, crowded round the table.

'Will you throw, ma'am?' said the presiding goddess, handing the dice-box to the eldest daughter of a stout lady, with four girls.

There was a profound silence among the lookers-on.

'Throw, Jane, my dear,' said the stout lady. An interesting display of bashfulness—a little blushing in a cambric handkerchief—a whispering to a younger sister.

'Amelia, my dear, throw for your sister,' said the stout lady; and then she turned to a walking advertisement of Rowlands' Macassar Oil,[6] who stood next her, and said, 'Jane is so *very* modest and retiring; but I can't be angry with her for it. An artless and unsophisticated girl is *so* truly amiable, that I often wish Amelia was more like her sister!'

The gentleman with the whiskers whispered his admiring approval.

'Now, my dear!' said the stout lady. Miss Amelia threw—eight for her sister, ten for herself.

'Nice figure, Amelia,' whispered the stout lady to a thin youth beside her.

'Beautiful!'

'And *such* a spirit! I am like you in that respect. I can *not* help admiring that life and vivacity. Ah! (a sigh) I wish I could make poor Jane a little more like my dear Amelia!'

The young gentleman cordially acquiesced in the sentiment; both he, and the individual first addressed, were perfectly contented.

[6] Hair-oil.

'Who's this? inquired Mr. Cymon Tuggs of Mrs. Captain Waters, as a short female, in a blue velvet hat and feathers, was led into the orchestra, by a fat man in black tights and cloudy Berlins.[7]

'Mrs. Tippin, of the London theatres,' replied Belinda, referring to the programme of the concert.

The talented Tippin having condescendingly acknowledged the clapping of hands and shouts of 'bravo!' which greeted her appearance, proceeded to sing the popular cavatina of 'Bid me discourse,' accompanied on the piano by Mr. Tippin; after which, Mr. Tippin sang a comic song, accompanied on the piano by Mrs. Tippin: the applause consequent upon which, was only to be exceeded by the enthusiastic approbation bestowed upon an air with variations on the guitar, by Miss Tippin, accompanied on the chin by Master Tippin.

Thus passed the evening; thus passed the days and evenings of the Tuggses, and the Waterses, for six weeks. Sands in the morning—donkeys at noon—pier in the afternoon—library at night—and the same people everywhere.

On that very night six weeks, the moon was shining brightly over the calm sea, which dashed against the feet of the tall gaunt cliffs, with just enough noise to lull the old fish to sleep, without disturbing the young ones, when two figures were discernible—or would have been, if anybody had looked for them—seated on one of the wooden benches which are stationed near the verge of the western cliff. The moon had climbed higher into the heavens, by two hours' journeying, since those figures first sat down—and yet they had moved not. The crowd of loungers had thinned and dispersed; the noise of itinerant musicians had died away; light after light had appeared in the windows of the different houses in the distance; blockade-man[8] after blockade-man had passed the spot, wending his way towards his solitary post; and yet those figures had remained stationary. Some portions of the two forms were in deep shadow, but the light of the moon fell strongly on a puce-coloured boot and a glazed stock. Mr. Cymon Tuggs and Mrs. Captain Waters were seated on that bench. They spoke not, but were silently gazing on the sea.

[7] Knitted gloves. [8] Coast-guard.

'Walter will return to-morrow,' said Mrs. Captain Waters, mournfully breaking silence.

Mr. Cymon Tuggs sighed like a gust of wind through a forest of gooseberry bushes, as he replied, 'Alas! he will.'

'Oh, Cymon!' resumed Belinda, 'the chaste delight, the calm happiness, of this one week of Platonic love, is too much for me!'

Cymon was about to suggest that it was too little for him, but he stopped himself, and murmured unintelligibly.

'And to think that even this gleam of happiness, innocent as it is,' exclaimed Belinda, 'is now to be lost for ever!'

'Oh, do not say for ever, Belinda,' exclaimed the excitable Cymon, as two strongly-defined tears chased each other down his pale face—it was so long that there was plenty of room for a chase. 'Do not say for ever!'

'I must,' replied Belinda.

'Why?' urged Cymon, 'oh why? Such Platonic acquaintance as ours is so harmless, that even your husband can never object to it.'

'My husband!' exclaimed Belinda. 'You little know him. Jealous and revengeful; ferocious in his revenge—a maniac in his jealousy! Would you be assassinated before my eyes?' Mr. Cymon Tuggs, in a voice broken by emotion, expressed his disinclination to undergo the process of assassination before the eyes of anybody.

'Then leave me,' said Mrs. Captain Waters. 'Leave me, this night, for ever. It is late: let us return.'

Mr. Cymon Tuggs sadly offered the lady his arm, and escorted her to her lodgings. He paused at the door—he felt a Platonic pressure of his hand. 'Good night,' he said, hesitating.

'Good night,' sobbed the lady. Mr. Cymon Tuggs paused again.

'Won't you walk in, sir?' said the servant. Mr. Tuggs hesitated. Oh, that hesitation! He *did* walk in.

'Good night!' said Mr. Cymon Tuggs again, when he reached the drawing-room.

'Good night!' replied Belinda; 'and, if at any period of my life, I—Hush!' The lady paused and stared, with a steady gaze of horror, on the ashy countenance of Mr. Cymon Tuggs. There was a double knock at the street-door.

'It is my husband!' said Belinda, as the captain's voice was heard below.

'And my family!' added Cymon Tuggs, as the voices of his relatives floated up the staircase.

'The curtain! The curtain!' gasped Mrs. Captain Waters, pointing to the window, before which some chintz hangings were closely drawn.

'But I have done nothing wrong,' said the hesitating Cymon.

'The curtain!' reiterated the frantic lady: 'you will be murdered.' This last appeal to his feelings was irresistible. The dismayed Cymon concealed himself behind the curtain with pantomimic suddenness.

Enter the captain, Joseph Tuggs, Mrs. Tuggs, and Charlotta.

'My dear,' said the captain, 'Lieutenant Slaughter.' Two iron-shod boots and one gruff voice was heard by Mr. Cymon to advance, and acknowledge the honour of the introduction. The sabre of the lieutenant rattled heavily upon the floor, as he seated himself at the table. Mr. Cymon's fears almost overcame his reason.

'The brandy, my dear!' said the captain. Here was a situation! They were going to make a night of it! And Mr. Cymon Tuggs was pent up behind the curtain and afraid to breathe!

'Slaughter,' said the captain, 'a cigar?'

Now, Mr. Cymon Tuggs never could smoke without feeling it indispensably necessary to retire immediately, and never could smell smoke without a strong disposition to cough. The cigars were introduced; the captain was a professed smoker; so was the lieutenant; so was Joseph Tuggs. The apartment was small, the door was closed, the smoke powerful: it hung in heavy wreaths over the room, and at length found its way behind the curtain. Cymon Tuggs held his nose, his mouth, his breath. It was all of no use—out came the cough.

'Bless my soul!' said the captain, 'I beg your pardon, Miss Tuggs. You dislike smoking?'

'Oh, no; I don't indeed,' said Charlotta.

'It makes you cough.'

'Oh dear no.'

'You coughed just now.'

'Me, Captain Waters! Lor! how can you say so?'

'Somebody coughed,' said the captain.

'I certainly thought so,' said Slaughter. No; everybody denied it.

'Fancy,' said the captain.

'Must be,' echoed Slaughter.

Cigars resumed—more smoke—another cough—smothered, but violent.

'Damned odd!' said the captain, staring about him.

'Sing'ler!' ejaculated the unconscious Mr. Joseph Tuggs.

Lieutenant Slaughter looked first at one person mysteriously, then at another: then laid down his cigar, then approached the window on tiptoe, and pointed with his right thumb over his shoulder, in the direction of the curtain.

'Slaughter!' ejaculated the captain, rising from table, 'what do you mean?'

The lieutenant, in reply, drew back the curtain and discovered Mr. Cymon Tuggs behind it: pallid with apprehension, and blue with wanting to cough.

'Aha!' exclaimed the captain, furiously. 'What do I see? Slaughter, your sabre!'

'Cymon!' screamed the Tuggses.

'Mercy!' said Belinda.

'Platonic!' gasped Cymon.

'Your sabre!' roared the captain: 'Slaughter—unhand me—the villain's life!'

'Murder!' screamed the Tuggses.

'Hold him fast, sir!' faintly articulated Cymon.

'Water!' exclaimed Joseph Tuggs—and Mr. Cymon Tuggs and all the ladies forthwith fainted away, and formed a tableau.

Most willingly would we conceal the disastrous termination of the six weeks' acquaintance. A troublesome form, and an arbitrary custom, however, prescribe that a story should have a conclusion, in addition to a commencement; we have therefore no alternative. Lieutenant Slaughter brought a message—the captain brought an action. Mr. Joseph Tuggs interposed—the lieutenant negotiated. When Mr. Cymon Tuggs recovered from the nervous disorder into which misplaced affection, and exciting circumstances, had plunged him, he found that his family had lost their pleasant acquaintance; that his father was minus fifteen hundred pounds; and the captain plus the precise sum. The money was paid to hush the matter up, but it got abroad notwithstanding; and there are not wanting some who affirm that three designing impostors never found more easy dupes, than did Captain Waters, Mrs. Waters, and Lieutenant Slaughter, in the Tuggses at Ramsgate.

The Signal-man

'Halloa! Below there!'

When he heard a voice thus calling to him, he was standing at the door of his box, with a flag in his hand, furled round its short pole. One would have thought, considering the nature of the ground, that he could not have doubted from what quarter the voice came; but instead of looking up to where I stood on the top of the steep cutting nearly over his head, he turned himself about, and looked down the Line. There was something remarkable in his manner of doing so, though I could not have said for my life what. But I know it was remarkable enough to attract my notice, even though his figure was foreshortened and shadowed, down in the deep trench, and mine was high above him, so steeped in the glow of an angry sunset, that I had shaded my eyes with my hand before I saw him at all.

'Halloa! Below!'

From looking down the Line, he turned himself about again, and, raising his eyes, saw my figure high above him.

'Is there any path by which I can come down and speak to you?'

He looked up at me without replying, and I looked down at him without pressing him too soon with a repetition of my idle question. Just then there came a vague vibration in the earth and air, quickly changing into a violent pulsation, and an oncoming rush that caused me to start back, as though it had force to draw me down. When such vapour as rose to my height from this rapid train had passed me, and was skimming away over the landscape, I looked down again, and saw him refurling the flag he had shown while the train went by.

I repeated my inquiry. After a pause, during which he seemed to regard me with fixed attention, he motioned with his rolled-up flag towards a point on my level, some two or three hundred yards distant. I called down to him, 'All right!' and made for that point. There, by dint of looking closely about me, I found a rough zigzag descending path notched out, which I followed.

The cutting was extremely deep, and unusually precipitate. It was made through a clammy stone, that became oozier and wetter as I went down. For these reasons, I found the way long enough to give me time to recall a singular air of reluctance or compulsion with which he had pointed out the path.

When I came down low enough upon the zigzag descent to see him again, I saw that he was standing between the rails on the way by which the train had lately passed, in an attitude as if he were waiting for me to appear. He had his left hand at his chin, and that left elbow rested on his right hand, crossed over his breast. His attitude was one of such expectation and watchfulness that I stopped a moment, wondering at it.

I resumed my downward way, and stepping out upon the level of the railroad, and drawing nearer to him, saw that he was a dark sallow man, with a dark beard and rather heavy eyebrows. His post was in as solitary and dismal a place as ever I saw. On either side, a dripping-wet wall of jagged stone, excluding all view but a strip of sky; the perspective one way only a crooked prolongation of this great dungeon; the shorter perspective in the other direction terminating in a gloomy red light, and the gloomier entrance to a black tunnel, in whose massive architecture there was a barbarous, depressing, and forbidding air. So little sunlight ever found its way to this spot, that it had an earthy, deadly smell; and so much cold wind rushed through it, that it struck chill to me, as if I had left the natural world.

Before he stirred, I was near enough to him to have touched him. Not even then removing his eyes from mine, he stepped back one step, and lifted his hand.

This was a lonesome post to occupy (I said), and it had riveted my attention when I looked down from up yonder. A visitor was a rarity, I should suppose; not an unwelcome rarity, I hoped? In me, he merely saw a man who had been shut up within narrow limits all his life, and who, being at last set free, had a newly-awakened interest in these great works. To such purpose I spoke to him; but I am far from sure of the terms I used; for, besides that I am not happy in opening any conversation, there was something in the man that daunted me.

He directed a most curious look towards the red light near the tunnel's mouth, and looked all about it, as if something were missing from it, and then looked at me.

That light was part of his charge? Was it not?

He answered in a low voice,—'Don't you know it is?'

The monstrous thought came into my mind, as I perused the fixed eyes and the saturnine face, that this was a spirit, not a man. I have speculated since, whether there may have been infection in his mind.

In my turn, I stepped back. But in making the action, I detected in his eyes some latent fear of me. This put the monstrous thought to flight.

'You look at me,' I said, forcing a smile, 'as if you had a dread of me.'

'I was doubtful,' he returned, 'whether I had seen you before.'

'Where?'

He pointed to the red light he had looked at.

'There?' I said.

Intently watchful of me, he replied (but without sound), 'Yes.'

'My good fellow, what should I do there? However, be that as it may, I never was there, you may swear.'

'I think I may,' he rejoined. 'Yes. I am sure I may.'

His manner cleared, like my own. He replied to my remarks with readiness, and in well-chosen words. Had he much to do there? Yes; that was to say, he had enough responsibility to bear; but exactness and watchfulness were what was required of him, and of actual work—manual labour—he had next to none. To change that signal, to trim those lights, and to turn this iron handle now and then, was all he had to do under that head.

Regarding those many long and lonely hours of which I seemed to make so much, he could only say that the routine of his life had shaped itself into that form, and he had grown used to it. He had taught himself a language down here,—if only to know by sight, and to have formed his own crude ideas of its pronunciation, could be called learning it. He had also worked at fractions and decimals, and tried a little algebra; but he was, and had been as a boy, a poor hand at figures. Was it necessary for him when on duty always to remain in that channel of damp air, and could he never rise into the sunshine from between those high stone walls? Why, that depended upon times and circumstances. Under some conditions there would be less upon the Line than under others, and the same held good as to certain hours of the day and night. In bright weather, he did choose occasions for getting a little above these lower shadows; but, being at all times liable to be called by his electric bell, and at such times listening for it with redoubled anxiety, the relief was less than I would suppose.

He took me into his box, where there was a fire, a desk for an official book in which he had to make certain entries, a telegraphic instrument with its dial, face, and needles, and the little bell of which he had spoken. On my trusting that he would excuse the remark that he had been well educated, and (I hoped I might say without offence), perhaps educated above that station, he observed that instances of slight incongruity in such wise would rarely be found wanting among large bodies of men; that he had heard it was so in workhouses, in the police force, even in that last desperate resource, the army; and that he knew it was so, more or less, in any great railway staff. He had been, when young (if I could believe it, sitting in that hut,—he scarcely could), a student of natural philosophy, and had attended lectures; but he had run wild, misused his opportunities, gone down, and never risen again. He had no complaint to offer about that. He had made his bed, and he lay upon it. It was far too late to make another.

All that I have here condensed he said in a quiet manner, with his grave dark regards divided between me and the fire. He threw in the word, 'Sir,' from time to time, and especially when he referred to his youth,—as though to request me to understand that he claimed to be nothing but what I found him. He was several times interrupted by the little bell, and had to read off messages, and send replies. Once he had to stand without the door, and display a flag as a train passed, and make some verbal communication to the driver. In the discharge of his duties, I observed him to be remarkably exact and vigilant, breaking off his discourse at a syllable, and remaining silent until what he had to do was done.

In a word, I should have set this man down as one of the safest of men to be employed in that capacity, but for the circumstance that while he was speaking to me he twice broke off with a fallen colour, turned his face towards the little bell when it did NOT ring, opened the door of the hut (which was kept shut to exclude the unhealthy damp), and looked out towards the red light near the mouth of the tunnel. On both of those occasions, he came back to the fire with the inexplicable air upon him which I had remarked, without being able to define, when we were so far asunder.

Said I, when I rose to leave him, 'You almost make me think that I have met with a contented man.'

(I am afraid I must acknowledge that I said it to lead him on.)

'I believe I used to be so,' he rejoined, in the low voice in which he had first spoken; 'but I am troubled, sir, I am troubled.'

He would have recalled the words if he could. He had said them, however, and I took them up quickly.

'With what? What is your trouble?'

'It is very difficult to impart, sir. It is very, very difficult to speak of. If ever you make me another visit, I will try to tell you.'

'But I expressly intend to make you another visit. Say, when shall it be?'

'I go off early in the morning, and I shall be on again at ten to-morrow night, sir.'

'I will come at eleven.'

He thanked me, and went out at the door with me. 'I'll show my white light, sir,' he said, in his peculiar low voice, 'till you have found the way up. When you have found it, don't call out! And when you are at the top, don't call out!'

His manner seemed to make the place strike colder to me, but I said no more than, 'Very well.'

'And when you come down to-morrow night, don't call out! Let me ask you a parting question. What made you cry, "Halloa! Below there!" tonight?'

'Heaven knows,' said I. 'I cried something to that effect——'

'Not to that effect, sir. Those were the very words. I know them well.'

'Admit those were the very words. I said them, no doubt, because I saw you below.'

'For no other reason?'

'What other reason could I possibly have?'

'You had no feeling that they were conveyed to you in any supernatural way?'

'No.'

He wished me good night, and held up his light. I walked by the side of the down Line of rails (with a very disagreeable sensation of a train coming behind me) until I found the path. It was easier to mount than to descend, and I got back to my inn without any adventure.

Punctual to my appointment, I placed my foot on the first notch of the zigzag next night, as the distant clocks were striking eleven. He was waiting for me at the bottom, with his white light on. 'I have not called out,' I said, when we came close together; 'may I speak now?' 'By all means, sir.' 'Good night, then, and here's my hand.' 'Good night, sir, and here's mine.' With that we walked side by side to his box, entered it, closed the door, and sat down by the fire.

'I have made up my mind, sir,' he began, bending forward as soon as we were seated, and speaking in a tone but a little above a whisper, 'that you shall not have to ask me twice what troubles me. I took you for some one else yesterday evening. That troubles me.'

'That mistake?'

'No. That some one else.'

'Who is it?'

'I don't know.'

'Like me?'

'I don't know. I never saw the face. The left arm is across the face, and the right arm is waved,—violently waved. This way.'

I followed his action with my eyes, and it was the action of an arm gesticulating, with the utmost passion and vehemence, 'For God's sake, clear the way!'

'One moonlight night,' said the man, 'I was sitting here, when I heard a voice cry, "Halloa! Below there!" I started up, looked from that door, and saw this Some-one else standing by the red light near the tunnel, waving as I just now showed you. The voice seemed hoarse with shouting, and it cried, "Look out! Look out!" And then again, "Halloa! Below there! Look out!" I caught up my lamp, turned it on red, and ran towards the figure, calling, "What's wrong? What has happened? Where?" It stood just outside the blackness of the tunnel. I advanced so close upon it that I wondered at its keeping the sleeve across its eyes. I ran right up at it, and had my hand stretched out to pull the sleeve away, when it was gone.'

'Into the tunnel?' said I.

'No. I ran on into the tunnel, five hundred yards. I stopped, and held my lamp above my head, and saw the figures of the measured distance, and saw the wet stains stealing down the walls and trickling through the arch. I ran out again faster than I had run in (for I had a mortal abhorrence of the place upon me), and I looked all round the red light with my own red light, and I went up the iron ladder to the gallery atop of it, and I came down again, and ran back here. I telegraphed both ways, "An alarm has been given. Is anything wrong?" The answer came back, both ways, "All well."'

Resisting the slow touch of a frozen finger tracing out my spine, I showed him how that this figure must be a deception of his sense of sight; and how that figures, originating in disease of the delicate nerves that minister to the functions of the eye, were known to have often troubled patients, some of whom had become conscious of the nature of their affliction, and had even proved it by experiments upon themselves. 'As to an imaginary cry,' said I, 'do but listen for a moment to the wind in this unnatural valley while we speak so low, and to the wild harp it makes of the telegraph wires.'

That was all very well, he returned, after we had sat listening for a while, and he ought to know something of the wind and the wires,—he who so often passed long winter nights there, alone and watching. But he would beg to remark that he had not finished.

I asked his pardon, and he slowly added these words, touching my arm,—

'Within six hours after the Appearance, the memorable accident on this Line happened, and within ten hours the dead and wounded were brought along through the tunnel over the spot where the figure had stood.'

A disagreeable shudder crept over me, but I did my best against it. It was not to be denied, I rejoined, that this was a remarkable coincidence, calculated deeply to impress his mind. But it was unquestionable that remarkable coincidences did continually occur, and they must be taken into account in dealing with such a subject. Though to be sure I must admit, I added (for I thought I saw that he was going to bring the objection to bear upon me), men of common sense did not allow much for coincidences in making the ordinary calculations of life.

He again begged to remark that he had not finished.

I again begged his pardon for being betrayed into interruptions.

'This,' he said, again laying his hand upon my arm, and glancing over his shoulder with hollow eyes, 'was just a year ago. Six or seven months passed, and I had recovered from the surprise and shock, when one morning, as the day was breaking, I, standing at the door, looked towards the red light, and saw the spectre again.' He stopped, with a fixed look at me.

'Did it cry out?'

'No. It was silent.'

'Did it wave its arm?'

'No. It leaned against the shaft of the light, with both hands before the face. Like this.'

Once more I followed his action with my eyes. It was an action of mourning. I have seen such an attitude in stone figures on tombs.

'Did you go up to it?'

'I came in and sat down, partly to collect my thoughts, partly because it had turned me faint. When I went to the door again, daylight was above me, and the ghost was gone.'

9110212 E

'But nothing followed? Nothing came of this?'

He touched me on the arm with his forefinger twice or thrice, giving a ghastly nod each time:

'That very day, as a train came out of the tunnel, I noticed, at a carriage window on my side, what looked like a confusion of hands and heads, and something waved. I saw it just in time to signal the driver, Stop! He shut off, and put his brake on, but the train drifted past here a hundred and fifty yards or more. I ran after it, and, as I went along, heard terrible screams and cries. A beautiful young lady had died instantaneously in one of the compartments, and was brought in here, and laid down on this floor between us.'

Involuntarily I pushed my chair back, as I looked from the boards at which he pointed to himself.

'True, sir. True. Precisely as it happened, so I tell it you.'

I could think of nothing to say, to any purpose, and my mouth was very dry. The wind and the wires took up the story with a long lamenting wail.

He resumed. 'Now, sir, mark this, and judge how my mind is troubled. The spectre came back a week ago. Ever since, it has been there, now and again, by fits and starts.'

'At the light?'

'At the Danger-light.'

'What does it seem to do?'

He repeated, if possible with increased passion and vehemence, that former gesticulation of, 'For God's sake, clear the way!'

Then he went on. 'I have no peace or rest for it. It calls to me, for many minutes together, in an agonised manner, "Below there! Look out! Look out!" It stands waving to me. It rings my little bell—'

I caught at that. 'Did it ring your bell yesterday evening when I was here, and you went to the door?'

'Twice.'

'Why, see,' said I, 'how your imagination misleads you. My eyes were on the bell, and my ears were open to the bell, and if I am a living man, it did NOT ring at those times. No, nor at any other time, except when it was rung in the natural course of physical things by the station communicating with you.'

He shook his head. 'I have never made a mistake as to that yet, sir. I have never confused the spectre's ring with the man's. The ghost's ring is a strange vibration in the bell that it derives from nothing else, and I have not asserted that the bell stirs to the eye. I don't wonder that you failed to hear it. But *I* heard it.'

'And did the spectre seem to be there, when you looked out?'

'It WAS there.'

'Both times?'

He repeated firmly: 'Both times.'

'Will you come to the door with me, and look for it now?'

He bit his under lip as though he were somewhat unwilling, but arose. I opened the door, and stood on the step, while he stood in the doorway. There was the Danger-light. There was the dismal mouth of the tunnel. There were the high, wet stone walls of the cutting. There were the stars above them.

'Do you see it?' I asked him, taking particular note of his face. His eyes were prominent and strained, but not very much more so, perhaps, than my own had been when I had directed them earnestly towards the same spot.

'No,' he answered. 'It is not there.'

'Agreed,' said I.

We went in again, shut the door, and resumed our seats. I was thinking how best to improve this advantage, if it might be called one, when he took up the conversation in such a matter-of-course way, so assuming that there could be no serious question of fact between us, that I felt myself placed in the weakest of positions.

'By this time you will fully understand, sir,' he said, 'that what troubles me so dreadfully is the question, What does the spectre mean?'

I was not sure, I told him, that I did fully understand.

'What is its warning against?' he said, ruminating, with his eyes on the fire, and only by times turning them on me. 'What is the danger? Where is the danger? There is danger overhanging somewhere on the Line. Some dreadful calamity will happen. It is not to be doubted this third time, after what has gone before. But surely this a cruel haunting of *me*. What can *I* do?'

He pulled out his handkerchief, and wiped the drops from his heated forehead.

'If I telegraph Danger, on either side of me, or on both, I can give no reason for it,' he went on, wiping the palms of his hands. 'I should get into trouble, and do no good. They would think I was mad. This is the way it would work,—Message: "Danger! Take care!" Answer: "What Danger? Where?" Message: "Don't know. But, for God's sake, take care!" They would displace me. What else could they do?'

His pain of mind was most pitiable to see. It was the mental torture of a conscientious man, oppressed beyond endurance by an unintelligible responsibility involving life.

'When it first stood under the Danger-light,' he went on, putting his dark hair back from his head, and drawing his hands outward across and across his temples in an extremity of feverish distress, 'why not tell me where that accident was to happen,—if it must happen? Why not tell me how it could be averted,—if it could have been averted? When on its second coming it hid its face, why not tell me, instead, "She is going to die. Let them keep her at home"? If it came, on those two occasions, only to show me that its warnings were true, and so to prepare me for the third, why not warn me plainly now? And I, Lord help me! A mere poor signal-man on this solitary station! Why not go to somebody with credit to be believed, and power to act?'

When I saw him in this state, I saw that for the poor man's sake, as well as for the public safety, what I had to do for the time was to compose his mind. Therefore, setting aside all questions of reality or unreality between us, I represented to him that whoever thoroughly discharged his duty must do well, and that at least it was his comfort that he understood his duty, though he did not understand these confounding Appearances. In this effort I succeeded far better than in the attempt to reason him out of his conviction. He became calm; the occupations incidental to his post as the night advanced began to make larger demands on his attention and I left him at two in the morning. I had offered to stay through the night, but he would not hear of it.

That I more than once looked back at the red light as I ascended the pathway, that I did not like the red light, and that

I should have slept but poorly if my bed had been under it, I see no reason to conceal. Nor did I like the two sequences of the accident and the dead girl. I see no reason to conceal that either.

But what ran most in my thoughts was the consideration how ought I to act, having become the recipient of this disclosure? I had proved the man to be intelligent, vigilant, painstaking, and exact; but how long might he remain so, in his state of mind? Though in a subordinate position, still he held a most important trust, and would I (for instance) like to stake my own life on the chances of his continuing to execute it with precision?

Unable to overcome a feeling that there would be something treacherous in my communicating what he had told me to his superiors in the Company, without first being plain with himself and proposing a middle course to him, I ultimately resolved to offer to accompany him (otherwise keeping his secret for the present) to the wisest medical practitioner we could hear of in those parts, and to take his opinion. A change in his time of duty would come round next night, he had apprised me, and he would be off an hour or two after sunrise, and on again soon after sunset. I had appointed to return accordingly.

Next evening was a lovely evening, and I walked out early to enjoy it. The sun was not yet quite down when I traversed the field-path near the top of the deep cutting. I would extend my walk for an hour, I said to myself, half an hour on and half an hour back, and it would then be time to go to my signal-man's box.

Before pursuing my stroll, I stepped to the brink, and mechanically looked down, from the point from which I had first seen him. I cannot describe the thrill that seized upon me, when, close at the mouth of the tunnel, I saw the appearance of a man, with his left sleeve across his eyes, passionately waving his right arm.

The nameless horror that oppressed me passed in a moment, for in a moment I saw that this appearance of a man was a man indeed, and that there was a little group of other men, standing at a short distance, to whom he seemed to be rehearsing the gesture he made. The Danger-light was not yet lighted. Against its shaft, a little low hut, entirely new to me, had been made of some wooden supports and tarpaulin. It looked no bigger than a bed.

With an irresistible sense that something was wrong,—with a flashing self-reproachful fear that fatal mischief had come of my leaving the man there, and causing no one to be sent to overlook or correct what he did,—I descended the notched path with all the speed I could make.

'What is the matter?' I asked the men.

'Signal-man killed this morning, sir.'

'Not the man belonging to that box?'

'Yes, sir.'

'Not the man I know?'

'You will recognize him, sir, if you knew him,' said the man who spoke for the others, solemnly uncovering his own head, and raising an end of the tarpaulin, 'for his face is quite composed.'

'O, how did this happen, how did this happen?' I asked, turning from one to another as the hut closed in again.

'He was cut down by an engine, sir. No man in England knew his work better. But somehow he was not clear of the outer rail. It was just at broad day. He had struck the light, and had the lamp in his hand. As the engine came out of the tunnel, his back was towards her, and she cut him down. That man drove her, and was showing how it happened. Show the gentleman, Tom.'

The man, who wore a rough dark dress, stepped back to his former place at the mouth of the tunnel.

'Coming round the curve in the tunnel, sir,' he said, 'I saw him at the end, like as if I saw him down a perspective-glass. There was no time to check speed, and I knew him to be very careful. As he didn't seem to take heed of the whistle, I shut it off when we were running down upon him, and called to him as loud as I could call.'

'What did you say?'

'I said, "Below there! Look out! Look out! For God's sake, clear the way!"'

I started.

'Ah! it was a dreadful time, sir. I never left off calling to him. I put this arm before my eyes not to see, and I waved this arm to the last; but it was no use.'

Without prolonging the narrative to dwell on any one of its curious circumstances more than on any other, I may, in closing it, point out the coincidence that the warning of the engine-driver included, not only the words which the unfortunate signal-man had repeated to me as haunting him, but also the words which I myself—not he—had attached, and that only in my own mind, to the gesticulation he had imitated.

WILLIAM MAKEPEACE THACKERAY
(1811–1863)

'Mr. and Mrs. Frank Berry' and 'Dennis Haggarty's Wife' both appeared in the series *Men's Wives*, contributed by Thackeray to *Fraser's Magazine* under the pseudonym of George Savage Fitz-Boodle in 1843. They are thus early works, although within five years *Vanity Fair* appeared. 'Fitz-Boodle' was a bachelor, and *Men's Wives* describes a series of unfortunate marriages. Thackeray's own marriage had come sadly to grief after four years with his wife's insanity, and probably Mrs. Major Gam that 'odious Irishwoman' in 'Dennis Haggarty's Wife' with her snobbish claims of distinguished family and her domination of her daughter, in some way reflects his Irish mother-in-law, Isabella Shawe, whom the novelist called in a letter 'a singular old deevil' with a tendency to talk 'as big as St. Paul's'.

I have regretfully omitted Chapter I of 'Mr. and Mrs. Frank Berry'. It is called 'The Fight at Slaughter House'—a glance at Charterhouse where Thackeray was at school—and Chapter II is called 'The Combat at Versailles'. Although the author asked at the end of Chapter I 'What has this horrid description of a battle and a parcel of school-boys to do with *Men's Wives*?' and answered, 'A great deal more than you think, for only read Chapter II, and you shall hear', there is no continuity and little real connection, save that the honourable and manly Frank Berry is not victorious in either combat.

Mr. and Mrs. Frank Berry

I AFTERWARDS came to be Berry's fag, and, though beaten by him daily, he allowed, of course, no one else to lay a hand upon me, and I got no more thrashing than was good for me. Thus an intimacy grew up between us, and after he left Slaughter House[1] and went into the dragoons, the honest fellow did not forget his old friend, but actually made his appearance one day in the play-

[1] Charterhouse (Thackeray's own old school). The great fight between Berry and Biggs was described in Chapter I of 'Mr. and Mrs. Frank Berry'.

ground in moustaches and a braided coat, and gave me a gold pencil-case and a couple of sovereigns. I blushed when I took them, but take them I did; and I think the thing I almost best recollect in my life, is the sight of Berry getting behind an immense bay cab-horse, which was held by a correct little groom, and was waiting near the school in Slaughter House Square. He proposed, too, to have me to 'Long's,' where he was lodging for the time; but this invitation was refused on my behalf by Dr. Buckle, who said, and possibly with correctness, that I should get little good by spending my holiday with such a scapegrace.

Once afterwards he came to see me at Christ Church,[2] and we made a show of writing to one another, and didn't, and always had a hearty mutual goodwill; and, though we did not quite burst into tears on parting, were yet quite happy when occasion threw us together, and so almost lost sight of each other. I heard lately that Berry was married, and am rather ashamed to say, that I was not so curious as even to ask the maiden name of his lady.

Last summer I was at Paris, and had gone over to Versailles to meet a party, one of which was a young lady to whom I was tenderly . . . But, never mind. The day was rainy, and the party did not keep its appointment; and after yawning through the interminable palace picture-galleries, and then making an attempt to smoke a cigar in the Palace garden—for which crime I was nearly run through the body by a rascally sentinel—I was driven, perforce, into the great bleak, lonely *Place* before the Palace, with its roads branching off to all the towns in the world, which Louis and Napoleon once intended to conquer, and there enjoyed my favourite pursuit at leisure, and was meditating whether I should go back to 'Véfour's' for dinner, or patronize my friend M. Duboux of the 'Hôtel des Réservoirs,' who gives not only a good dinner, but as dear a one as heart can desire. I was, I say, meditating these things, when a carriage passed by. It was a smart, low calash,[3] with a pair of bay horses and a postilion in a drab jacket, that twinkled with innumerable buttons, and I was too much occupied in admiring the build of the machine, and the extreme tightness of the fellow's inexpressibles,[4] to look at the

[2] College at Oxford. [3] A light carriage. [4] Facetious for trousers.

personages within the carriage, when the gentleman roared out 'Fitz!' and the postilion pulled up, and the lady gave a shrill scream, and a little black-muzzled spaniel began barking and yelling with all his might, and a man with moustaches jumped out of the vehicle, and began shaking me by the hand.

'Drive home, John,' said the gentleman: 'I'll be with you, my love, in an instant—it's an old friend. Fitz, let me present you to Mrs. Berry.'

The lady made an exceedingly gentle inclination of her black-velvet bonnet, and said, 'Pray, my love, remember that it is just dinner-time. However, never mind *me*.' And with another slight toss and a nod to the postilion, that individual's white leather breeches began to jump up and down again in the saddle, and the carriage disappeared, leaving me shaking my old friend Berry by the hand.

He had long quitted the army, but still wore his military beard, which gave to his fair pink face a fierce and lion-like look. He was extraordinarily glad to see me, as only men are glad who live in a small town, or in dull company. There is no destroyer of friendships like London, where a man has no time to think of his neighbour, and has far too many friends to care for them. He told me in a breath of his marriage, and how happy he was, and straight insisted that I must come home to dinner, and see more of Angelica, who had invited me herself—didn't I hear her?

'Mrs. Berry asked *you*, Frank; but I certainly did not hear her ask *me!*'

'She would not have mentioned the dinner but that she meant me to ask you. I know she did,' cried Frank Berry. 'And, besides—hang it—I'm master of the house. So come you shall. No ceremony, old boy—one or two friends—snug family party—and we'll talk of old times over a bottle of claret.'

There did not seem to me to be the slightest objection to this arrangement, except that my boots were muddy, and my coat of the morning sort. But as it was quite impossible to go to Paris and back in a quarter of an hour, and as a man may dine with perfect comfort to himself in a frock-coat, it did not occur to me to be particularly squeamish, or to decline an old friend's invitation upon a pretext so trivial.

Accordingly we walked to a small house in the Avenue de Paris, and were admitted first into a small garden ornamented by a grotto, a fountain, and several nymphs in plaster-of-Paris, then up a mouldy old steep stair into a hall, where a statue of Cupid and another of Venus welcomed us with their eternal simper; then through a *salle-à-manger*, where covers were laid for six; and finally to a little saloon, where Fido the dog began to howl furiously according to his wont.

It was one of the old pavilions that had been built for a pleasure-house in the gay days of Versailles, ornamented with abundance of damp Cupids and cracked gilt cornices, and old mirrors let into the walls, and gilded once, but now painted a dingy French white. The long low windows looked into the court, where the fountain played its ceaseless dribble, surrounded by numerous rank creepers and weedy flowers, but in the midst of which the statues stood with their bases quite moist and green.

I hate fountains and statues in dark, confined places: that cheerless, endless plashing of water is the most inhospitable sound ever heard. The stiff grin of those French statues, or ogling Canova Graces,[5] is by no means more happy, I think, than the smile of a skeleton, and not so natural. Those little pavilions in which the old *roués*[6] sported, were never meant to be seen by daylight, depend on't. They were lighted up with a hundred wax-candles, and the little fountain yonder was meant only to cool their claret. And so, my first impression of Berry's place of abode was rather a dismal one. However, I heard him in the *salle-à-manger* drawing the corks, which went off with a *cloop*, and that consoled me.

As for the furniture of the rooms appertaining to the Berrys, there was a harp in a leather case, and a piano, and a flute-box, and a huge tambour[7] with a Saracen's nose just begun, and likewise on the table a multiplicity of those little gilt books, half sentimental and half religious, which the wants of the age and of our young ladies have produced in such numbers of late. I

[5] Group of the Graces (three goddesses in Greek mythology personifying loveliness, grace, and generosity); Canova (1757–1822), Venetian neo-classical sculptor whom Napoleon invited to Paris and greatly patronized.
[6] Rakes, libertines.
[7] Frame for embroidery.

quarrel with no lady's taste in that way; but heigho! I had rather that Mrs. Fitzboodle should read 'Humphrey Clinker!'

Beside these works, there was a 'Peerage' of course. What genteel family was ever without one?

I was making for the door to see Frank drawing the corks, and was bounced at by the amiable little black-muzzled spaniel, who fastened his teeth in my pantaloons, and received a polite kick in consequence, which sent him howling to the other end of the room, and the animal was just in the act of performing that feat of agility, when the door opened and madame made her appearance. Frank came behind her, peering over her shoulder with rather an anxious look.

Mrs. Berry is an exceedingly white and lean person. She has thick eyebrows, which meet rather dangerously over her nose, which is Grecian, and a small mouth with no lips—a sort of feeble pucker in the face as it were. Under her eyebrows are a pair of enormous eyes, which she is in the habit of turning constantly ceiling-wards. Her hair is rather scarce, and worn in bandeaux, and she commonly mounts a sprig of laurel, or a dark flower or two, which, with the sham *tour*—I believe that is the name of the knob of artificial hair that many ladies sport—gives her a rigid and classical look. She is dressed in black, and has invariably the neatest of silk stockings and shoes; for, forsooth her foot is a fine one, and she always sits with it before her looking at it, stamping it, and admiring it a great deal. 'Fido,' she says to her spaniel, 'you have almost crushed my poor foot;' or, 'Frank,' to her husband, 'bring me a footstool;' or, 'I suffer so from cold in the feet,' and so forth; but be the conversation what it will, she is always sure to put *her foot* into it.

She invariably wears on her neck the miniature of her late father, Sir George Catacomb, apothecary to George III; and she thinks those two men the greatest the world ever saw. She was born in Baker Street, Portman Square, and that is saying almost enough of her. She is as long, as genteel, and as dreary as the deadly-lively place, and sports, by way of ornament, her papa's hatchment,[8] as it were, as every tenth Baker Street house has taught her.

[8] Armorial shield (technically, a hatchment was one hung up outside the house of a dead person).

What induced such a jolly fellow as Frank Berry to marry Miss Angelica Catacomb no one can tell. He met her, he says, at a ball at Hampton Court, where his regiment was quartered, and where, to this day, lives 'her aunt, Lady Pash.' She alludes perpetually in conversation to that celebrated lady; and if you look in the 'Baronetage' to the pedigree of the Pash family, you may see manuscript notes by Mrs. Frank Berry, relative to them and herself. Thus, when you see in print that Sir John Pash married Angelica, daughter of Graves Catacomb, Esq., in a neat hand you find written, *and sister of the late Sir George Catacomb, of Baker Street, Portman Square:* 'A. B.' follows of course. It is a wonder how fond ladies are of writing in books and signing their charming initials! Mrs. Berry's before-mentioned little gilt books are scored with pencil-marks, or occasionally at the margin with a !—note of interjection, or the words '*Too true, A. B.*,' and so on. Much may be learned with regard to lovely woman by a look at the book she reads in; and I had gained no inconsiderable knowledge of Mrs. Berry by the ten minutes spent in the drawing-room, while she was at her toilet in the adjoining bed-chamber.

'You have often heard me talk of George Fitz,' says Berry, with an appealing look to madame.

'Very often,' answered his lady, in a tone which clearly meant 'a great deal too much.' 'Pray, sir,' continued she, looking at my boots with all her might, 'are we to have your company at dinner?'

'Of course you are, my dear; what else do you think he came for? You would not have the man go back to Paris to get his evening coat, would you?'

'At least, my love, I hope you will go and put on *yours*, and change those muddy boots. Lady Pash will be here in five minutes, and you know Dobus is as punctual as clock-work.' Then turning to me with a sort of apology that was as consoling as a box on the ear, 'We have some friends at dinner, sir, who are rather particular persons; but I am sure when they hear that you only came on a sudden invitation, they will excuse your morning dress.—Bah, what a smell of smoke!'

With this speech madame placed herself majestically on a sofa, put out her foot, called Fido, and relapsed into an icy silence. Frank had long since evacuated the premises, with a rueful look at his wife, but never daring to cast a glance at me. I saw the whole business at once; here was this lion of a fellow tamed down by a she Van Amburgh,[9] and fetching and carrying at her orders a great deal more obediently than her little yowling, black-muzzled darling of a Fido.

I am not, however, to be tamed so easily, and was determined in this instance not to be in the least disconcerted, or to show the smallest sign of ill-humour: so to *renouer* the conversation, I began about Lady Pash.

'I heard you mention the name of Pash, I think?' said I. 'I know a lady of that name, and a very ugly one it is too.'

'It is most probably not the same person,' answered Mrs. Berry, with a look which intimated that a fellow like me could never have had the honour to know so exalted a person.

'I mean old Lady Pash of Hampton Court. Fat woman—fair, ain't she?—and wears an amethyst in her forehead, has one eye, a blond wig, and dresses in light green?'

'Lady Pash, sir, is MY AUNT,' answered Mrs. Berry (not altogether displeased, although she expected money from the old lady; but you know we love to hear our friends abused when it can be safely done).

'Oh, indeed! she was a daughter of old Catacomb's of Windsor, I remember, the undertaker. They called her husband Callipash, and her ladyship Pishpash. So you see, madam, that I know the whole family!'

'Mr. Fitz-Simons!' exclaimed Mrs. Berry, rising, 'I am not accustomed to hear nicknames applied to myself and my family; and must beg you, when you honour us with your company, to spare our feelings as much as possible. Mr. Catacomb had the confidence of his SOVEREIGN, sir, and Sir John Pash was of Charles II.'s creation. The one was my uncle, sir, the other my grandfather!'

'My dear madam, I am extremely sorry, and most sincerely apologize for my inadvertence. But you owe me an apology too: my name is not Fitz-Simons, but Fitz-Boodle.'

'What! of Boodle Hall—my husband's old friend; of Charles I.'s creation? My dear sir, I beg you a thousand pardons, and am

[9] A contemporary American lion-tamer.

delighted to welcome a person of whom I have heard Frank say so much. Frank!' (to Berry, who soon entered in very glossy boots and a white waistcoat), 'do you know, darling, I mistook Mr. Fitz-Boodle for Mr. Fitz-Simons—that horrid Irish horse-dealing person; and I never, never, never can pardon myself for being so rude to him.'

The big eyes here assumed an expression that was intended to kill me outright with kindness: from being calm, still, reserved, Angelica suddenly became gay, smiling, confidential, and *folâtre.*[10] She told me she had heard I was a sad creature, and that she intended to reform me, and that I must come and see Frank a great deal.

Now, although Mr. Fitz-Simons, for whom I was mistaken, is as low a fellow as ever came out of Dublin, and having been a captain in somebody's army, is now a black-leg[11] and horse-dealer by profession; yet if I had brought him home to Mrs. Fitz-Boodle to dinner, I should have liked far better that that imaginary lady should have received him with decent civility, and not insulted the stranger within her husband's gates. And, although it was delightful to be received so cordially when the mistake was discovered, yet I found that *all* Berry's old acquaintances were by no means so warmly welcomed; for another old school-chum presently made his appearance, who was treated in a very different manner.

This was no other than poor Jack Butts, who is a sort of small artist and picture-dealer by profession, and was a day-boy at Slaughter House when we were there, and very serviceable in bringing in sausages, pots of pickles, and other articles of mechandise, which we could not otherwise procure. The poor fellow has been employed, seemingly, in the same office of fetcher and carrier ever since, and occupied that post for Mrs. Berry. It was 'Mr. Butts, have you finished that drawing for Lady Pash's album?' and Butts produced it; and 'Did you match the silk for me at Delille's?' and there was the silk, bought, no doubt, with the poor fellow's last five francs; and 'Did you go to the furniture-man in the Rue St. Jacques; and bring the canary-seed, and call about

[10] Playful.
[11] Swindler, race-course cheat.

my shawl at that odious, dawdling Madame Fichet's; and have you brought the guitar-strings?'

Butts hadn't brought the guitar-strings; and thereupon Mrs. Berry's countenance assumed the same terrible expression which I had formerly remarked in it, and which made me tremble for Berry.

'My dear Angelica,' though said he with some spirit, 'Jack Butts isn't a baggage-waggon, nor a Jack-of-all-trades; you make him paint pictures for your women's albums, and look after your upholsterer, and your canary-bird, and your milliners, and turn rusty because he forgets your last message.'

'I did not turn *rusty*, Frank, as you call it elegantly. I'm very much obliged to Mr. Butts for performing my commissions—very much obliged. And as for not paying for the pictures to which you so kindly allude, Frank, *I* should never have thought of offering payment for so paltry a service; but I'm sure I shall be happy to pay if Mr. Butts will send me in his bill.'

'By Jove, Angelica, this is too much!' bounced out Berry; but the little matrimonial squabble was abruptly ended, by Berry's French man flinging open the door and announcing MILADI PASH and Doctor Dobus, which two personages made their appearance.

The person of old Pash has been already parenthetically described. But, quite different from her dismal niece in temperament, she is as jolly an old widow as ever wore weeds. She was attached somehow to the court, and has a multiplicity of stories about the princesses and the old king, to which Mrs. Berry never fails to call your attention in her grave, important way. Lady Pash has ridden many a time to the Windsor hounds; she made her husband become a member of the Four-in-hand Club, and has numberless stories about Sir Godfrey Webster, Sir John Lade, and the old heroes of those times. She has lent a rouleau[12] to Dick Sheridan, and remembers Lord Byron when he was a sulky slim young lad. She says Charles Fox was the pleasantest fellow she ever met with, and has not the slightest objection to inform you that one of the princes was very much in love with her. Yet somehow she is only fifty-two years old, and I have never been able to understand her calculation. One day or other before her

[12] A cylindrical packet of gold coins.

eye went out, and before those pearly teeth of of hers were stuck to her gums by gold, she must have been a pretty-looking body enough. Yet in spite of the latter inconvenience, she eats and drinks too much every day, and tosses off a glass of maraschino[13] with a trembling pudgy hand, every finger of which twinkles with a dozen, at least, of old rings. She has a story about every one of those rings, and a stupid one too. But there is always something pleasant, I think, in stupid family stories: they are good-hearted people who tell them.

As for Mrs. Muchit, nothing need be said of her: she is Pash's companion, she has lived with Lady Pash since the peace. Nor does my lady take any more notice of her than of the dust of the earth. She calls her 'poor Muchit,' and considers her a half-witted creature. Mrs. Berry hates her cordially, and thinks she is a designing toad-eater,[14] who has formed a conspiracy to rob her of her aunt's fortune. She never spoke a word to poor Muchit during the whole of dinner, or offered to help her to anything on the table.

In respect to Dobus, he is an old Peninsular man, as you are made to know before you have been very long in his company; and, like most army surgeons, is a great deal more military in his looks and conversation than the combatant part of the forces. He has adopted the sham-Duke-of-Wellington air, which is by no means uncommon in veterans; and though one of the easiest and softest fellows in existence, speaks slowly and briefly, and raps out an oath or two occasionally, as it is said a certain great captain does. Besides the above, we sat down to the table with Captain Goff, late of the —— Highlanders; the Rev. Lemuel Whey, who preaches at St. Germains; little Cutler, and the Frenchman, who always *will* be at English parties on the Continent, and who, after making some frightful efforts to speak English, subsides and is heard of no more. Young married ladies and heads of families generally have him for the purpose of waltzing, and in return he informs his friends of the club or the *café* that he has made the conquest of a *charmante Anglaise.* Listen to me, all family men who read this! and never *let an unmarried Frenchman into your doors.* This lecture alone is worth the price of the book. It is not

[13] A liqueur made from black cherries. [14] Sycophant, flatterer.

that they do any harm in one case out of a thousand, heaven forbid! but they mean harm. They look on our Susannahs[15] with unholy, dishonest eyes. Hearken to two of the grinning rogues chattering together as they clink over the asphalte of the Boulevard with lacquered boots, and plastered hair, and waxed moustaches, and turned-down shirt-collars, and stays and goggling eyes, and hear how they talk of a good, simple, giddy, vain, dull Baker Street creature, and canvass her points, and show her letters, and insinuate—never mind, but I tell you my soul grows angry when I think of the same; and I can't hear of an Englishwoman marrying a Frenchman, without feeling a sort of shame and pity for her.*

To return to the guests. The Rev. Lemuel Whey is a tea-party man, with a curl on his forehead and a scented pocket-handkerchief. He ties his white neckcloth to a wonder, and I believe sleeps in it. He brings his flute with him; and prefers Handel, of course; but has one or two pet profane songs of the sentimental kind, and will occasionally lift up his little pipe in a glee. He does not dance, but the honest fellow would give the world to do it; and he leaves his clogs in the passage, though it is a wonder he wears them, for in the muddiest weather he never has a speck on his foot. He was at St. John's College, Cambridge, and was rather gay for a term or two, he says. He is, in a word, full of the milk-and-water of human kindness, and his family lives near Hackney.

As for Goff, he has a huge, shining, bald forehead, and immense bristling, Indian-red whiskers. He wears white wash-leather gloves, drinks fairly, likes a rubber, and has a story for after dinner, beginning, 'Doctor, ye racklackt Sandy M'Lellan, who joined us in the West Indies, Wal, sir,' &c. These and little Cutler made up the party.

[15] Susannah on whom the elders looked lustfully when she was bathing (in the *Apocrypha*).

* Every person who has lived abroad, can, of course, point out a score of honourable exceptions to the case above hinted at, and knows many such unions in which it is the Frenchman who honours the English lady by marrying her. But it must be remembered that marrying in France means commonly *fortune-hunting:* and as for the respect in which marriage is held in France, let all the French novels in M. Rolandi's library be perused by those who wish to come to a decision upon the question.

Now it may not have struck all readers, but any sharp fellow conversant with writing must have found out long ago, that if there had been something exceedingly interesting to narrate with regard to this dinner at Frank Berry's, I should have come out with it a couple of pages since, nor have kept the public looking for so long a time at the dish-covers and ornaments of the table.

But the simple fact must now be told, that there was nothing of the slightest importance occurred at this repast, except that it gave me an opportunity of studying Mrs. Berry in many different ways; and, in spite of the extreme complaisance which she now showed me, of forming, I am sorry to say, a most unfavourable opinion of that fair lady. Truth to tell, I would much rather she should have been civil to Mrs. Muchit, than outrageously complimentary to your humble servant; and, as she professed not to know what on earth there was for dinner, would it not have been much more natural for her not to frown, and bob, and wink, and point, and pinch her lips as often as Monsieur Anatole, her French domestic, not knowing the ways of English dinner-tables, placed anything out of its due order? The allusions to Boodle Hall were innumerable, and I don't know any greater bore than to be obliged to talk of a place which belongs to one's elder brother. Many questions were likewise asked about the dowager and her Scotch relatives, the Plumduffs, about whom Lady Pash knew a great deal, having seen them at court and at Lord Melville's. Of course she had seen them at court and at Lord Melville's, as she might have seen thousands of Scotchmen besides; but what mattered it to me, who care not a jot for old Lady Fitz-Boodle? 'When you write, you'll say you met an old friend of her ladyship's,' says Mrs. Berry, and I faithfully promised I would when I wrote; but if the New Post Office paid us for writing letters (as very possibly it will soon), I could not be bribed to send a line to old Lady Fitz.

In a word I found that Berry, like many simple fellows before him, had made choice of an imperious, ill-humoured, and underbred female for a wife, and could see with half an eye that he was a great deal too much her slave.

The struggle was not over yet, however. Witness that little encounter before dinner; and once or twice the honest fellow replied rather smartly during the repast, taking especial care to atone as much as possible for his wife's inattention to Jack and Mrs. Muchit, by particular attention to those personages, whom he helped to everything round about and pressed perpetually to champagne; he drank but little himself, for his amiable wife's eye was constantly fixed on him.

Just at the conclusion of the dessert, madame, who had *boudé*'d[16] Berry during dinner-time, became particularly gracious to her lord and master, and tenderly asked me if I did not think the French custom was a good one, of men leaving table with the ladies.

'Upon my word, ma'am,' says I, 'I think it's a most abominable practice.'

'And so do I,' says Cutler.

'A most abominable practice! Do you hear *that?*' cries Berry, laughing, and filling his glass.

'I'm sure, Frank, when we are alone you always come to the drawing-room,' replies the lady, sharply.

'Oh, yes! when we're alone, darling,' says Berry, blushing; 'but now we're *not* alone—ha, ha! Anatole, du Bordeaux!'

'I'm sure they sat after the ladies at Carlton House; didn't they, Lady Pash?' says Dobus, who likes his glass.

'*That* they did!' says my lady, giving him a jolly nod.

'I racklackt,' exclaims Captain Goff, 'when I was in the Mauritius, that Mestress MacWhirter, who commanded the Saxty-Sackond, used to say, "Mac, if ye want to get lively, ye'll not stop for more than two hours after the leddies have laft ye: if ye want to get drunk, ye'll just dine at the mass." So ye see, Mestress Barry, what was Mac's allowance—haw, haw! Mester Whey, I'll trouble ye for the o-lives.'

But although we were in a clear majority, that indomitable woman, Mrs. Berry, determined to make us all as uneasy as possible, and would take the votes all round. Poor Jack, of course, sided with her, and Whey said he loved a cup of tea and a little music better than all the wine of Bordeaux. As for the Frenchman, when Mrs. Berry said, 'And what do you think, M. le Vicomte?'

[16] Been sulky with.

'Vat you speak?' said M. de Blagueval, breaking silence for the first time during two hours; 'yase—eh? to me you speak?'

'Apry deeny, aimy-voo ally avec les dam?'

'Comment avec les dames?'

'Ally avec les dam com à Parry, ou resty avec les Messew com on Onglyterre?'

'Ah, madame! vous me le démandez?' cries the little wretch, starting up in a theatrical way, and putting out his hand, which Mrs. Berry took, and with this the ladies left the room. Old Lady Pash trotted after her niece with her hand in Whey's, very much wondering at such practices, which were not in the least in vogue in the reign of George III.

Mrs. Berry cast a glance of triumph at her husband, at the defection; and Berry was evidently annoyed that three-eighths of his male forces had left him.

But fancy our delight and astonishment, when in a minute they all three came back again; the Frenchman looking entirely astonished, and the parson and the painter both very queer. The fact is, old downright Lady Pash, who had never been in Paris in her life before, and had no notion of being deprived of her usual hour's respite and nap, said at once to Mrs. Berry, 'My dear Angelica, you're surely not going to keep these three men here? Send them back to the dining-room, for I've a thousand things to say to you.' And Angelica, who expects to inherit her aunt's property, of course did as she was bid; on which the old lady fell into an easy chair, and fell asleep immediately,—so soon, that is, as the shout caused by the reappearance of the three gentlemen in the dining-room had subsided.

I had meanwhile had some private conversation with little Cutler regarding the character of Mrs. Berry. 'She's a regular screw,'[17] whispered he; 'a regular Tartar. Berry shows fight, though, sometimes, and I've known him have his own way for a week together. After dinner he is his own master, and hers when he has had his share of wine; and that's why she will never allow him to drink any.'

Was it a wicked or was it a noble and honourable thought which came to us both at the same minute, to rescue Berry from

[17] A horsy term, meaning rough and not well trained.

his captivity? The ladies, of course, will give their verdict according to their gentle natures; but I know what men of courage will think, and by their jovial judgment will abide.

We received, then, the three lost sheep back into our innocent fold again with the most joyous shouting and cheering. We made Berry (who was, in truth, nothing loth) order up I don't know how much more claret. We obliged the Frenchman to drink *malgré lui*, and in the course of a short time we had poor Whey in such a state of excitement, that he actually volunteered to sing a song, which he said he had heard at some very gay supper-party at Cambridge, and which begins:—

> 'A pye sat on a pear-tree,
> A pye sat on a pear-tree,
> A pye sat on a pear-tree,
> Heigh-ho, heigh-ho, heigh-ho!'

Fancy Mrs. Berry's face as she looked in, in the midst of that Bacchanalian ditty, when she saw no less a person than the Rev. Lemuel Whey carolling it!

'Is it you, my dear?' cries Berry, as brave now as any Petruchio.[18] 'Come in and sit down, and hear Whey's song.'

'Lady Pash is asleep, Frank,' said she.

'Well, darling; that's the very reason. Give Mrs. Berry a glass, Jack, will you?'

'Would you wake your aunt, sir?' hissed out madam.

'Never mind me, love! I'm awake, and like it!' cried the venerable Lady Pash from the *salon*. 'Sing away, gentlemen!'

At which we all set up an audacious cheer; and Mrs. Berry flounced back to the drawing-room, but did not leave the door open that her aunt might hear our melodies.

Berry had by this time arrived at that confidential state to which a third bottle always brings the well-regulated mind; and he made a clean confession to Cutler and myself of his numerous matrimonial annoyances. He was not allowed to dine out, he said, and but seldom to ask his friends to meet him at home. He never dared smoke a cigar for the life of him, not even in the

[18] Who tamed his wife in Shakespeare's comedy, *The Taming of the Shrew*.

stables. He spent the mornings dawdling in eternal shops, the evenings at endless tea-parties, or in reading poems or missionary tracts to his wife. He was compelled to take physic whenever she thought he looked a little pale, to change his shoes and stockings whenever he came in from a walk. 'Look here,' said he, opening his chest, and shaking his fist at Dobus; 'look what Angelica and that infernal Dobus have brought me to.'

I thought it might be a flannel waistcoat into which madam had forced him: but it was worse: I give you my word of honour it was a *pitch-plaster!*[19]

We all roared at this, and the doctor as loud as any one; but he vowed that he had no hand in the pitch-plaster. It was a favourite family remedy of the late apothecary, Sir George Catacomb, and had been put on by Mrs. Berry's own fair hands.

When Anatole came in with coffee, Berry was in such high courage, that he told him to go to the deuce with it; and we never caught sight of Lady Pash more, except when, muffled up to the nose, she passed through the *salle-à manger* to go to her carriage, in which Dobus and the parson were likewise to be transported to Paris. 'Be a man, Frank,' says she, 'and hold your own'—for the good old lady had taken her nephew's part in the matrimonial business—'and you, Mr. Fitz-Boodle, come and see him often. You're a good fellow, take old one-eyed Callipash's word for it. Shall I take you to Paris?'

Dear, kind Angelica, she had told her aunt all I said!

'Don't go, George,' says Berry, squeezing me by the hand. So I said I was going to sleep at Versailles that night; but if she would give a convoy to Jack Butts, it would be conferring a great obligation on him; with which favour the old lady accordingly complied, saying to him, with great coolness, 'Get up and sit with John in the rumble,[20] Mr. What-d'ye-call-'im.' The fact is, the good old soul despises an artist as much as she does a tailor.

Jack tripped to his place very meekly; and 'Remember Saturday,' cried the doctor; and 'Don't forget Thursday,' exclaimed the divine,—'a bachelor's party, you know.' And so the cavalcade drove thundering down the gloomy old Avenue de Paris.

[19] A tight dressing soaked in resin or tar.
[20] Rear part of a carriage, meant for luggage or an extra passenger.

The Frenchman, I forgot to say, had gone away exceedingly ill long before; and the reminiscences of 'Thursday' and 'Saturday' evoked by Dobus and Whey were, to tell the truth, parts of our conspiracy: for in the heat of Berry's courage, we had made him promise to dine with us all round *en garçon;* with all except Captain Goff, who 'racklacted' that he was engaged every day for the next three weeks: as indeed he is, to a thirty-sous ordinary[21] which the gallant officer frequents, when not invited elsewhere.

Cutler and I then were the last on the field; and though we were for moving away, Berry, whose vigour had, if possible, been excited by the bustle and colloquy in the night air, insisted upon dragging us back again, and actually proposed a grill for supper.

We found in the *salle-à-manger* a strong smell of an extinguished lamp, and Mrs. Berry was snuffing out the candles on the sideboard.

'Hullo, my dear!' shouts Berry: 'easily, if you please! we've not done yet!'

'Not done yet, Mr. Berry!' groans the lady, in a hollow, sepulchral tone.

'No, Mrs. B., not done yet. We are going to have some supper, ain't we, George?'

'I think it's quite time to go home,' said Mr. Fitz-Boodle (who, to say the truth, began to tremble himself).

'I think it is, sir; you are quite right sir; you will pardon me, gentlemen, I have a bad headache, and will retire.'

'Good-night, my dear!' said that audacious Berry. 'Anatole, tell the cook to broil a fowl and bring some wine.'

If the loving couple had been alone, or if Cutler had not been an attaché to the Embassy, before whom she was afraid of making herself ridiculous, I am confident that Mrs. Berry would have fainted away on the spot; and that all Berry's courage would have tumbled down lifeless by the side of her. So she only gave a martyrised look, and left the room; and while we partook of the very unnecessary repast, was good enough to sing some hymn tunes to an exceedingly slow movement in the next room, intimating that she was awake, and that, though suffering, she found her consolations in religion.

[21] Cheap public restaurant-meal at a fixed time and price.

These melodies did not in the least add to our friend's courage. The devilled[22] fowl had, somehow, no devil in it. The champagne in the glasses looked exceedingly flat and blue. The fact is, that Cutler and I were now both in a state of dire consternation, and soon made a move for our hats, and lighting each a cigar in the hall, made across the little green where the Cupids and nymphs were listening to the dribbling fountain in the dark.

'I'm hanged if I don't have a cigar too!' says Berry, rushing after us; and accordingly putting in his pocket a key about the size of a shovel, which hung by the little handle of the outer grille, forth he sallied, and joined us in our fumigation.

He stayed with us a couple of hours, and returned homewards in perfect good spirits, having given me his word of honour he would dine with us the next day. He put in his immense key into the grille, and unlocked it; but the gate would not open: *it was bolted within.*

He began to make a furious jangling and ringing at the bell; and in oaths, both French and English, called upon the recalcitrant Anatole.

After much tolling of the bell, a light came cutting across the crevices of the inner door; it was thrown open, and a figure appeared with a lamp,—a tall, slim figure of a woman, clothed in white from head to foot.

It was Mrs. Berry, and when Cutler and I saw her, we both ran away as fast as our legs could carry us.

Berry, at this, shrieked with a wild laughter. 'Remember tomorrow, old boys,' shouted he,—'six o'clock;' and we were a quarter of a mile off when the gate closed, and the little mansion of the Avenue de Paris was once more quiet and dark.

The next afternoon, as we were playing at billiards, Cutler saw Mrs. Berry drive by in her carriage; and as soon as rather a long rubber was over, I thought I would go and look for our poor friend, and so went down to the Pavilion. Every door was open, as the wont is in France, and I walked in unannounced, and saw this:

He was playing a duet with her on the flute. She had been out

[22] Grilled with a mustard and pepper (etc.) sauce.

but for half-an-hour, after not speaking all the morning; and having seen Cutler at the billiard-room window, and suspecting we might take advantage of her absence, she had suddenly returned home again, and had flung herself, weeping, into Frank's arms, and said she could not bear to leave him in anger. And so, after sitting for a little while sobbing on his knee, she had forgotten and forgiven everything!

The dear angel! I met poor Frank in Bond Street only yesterday; but he crossed over to the other side of the way. He had on goloshes, and is grown very fat and pale. He has shaved off his moustaches and instead, wears a respirator.[23] He has taken his name off all his clubs, and lives very grimly in Baker Street. Well, ladies, no doubt you say he is right: and what are the odds, so long as *you* are happy?

[23] A gauze worn over the mouth and nose to warm or filter the air breathed in.

Dennis Haggarty's Wife

THERE was an odious Irishwoman and her daughter who used to frequent the 'Royal Hotel' at Leamington some years ago, and who went by the name of Mrs. Major Gam. Gam had been a distinguished officer in his Majesty's service, whom nothing but death and his own amiable wife could overcome. The widow mourned her husband in the most becoming bombazeen[1] she could muster, and had at least half-an-inch of lampblack round the immense visiting-tickets which she left at the houses of the nobility and gentry her friends.

Some of us, I am sorry to say, used to call her Mrs. Major Gammon; for if the worthy widow had a propensity, it was to talk largely of herself and family (of her own family, for she held her husband's very cheap), and of the wonders of her paternal mansion, Molloyville, county of Mayo. She was of the Malloys of that county; and though I never heard of the family before, I

[1] A dress-material.

have little doubt, from what Mrs. Major Gam stated, that they were the most ancient and illustrious family of that part of Ireland. I remember there came down to see his aunt a young fellow with huge red whiskers and tight nankeens,[2] a green coat and an awful breastpin, who, after two days' stay at the Spa, proposed marriage to Miss S——, or, in default, a duel with her father; and who drove a flash curricle[3] with a bay and a grey, and who was presented with much pride by Mrs. Gam as Castlereagh Molloy of Molloyville. We all agreed that he was the most insufferable snob of the whole season, and were delighted when a bailiff came down in search of him.

Well, this is all I know personally of the Molloyville family; but at the house if you met the widow Gam, and talked on any subject in life, you were sure to hear of it. If you asked her to have pease at dinner, she would say, 'Oh, sir, after the pease at Molloyville, I really don't care for any others,—do I, dearest Jemima? We always had a dish in the month of June, when my father gave his head gardener a guinea (we had three at Molloyville), and sent him with his compliments and a quart of pease to our neighbour, dear Lord Marrowfat. What a sweet place Marrowfat Park is! isn't it, Jemima?' If a carriage passed by the window, Mrs. Major Gammon would be sure to tell you that there were three carriages at Molloyville, 'the barouche,[4] the chawiot, and the covered cyar.' In the same manner she would favour you with the number and names of the footmen of the establishment; and on a visit to Warwick Castle (for this bustling woman made one in every party of pleasure that was formed from the hotel), she gave us to understand that the great walk by the river was altogether inferior to the principal avenue of Molloyville Park. I should not have been able to tell so much about Mrs. Gam and her daughter, but that, between ourselves, I was particularly sweet upon a young lady at the time, whose papa lived at the 'Royal,' and was under the care of Dr. Jephson.

The Jemima appealed to by Mrs. Gam in the above sentence was, of course, her daughter, apostrophized by her mother, 'Jemima, my soul's darling!' or, 'Jemima, my blessed child!' or,

[2] Light-coloured trousers (from *Nanking* cloth).
[3] Light two-wheeled carriage. [4] Four-wheeled four-seater carriage.

'Jemima, my own love!' The sacrifices that Mrs. Gam had made for that daughter were, she said, astonishing. The money she had spent in masters upon her, the illnesses through which she had nursed her, the ineffable love the mother bore her, were only known to heaven, Mrs. Gam said. They used to come into the room with their arms round each other's waists: at dinner between the courses the mother would sit with one hand locked in her daughter's; and if only two or three young men were present at the time, would be pretty sure to kiss her Jemima more than once during the time whilst the bohea[5] was poured out.

As for Miss Gam, if she was not handsome, candour forbids me to say she was ugly. She was neither one nor t'other. She was a person who wore ringlets and a band round her forehead; she knew four songs, which became rather tedious at the end of a couple of months' acquaintance; she had excessively bare shoulders; she inclined to wear numbers of cheap ornaments, rings, brooches, *ferronnières*,[6] smelling-bottles, and was always, we thought, very smartly dressed: though old Mrs. Lynx hinted that her gowns and her mother's were turned over and over again, and that her eyes were almost put out by darning stockings.

These eyes Miss Gam had very large, though rather red and weak, and used to roll them about at every eligible unmarried man in the place. But though the widow subscribed to all the balls, though she hired a fly to go to the meet of the hounds, though she was constant at church, and Jemima sang louder than any person there except the clerk, and though, probably, any person who made her a happy husband would be invited down to enjoy the three footmen, gardeners and carriages at Molloyville, yet no English gentleman was found sufficiently audacious to propose. Old Lynx used to say that the pair had been at Tunbridge, Harrogate, Brighton, Ramsgate, Cheltenham,[7] for this eight years past; where they had met, it seemed, with no better fortune. Indeed, the widow looked rather high for her blessed child: and as she looked with the contempt which no small number of Irish people feel upon all persons who get their bread by labour or commerce: and as she was a person whose energetic manners,

[5] Black China tea of the poorest quality. [6] Frontlets or coronets.
[7] The spa and resort towns of the late eighteenth and nineteenth century.

costume, and brogue were not much to the taste of quiet English country gentlemen, Jemima—sweet, spotless flower,—still remained on her hands, a thought withered, perhaps, and seedy.

Now, at this time, the 120th Regiment was quartered at Weedon Barracks, and with the corps was a certain Assistant-Surgeon Haggarty, a large, lean, tough, raw-boned man, with big hands, knock-knees, and carroty whiskers, and, withal, as honest a creature as ever handled a lancet. Haggarty, as his name imports, was of the very same nation as Mrs. Gam, and, what is more, the honest fellow had some of the peculiarities which belonged to the widow, and bragged about his family almost as much as she did. I do not know of what particular part of Ireland they were kings, but monarchs they must have been, as have been the ancestors of so many thousand Hibernian families; but they had been men of no small consideration in Dublin, 'where my father,' Haggarty said, 'is as well known as King William's statue, and where he "rowls his carriage, too," let me tell ye.'

Hence, Haggarty was called by the wags 'Rowl the carriage,' and several of them made inquiries of Mrs. Gam regarding him: 'Mrs. Gam, when you used to go up from Molloyville to the Lord Lieutenant's balls, and had your town-house in Fitzwilliam Square, used you to meet the famous Doctor Haggarty in society?'

'Is it Surgeon Haggarty of Gloucester Street ye mean? The black Papist! D'ye suppose that the Molloys would sit down to table with a creature of that sort?'

'Why, isn't he the most famous physician in Dublin, and doesn't he rowl his carriage there?'

'The horrid wretch! He keeps a shop, I tell ye, and sends his sons out with the medicine. He's got four of them off into the army, Ulick and Phil, and Terence and Denny, and now it's Charles that takes out the physic. But how should I know about these odious creatures? Their mother was a Burke, of Burke's Town, county Cavan, and brought Surgeon Haggarty two thousand pounds. She was a Protestant; and I am surprised how she could have taken up with a horrid, odious, Popish apothecary!'

From the extent of the widow's information, I am led to suppose that the inhabitants of Dublin are not less anxious about their neighbours than are the natives of English cities; and I think it is very probable that Mrs. Gam's account of the young Haggartys who carried out the medicine is perfectly correct, for a lad in the 120th made a caricature of Haggarty coming out of a chemist's shop with an oilcloth basket under his arm, which set the worthy surgeon in such a fury that there would have been a duel between him and the ensign, could the fiery doctor have had his way.

Now, Dionysius Haggarty was of an exceedingly inflammable temperament, and it chanced that of all the invalids, the visitors, the young squires of Warwickshire, the young manufacturers from Birmingham, the young officers from the barracks—it chanced, unluckily for Miss Gam and himself, that he was the only individual who was in the least smitten by her personal charms. He was very tender and modest about his love, however, for it must be owned that he respected Mrs. Gam hugely, and fully admitted, like a good simple fellow as he was, the superiority of that lady's birth and breeding to his own. How could he hope that he, a humble assistant-surgeon, with a thousand pounds his aunt Kitty left him for all his fortune,—how could he hope that one of the race of Molloyville would ever condescend to marry him?

Inflamed, however, by love, and inspired by wine, one day at a picnic at Kenilworth, Haggarty, whose love and raptures were the talk of the whole regiment, was induced by his waggish comrades to make a proposal in form.

'Are you aware, Mr. Haggarty, that you are speaking to a Molloy?' was all the reply majestic Mrs. Gam made when, according to the usual formula, the fluttering Jemima referred her suitor to 'mamma.' She left him with a look which was meant to crush the poor fellow to earth; she gathered up her cloak and bonnet, and precipitately called for her fly. She took care to tell every single soul in Leamington that the son of the odious Papist apothecary had had the audacity to propose for her daughter (indeed, a proposal, coming from whatever quarter it may, does no harm), and left Haggarty in a state of extreme depression and despair.

His down-heartedness, indeed, surprised most of his acquaintances in and out of the regiment, for the young lady was no beauty, and a doubtful fortune, and Dennis was a man outwardly of an unromantic turn, who seemed to have a great deal more liking for beef-steak and whisky-punch than for women, however fascinating.

But there is no doubt this shy, uncouth, rough fellow had a warmer and more faithful heart hid within him than many a dandy who is as handsome as Apollo. I, for my part, never can understand why a man falls in love, and heartily give him credit for so doing, never mind with what or whom. *That* I take to be a point quite as much beyond an individual's own control as the catching of the small-pox or the colour of his hair. To the surprise of all, Assistant-Surgeon Dionysius Haggarty was deeply and seriously in love; and I am told that one day he very nearly killed the before-mentioned young ensign with a carving-knife, for venturing to make a second caricature, representing Lady Gammon and Jemima in a fantastical park, surrounded by three gardeners, three carriages, three footmen, and the covered cyar. He would have no joking concerning them. He became moody and quarrelsome of habit. He was for some time much more in the surgery and hospital than in the mess. He gave up the eating, for the most part, of those vast quantities of beef and pudding, for which his stomach had used to afford such ample and swift accommodation; and when the cloth was drawn, instead of taking twelve tumblers, and singing Irish melodies, as he used to do, in a horrible cracked yelling voice, he would retire to his own apartment, or gloomily pace the barrack-yard, or madly whip and spur a grey mare he had on the road to Leamington, where his Jemima (although invisible for him) still dwelt.

The season at Leamington coming to a conclusion by the withdrawal of the young fellows who frequented that watering-place, the Widow Gam retired to her usual quarters for the other months of the year. Where these quarters were, I think we have no right to ask, for I believe she had quarrelled with her brother at Molloyville, and besides, was a great deal too proud to be a burden on anybody.

Not only did the widow quit Leamington, but very soon afterwards the 120th received its marching orders, and left Weedon and Warwickshire. Haggarty's appetite was by this time partially restored, but his love was not altered, and his humour was still morose and gloomy. I am informed that at this period of his life he wrote some poems relative to his unhappy passion; a wild set of verses of several lengths, and in his handwriting, being discovered upon a sheet of paper in which a pitch-plaster was wrapped up, which Lieutenant and Adjutant Wheezer was compelled to put on for a cold.

Fancy, then, three years afterwards, the surprise of all Haggarty's acquaintances on reading in the public papers the following announcement:—

'Married, at Monkstown on the 12th instant, Dionysius Haggarty, Esq., of H.M. 120th Foot, to Jemima Amelia Wilhelmina Molloy, daughter of the late Major Lancelot Gam, R.M., and granddaughter of the late, and niece of the present Burke Bodkin Blake Molloy, Esq., Molloyville, county Mayo.'

'Has the course of true love at last begun to run smooth?' thought I, as I laid down the paper; and the old times, and the old leering, bragging widow, and the high shoulders of her daughter, and the jolly days with the 120th, and Dr. Jephson's one-horse chaise, and the Warwickshire hunt, and—and Louisa S——, but never mind *her*,—came back to my mind. Has that good-natured, simple fellow at last met with his reward? Well, if he has not to marry the mother-in-law too, he may get on well enough.

Another year announced the retirement of Assistant-Surgeon Haggarty from the 120th, where he was replaced by Assistant-Surgeon Angus Rothsay Leech, a Scotchman, probably; with whom I have not the least acquaintance, and who has nothing whatever to do with this little history.

Still more years passed on, during which time I will not say that I kept a constant watch upon the fortunes of Mr. Haggarty and his lady, for, perhaps, if the truth were known, I never thought for a moment about them; until one day, being at Kingstown, near Dublin, dawdling on the beach, and staring at the Hill of Howth, as most people at that watering-place do, I saw coming towards me a tall gaunt man, with a pair of bushy red whiskers, of which I thought I had seen the like in former years, and a face which could be no other than Haggarty's. It was Haggarty, ten years older than when we last met, and greatly more grim and thin. He had on one shoulder a young gentleman in a dirty tartan costume, and a face exceedingly like his own peeping from under a battered plume of black feathers, while with his other hand he was dragging a light green go-cart, in which reposed a female infant of some two years old. Both were roaring with great power of lungs.

As soon as Dennis saw me, his face lost the dull, puzzled expression which had seemed to characterize it; he dropped the pole of the go-cart from one hand, and his son from the other, and came jumping forward to greet me with all his might, leaving his progeny roaring in the road.

'Bless my sowl,' says he, 'sure it's Fitz-Boodle? Fitz, don't you remember me? Dennis Haggarty of the 120th? Leamington, you know? Molloy, my boy, hould your tongue, and stop your screeching, and Jemima's too; d'ye hear? Well, it does good to sore eyes to see an old face. How fat you're grown, Fitz; and were ye ever in Ireland before? and a'n't ye delighted with it? Confess, now, isn't it beautiful?'

This question regarding the merits of their country, which I have remarked is put by most Irish persons, being answered in a satisfactory manner, and the shouts of the infants appeased from an apple-stall hard by, Dennis and I talked of old times; I congratulated him on his marriage with the lovely girl whom we all admired, and hoped he had a fortune with her, and so forth. His appearance, however, did not bespeak a great fortune: he had an old grey hat, short old trousers, an old waistcoat with regimental buttons, and patched Blucher boots,[8] such as are not usually sported by persons in easy life.

'Ah!' says he, with a sigh, in reply to my queries, 'times are changed since them days, Fitz-Boodle. My wife's not what she was—the beautiful creature you knew her. Molloy my boy, run off in a hurry to your mamma, and tell her an English gentleman is coming home to dine; for you'll dine with me, Fitz, in course?' And I agreed to partake of that meal; though Master

[8] Low boots: named after the Prussian field-marshal who fought at Waterloo.

9110212 F

Molloy altogether declined to obey his papa's orders with respect to announcing the stranger.

'Well, I must announce you myself,' says Haggarty, with a smile. 'Come, it's just dinner-time, and my little cottage is not a hundred yards off.' Accordingly, we all marched in procession to Dennis's little cottage, which was one of a row and a half of one-storied houses, with little court-yards before them, and mostly with very fine names on the door-posts of each. 'Surgeon Haggarty' was emblazoned on Dennis's gate, on a stained green copper-plate; and, not content with this, on the door-post above the bell was an oval with the inscription of 'New Molloyville'. The bell was broken, of course; the court, or garden-path, was mouldy, weedy, seedy; there were some dirty rocks, by way of ornament, round a faded grass-plot in the centre, some clothes and rags hanging out of most part of the windows of New Molloyville, the immediate entrance to which was by a battered scraper,[9] under a broken trellis-work, up which a withered creeper declined any longer to climb.

'Small, but snug,' says Haggarty: 'I'll lead the way, Fitz; put your hat on the flower-pot there, and turn to the left into the drawing-room.' A fog of onions and turf-smoke filled the whole of the house, and gave signs that dinner was not far off. Far off? You could hear it frizzling in the kitchen, where the maid was also endeavouring to hush the crying of a third refractory child. But as we entered, all three of Haggarty's darlings were in full war.

'Is it you, Dennis?' cried a sharp raw voice, from a dark corner in the drawing-room to which we were introduced, and in which a dirty tablecloth was laid for dinner, some bottles of porter[10] and a cold mutton-bone being laid out on a rickety grand-piano hard by. 'Ye're always late, Mr. Haggarty. Have you brought the whisky from Nowlan's? I'll go bail ye've not now.'

'My dear, I've brought an old friend of yours and mine to take pot-luck with us to-day,' said Dennis.

'When is he to come?' said the lady. At which speech I was rather surprised, for I stood before her.

[9] To scrape the dirt off boots and shoes before going in.
[10] A dark brown bitter beer.

'Here he is, Jemima my love,' answered Dennis, looking at me. 'Mr. Fitz-Boodle; don't you remember him in Warwickshire, darling?'

'Mr. Fitz-Boodle! I am very glad to see him,' said the lady, rising and curtseying with much cordiality.

Mrs. Haggarty was blind.

Mrs. Haggarty was not only blind, but it was evident that smallpox had been the cause of her loss of vision. Her eyes were bound with a bandage, her features were entirely swollen, scarred, and distorted by the horrible effects of the malady. She had been knitting in a corner when we entered, and was wrapped in a very dirty bed-gown. Her voice to me was quite different to that in which she addressed her husband. She spoke to Haggarty in broad Irish: she addressed me in that most odious of all languages—Irish-English, endeavouring to the utmost to disguise her brogue, and to speak with the true dawdling *distingué* English air.

'Are you long in I-a-land?' said the poor creature in this accent. 'You must faind it a sad ba'ba'ous place, Mr. Fitz-Boodle, I'm shu-ah! It was vary kaind of you to come upon us *en famille*, and accept a dinner *sans cérémonie*. Mr. Haggarty, I hope you'll put the waine into aice, Mr. Fitz-Boodle must be melted with this hot weathah.'

For some time she conducted the conversation in this polite strain, and I was obliged to say, in reply to a query of hers, that I did not find her the least altered, though I should never have recognized her but for this rencontre.[11] She told Haggarty with a significant air to get the wine from the cellah, and whispered to me that he was his own butlah; and the poor fellow, taking the hint, scudded away into the town for a pound of veal cutlets and a couple of bottles of wine from the tavern.

'Will the childhren get their potatoes and butther here?' said a barefoot girl, with long black hair flowing over her face, which she thrust in at the door.

'Let them sup in the nursery, Elizabeth, and send—ah! Edwards to me.'

'It it cook you mane, ma'am?' said the girl.

'Send her at once!' shrieked the unfortunate woman; and the

[11] Chance meeting.

noise of frying presently ceasing, a hot woman made her appearance, wiping her brows with her apron, and asking, with an accent decidedly Hibernian, what the misthress wanted.

'Lead me up to my dressing-room, Edwards: I really am not fit to be seen in this dishabille[12] by Mr. Fitz-Boodle.'

'Fait' I can't!' says Edwards; 'sure the masther's out at the butcher's, and can't look to the kitchen-fire!'

'Nonsense, I must go!' cried Mrs. Haggarty; and so Edwards, putting on a resigned air, and giving her arm and face a further rub with her apron, held out her arm to Mrs. Dennis, and the pair went upstairs.

She left me to indulge my reflections for half-an-hour, at the end of which period she came downstairs dressed in an old yellow satin, with the poor shoulders exposed just as much as ever. She had mounted a tawdry cap, which Haggarty himself must have selected for her. She had all sorts of necklaces, bracelets, and earrings in gold, in garnets, in mother-of-pearl, in ormolu. She brought in a furious savour of musk, which drove the odours of onions and turf-smoke before it; and she waved across her wretched, angular, mere, scarred features, an old cambric handkerchief with a yellow-lace border.

'And so you would have known me anywhere, Mr. Fitz-Boodle?' said she, with a grin that was meant to be most fascinating. 'I was sure you would; for though my dreadful illness deprived me of my sight, it is a mercy that it did not change my features or complexion at all!'

This mortification had been spared the unhappy woman; but I don't know whether, with all her vanity, her infernal pride, folly, and selfishness, it was charitable to leave her in her error.

Yet why correct her? There is a quality in certain people which is above all advice, exposure, or correction. Only let a man or woman have DULNESS sufficient, and they need bow to no extant authority. A dullard recognizes no betters; a dullard can't see that he is in the wrong; a dullard has no scruples of conscience, no doubts of pleasing, or succeeding, or doing right; no qualms for other people's feelings, no respect but for the fool himself. How can you make a fool perceive that he is a fool? Such a personage

[12] Partly undressed state.

can no more see his own folly than he can see his own ears. And the great quality of dulness is to be unalterably contented with itself. What myriads of souls are there of this admirable sort—selfish, stingy, ignorant, passionate, brutal; bad sons, mothers, fathers, never known to do kind actions!

To pause, however, in this disquisition which was carrying us far off Kingstown, New Molloyville, Ireland,—nay, into the wide world wherever Dulness inhabits, let it be stated that Mrs. Haggarty, from my brief acquaintance with her and her mother, was of the order of persons just mentioned. There was an air of conscious merit about her, very hard to swallow along with the infamous dinner poor Dennis managed, after much delay, to get on the table. She did not fail to invite me to Molloyville, where she said her cousin would be charmed to see me; and she told me almost as many anecdotes about that place as her mother used to impart in former days. I observed, moreover, that Dennis cut her the favourite pieces of the beefsteak, that she ate thereof with great gusto, and that she drank with similar eagerness of the various strong liquors at table. 'We Irish ladies are all fond of a leetle glass of punch,' she said, with a playful air, and Dennis mixed her a powerful tumbler of such violent grog as I myself could swallow only with some difficulty. She talked of her suffering a great deal, of her sacrifices, of the luxuries to which she had been accustomed before marriage,—in a word, of a hundred of those themes on which some ladies are in the custom of enlarging when they wish to plague some husbands.

But honest Dennis, far from being angry at this perpetual, wearisome, impudent recurrence to her own superiority, rather encouraged the conversation than otherwise. It pleased him to hear his wife discourse about her merits and family splendours. He was so thoroughly beaten down and henpecked, that he, as it were, gloried in his servitude, and fancied that his wife's magnificence reflected credit on himself. He looked towards me, who was half sick of the woman and her egotism, as if expecting me to exhibit the deepest sympathy, and flung me glances across the table as much as to say, 'What a gifted creature my Jemima is, and what a fine fellow I am to be in possession of her!' When the children came down she scolded them, of course, and dismissed them abruptly (for which circumstance, perhaps, the writer of these pages was not in his heart very sorry), and, after having sat a preposterously long time, left us, asking whether we would have coffee there or in her boudoir.

'Oh! here, of course,' said Dennis, with rather a troubled air, and in about ten minutes the lovely creature was led back to us again by 'Edwards,' and the coffee made its appearance. After coffee her husband begged her to let Mr. Fitz-Boodle hear her voice: 'He longs for some of his old favourites.'

'No! *do* you?' said she; and was led in triumph to the jingling old piano, and with a screechy, wiry voice, sung those very abominable old ditties which I had heard her sing at Leamington ten years back.

Haggarty, as she sang, flung himself back in the chair delighted. Husbands always are, and with the same song, one that they have heard when they were nineteen years old, probably; most Englishmen's tunes have that date, and it is rather affecting, I think, to hear an old gentleman of sixty or seventy quavering the old ditty that was fresh when *he* was fresh and in his prime. If he has a musical wife, depend on it he thinks her old songs of 1788 are better than any he has heard since: in fact he has heard *none* since. When the old couple are in high good-humour the old gentleman will take the old lady round the waist, and say, 'My dear, do sing me one of your own songs,' and she sits down and sings with her old voice, and, as she sings, the roses of her youth bloom again for a moment, Ranelagh[13] resuscitates, and she is dancing a minuet in powder and a train.

This is another digression. It was occasioned by looking at poor Dennis's face while his wife was screeching (and, believe me, the former was the most pleasant occupation). Bottom tickled by the fairies could not have been in greater ecstacies. He thought the music was divine; and had further reason for exulting in it, which was, that his wife was always in a good humour after singing, and never would sing but in that happy frame of mind. Dennis had hinted so much in our little colloquy during the ten minutes of his lady's absence in the 'boudoir;' so, at the

[13] In Chelsea, a place of public amusement in the grounds of the Earl of Ranelagh where music and dancing took place. It closed in 1804.

conclusion of each piece, we shouted 'Bravo!' and clapped our hands like mad.

Such was my insight into the life of Surgeon Dionysius Haggarty and his wife; and I must have come upon him at a favourable moment too, for poor Dennis has spoken, subsequently, of our delightful evening at Kingstown, and evidently thinks to this day that his friend was fascinated by the entertainment there. His inward economy was as follows: he had his half-pay, a thousand pounds, about a hundred a year that his father left, and his wife had sixty pounds a year from the mother; which the mother, of course, never paid. He had no practice, for he was absorbed in attention to his Jemima and the children, whom he used to wash, to dress, to carry out, to walk, or to ride, as we have seen, and who could not have a servant, as their dear blind mother could never be left alone. Mrs. Haggarty, a great invalid, used to lie in bed till one, and have breakfast and hot luncheon there. A fifth part of his income was spent in having her wheeled about in a chair, by which it was his duty to walk daily for an allotted number of hours. Dinner would ensue, and the amateur clergy, who abound in Ireland, and of whom Mrs. Haggarty was a great admirer, lauded her everywhere as a model of resignation and virtue, and praised beyond measure the admirable piety with which she bore her sufferings.

Well, every man to his taste. It did not certainly appear to me that *she* was the martyr of the family.

'The circumstances of my marriage with Jemima,' Dennis said to me, in some after conversations we had on this interesting subject, 'were the most romantic and touching you can conceive. You saw what an impression the dear girl had made upon me when we were at Weedon; for from the first day I set eyes on her, and heard her sing her delightful song of "Dark-eyed Maiden of Araby," I felt, and said to Turniquet of ours, that every night, that *she* was the dark-eyed maid of Araby for *me*,—not that she was, you know, for she was born in Shropshire. But I felt that I had seen the woman who was to make me happy or miserable for life. You know how I proposed for her at Kenilworth, and how I was rejected, and how I almost shot myself in consequence,—no, you don't know that, for I said nothing about it to any one, but I can tell you it was a very near thing; and a very lucky thing for me I didn't do it: for,—would you believe it?—the dear girl was in love with me all the time.'

'Was she really?' said I, who recollected that Miss Gam's love of those days showed itself in a very singular manner; but the fact is, when women are most in love they most disguise it.

'Over head and ears in love with poor Dennis,' resumed that worthy fellow, 'who'd ever have thought it? But I have it from the best authority, from her own mother, with whom I'm not over and above good friends now; but of this fact she assured me, and I'll tell you when and how.

'We were quartered at Cork three years after we were at Weedon, and it was our last year at home; and a great mercy that my dear girl spoke in time, or where should we have been *now?* Well, one day, marching home from parade, I saw a lady seated at an open window by another who seemed an invalid, and the lady at the window, who was dressed in the profoundest mourning, cried out, with a scream, "Gracious heavens! it's Mr. Haggarty of the 120th."

'"Sure I know that voice," says I to Whiskerton.

'"It's a great mercy you don't know it a deal too well," says he: "it's Lady Gammon. She's on some husband-hunting scheme, depend on it, for that daughter of hers. She was at Bath last year on the same errand, and at Cheltenham the year before, where, heaven bless you! she's as well known as the 'Hen and Chickens.'"

'"I'll thank you not to speak disrespectfully of Miss Jemima Gam," said I to Whiskerton; "she's of one of the first families in Ireland, and whoever says a word against a woman I once proposed for, insults me—do you understand?"

'"Well, marry her, if you like," says Whiskerton, quite peevish: "marry her, and be hanged!"

'Marry her! the very idea of it set my brain a-whirling, and made me a thousand times more mad than I am by nature.

'You may be sure I walked up the hill to the parade-ground that afternoon, and with a beating heart too. I came to the widow's house. It was called "New Molloyville," as this is. Wherever she takes a house for six months, she calls it "New Molloyville;" and has had one in Mallow, in Bandon, in Sligo, in Castlebar, in

Fermoy, in Drogheda, and the deuce knows where besides: but the blinds were down, and though I thought I saw somebody behind 'em, no notice was taken of poor Denny Haggarty, and I paced up and down all mess-time in hopes of catching a glimpse of Jemima, but in vain. The next day I was on the ground again; I was just as much in love as ever, that's the fact. I'd never been in that way before, look you; and when once caught, I knew it was for life.

'There's no use in telling you how long I beat about the bush, but when I *did* get admittance to the house (it was through the means of young Castlereagh Molloy, whom you may remember at Leamington, and who was at Cork for the regatta, and used to dine at our mess, and had taken a mighty fancy to me)—when I *did* get into the house, I say, I rushed *in medias res*[14] at once: I couldn't keep myself quiet, my heart was too full.

'Oh, Fitz! I shall never forget the day,—the moment I was inthrojuiced into the dthrawing-room' (as he began to be agitated, Dennis's brogue broke out with greater richness than ever; but though a stranger may catch, and repeat from memory, a few words, it is next to impossible for him to *keep up a conversation* in Irish, so that we had best give up all attempts to imitate Dennis). 'When I saw old Mother Gam,' said he, 'my feelings overcame me all at once. I rowled down on the ground, sir, as if I'd been hit by a musket-ball. "Dearest madam," says I, "I'll die if you don't give me Jemima."

'"Heavens, Mr. Haggarty!" says she, "how you seize me with surprise! Castlereagh, my dear nephew, had you not better leave us?" and away he went, lighting a cigar, and leaving me still on the floor.

'"Rise, Mr. Haggarty," continued the widow. "I will not attempt to deny that this constancy towards my daughter is extremely affecting, however sudden your present appeal may be. I will not attempt to deny that, perhaps, Jemima may have a similar feeling; but, as I said, I never could give my daughter to a Catholic.'

'"I'm as good a Protestant as yourself, ma'am," says I; "my mother was an heiress, and we were all brought up her way."

'"That makes the matter very different," says she, turning up

[14] Into the middle of things.

the whites of her eyes. "How could I ever have reconciled it to my conscience to see my blessed child married to a Papist? How could I ever have taken him to Molloyville? Well, this obstacle being removed, *I* must put myself no longer in the way between two young people. *I* must sacrifice myself; as I always have when my darling girl was in question. You shall see her, the poor dear, lovely, gentle sufferer, and learn your fate from her own lips."

'"The sufferer, ma'am," says I; "has Miss Gam been ill?"

'"What! haven't you heard?" cried the widow. "Haven't you heard of the dreadful illness which so nearly carried her from me? For nine weeks, Mr. Haggarty, I watched her day and night, without taking a wink of sleep,—for nine weeks she lay trembling between death and life; and I paid the doctor eighty-three guineas. She is restored now; but she is the wreck of the beautiful creature she was. Suffering, and, perhaps, *another disappointment*—but we won't mention that *now*—have so pulled her down. But I will leave you, and prepare my sweet girl for this strange, this entirely unexpected visit."

'I won't tell you what took place between me and Jemima, to whom I was introduced as she sat in the darkened room, poor sufferer! nor describe to you with what a thrill of joy I seized (after groping about for it) her poor emaciated hand. She did not withdraw it; I came out of that room an engaged man, sir; and *now* I was enabled to show her that I had always loved her sincerely, for there was my will, made three years back, in her favour: that night she refused me, as I told you. I would have shot myself, but they'd have brought me in *non compos*,[15] and my brother Mick would have contested the will, and so I determined to live, in order that she might benefit by my dying. I had but a thousand pounds then: since that my father has left me two more. I willed every shilling to her, as you may fancy, and settled it upon her when we married, as we did soon after. It was not for some time that I was allowed to see the poor girl's face, or, indeed, was aware of the horrid loss she had sustained. Fancy my agony, my dear fellow, when I saw that beautiful wreck!'

There was something not a little affecting to think, in the conduct of this brave fellow, that he never once, as he told his story,

[15] Of unsound mind.

seemed to allude to the possibility of his declining to marry a woman who was not the same as the woman he loved; but that he was quite as faithful to her now, as he had been when captivated by the poor tawdry charms of the silly Miss of Leamington. It was hard that such a noble heart as this should be flung away upon yonder foul mass of greedy vanity. Was it hard, or not, that he should remain deceived in his obstinate humility, and continue to admire the selfish, silly being whom he had chosen to worship?

'I should have been appointed surgeon of the regiment,' continued Dennis 'soon after, when it was ordered abroad to Jamaica, where it now is. But my wife would not hear of going, and said she would break her heart if she left her mother. So I retired on half-pay, and took this cottage; and in case any practice should fall in my way—why, there is my name on the brass plate, and I'm ready for anything that comes. But the only case that ever *did* come was one day when I was driving my wife in the chaise, and another, one night, of a beggar with a broken head. My wife makes me a present of a baby every year, and we've no debts; and between you and me and the post, as long as my mother-in-law is out of the house, I'm as happy as I need be.'

'What! you and the old lady don't get on well?' said I.

'I can't say we do; it's not in nature, you know,' said Dennis, with a faint grin. 'She comes into the house, and turns it topsy-turvy. When she's here I'm obliged to sleep in the scullery. She's never paid her daughter's income since the first year, though she brags about her sacrifices as if she had ruined herself for Jemima; and besides, when she's here, there's a whole clan of the Molloys, horse, foot, and dragoons, that are quartered upon us, and eat me out of house and home.'

'And is Molloyville such a fine place as the widow described it?' asked I, laughing, and not a little curious.

'Oh, a mighty fine place entirely!' said Dennis. 'There's the oak park of two hundred acres, the finest land ye ever saw, only they've cut all the wood down. The garden in the old Molloy's time, they say, was the finest ever seen in the West of Ireland; but they've taken all the glass to mend the house windows: and small blame to them either. There's a clear rent-roll of three and fifty hundred a year, only it's in the hand of receivers; besides other debts, on which there is no land security.'

'Your cousin-in-law, Castlereagh Molloy, won't come into a large fortune?'

'Oh, he'll do very well,' said Dennis. 'As long as he can get credit, he's not the fellow to stint himself. Faith, I was fool enough to put my name to a bit of paper for him, and as they could not catch him in Mayo, they laid hold of me at Kingstown here. And there was a pretty to do. Didn't Mrs. Gam say I was ruining her family, that's all! I paid it by instalments (for all my money is settled on Jemima); and Castlereagh, who's an honourable fellow, offered me any satisfaction in life. Anyhow, he couldn't do more than *that.*'

'Of course not, and now you're friends?'

'Yes, and he and his aunt have had a tiff, too; and he abuses her properly, I warrant ye. He says that she carried about Jemima from place to place, and flung her at the head of every unmarried man in England a'most,—my poor Jemima, and she all the while dying in love with me! As soon as she got over the small-pox—she took it at Fermoy—God bless her, I wish I'd been by to be her nurse-tender,—as soon as she was rid of it, the old lady said to Castlereagh, 'Castlereagh, go to the bar'cks, and find out in the Army List where the 120th is.' Off she came to Cork hot foot. It appears that while she was ill, Jemima's love for me showed itself in such a violent way that her mother was overcome, and promised that, should the dear child recover, she would try and bring us together. Castlereagh says she would have gone after us to Jamaica.'

'I have no doubt she would,' said I.

'Could you have a stronger proof of love than that?' cried Dennis. My dear girl's illness and frightful blindness have, of course, injured her health and her temper. She cannot in her position look to the children, you know, and so they come under my charge for the most part; and her temper is unequal, certainly. But you see what a sensitive, refined, elegant creature she is, and may fancy that she's often put out by a rough fellow like me.'

Here Dennis left me, saying it was time to go and walk out the children; and I think his story has matter of some wholesome reflection in it for bachelors who are about to change their condition, or may console some who are mourning their celibacy. Marry, gentlemen, if you like; leave your comfortable dinner at the club for cold mutton and curl-papers at your home; give up your books or pleasures, and take to yourselves wives and children; but think well on what you do first, as I have no doubt you will after this advice and example. Advice is always useful in matters of love; men always take it; they always follow other people's opinions, not their own: they always profit by example. When they see a pretty woman, and feel the delicious madness of love coming over them, they always stop to calculate her temper, her money, their own money, or suitableness for the married life. . . . Ha, ha, ha! Let us fool in this way no more. I have been in love forty-three times with all ranks and conditions of women, and would have married every time if they would have let me. How many wives had King Solomon, the wisest of men? And is not that story a warning to us that Love is master of the wisest? It is only fools who defy him.

I must come, however, to the last, and perhaps the saddest, part of poor Denny Haggarty's history. I met him once more, and in such a condition as made me determine to write this history.

In the month of June last I happened to be at Richmond, a delightful little place of retreat; and there, sunning himself upon the terrace, was my old friend of the 120th: he looked older, thinner, poorer, and more wretched than I had ever seen him. 'What! you have given up Kingstown?' said I, shaking him by the hand.

'Yes,' says he.

'And is my lady and your family here at Richmond?'

'No,' says he, with a sad shake of the head; and the poor fellow's hollow eyes filled with tears.

'Good heavens, Denny! what's the matter?' said I. He was squeezing my hand like a vice as I spoke.

'They've LEFT me!' he burst out with a dreadful shout of passionate grief—a horrible scream which seemed to be wrenched out of his heart. 'Left me!' said he, sinking down on a seat, and clenching his great fists, and shaking his lean arms wildly. 'I'm a wise man now, Mr. Fitz-Boodle. Jemima has gone away from me, and yet you know how I loved her, and how happy we were! I've got nobody now; but I'll die soon, that's one comfort: and to think it's she that'll kill me after all!'

The story, which he told with a wild and furious lamentation such as is not known among men of our cooler country, and such as I don't like now to recall, was a very simple one. The mother-in-law had taken possession of the house, and had driven him from it. His property at his marriage was settled on his wife. She had never loved him, and told him this secret at last, and drove him out of doors with her selfish scorn and ill-temper. The boy had died; the girls were better, he said, brought up among the Molloys than they could be with him; and so he was quite alone in the world, and was living, or rather dying, on forty pounds a year.

His troubles are very likely over by this time. The two fools who caused his misery will never read this history of him; *they* never read godless stories in magazines; and I wish, honest reader, that you and I went to church as much as they do. These people are not wicked *because* of their religious observances, but *in spite* of them. They are too dull to understand humility, too blind to see a tender and simple heart under a rough ungainly bosom. They are sure that all their conduct towards my poor friend here has been perfectly righteous, and that they have given proofs of the most Christian virtue. Haggarty's wife is considered by her friends as a martyr to a savage husband, and her mother is the angel that has come to rescue her. All they did was to cheat him and desert him. And safe in that wonderful self-complacency with which the fools of this earth are endowed, they have not a single pang of conscience for their villany towards him, and consider their heartlessness as a proof and consequence of their spotless piety and virtue.

ANTHONY TROLLOPE
(1815–1882)

'La Mère Bauche' first appeared in *Harper's New York Magazine* in May 1860, and was then published with others in 1861 in *Tales From All Countries*.

'Malachi's Cove' is taken from *Lotta Schmidt, and other Stories*, published in 1867.

La Mère Bauche

THE Pyrenean valley in which the baths of Vernet are situated is not much known to English, or indeed to any travellers. Tourists in search of good hotels and picturesque beauty combined do not generally extend their journeys to the Eastern Pyrenees. They rarely get beyond Luchon; and in this they are right, as they thus end their peregrinations at the most lovely spot among these mountains, and are as a rule so deceived, imposed on, and bewildered by guides, innkeepers, and horse-owners, at this otherwise delightful place, as to become undesirous of further travel. Nor do invalids from distant parts frequent Vernet. People of fashion go to the Eaux Bonnes and to Luchon, and people who are really ill to Barèges and Cauterets. It is at these places that one meets crowds of Parisians, and the daughters and wives of rich merchants from Bordeaux, with an admixture, now by no means inconsiderable, of Englishmen and Englishwomen. But the Eastern Pyrenees are still unfrequented. And probably they will remain so; for though there are among them lovely valleys—and of all such the valley of Vernet is perhaps the most lovely—they cannot compete with the mountain scenery of other tourist-loved regions in Europe. At the Port de Venasquez and the Brèche de Roland[1] in the Western Pyrenees, or rather, to speak more

[1] A narrow pass said to have been cut by a sword-blow by the epic hero Roland of the French *Chansons de Geste*.

truly, at spots in the close vicinity of these famous mountain entrances from France into Spain, one can make comparisons with Switzerland, Northern Italy, the Tyrol, and Ireland, which will not be injurious to the scenes then under view. But among the eastern mountains this can rarely be done. The hills do not stand thickly together so as to group themselves; the passes from one valley to another, though not wanting in altitude, are not close pressed together with overhanging rocks, and are deficient in grandeur as well as loveliness. And then, as a natural consequence of all this, the hotels—are not quite as good as they should be.

But there is one mountain among them which can claim to rank with the Pic du Midi or the Maledetta. No one can pooh-pooh the stern old Canigou, standing high and solitary, solemn and grand, between the two roads which run from Perpignan into Spain, the one by Prades and the other by Le Boulon. Under the Canigou, towards the west, lie the hot baths of Vernet, in a close secluded valley, which, as I have said before, is, as far as I know, the sweetest spot in these Eastern Pyrenees.

The frequenters of these baths were a few years back gathered almost entirely from towns not very far distant, from Perpignan, Narbonne, Carcassonne, and Béziers, and the baths were not therefore famous, expensive, or luxurious; but those who believed in them believed with great faith; and it was certainly the fact that men and women who went thither worn with toil, sick with excesses, and nervous through overcare, came back fresh and strong, fit once more to attack the world with all its woes. Their character in latter days does not seem to have changed, though their circle of admirers may perhaps be somewhat extended.

In those days, by far the most noted and illustrious person in the village of Vernet was La Mère Bauche. That there had once been a Père Bauche was known to the world, for there was a Fils Bauche who lived with his mother; but no one seemed to remember more of him than that he had once existed. At Vernet he had never been known. La Mère Bauche was a native of the village, but her married life had been passed away from it, and she had returned in her early widowhood to become proprietress and manager, or, as one may say, the heart and soul of the Hôtel Bauche at Vernet.

This hotel was a large and somewhat rough establishment, intended for the accommodation of invalids who came to Vernet for their health. It was built immediately over one of the thermal springs, so that the water flowed from the bowels of the earth directly into the baths. There was accommodation for seventy people, and during the summer and autumn months the place was always full. Not a few also were to be found there during the winter and spring, for the charges of Madame Bauche were low, and the accommodation reasonably good.

And in this respect, as indeed in all others, Madame Bauche had the reputation of being an honest woman. She had a certain price, from which no earthly consideration would induce her to depart; and there were certain returns from this price in the shape of *déjeuners* and dinners, baths and beds, which she never failed to give in accordance with the dictates of a strict conscience. These were traits in the character of an hotel-keeper which cannot be praised too highly, and which had met their due reward in the custom of the public. But nevertheless there were those who thought that there was occasionally ground for complaint in the conduct even of Madame Bauche.

In the first place she was deficient in that pleasant smiling softness which should belong to any keeper of a house of public entertainment. In her general mode of life she was stern and silent with her guests, autocratic, authoritative, and sometimes contradictory in her house, and altogether irrational and unconciliatory when any change even for a day was proposed to her, or when any shadow of a complaint reached her ears.

Indeed of complaint, as made against the establishment, she was altogether intolerant. To such she had but one answer. He or she who complained might leave the place at a moment's notice if it so pleased them. There were always others ready to take their places. The power of making this answer came to her from the lowness of her prices; and it was a power which was very dear to her.

The baths were taken at different hours according to medical advice, but the usual time was from five to seven in the morning. The *déjeuner* or early meal was at nine o'clock, the dinner was at four. After that, no eating or drinking was allowed in the

Hôtel Bauche. There was a *café* in the village, at which ladies and gentlemen could get a cup of coffee or a glass of *eau sucrée*; but no such accommodation was to be had in the establishment. Not by any possible bribery or persuasion could any meal be procured at any other than the authorized hours. A visitor who should enter the *salle à manger* more than ten minutes after the last bell would be looked at very sourly by Madame Bauche, who on all occasions sat at the top of her own table. Should anyone appear as much as half an hour late, he would receive only his share of what had not been handed round. But after the last dish had been so handed, it was utterly useless for anyone to enter the room at all.

Her appearance at the period of our tale was perhaps not altogether in her favour. She was about sixty years of age and was very stout and short in the neck. She wore her own grey hair, which at dinner was always tidy enough; but during the whole day previous to that hour she might be seen with it escaping from under her cap in extreme disorder. Her eyebrows were large and bushy, but those alone would not have given to her face that look of indomitable sternness which it possessed. Her eyebrows were serious in their effect, but not so serious as the pair of green spectacles which she always wore under them. It was thought by those who had analysed the subject that the great secret of Madame Bauche's power lay in her green spectacles.

Her custom was to move about and through the whole establishment every day from breakfast till the period came for her to dress for dinner. She would visit every chamber and every bath, walk once or twice round the *salle à manger*, and very repeatedly round the kitchen; she would go into every hole and corner, and peer into everything through her green spectacles; and in these walks it was not always thought pleasant to meet her. Her custom was to move very slowly, with her hands generally clasped behind her back: she rarely spoke to the guests unless she was spoken to, and on such occasions she would not often diverge into general conversation. If anyone had aught to say connected with the business of the establishment, she would listen, and then she would make her answers,—often not pleasant in the hearing.

And thus she walked her path through the world, a stern, hard, solemn old woman, not without gusts of passionate explosion; but honest withal, and not without some inward benevolence and true tenderness of heart. Children she had had many, some seven or eight. One or two had died, others had been married; she had sons settled far away from home, and at the time of which we are now speaking but one was left in any way subject to maternal authority.

Adolphe Bauche was the only one of her children of whom much was remembered by the present denizens and hangers-on of the hotel. He was the youngest of the number, and having been born only very shortly before the return of Madame Bauche to Vernet, had been altogether reared there. It was thought by the world of those parts, and rightly thought, that he was his mother's darling—more so than had been any of his brothers and sisters—the very apple of her eye and gem of her life. At this time he was about twenty-five years of age, and for the last two years had been absent from Vernet—for reasons which will shortly be made to appear. He had been sent to Paris to see something of the world and learn to talk French instead of the *patois* of his valley; and having left Paris had come down south in Languedoc, and remained there picking up some agricultural lore which it was thought might prove useful in the valley farms of Vernet. He was now expected home again very speedily, much to his mother's delight.

That she was kind and gracious to her favourite child does not perhaps give much proof of her benevolence; but she had also been kind and gracious to the orphan child of a neighbour; nay, to the orphan child of a rival innkeeper. At Vernet there had been more than one water establishment, but the proprietor of the second had died some few years after Madame Bauche had settled herself at the place. His house had not thrived, and his only child, a little girl, was left altogether without provision.

This little girl, Marie Clavert, La Mère Bauche had taken into her own house immediately after the father's death, although she had most cordially hated that father. Marie was then an infant, and Madame Bauche had accepted the charge without much thought, perhaps, as to what might be the child's ultimate destiny. But since then she had thoroughly done the duty of a mother by the little girl, who had become the pet of the whole establishment, the favourite plaything of Adolphe Bauche,—and at last of course his early sweetheart.

And then and therefore there had come troubles at Vernet. Of course all the world of the valley had seen what was taking place and what was likely to take place, long before Madame Bauche knew anything about it. But at last it broke upon her senses that her son, Adolphe Bauche, the heir to all her virtues and all her riches, the first young man in that or any neighbouring valley, was absolutely contemplating the idea of marrying that poor little orphan, Marie Clavert!

That anyone should ever fall in love with Marie Clavert had never occurred to Madame Bauche. She had always regarded the child as a child, as the object of her charity, and as a little thing to be looked on as poor Marie by all the world. She, looking through her green spectacles, had never seen that Marie Clavert was a beautiful creature, full of ripening charms, such as young men love to look on. Marie was of infinite daily use to Madame Bauche in a hundred little things about the house, and the old lady thoroughly recognised and appreciated her ability. But for this very reason she had never taught herself to regard Marie otherwise than as a useful drudge. She was very fond of her *protégée*—so much so that she would listen to her in affairs about the house when she would listen to no one else; but Marie's prettiness and grace and sweetness as a girl had all been thrown away upon 'Maman Bauche,' as Marie used to call her.

But unluckily it had not been thrown away upon Adolphe. He had appreciated, as it was natural that he should do, all that had been so utterly indifferent to his mother; and consequently had fallen in love. Consequently also he had told his love; and consequently also Marie had returned his love.

Adolphe had been hitherto contradicted but in few things, and thought that all difficulty would be prevented by his informing his mother that he wished to marry Marie Clavert. But Marie, with a woman's instinct, had known better. She had trembled and almost crouched with fear when she confessed her love, and had absolutely hid herself from sight when Adolphe went forth, prepared to ask his mother's consent to his marriage.

The indignation and passionate wrath of Madame Bauche were past and gone two years before the date of this story, and I need not therefore much enlarge upon that subject. She was at first abusive and bitter, which was bad for Marie; and afterwards bitter and silent, which was worse. It was, of course, determined that poor Marie should be sent away to some asylum for orphans or penniless paupers—in short, anywhere out of the way. What mattered her outlook into the world, her happiness, or indeed her very existence? The outlook and happiness of Adolphe Bauche,—was not that to be considered as everything at Vernet?

But this terrible sharp aspect of affairs did not last very long. In the first place, La Mère Bauche had under those green spectacles a heart that in truth was tender and affectionate, and after the first two days of anger she admitted that something must be done for Marie Clavert; and after the fourth day she acknowledged that the world of the hotel, her world, would not go as well without Marie Clavert as it would with her. And in the next place, Madame Bauche had a friend whose advice in grave matters she would sometimes take. This friend had told her that it would be much better to send away Adolphe, since it was so necessary that there should be a sending away of some one; that he would be much benefited by passing some months of his life away from his native valley; and that an absence of a year or two would teach him to forget Marie, even if it did not teach Marie to forget him.

And we must say a word or two about this friend. At Vernet he was usually called M. le Capitaine, though in fact he had never reached that rank. He had been in the army, and having been wounded in the leg while still a *sous-lieutenant*, had been pensioned, and had thus been interdicted from treading any further the thorny path that leads to glory. For the last fifteen years he had resided under the roof of Madame Bauche, at first as a casual visitor, going and coming, but now for many years as constant there as she was herself.

He was so constantly called Le Capitaine that his real name was seldom heard. It may, however, as well be known to us that this was Theodore Campan. He was a tall, well-looking man; always dressed in black garments, of a coarse description certainly, but scrupulously clean and well brushed; of perhaps fifty years of age, and conspicuous for the rigid uprightness of his back—and for a black wooden leg.

This wooden leg was perhaps the most remarkable trait in his character. It was always jet black, being painted, or polished, or japanned, as occasion might require, by the hands of the Capitaine himself. It was longer than ordinary wooden legs, as indeed the Capitaine was longer than ordinary men; but nevertheless it never seemed in any way to impede the rigid punctilious propriety of his movements. It was never in his way as wooden legs usually are in the way of their wearers. And then to render it more illustrious it had round its middle, round the calf of the leg we may so say, a band of bright brass which shone like burnished gold.

It had been the Capitaine's custom, now for some years past, to retire every evening at about seven o'clock into the *sanctum sanctorum*[2] of Madame Bauche's habitation, the dark little private sitting-room in which she made out her bills and calculated her profits, and there regale himself in her presence—and indeed at her expense, for the items never appeared in the bill—with coffee and cognac. I have said that there was never eating or drinking at the establishment after the regular dinner-hours, but in so saying I spoke of the world at large. Nothing further was allowed in the way of trade; but in the way of friendship so much was nowadays always allowed to the Capitaine.

It was at these moments that Madame Bauche discussed her private affairs, and asked for and received advice. For even Madame Bauche was mortal; nor could her green spectacles without other aid carry her through all the troubles of life. It was now five years since the world of Vernet discovered that La Mère Bauche was going to marry the Capitaine, and for eighteen months the world of Vernet had been full of this matter; but any amount of patience is at last exhausted, and as no further steps in that direction were ever taken beyond the daily cup of coffee, that subject died away—very much unheeded by La Mère Bauche.

[2] 'The holy of holies', the most sacred sanctuary.

But she, though she thought of no matrimony for herself, thought much of matrimony for other people; and over most of those cups of evening coffee and cognac a matrimonial project was discussed in these latter days. It has been seen that the Capitaine pleaded in Marie's favour when the fury of Madame Bauche's indignation broke forth; and that ultimately Marie was kept at home, and Adolphe sent away by his advice.

'But Adolphe cannot always stay away,' Madame Bauche had pleaded in her difficulty. The truth of this the Capitaine had admitted, but Marie, he said, might be married to some one else before two years were over. And so the matter had commenced.

But to whom should she be married? To this question the Capitaine had answered in perfect innocence of heart, that La Mère Bauche would be much better able to make such a choice than himself. He did not know how Marie might stand with regard to money. If madame would give some little *dot*,[3] the affair, the Capitaine thought, would be more easily arranged.

All these things took months to say, during which period Marie went on with her work in melancholy listlessness. One comfort she had. Adolphe, before he went, had promised to her, holding in his hand as he did so a little cross which she had given him, that no earthly consideration should sever them;—that sooner or later he would certainly be her husband. Marie felt that her limbs could not work nor her tongue speak were it not for this one drop of water in her cup.

And then, deeply meditating, La Mère Bauche hit upon a plan, and herself communicated it to the Capitaine over a second cup of coffee, into which she poured a full teaspoonful more than the usual allowance of cognac. Why should not he, the Capitaine himself, be the man to marry Marie Clavert?

It was a very startling proposal, the idea of matrimony for himself never having as yet entered into the Capitaine's head at any period of his life; but La Mère Bauche did contrive to make it not altogether unacceptable. As to that matter of dowry she was prepared to be more than generous. She did love Marie well, and could find it in her heart to give her anything—anything except her son, her own Adolphe. What she proposed was this. Adolphe,

[3] Marriage-portion given by a girl's family to secure a husband.

himself, would never keep the baths. If the Capitaine would take Marie for his wife, Marie, Madame Bauche declared, should be the mistress after her death; subject of course to certain settlements as to Adolphe's pecuniary interests.

The plan was discussed a thousand times, and at last so far brought to bear that Marie was made acquainted with it—having been called in to sit in presence with La Mère Bauche and her future proposed husband. The poor girl manifested no disgust to the stiff ungainly lover whom they assigned to her,—who through his whole frame was in appearance almost as wooden as his own leg. On the whole, indeed, Marie liked the Capitaine, and felt that he was her friend; and in her country such marriages were not uncommon. The Capitaine was perhaps a little beyond the age at which a man might usually be thought justified in demanding the services of a young girl as his nurse and wife, but then Marie of herself had so little to give—except her youth, and beauty, and goodness.

But yet she could not absolutely consent, for was she not absolutely pledged to her own Adolphe? And therefore, when the great pecuniary advantages were, one by one, displayed before her, and when La Mère Bauche, as a last argument, informed her that as wife of the Capitaine she would be regarded as second mistress in the establishment and not as a servant, she could only burst out into tears and say that she did not know.

'I will be very kind to you,' said the Capitaine; 'as kind as a man can be.'

Marie took his hard withered hand and kissed it, and then looked up into his face with beseeching eyes which were not without avail upon his heart.

'We will not press her now,' said the Capitaine. 'There is time enough.'

But let his heart be touched ever so much, one thing was certain. It could not be permitted that she should marry Adolphe. To that view of the matter he had given in his unrestricted adhesion, nor could he by any means withdraw it without losing altogether his position in the establishment of Madame Bauche. Nor, indeed, did his conscience tell him that such a marriage should be permitted. That would be too much. If every pretty girl were allowed to marry the first young man that might fall in love with her, what would the world come to?

And it soon appeared that there was not time enough—that the time was growing very scant. In three months Adolphe would be back. And if everything was not arranged by that time matters might still go astray.

And then Madame Bauche asked her final question: 'You do not think, do you, that you can ever marry Adolphe?' And as she asked it the accustomed terror of her green spectacles magnified itself tenfold. Marie could only answer by another burst of tears.

The affair was at last settled among them. Marie said that she would consent to marry the Capitaine when she should hear from Adolphe's own mouth that he, Adolphe, loved her no longer. She declared with many tears that her vows and pledges prevented her from promising more than this. It was not her fault, at any rate not now, that she loved her lover. It was not her fault—not now at least—that she was bound by these pledges. When she heard from his own mouth that he had discarded her, then she would marry the Capitaine—or, indeed, sacrifice herself in any other way that La Mère Bauche might desire. What would anything signify then?

Madame Bauche's spectacles remained unmoved, but not her heart. Marie, she told the Capitaine, should be equal to herself in the establishment, when once she was entitled to be called Madame Campan, and she should be to her quite as a daughter. She should have her cup of coffee every evening, and dine at the big table, and wear a silk gown at church, and the servants should all call her madame; a great career should be open to her, if she would only give up her foolish, girlish, childish love for Adolphe. And all these great promises were repeated to Marie by the Capitaine.

But nevertheless there was but one thing in the world which in Marie's eyes was of any value, and that one thing was the heart of Adolphe Bauche. Without that she would be nothing; with that,—with that assured, she could wait patiently till doomsday.

Letters were written to Adolphe during all these eventful doings; and a letter came from him saying that he greatly valued

Marie's love, but that as it had been clearly proved to him that their marriage would be neither for her advantage, nor for his, he was willing to give it up. He consented to her marriage with the Capitaine, and expressed his gratitude to his mother for the pecuniary advantages which she had held out to him. Oh, Adolphe, Adolphe! But, alas, alas! is not such the way of most men's hearts—and of the hearts of some women?

This letter was read to Marie, but it had no more effect upon her than would have had some dry legal document. In those days and in those places men and women did not depend much upon letters; nor when they were written was there expressed in them much of heart or of feeling. Marie would understand, as she was well aware, the glance of Adolphe's eye and the tone of Adolphe's voice; she would perceive at once from them what her lover really meant, what he wished, what in the innermost corner of his heart he really desired that she should do. But from that stiff, constrained written document she could understand nothing.

It was agreed therefore that Adolphe should return, and that she would accept her fate from his mouth. The Capitaine, who knew more of human nature than poor Marie, felt tolerably sure of his bride. Adolphe, who had seen something of the world, would not care very much for the girl of his own valley. Money and pleasure, and some little position in the world, would soon wean him from his love; and then Marie would accept her destiny —as other girls in the same position had done since the French world began.

And now it was the evening before Adolphe's expected arrival. La Mère Bauche was discussing the matter with the Capitaine over the usual cup of coffee. Madame Bauche had of late become rather nervous on the matter, thinking that they had been somewhat rash in acceding so much to Marie. It seemed to her that it was absolutely now left to the two young lovers to say whether or no they would have each other or not. Now nothing on earth could be further from Madame Bauche's intention than this. Her decree and resolve was to heap down blessings on all persons concerned—provided always that she could have her own way; but, provided she did not have her own way, to heap down,—anything but blessings. She had her code of morality in this matter. She would do good if possible to everybody around her. But she would not on any score be induced to consent that Adolphe should marry Marie Clavert. Should that be in the wind she would rid the house of Marie, of the Capitaine, and even of Adolphe himself.

She had become therefore somewhat querulous and self-opinionated in her discussions with her friend.

'I don't know,' she said on the evening in question; 'I don't know. It may be all right; but if Adolphe turns against me, what are we to do then?'

'Mère Bauche,' said the Capitaine, sipping his coffee and puffing out the smoke of his cigar, 'Adolphe will not turn against us.' It had been somewhat remarked by many that the Capitaine was more at home in the house, and somewhat freer in his manner of talking with Madame Bauche, since this matrimonial alliance had been on the *tapis*[4] than he had ever been before. La Mère herself observed it, and did not quite like it; but how could she prevent it now? When the Capitaine was once married she would make him know his place, in spite of all her promises to Marie.

'But if he says he likes the girl?' continued Madame Bauche.

'My friend, you may be sure that he will say nothing of the kind. He has not been away two years without seeing girls as pretty as Marie. And then you have his letter.'

'That is nothing, Capitaine; he would eat his letter as quick as you would eat an omelet *aux fines herbes*.' Now the Capitaine was especially quick over an omelet *aux fines herbes*.

'And, Mère Bauche, you also have the purse; he will know that he cannot eat that, except with your good will.'

'Ah!' exclaimed Madame Bauche, 'poor lad! He has not a *sou* in the world unless I give it to him.' But it did not seem that this reflection was in itself displeasing to her.

'Adolphe will now be a man of the world,' continued the Capitaine. 'He will know that it does not do to throw away everything for a pair of red lips. That is the folly of a boy, and Adolphe will be no longer a boy. Believe me, Mère Bauche, things will be right enough.'

'And then we shall have Marie sick and ill and half dying on our hands,' said Madame Bauche.

[4] Literally on the carpet; we would say 'on the cards', a possibility.

This was not flattering to the Capitaine, and so he felt it.

'Perhaps so, perhaps not,' he said. 'But at any rate she will get over it. It is a malady which rarely kills young women—especially when another alliance awaits them.'

'Bah!' said Madame Bauche, and in saying that word she avenged herself for the too great liberty which the Capitaine had lately taken. He shrugged his shoulders, took a pinch of snuff, and, uninvited, helped himself to a teaspoonful of cognac. Then the conference ended, and on the next morning before breakfast Adolphe Bauche arrived.

On that morning poor Marie hardly knew how to bear herself. A month or two back, and even up to the last day or two, she had felt a sort of confidence that Adolphe would be true to her; but the nearer came that fatal day the less strong was the confidence of the poor girl. She knew that those two long-headed, aged counsellors were plotting against her happiness, and she felt that she could hardly dare hope for success with such terrible foes opposed to her. On the evening before the day Madame Bauche had met her in the passages, and kissed her as she wished her good night. Marie knew little about sacrifices, but she felt that it was a sacrificial kiss.

In those days a sort of diligence[5] with the mails for Olette passed through Prades early in the morning, and a conveyance was sent from Vernet to bring Adolphe to the baths. Never was prince or princess expected with more anxiety. Madame Bauche was up and dressed long before the hour, and was heard to say five several times that she was sure he would not come. The Capitaine was out and on the high road, moving about with his wooden leg, as perpendicular as a lamp-post and almost as black. Marie also was up, but nobody had seen her. She was up and had been out about the place before any of them were stirring; but now that the world was on the move she lay hidden like a hare in its form.

And then the old *char-à-banc*[6] clattered up to the door, and Adolphe jumped out of it into his mother's arms. He was fatter and fairer than she had last seen him, had a larger beard, was more fashionably clothed, and certainly looked more like a man.

[5] Public stage-coach. [6] Cart with benches for seats.

Marie also saw him out of her little window, and she thought that he looked like a god. Was it probable, she said to herself, that one so godlike would still care for her?

The mother was delighted with her son, who rattled away quite at his ease. He shook hands very cordially with the Capitaine—of whose intended alliance with his own sweetheart he had been informed, and then as he entered the house with his hand under his mother's arm, he asked one question about her. 'And where is Marie?' said he. 'Marie! oh upstairs; you shall see her after breakfast,' said La Mère Bauche. And so they entered the house, and went in to breakfast, among the guests. Everybody had heard something of the story, and they were all on the alert to see the young man whose love or want of love was considered to be of so much importance.

'You will see that it will be all right,' said the Capitaine, carrying his head very high.

'I think so, I think so,' said La Mère Bauche, who, now that the Capitaine was right, no longer desired to contradict him.

'I know that it will be all right,' said the Capitaine. 'I told you that Adolphe would return a man; and he is a man. Look at him; he does not care this for Marie Clavert'; and the Capitaine, with much eloquence in his motion, pitched over a neighbouring wall a small stone which he held in his hand.

And then they all went to breakfast with many signs of outward joy. And not without some inward joy; for Madame Bauche thought she saw that her son was cured of his love. In the meantime Marie sat upstairs still afraid to show herself.

'He has come,' said a young girl, a servant in the house, running up to the door of Marie's room.

'Yes,' said Marie; 'I could see that he has come.'

'And, oh, how beautiful he is!' said the girl, putting her hands together and looking up to the ceiling. Marie in her heart of hearts wished that he was not half so beautiful, as then her chance of having him might be greater.

'And the company are all talking to him as though he were the *préfet*,'[7] said the girl.

'Never mind who is talking to him,' said Marie; 'go away and

[7] Chief administrator of a district.

leave me—you are wanted for your work.' Why before this was he not talking to her? Why not, if he were really true to her? Alas, it began to fall upon her mind that he would be false! And what then? What should she do then? She sat still gloomily, thinking of that other spouse that had been promised to her.

As speedily after breakfast as was possible Adolphe was invited to a conference in his mother's private room. She had much debated in her own mind whether the Capitaine should be invited to this conference or no. For many reasons she would have wished to exclude him. She did not like to teach her son that she was unable to manage her own affairs, and she would have been well pleased to make the Capitaine understand that his assistance was not absolutely necessary to her. But then she had an inward fear that her green spectacles would not now be as efficacious on Adolphe, as they had once been, in old days, before he had seen the world and become a man. It might be necessary that her son, being a man, should be opposed by a man. So the Capitaine was invited to the conference.

What took place there need not be described at length. The three were closeted for two hours, at the end of which time they came forth together. The countenance of Madame Bauche was serene and comfortable; her hopes of ultimate success ran higher than ever. The face of the Capitaine was masked, as are always the faces of great diplomatists; he walked placid and upright, raising his wooden leg with an ease and skill that was absolutely marvellous. But poor Adolphe's brow was clouded. Yes, poor Adolphe! for he was poor in spirit. He had pledged himself to give up Marie, and to accept the liberal allowance which his mother tendered him; but it remained for him now to communicate these tidings to Marie herself.

'Could not you tell her?' he had said to his mother, with very little of that manliness in his face on which his mother now so prided herself. But La Mère Bauche explained to him that it was a part of the general agreement that Marie was to hear his decision from his own mouth.

'But you need not regard it,'[8] said the Capitaine, with the most indifferent air in the world. 'The girl expects it. Only she has

[8] Worry about it.

some childish idea that she is bound till you yourself release her. I don't think she will be troublesome.' Adolphe at that moment did feel that he should have liked to kick the Capitaine out of his mother's house.

And where should the meeting take place? In the hall of the bath-house, suggested Madame Bauche; because, as she observed, they could walk round and round, and nobody ever went there at that time of day. But to this Adolphe objected; it would be so cold and dismal and melancholy.

The Capitaine thought that Mère Bauche's little parlour was the place; but La Mère herself did not like this. They might be overheard, as she well knew; and she guessed that the meeting would not conclude without some sobs that would certainly be bitter and might perhaps be loud.

'Send her up to the grotto, and I will follow her,' said Adolphe. On this therefore they agreed. Now the grotto was a natural excavation in a high rock, which stood precipitously upright over the establishment of the baths. A steep zigzag path with almost never-ending steps had been made along the face of the rock from a little flower-garden attached to the house which lay immediately under the mountain. Close along the front of the hotel ran a little brawling river, leaving barely room for a road between it and the door; over this there was a wooden bridge leading to the garden, and some two or three hundred yards from the bridge began the steps by which the ascent was made to the grotto.

When the season was full and the weather perfectly warm the place was much frequented. There was a green table in it, and four or five deal chairs; a green garden seat also was there, which however had been removed into the innermost back corner of the excavation, as its hinder legs were somewhat at fault. A wall about two feet high ran along the face of it, guarding its occupants from the precipice. In fact it was no grotto, but a little chasm in the rock, such as we often see up above our heads in rocky valleys, and which by means of these steep steps had been turned into a source of exercise and amusement for the visitors at the hotel.

Standing at the wall one could look down into the garden, and down also upon the shining slate roof of Madame Bauche's house;

and to the left might be seen the sombre, silent, snow-capped top of stern old Canigou, king of mountains among those Eastern Pyrenees.

And so Madame Bauche undertook to send Marie up to the grotto, and Adolphe undertook to follow her thither. It was now spring; and though the winds had fallen and the snow was no longer lying on the lower peaks, still the air was fresh and cold, and there was no danger that any of the few guests at the establishment would visit the place.

'Make her put on her cloak, Mère Bauche,' said the Capitaine, who did not wish that his bride should have a cold in her head on her wedding-day. La Mère Bauche pished and pshawed, as though she were not minded to pay any attention to recommendations on such subjects from the Capitaine. But nevertheless when Marie was seen slowly to creep across the little bridge about fifteen minutes after this time, she had a handkerchief on her head, and was closely wrapped in a dark brown cloak.

Poor Marie herself little heeded the cold fresh air, but she was glad to avail herself of any means by which she might hide her face. When Madame Bauche sought her out in her own little room, and with a smiling face and kind kiss bade her go to the grotto, she knew, or fancied that she knew, that it was all over.

'He will tell you all the truth,—how it all is,' said La Mère. 'We will do all we can, you know, to make you happy, Marie. But you must remember what Monsieur le Curé told us the other day. In this vale of tears we cannot have everything; as we shall have some day, when our poor wicked souls have been purged of all their wickedness. Now go, dear, and take your cloak.'

'Yes, *maman*.'

'And Adolphe will come to you. And try and behave well, like a sensible girl.'

'Yes, *maman*,'—and so she went, bearing on her brow another sacrificial kiss,—and bearing in her heart such an unutterable load of woe!

Adolphe had gone out of the house before her; but standing in the stable yard, well within the gate so that she should not see him, he watched her slowly crossing the bridge and mounting the first flight of the steps. He had often seen her tripping up those stairs, and had, almost as often, followed her with his quicker feet. And she, when she would hear him, would run; and then he would catch her breathless at the top, and steal kisses from her when all power of refusing them had been robbed from her by her efforts at escape. There was no such running now, no such following, no thought of such kisses.

As for him, he would fain have skulked off and shirked the interview had he dared. But he did not dare; so he waited there, out of heart, for some ten minutes, speaking a word now and then to the bathman, who was standing by, just to show that he was at his ease. But the bathman knew that he was not at his ease. Such would-be lies as those rarely achieve deception;—are rarely believed. And then, at the end of the ten minutes, with steps as slow as Marie's had been, he also ascended to the grotto.

Marie had watched him from the top, but so that she herself should not be seen. He, however, had not once lifted up his head to look for her; but with eyes turned to the ground had plodded his way up to the cave. When he entered she was standing in the middle, with her eyes downcast and her hands clasped before her. She had retired some way from the wall, so that no eyes might possibly see her but those of her false lover. There she stood when he entered, striving to stand motionless, but trembling like a leaf in every limb.

It was only when he reached the top step that he made up his mind how he would behave. Perhaps after all, the Capitaine was right; perhaps she would not mind it.

'Marie,' said he, with a voice that attempted to be cheerful; 'this is an odd place to meet in after such a long absence,' and he held out his hand to her. But only his hand! He offered her no salute. He did not even kiss her cheek as a brother would have done! Of the rules of the outside world it must be remembered that poor Marie knew but little. He had been a brother to her before he had become her lover.

But Marie took his hand saying, 'Yes, it has been very long.'

'And now that I have come back,' he went on to say, 'it seems that we are all in a confusion together. I never knew such a piece of work. However, it is all for the best, I suppose.'

'Perhaps so,' said Marie, still trembling violently, and still looking down upon the ground. And then there was silence between them for a minute or so.

'I tell you what it is, Marie,' said Adolphe at last, dropping her hand and making a great effort to get through the work before him. 'I am afraid we two have been very foolish. Don't you think we have now? It seems quite clear that we can never get ourselves married. Don't you see it in that light?'

Marie's head turned round and round with her, but she was not of the fainting order. She took three steps backwards and leant against the wall of the cave. She also was trying to think how she might best fight her battle. Was there no chance for her? Could no eloquence, no love prevail? On her own beauty she counted but little; but might not prayers do something, and a reference to those old vows which had been so frequent, so eager, so solemnly pledged between them?

'Never get ourselves married!' she said, repeating his words. 'Never, Adolphe? Can we never be married?'

'Upon my word, my dear girl, I fear not. You see my mother is so dead against it.'

'But we could wait; could we not?'

'Ah, but that's just it, Marie. We cannot wait. We must decide now,—to-day. You see I can do nothing without money from her—and as for you, you see she won't even let you stay in the house unless you marry old Campan at once. He's a very good sort of fellow though, old as he is. And if you do marry him, why you see you'll stay here, and have it all your own way in everything. As for me, I shall come and see you all from time to time, and shall be able to push my way as I ought to do.'

'Then, Adolphe, you wish me to marry the Capitaine?'

'Upon my honour I think it is the best thing you can do; I do indeed.'

'Oh, Adolphe!'

'What can I do for you, you know? Suppose I was to go down to my mother and tell her that I had decided to keep you myself, what would come of it? Look at it in that light, Marie.'

'She could not turn you out—you her own son!'

'But she would turn you out; and deuced quick, too, I can assure you of that; I can, upon my honour.'

'I should not care that,' and she made a motion with her hand to show how indifferent she would be to such treatment as regarded herself. 'Not that——; if I still had the promise of your love.'

'But what would you do?'

'I would work. There are other houses beside that one,' and she pointed to the slate roof of the Bauche establishment.

'And for me—I should not have a penny in the world,' said the young man.

She came up to him and took his right hand between both of hers and pressed it warmly, oh, so warmly. 'You would have my love,' said she, 'my deepest, warmest, best heart's love. I should want nothing more, nothing on earth, if I could still have yours.' And she leaned against his shoulder and looked with all her eyes into his face.

'But, Marie, that's nonsense, you know.'

'No, Adolphe, it is not nonsense. Do not let them teach you so. What does love mean, if it does not mean that? Oh, Adolphe, you do love me, you do love me, you do love me?'

'Yes;—I love you,' he said slowly;—as though he would not have said it if he could have helped it. And then his arm crept slowly round her waist, as though in that also he could not help himself.

'And do not I love you?' said the passionate girl. 'Oh, I do, so dearly; with all my heart, with all my soul. Adolphe, I so love you, that I cannot give you up. Have I not sworn to be yours; sworn, sworn a thousand times? How can I marry that man! Oh, Adolphe, how can you wish that I should marry him?' And she clung to him, and looked at him, and besought him with her eyes.

'I shouldn't wish it;—only——' and then he paused. It was hard to tell her that he was willing to sacrifice her to the old man because he wanted money from his mother.

'Only what! But, Adolphe, do not wish it at all! Have you not sworn that I should be your wife? Look here, look at this'; and she brought out from her bosom a little charm that he had given her in return for that cross. 'Did you not kiss that when you swore before the figure of the Virgin that I should be your wife? And do you not remember that I feared to swear too, because your mother was so angry; and then you made me? After that, Adolphe! Oh, Adolphe! Tell me that I may have some hope. I will wait; oh, I will wait so patiently.'

He turned himself away from her and walked backwards and forwards uneasily through the grotto. He did love her;—love her as such men do love sweet, pretty girls. The warmth of her hand, the affection of her touch, the pure bright passion of her tear-laden eye had re-awakened what power of love there was within him. But what was he to do? Even if he were willing to give up the immediate golden hopes which his mother held out to him, how was he to begin, and then how carry out this work of self-devotion? Marie would be turned away, and he would be left a victim in the hands of his mother, and of that stiff, wooden-legged *militaire*;—a penniless victim, left to mope about the place without a grain of influence or a morsel of pleasure.

'But what can we do?' he exclaimed again, as he once more met Marie's searching eye.

'We can be true and honest, and we can wait,' she said, coming close up to him and taking hold of his arm. 'I do not fear it; and she is not my mother, Adolphe. You need not fear your own mother.'

'Fear! No, of course I don't fear. But I don't see how the very devil we can manage it.'

'Will you let me tell her that I will not marry the Capitaine; that I will not give up your promises; and then I am ready to leave the house?'

'It would do no good.'

'It would do every good, Adolphe, if I had your promised word once more; if I could hear from your own voice one more tone of love. Do you not remember this place? It was here that you forced me to say that I loved you. It is here also that you will tell me that I have been deceived.'

'It is not I that would deceive you,' he said. 'I wonder that you should be so hard upon me. God knows that I have trouble enough.'

'Well, if I am a trouble to you, be it so. Be it as you wish,' and she leaned back against the wall of the rock, and crossing her arms upon her breast looked away from him and fixed her eyes upon the sharp granite peaks of Canigou.

He again betook himself to walk backwards and forwards through the cave. He had quite enough of love for her to make him wish to marry her; quite enough now, at this moment, to make the idea of her marriage with the Capitaine very distasteful to him; enough probably to make him become a decently good husband to her, should fate enable him to marry her; but not enough to enable him to support all the punishment which would be the sure effects of his mother's displeasure. Besides, he had promised his mother that he would give up Marie;—had entirely given in his adhesion to that plan of the marriage with the Capitaine. He had owned that the path of life as marked out for him by his mother was the one which it behoved him, as a man, to follow. It was this view of his duties as a man which had been specially urged on him with all the Capitaine's eloquence. And old Campan had entirely succeeded. It is so easy to get the assent of such young men, so weak in mind and so weak in pocket, when the arguments are backed by a promise of two thousand francs a year.

'I'll tell you what I'll do,' at last he said. 'I'll get my mother by herself, and will ask her to let the matter remain as it is for the present.'

'Not if it be a trouble, M. Adolphe'; and the proud girl still held her hands upon her bosom, and still looked towards the mountain.

'You know what I mean, Marie. You can understand how she and the Capitaine are worrying me.'

'But, tell me, Adolphe, do you love me?'

'You know I love you, only——'

'And you will not give me up?'

'I will ask my mother. I will try and make her yield.'

Marie could not feel that she received much confidence from her lover's promise; but still, even that, weak and unsteady as it was, even that was better than absolute fixed rejection. So she thanked him, promised him with tears in her eyes that she would always, always be faithful to him, and then bade him go down to the house. She would follow, she said, as soon as his passing had ceased to be observed.

Then she looked at him as though she expected some sign of renewed love. But no sign was vouchsafed to her. Now that she thirsted for the touch of his lip upon her cheek, it was denied to her. He did as she bade him; he went down, slowly loitering, by himself; and in about half on hour she followed him, and unobserved crept to her chamber.

Again we will pass over what took place between the mother and the son; but late in the evening, after the guests had gone to bed, Marie received a message, desiring her to wait on Madame Bauche in a small *salon* which looked out from one end of the house. It was intended as a private sitting-room should any special stranger arrive who required such accommodation, and therefore was but seldom used. Here she found La Mère Bauche sitting in an armchair behind a small table on which stood two candles; and on a sofa against the wall sat Adolphe. The Capitaine was not in the room.

'Shut the door, Marie, and come in and sit down,' said Madame Bauche. It was easy to understand from the tone of her voice that she was angry and stern, in an unbending mood, and resolved to carry out to the very letter all the threats conveyed by those terrible spectacles.

Marie did as she was bid. She closed the door and sat down on the chair that was nearest to her.

'Marie,' said La Mère Bauche—and the voice sounded fierce in the poor girl's ears, and an angry fire glimmered through the green glasses—'what is all this about that I hear? Do you dare to say that you hold my son bound to marry you?' And then the august mother paused for an answer.

But Marie had no answer to give. She looked suppliantly towards her lover, as though beseeching him to carry on the fight for her. But if she could not do battle for herself, certainly he could not do it for her. What little amount of fighting he had had in him, had been thoroughly vanquished before her arrival.

'I will have an answer, and that immediately,' said Madame Bauche. 'I am not going to be betrayed into ignominy and disgrace by the object of my own charity. Who picked you out of the gutter, miss, and brought you up and fed you, when you would otherwise have gone to the foundling? And this is your gratitude for it all? You are not satisfied with being fed and clothed and cherished by me, but you must rob me of my son! Know this then, Adolphe shall never marry a child of charity such as you are.'

Marie sat still, stunned by the harshness of these words. La Mère Bauche had often scolded her; indeed, she was given to much scolding; but she had scolded her as a mother may scold a child. And when this story of Marie's love first reached her ears she had been very angry; but her anger had never brought her to such a pass as this. Indeed, Marie had not hitherto been taught to look at the matter in this light. No one had heretofore twitted her with eating the bread of charity. It had not occurred to her that on this account she was unfit to be Adolphe's wife. There, in that valley, they were all so nearly equal that no idea of her own inferiority had ever pressed itself upon her mind. But now——!

When the voice ceased she again looked at him; but it was no longer a beseeching look. Did he also altogether scorn her? That was now the inquiry which her eyes were called upon to make. No; she could not say that he did. It seemed to her that his energies were chiefly occupied in pulling to pieces the tassel on the sofa cushion.

'And now, miss, let me know at once whether this nonsense is to be over or not,' continued La Mère Bauche; 'and I will tell you at once I am not going to maintain you here, in my house, to plot against our welfare and happiness. As Marie Clavert you shall not stay here. Capitaine Campan is willing to marry you; and as his wife I will keep my word to you, though you little deserve it. If you refuse to marry him you must go. As to my son, he is there, and he will tell you now, in my presence, that he altogether declines the honour you propose for him.'

And then she ceased, waiting for an answer, drumming the table with a wafer stamp[9] which happened to be ready to her hand; but Marie said nothing. Adolphe had been appealed to; but Adolphe had not yet spoken.

'Well, miss?' said La Mère Bauche.

Then Marie rose from her seat, and walking round she touched

[9] For pressing down wafers—small discs of dried paste used for fastening letters.

Adolphe lightly on the shoulder. 'Adolphe,' she said, 'it is for you to speak now. I will do as you bid me.'

He gave a long sigh, looked first at Marie and then at his mother, shook himself lightly, and then spoke: 'Upon my word, Marie, I think mother is right. It would never do for us to marry; it would not indeed.'

'Then it is decided,' said Marie, returning to her chair.

'And you will marry the Capitaine?' said La Mère Bauche.

Marie merely bowed her head in token of acquiescence.

'Then we are friends again. Come here, Marie, and kiss me. You must know that it is my duty to take care of my own son. But I don't want to be angry with you if I can help it; I don't indeed. When once you are Madame Campan, you shall be my own child; and you shall have any room in the house you like to choose—there!' And she once more imprinted a kiss on Marie's cold forehead.

How they all got out of the room, and off to their own chambers, I can hardly tell. But in five minutes from the time of this last kiss they were divided. La Mère Bauche had patted Marie, and smiled on her, and called her her dear good little Madame Campan, her young little Mistress of the Hôtel Bauche; and had then got herself into her own room, satisfied with her own victory.

Nor must my readers be too severe on Madame Bauche. She had already done much for Marie Clavert; and when she found herself once more by her own bedside, she prayed to be forgiven for the cruelty which she felt that she had shown to the orphan. But in making this prayer, with her favourite crucifix in her hand and the little image of the Virgin before her, she pleaded her duty to her son. Was it not right, she asked the Virgin, that she should save her son from a bad marriage? And then she promised ever so much of recompense, both to the Virgin and to Marie; a new trousseau for each, with candles to the Virgin, with a gold watch and chain for Marie, as soon as she should be Marie Campan. She had been cruel; she acknowledged it. But at such a crisis was it not defensible? And then the recompense should be so full!

But there was one other meeting that night, very short indeed, but not the less significant. Not long after they had all separated, just so long as to allow of the house being quiet, Adolphe, still sitting in his room, meditating on what the day had done for him, heard a low tap at his door. 'Come in,' he said, as men always do say; and Marie opening the door, stood just within the verge of his chamber. She had on her countenance neither the soft look of entreating love which she had worn up there in the grotto, nor did she appear crushed and subdued as she had done before his mother. She carried her head somewhat more erect than usual, and looked boldly out at him from under her soft eyelashes. There might still be love there, but it was love proudly resolving to quell itself. Adolphe, as he looked at her, felt that he was afraid of her.

'It is all over then between us, M. Adolphe?' she said.

'Well, yes. Don't you think it had better be so, eh, Marie?'

'And this is the meaning of oaths and vows, sworn to each other so sacredly?'

'But, Marie, you heard what my mother said.'

'Oh, sir! I have not come to ask you again to love me. Oh no! I am not thinking of that. But this, this would be a lie if I kept it now; it would choke me if I wore it as that man's wife. Take it back'; and she tendered to him the little charm which she had always worn round her neck since he had given it to her. He took it abstractedly, without thinking what he did, and placed it on the dressing-table.

'And you,' she continued, 'can you still keep that cross? Oh, no! you must give me back that. It would remind you too often of vows that were untrue.'

'Marie,' he said, 'do not be so harsh to me.'

'Harsh!' said she, 'no; there has been enough of harshness. I would not be harsh to you, Adolphe. But give me the cross; it would prove a curse to you if you kept it.'

He then opened a little box which stood upon the table, and taking out the cross gave it to her.

'And now good-bye,' she said. 'We shall have but little more to say to each other. I know this now, that I was wrong ever to have loved you. I should have been to you as one of the other poor girls in the house. But, oh! how was I to help it?' To this he made no answer, and she, closing the door softly, went back to her chamber. And thus ended the first day of Adolphe Bauche's return to his own house.

On the next morning the Capitaine and Marie were formally betrothed. This was done with some little ceremony, in the presence of all the guests who were staying at the establishment, and with all manner of gracious acknowledgments of Marie's virtues. It seemed as though La Mère Bauche could not be courteous enough to her. There was no more talk of her being a child of charity; no more allusion now to the gutter. La Mère Bauche with her own hand brought her cake with a glass of wine after her betrothal was over, and patted her on the cheek, and called her her dear little Marie Campan. And then the Capitaine was made up of infinite politeness, and the guests all wished her joy, and the servants of the house began to perceive that she was a person entitled to respect. How different was all this from that harsh attack that was made on her the preceding evening! Only Adolphe, he alone kept aloof. Though he was present there he said nothing. He, and he only, offered no congratulations.

In the midst of all these gala doings Marie herself said little or nothing. La Mère Bauche perceived this, but she forgave it. Angrily as she had expressed herself at the idea of Marie's daring to love her son, she had still acknowledged within her own heart that such love had been natural. She could feel no pity for Marie as long as Adolphe was in danger; but now she knew how to pity her. So Marie was still petted and still encouraged, though she went through the day's work sullenly and in silence.

As to the Capitaine it was all one to him. He was a man of the world. He did not expect that he should really be preferred, *con amore*, to a young fellow like Adolphe. But he did expect that Marie, like other girls, would do as she was bid; and that in a few days she would regain her temper and be reconciled to her life.

And then the marriage was fixed for a very early day; for as La Mère said, 'What was the use of waiting? All their minds were made up now, and therefore the sooner the two were married the better. Did not the Capitaine think so?'

The Capitaine said that he did think so.

And then Marie was asked. It was all one to her, she said. Whatever Maman Bauche liked, that she would do; only she would not name a day herself. Indeed she would neither do nor say anything herself which tended in any way to a furtherance of these matrimonials. But then she acquiesced, quietly enough if not readily, in what other people did and said; and so the marriage was fixed for the day week after Adolphe's return.

The whole of that week passed much in the same way. The servants about the place spoke among themselves of Marie's perverseness, obstinacy, and ingratitude, because she would not look pleased, or answer Madame Bauche's courtesies with gratitude; but La Mère herself showed no signs of anger. Marie had yielded to her, and she required no more. And she remembered also the harsh words she had used to gain her purpose: and she reflected on all that Marie had lost. On these accounts she was forbearing and exacted nothing—nothing but that one sacrifice which was to be made in accordance to her wishes.

And it was made. They were married in the great *salon*, the dining-room, immediately after breakfast. Madame Bauche was dressed in a new puce silk dress, and looked very magnificent on the occasion. She simpered and smiled, and looked gay even in spite of her spectacles; and as the ceremony was being performed, she held fast clutched in her hand the gold watch and chain which were intended for Marie as soon as ever the marriage should be completed.

The Capitaine was dressed exactly as usual, only that all his clothes were new. Madame Bauche had endeavoured to persuade him to wear a blue coat; but he answered that such a change would not, he was sure, be to Marie's taste. To tell the truth, Marie would hardly have known the difference had he presented himself in scarlet vestments.

Adolphe, however, was dressed very finely, but he did not make himself prominent on the occasion. Marie watched him closely, though none saw that she did so; and of his garments she could have given an account with much accuracy—of his garments, ay! and of every look. 'Is he a man,' she said at last to herself, 'that he can stand by and see all this?'

She too was dressed in silk. They had put on her what they pleased, and she bore the burden of her wedding finery without complaint and without pride. There was no blush on her face as she walked up to the table at which the priest stood, nor hesitation in her low voice as she made the necessary answers. She put her hand into that of the Capitaine when required to do so; and when the ring was put on her finger she shuddered, but ever so slightly. No one observed it but La Mère Bauche. 'In one week she will be used to it, and then we shall all be happy,' said La Mère to herself. 'And I—I will be so kind to her!'

And so the marriage was completed, and the watch was at once given to Marie. 'Thank you, *maman,*' said she, as the trinket was fastened to her girdle. Had it been a pincushion that had cost three *sous,* it would have affected her as much.

And then there was cake and wine and sweetmeats; and after a few minutes Marie disappeared. For an hour or so the Capitaine was taken up with the congratulations of his friends, and with the efforts necessary to the wearing of his new honours with an air of ease; but after that time he began to be uneasy because his wife did not come to him. At two or three in the afternoon he went to La Mère Bauche to complain. 'This lackadaisical nonsense is no good,' he said. 'At any rate it is too late now. Marie had better come down among us and show herself satisfied with her husband.'

But Madame Bauche took Marie's part. 'You must not be too hard on Marie,' she said. 'She has gone through a good deal this week past, and is very young; whereas, Capitaine, you are not very young.'

The Capitaine merely shrugged his shoulders. In the meantime Mère Bauche went up to visit her *protégée* in her own room, and came down with a report that she was suffering from a headache. She could not appear at dinner, Madame Bauche said; but would make one at the little party which was to be given in the evening. With this the Capitaine was forced to be content.

The dinner therefore went on quietly without her, much as it did on other ordinary days. And then there was a little time for vacancy, during which the gentlemen drank their coffee and smoked their cigars at the *café,* talking over the event that had taken place that morning, and the ladies brushed their hair and added some ribbon or some brooch to their usual apparel. Twice during this time did Madam Bauche go up to Marie's room with offers to assist her. 'Not yet, *maman;* not quite yet,' said Marie piteously through her tears, and then twice did the green spectacles leave the room, covering eyes which also were not dry. Ah! what had she done? What had she dared to take upon herself to do? She could not undo it now.

And then it became quite dark in the passages and out of doors, and the guests assembled in the *salon*. La Mère came in and out three or four times, uneasy in her gait and unpleasant in her aspect, and everybody began to see that things were wrong. 'She is ill, I am afraid,' said one. 'The excitement has been too much,' said a second; 'and he is so old,' whispered a third. And the Capitaine stalked about erect on his wooden leg, taking snuff, and striving to look indifferent; but he also was uneasy in his mind.

Presently La Mère came in again, with a quicker step than before, and whispered something, first to Adolphe and then to the Capitaine, whereupon they both followed her out of the room.

'Not in her chamber,' said Adolphe.

'Then she must be in yours,' said the Capitaine.

'She is in neither,' said La Mère Bauche, with her sternest voice; 'nor is she in the house!'

And now there was no longer an affectation of indifference on the part of any of them. They were anything but indifferent. The Capitaine was eager in his demands that the matter should still be kept secret from the guests. She had always been romantic, he said, and had now gone out to walk by the riverside. They three and the old bathman would go out and look for her.

'But it is pitch dark,' said La Mère Bauche.

'We will take lanterns,' said the Capitaine. And so they sallied forth with creeping steps over the gravel, so that they might not be heard by those within, and proceeded to search for the young wife.

'Marie! Marie!' said La Mère Bauche, in piteous accents; 'do come to me; pray do!'

'Hush!' said the Capitaine. 'They'll hear you if you call.' He could not endure that the world should learn that a marriage with him had been so distasteful to Marie Clavert.

'Marie, dear Marie!' called Madame Bauche, louder than before, quite regardless of the Capitaine's feelings; but no Marie answered. In her innermost heart now did La Mère Bauche wish that this cruel marriage had been left undone.

Adolphe was foremost with his lamp, but he hardly dared to look in the spot where he felt that it was most likely that she should have taken refuge. How could he meet her again, alone, in that grotto? Yet he alone of the four was young. It was clearly for him to ascend. 'Marie,' he shouted, 'are you there?' as he slowly began the long ascent of the steps.

But he had hardly begun to mount when a whirring sound struck his ear, and he felt that the air near him was moved; and then there was a crash upon the lower platform of rock, and a moan, repeated twice, but so faintly, and a rustle of silk, and a slight struggle somewhere as he knew within twenty paces of him; and then all was again quiet and still in the night air.

'What was that?' asked the Capitaine in a hoarse voice. He made his way half across the little garden, and he also was within forty or fifty yards of the flat rock. But Adolphe was unable to answer him. He had fainted, and the lamp had fallen from his hands and rolled to the bottom of the steps.

But the Capitaine, though even his heart was all but quenched within him, had still strength enough to make his way up to the rock; and there, holding the lantern above his eyes, he saw all that was left for him to see of his bride.

As for La Mère Bauche, she never again sat at the head of that table,—never again dictated to guests,—never again laid down laws for the management of anyone. A poor bedridden old woman, she lay there in her house at Vernet for some seven tedious years, and then was gathered to her fathers.

As for the Capitaine—but what matters? He was made of sterner stuff. What matters either the fate of such a one as Adolphe Bauche?

Malachi's Cove

On the northern coast of Cornwall, between Tintagel and Bossiney, down on the very margin of the sea, there lived not long since an old man who got his living by saving sea-weed from the waves, and selling it for manure. The cliffs there are bold and fine, and the sea beats in upon them from the north with a grand violence. I doubt whether it be not the finest morsel of cliff scenery in England, though it is beaten by many portions of the west coast of Ireland, and perhaps also by spots in Wales and Scotland. Cliffs should be nearly precipitous, they should be broken in their outlines, and should barely admit here and there of an insecure passage from their summit to the sand at their feet. The sea should come, if not up to them, at least very near to them, and then, above all things, the water below them should be blue, and not of that dead leaden colour which is so familiar to us in England. At Tintagel all these requisites are there, except that bright blue colour which is so lovely. But the cliffs themselves are bold and well broken, and the margin of sand at high water is very narrow,—so narrow that at spring-tides there is barely a footing there.

Close upon this margin was the cottage or hovel of Malachi Trenglos, the old man of whom I have spoken. But Malachi, or old Glos, as he was commonly called by the people around him, had not built his house absolutely upon the sand. There was a fissure in the rock so great that at the top it formed a narrow ravine, and so complete from the summit to the base that it afforded an opening for a steep and rugged track from the top of the rock to the bottom. This fissure was so wide at the bottom that it had afforded space for Trenglos to fix his habitation on a foundation of rock, and here he had lived for many years. It was told of him that in the early days of his trade he had always carried the weed in a basket on his back to the top, but latterly he had been possessed of a donkey which had been trained to go up and down the steep track with a single pannier over his loins, for the rocks would not admit of panniers hanging by his side; and for this assistant he had built a shed adjoining his own, and almost as large as that in which he himself resided.

But, as years went on, old Glos procured other assistance than that of the donkey, or, as I should rather say, Providence supplied him with other help; and, indeed, had it not been so, the old man must have given up his cabin and his independence and gone into the workhouse at Camelford. For rheumatism had afflicted him, old age had bowed him till he was nearly double, and by degrees he became unable to attend the donkey on its upward passage to the world above, or even to assist in rescuing the coveted weed from the waves.

At the time to which our story refers Trenglos had not been up the cliff for twelve months, and for the last six months he had done nothing towards the furtherance of his trade, except to take the money and keep it, if any of it was kept, and occasionally to shake down a bundle of fodder for the donkey. The real work of the business was done altogether by Mahala Trenglos, his granddaughter.

Mally Trenglos was known to all the farmers round the coast, and to all the small tradespeople in Camelford. She was a wild-looking, almost unearthly creature, with wild-flowing, black, uncombed hair, small in stature, with small hands and bright black eyes; but people said that she was very strong, and the children around declared that she worked day and night, and knew nothing of fatigue. As to her age there were many doubts. Some said she was ten, and others five-and-twenty, but the reader may be allowed to know that at this time she had in truth passed her twentieth birthday. The old people spoke well of Mally, because she was so good to her grandfather; and it was said of her that though she carried to him a little gin and tobacco almost daily, she bought nothing for herself;—and as to the gin, no one who looked at her would accuse her of meddling with that. But she had no friends, and but few acquaintances among people of her own age. They said that she was fierce and ill-natured, that she had not a good word for any one, and that she was, complete at all points, a thorough little vixen. The young men did not care for her; for, as regarded dress, all days were alike with her. She never made herself smart on Sundays. She was generally without stockings, and seemed to care not at all to exercise any of those feminine attractions which might have been hers had she studied to attain them. All days were the same to her in regard to dress; and, indeed, till lately, all days had, I fear, been the same to her in other respects. Old Malachi had never been seen inside a place of worship since he had taken to live under the cliff.

But within the last two years Mally had submitted herself to the teaching of the clergyman at Tintagel, and had appeared at church on Sundays, if not absolutely with punctuality, at any rate so often that no one who knew the peculiarity of her residence was disposed to quarrel with her on that subject. But she made no difference in her dress on these occasions. She took her place on a low stone seat just inside the church door, clothed as usual in her thick red serge petticoat and loose brown serge jacket, such being the apparel which she had found to be best adapted for her hard and perilous work among the waters. She had pleaded to the clergyman when he attacked her on the subject of church attendance with vigour that she had got no church-going clothes. He had explained to her that she would be received there without distinction to her clothing. Mally had taken him at his word, and had gone, with a courage which certainly deserved admiration, though I doubt whether there was not mingled with it an obstinacy which was less admirable.

For people said that old Glos was rich, and that Mally might have proper clothes if she chose to buy them. Mr. Polwarth, the clergyman, who, as the old man could not come to him, went down the rocks to the old man, did make some hint on the matter in Mally's absence. But old Glos, who had been patient with him on other matters, turned upon him so angrily when he made an allusion to money, that Mr. Polwarth found himself obliged to give that matter up, and Mally continued to sit upon the stone bench in her short serge petticoat, with her long hair streaming down her face. She did so far sacrifice to decency as on such occasions to tie up her back hair with an old shoe-string. So tied it would remain through the Monday and Tuesday, but by Wednesday afternoon Mally's hair had generally managed to escape.

As to Mally's indefatigable industry there could be no manner of doubt, for the quantity of seaweed which she and the donkey amassed between them was very surprising. Old Glos, it was declared, had never collected half what Mally gathered together; but then the article was becoming cheaper, and it was necessary that the exertion should be greater. So Mally and the donkey toiled and toiled, and the seaweed came up in heaps which surprised those who looked at her little hands and light form. Was there not some one who helped her at nights, some fairy, or demon, or the like? Mally was so snappish in her answers to people that she had no right to be surprised if ill-natured things were said of her.

No one ever heard Mally Trenglos complain of her work, but about this time she was heard to make great and loud complaints of the treatment she received from some of her neighbours. It was known that she went with her plaints to Mr. Polwarth; and when he could not help her, or did not give her such instant help as she needed, she went—ah, so foolishly! to the office of a certain attorney at Camelford, who was not likely to prove himself a better friend than Mr. Polwarth.

Now the nature of her injury was as follows. The place in which she collected her seaweed was a little cove; the people had come to call it Malachi's Cove from the name of the old man who lived there;—which was so formed, that the margin of the sea therein could only be reached by the passage from the top down to Trenglos's hut. The breadth of the cove when the sea was out might perhaps be two hundred yards, and on each side the rocks ran out in such a way that both from north and south the domain of Trenglos was guarded from intruders. And this locality had been well chosen for its intended purpose.

There was a rush of the sea into the cove, which carried there large, drifting masses of seaweed, leaving them among the rocks when the tide was out. During the equinoctial winds of the spring and autumn the supply would never fail; and even when the sea was calm, the long, soft, salt-bedewed, trailing masses of the weed, could be gathered there when they could not be found elsewhere for miles along the coast. The task of getting the weed from the breakers was often difficult and dangerous,—so difficult that much of it was left to be carried away by the next incoming tide.

Mally doubtless did not gather half the crop that was there at her feet. What was taken by the returning waves she did not regret; but when interlopers came upon her cove, and gathered her wealth,—her grandfather's wealth, beneath her eyes, then her heart was broken. It was this interloping, this intrusion, that drove poor Mally to the Camelford attorney. But, alas, though the Camelford attorney took Mally's money, he could do nothing for her, and her heart was broken!

She had an idea, in which no doubt her grandfather shared, that the path to the cove was, at any rate, their property. When she was told that the cove, and sea running into the cove, were not the freeholds of her grandfather, she understood that the statement might be true. But what then as to the use of the path? Who had made the path what it was? Had she not painfully, wearily, with exceeding toil, carried up bits of rocks with her own little hands, that her grandfather's donkey might have footing for his feet? Had she not scraped together crumbs of earth along the face of the cliff that she might make easier to the animal the track of that rugged way? And now, when she saw big farmers' lads coming down with other donkeys,—and, indeed, there was one who came with a pony; no boy, but a young man, old enough to know better than rob a poor old man and a young girl,—she reviled the whole human race, and swore that the Camelford attorney was a fool.

Any attempt to explain to her that there was still weed enough for her was worse than useless. Was it not all hers and his, or, at any rate, was not the sole way to it his and hers? And was not her trade stopped and impeded? Had she not been forced to back her laden donkey down, twenty yards she said, but it had, in truth, been five, because Farmer Gunliffe's son had been in the way with his thieving pony? Farmer Gunliffe had wanted to buy her weed at his own price, and because she had refused he had set on his thieving son to destroy her in this wicked way.

'I'll hamstring[1] the beast the next time as he's down here!' said Mally to old Glos, while the angry fire literally streamed from her eyes.

Farmer Gunliffe's small homestead—he held about fifty acres of land—was close by the village of Tintagel, and not a mile from the cliff. The sea-wrack, as they call it, was pretty well the only manure within his reach, and no doubt he thought it hard that he should be kept from using it by Mally Trenglos and her obstinacy.

'There's heaps of other coves, Barty,' said Mally to Barty Gunliffe, the farmer's son.

[1] **Lame by cutting the tendons at the back of the leg which control the thigh-muscles.**

'But none so nigh, Mally, nor yet none that fills 'emselves as this place.'

Then he explained to her that he would not take the weed that came up close to hand. He was bigger than she was, and stronger, and would get it from the outer rocks, with which she never meddled. Then, with scorn in her eye, she swore that she could get it where he durst not venture, and repeated her threat of hamstringing the pony. Barty laughed at her wrath, jeered her because of her wild hair, and called her a mermaid.

'I'll mermaid you!' she cried. 'Mermaid, indeed! I wouldn't be a man to come and rob a poor girl and an old cripple. But you're no man, Barty Gunliffe! You're not half a man.'

Nevertheless, Bartholomew Gunliffe was a very fine young fellow, as far as the eye went. He was about five feet eight inches high, with strong arms and legs, with light curly brown hair and blue eyes. His father was but in a small way as a farmer, but nevertheless, Barty Gunliffe was well thought of among the girls around. Everybody liked Barty,—excepting only Mally Trenglos, and she hated him like poison.

Barty, when he was asked why so good-natured a lad as he persecuted a poor girl and an old man, threw himself upon the justice of the thing. It wouldn't do at all, according to his view, that any single person should take upon himself to own that which God Almighty sent as the common property of all. He would do Mally no harm, and so he had told her. But Mally was a vixen,—a wicked little vixen; and she must be taught to have a civil tongue in her head. When once Mally would speak him civil as he went for weed, he would get his father to pay the old man some sort of toll for the use of the path.

'Speak him civil?' said Mally. 'Never; not while I have a tongue in my mouth!' And I fear old Glos encouraged her rather than otherwise in her view of the matter.

But her grandfather did not encourage her to hamstring the pony. Hamstringing a pony would be a serious thing, and old Glos thought it might be very awkward for both of them if Mally were put into prison. He suggested, therefore, that all manner of impediments should be put in the way of the pony's feet, surmising that the well-trained donkey might be able to work in spite of them. And Barty Gunliffe, on his next descent, did find the passage very awkward when he came near to Malachi's hut, but he made his way down, and poor Mally saw the lumps of rock at which she had laboured so hard pushed on one side or rolled out of the way with a steady persistency of injury towards herself that almost drove her frantic.

'Well, Barty, you're a nice boy,' said old Glos, sitting in the doorway of the hut, as he watched the intruder.

'I ain't a doing no harm to none as doesn't harm me,' said Barty. 'The sea's free to all, Malachi.'

'And the sky's free to all, but I mustn't get up on the top of your big barn to look at it,' said Mally, who was standing among the rocks with a long hook in her hand. The long hook was the tool with which she worked in dragging the weed from the waves. 'But you ain't got no justice nor yet no sperrit, or you wouldn't come here to vex an old man like he.'

'I didn't want to vex him, nor yet to vex you, Mally. You let me be for a while, and we'll be friends yet.'

'Friends!' exclaimed Mally. 'Who'd have the likes of you for a friend? What are you moving them stones for? Them stones belongs to grandfather.' And in her wrath she made a movement as though she were going to fly at him.

'Let him be, Mally,' said the old man; 'let him be. He'll get his punishment. He'll come to be drowned some day if he comes down here when the wind is in shore.'

'That he may be drowned then!' said Mally, in her anger. 'If he was in the big hole there among the rocks, and the sea running in at half tide, I wouldn't lift a hand to help him out.'

'Yes, you would, Mally; you'd fish me up with your hook like a big stick of seaweed.'

She turned from him with scorn as he said this, and went into the hut. It was time for her to get ready for her work, and one of the great injuries done her lay in this,—that such a one as Barty Gunliffe should come and look at her during her toil among the breakers.

It was an afternoon in April, and the hour was something after four o'clock. There had been a heavy wind from the north-west all the morning, with gusts of rain, and the sea-gulls had been in and out of the cove all the day, which was a sure sign to Mally that the incoming tide would cover the rocks with weed.

The quick waves were now returning with wonderful celerity over the low reefs, and the time had come at which the treasure must be seized, if it was to be garnered on that day. By seven o'clock it would be growing dark, at nine it would be high water, and before daylight the crop would be carried out again if not collected. All this Mally understood very well, and some of this Barty was beginning to understand also.

As Mally came down with her bare feet, bearing her long hook in her hand, she saw Barty's pony standing patiently on the sand, and in her heart she longed to attack the brute. Barty at this moment, with a common three-pronged fork in his hand, was standing down on a large rock, gazing forth towards the waters. He had declared that he would gather the weed only at places which were inaccessible to Mally, and he was looking out that he might settle where he would begin.

'Let 'un be, let 'un be,' shouted the old man to Mally, as he saw her take a step towards the beast, which she hated almost as much as she hated the man.

Hearing her grandfather's voice through the wind, she desisted from her purpose, if any purpose she had had, and went forth to her work. As she passed down the cove, and scrambled in among the rocks, she saw Barty still standing on his perch; out beyond, the white-curling waves were cresting and breaking themselves with violence, and the wind was howling among the caverns and abutments of the cliff.

Every now and then there came a squall of rain, and though there was sufficient light, the heavens were black with clouds. A scene more beautiful might hardly be found by those who love the glories of the coast. The light for such objects was perfect. Nothing could exceed the grandeur of the colours,—the blue of the open sea, the white of the breaking waves, the yellow sands, or the streaks of red and brown which gave such richness to the cliff.

But neither Mally nor Barty were thinking of such things as these. Indeed they were hardly thinking of their trade after its ordinary forms. Barty was meditating how he might best accomplish his purpose of working beyond the reach of Mally's feminine powers, and Mally was resolving that wherever Barty went she would go farther.

And, in many respects, Mally had the advantage. She knew every rock in the spot, and was sure of those which gave a good foothold, and sure also of those which did not. And then her activity had been made perfect by practice for the purpose to which it was to be devoted. Barty, no doubt, was stronger than she, and quite as active. But Barty could not jump among the waves from one stone to another as she could do, nor was he as yet able to get aid in his work from the very force of the water as she could get it. She had been hunting seaweed in that cove since she had been an urchin of six years old, and she knew every hole and corner and every spot of vantage. The waves were her friends, and she could use them. She could measure their strength, and knew when and where it would cease.

Mally was great down in the salt pools of her own cove,—great, and very fearless. As she watched Barty make his way forward from rock to rock, she told herself, gleefully, that he was going astray. The curl of the wind as it blew into the cove would not carry the weed up to the northern buttresses of the cove; and then there was the great hole just there,—the great hole of which she had spoken when she wished him evil.

And now she went to work, hooking up the dishevelled hairs of the ocean, and landing many a cargo on the extreme margin of the sand, from whence she would be able in the evening to drag it back before the invading waters would return to reclaim the spoil.

And on his side also Barty made his heap up against the northern buttresses of which I have spoken. Barty's heap became big and still bigger, so that he knew, let the pony work as he might, he could not take it all up that evening. But still it was not as large as Mally's heap. Mally's hook was better than his fork, and Mally's skill was better than his strength. And when he failed in some haul Mally would jeer him with a wild, weird laughter, and shriek to him through the wind that he was not half a man. At first he answered her with laughing words, but before long, as she boasted of her success and pointed to his failure, he became angry, and then he answered her no more. He became angry with himself, in that he missed so much of the plunder before him.

The broken sea was full of the long straggling growth which the waves had torn up from the bottom of the ocean, but the masses were carried past him, away from him,—nay, once or twice over him; and then Mally's weird voice would sound in his ear, jeering him. The gloom among the rocks was now becoming thicker and thicker, the tide was beating in with increased strength, and the gusts of wind came with quicker and greater violence. But still he worked on. While Mally worked he would work, and he would work for some time after she was driven in. He would not be beaten by a girl.

The great hole was now full of water, but of water which seemed to be boiling as though in a pot. And the pot was full of floating masses,—large treasures of seaweed which were thrown to and fro upon its surface, but lying there so thick that one would seem almost able to rest upon it without sinking.

Mally knew well how useless it was to attempt to rescue aught from the fury of that boiling cauldron. The hole went in under the rocks, and the side of it towards the shore lay high, slippery, and steep. The hole, even at low water, was never empty; and Mally believed that there was no bottom to it. Fish thrown in there could escape out to the ocean, miles away,—so Mally in her softer moods would tell the visitors to the cove. She knew the hole well. Poulnadioul she was accustomed to call it; which was supposed, when translated, to mean that this was the hole of the Evil One. Never did Mally attempt to make her own of weed which had found its way into that pot.

But Barty Gunliffe knew no better, and she watched him as he endeavoured to steady himself on the treacherously slippery edge of the pool. He fixed himself there and made a haul, with some small success. How he managed it she hardly knew, but she stood still for a while watching him anxiously, and then she saw him slip. He slipped, and recovered himself;—slipped again, and again recovered himself.

'Barty, you fool!' she screamed; 'if you get yourself pitched in there, you'll never come out no more.'

Whether she simply wished to frighten him, or whether her

heart relented and she had thought of his danger with dismay, who shall say? She could not have told herself. She hated him as much as ever,—but she could hardly have wished to see him drowned before her eyes.

'You go on, and don't mind me,' said he, speaking in a hoarse, angry tone.

Mind you!—who minds you?' retorted the girl. And then she again prepared herself for her work.

But as she went down over the rocks with her long hook balanced in her hands, she suddenly heard a splash, and, turning quickly round, saw the body of her enemy tumbling amidst the eddying waves in the pool. The tide had now come up so far that every succeeding wave washed into it and over it from the side nearest to the sea, and then ran down again back from the rocks, as the rolling wave receded, with a noise like the fall of a cataract. And then, when the surplus water had retreated for a moment, the surface of the pool would be partly calm, though the fretting bubbles would still boil up and down, and there was ever a simmer on the surface, as though, in truth, the cauldron were heated. But this time of comparative rest was but a moment, for the succeeding breaker would come up almost as soon as the foam of the preceding one had gone, and then again the waters would be dashed upon the rocks, and the sides would echo with the roar of the angry wave.

Instantly Mally hurried across to the edge of the pool, crouching down upon her hands and knees for security as she did so. As a wave receded, Barty's head and face was carried round near to her, and she could see that his forehead was covered with blood. Whether he were alive or dead she did not know. She had seen nothing but his blood, and the light-coloured hair of his head lying amidst the foam. Then his body was drawn along by the suction of the retreating wave; but the mass of water that escaped was not on this occasion large enough to carry the man out with it.

Instantly Mally was at work with her hook, and getting it fixed into his coat, dragged him towards the spot on which she was kneeling. During the half minute of repose she got him so close that she could touch his shoulder. Straining herself down, laying herself over the long bending handle of the hook, she strove to grasp him with her right hand. But she could not do it; she could only touch him.

Then came the next breaker, forcing itself on with a roar, looking to Mally as though it must certainly knock her from her resting-place, and destroy them both. But she had nothing for it but to kneel, and hold by her hook.

What prayer passed through her mind at that moment for herself or for him, or for that old man who was sitting unconsciously up at the cabin, who can say? The great wave came and rushed over her as she lay almost prostrate, and when the water was gone from her eyes, and the tumult of the foam, and the violence of the roaring breaker had passed by her, she found herself at her length upon the rock, while his body had been lifted up, free from her hook, and was lying upon the slippery ledge, half in the water and half out of it. As she looked at him, in that instant, she could see that his eyes were open and that he was struggling with his hands.

'Hold by the hook, Barty,' she cried, pushing the stick of it before him, while she seized the collar of his coat in her hands.

Had he been her brother, her lover, her father, she could not have clung to him with more of the energy of despair. He did contrive to hold by the stick which she had given him, and when the succeeding wave had passed by, he was still on the ledge. In the next moment she was seated a yard or two above the hole, in comparative safety, while Barty lay upon the rocks with his still bleeding head resting upon her lap.

What could she do now? She could not carry him; and in fifteen minutes the sea would be up where she was sitting. He was quite insensible and very pale, and the blood was coming slowly,—very slowly,—from the wound on his forehead. Ever so gently she put her hand upon his hair to move it back from his face; and then she bent over his mouth to see if he breathed, and as she looked at him she knew that he was beautiful.

What would she not give that he might live? Nothing now was so precious to her as his life,—as this life which she had so far rescued from the waters. But what could she do? Her grandfather could scarcely get himself down over the rocks, if indeed he could succeed in doing so much as that. Could she drag the wounded man backwards, if it were only a few feet, so that he might lie above the reach of the waves till further assistance could be procured?

She set herself to work and she moved him, almost lifting him. As she did so she wondered at her own strength, but she was very strong at that moment. Slowly, tenderly, falling on the rocks herself so that he might fall on her, she got him back to the margin of the sand, to a spot which the waters would not reach for the next two hours.

Here her grandfather met them, having seen at last what had happened from the door.

'Dada,' she said, 'he fell into the pool yonder, and was battered against the rocks. See there at his forehead.'

'Mally, I'm thinking that he's dead already,' said old Glos, peering down over the body.

'No, dada; he is not dead; but mayhap he's dying. But I'll go at once up to the farm.'

'Mally,' said the old man, 'look at his head. They'll say we murdered him.'

'Who'll say so? Who'll lie like that? Didn't I pull him out of the hole?'

'What matters that? His father'll say we killed him.'

It was manifest to Mally that whatever any one might say hereafter, her present course was plain before her. She must run up the path to Gunliffe's farm and get necessary assistance. If the world were as bad as her grandfather said, it would be so bad that she would not care to live longer in it. But be that as it might, there was no doubt as to what she must do now.

So away she went as fast as her naked feet could carry her up the cliff. When at the top she looked round to see if any person might be within ken, but she saw no one. So she ran with all her speed along the headland of the corn-field which led in the direction of old Gunliffe's house, and as she drew near to the homestead she saw that Barty's mother was leaning on the gate. As she approached, she attempted to call, but her breath failed her for any purpose of loud speech, so she ran on till she was able to grasp Mrs. Gunliffe by the arm.

'Where's himself?' she said, holding her hand upon her beating heart that she might husband her breath.

'Who is it you mean?' said Mrs. Gunliffe, who participated in the family feud against Trenglos and his granddaughter. 'What does the girl clutch me for in that way?'

'He's dying then, that's all.'

'Who is dying? Is it old Malachi? If the old man's bad, we'll send some one down.'

'It ain't dad, it's Barty! Where's himself? where's the master?' But by this time Mrs. Gunliffe was in an agony of despair, and was calling out for assistance lustily. Happily Gunliffe, the father, was at hand, and with him a man from the neighbouring village.

'Will you not send for the doctor?' said Mally. 'Oh, man, you should send for the doctor!'

Whether any orders were given for the doctor she did not know, but in a very few minutes she was hurrying across the field again towards the path to the cove, and Gunliffe and the other man and his wife were following her.

As Mally went along she recovered her voice, for their step was not so quick as hers, and that which to them was a hurried movement, allowed her to get her breath again. And as she went she tried to explain to the father what had happened, saying but little, however, of her own doings in the matter. The wife hung behind listening, exclaiming every now and again that her boy was killed, and then asking wild questions as to his being yet alive. The father, as he went, said little. He was known as a silent, sober man, well spoken of for diligence and general conduct, but supposed to be stern and very hard when angered.

As they drew near to the top of the path, the other man whispered something to him, and then he turned round upon Mally and stopped her.

'If he has come by his death between you, your blood shall be taken for his,' said he.

Then the wife shrieked out that her child had been murdered, and Mally, looking round into the faces of the three, saw that her grandfather's words had come true. They suspected her of having taken the life, in saving which she had nearly lost her own.

She looked round at them with awe in her face, and then,

without saying a word, preceded them down the path. What had she to answer when such a charge as that was made against her? If they chose to say that she pushed him into the pool, and hit him with her hook as he lay amidst the waters, how could she show that it was not so?

Poor Mally knew little of the law of evidence, and it seemed to her that she was in their hands. But as she went down the steep track with a hurried step,—a step so quick that they could not keep up with her,—her heart was very full,—very full and very high. She had striven for the man's life as though he had been her brother. The blood was yet not dry on her own legs and arms, where she had torn them in his service. At one moment she had felt sure that she would die with him in that pool. And now they said that she had murdered him! It may be that he was not dead, and what would he say if ever he should speak again? Then she thought of that moment when his eyes had opened, and he had seemed to see her. She had no fear for herself, for her heart was very high. But it was full also,—full of scorn, disdain, and wrath.

When she had reached the bottom, she stood close to the door of the hut waiting for them, so that they might precede her to the other group, which was there in front of them, at a little distance on the sand.

'He is there, and dada is with him. Go and look at him,' said Mally.

The father and mother ran on stumbling over the stones, but Mally remained behind by the door of the hut.

Barty Gunliffe was lying on the sand where Mally had left him, and old Malachi Trenglos was standing over him, resting himself with difficulty upon a stick.

'Not a move he's moved since she left him,' said he, 'not a move. I put his head on the old rug as you see, and I tried 'un with a drop of gin, but he wouldn't take it,—he wouldn't take it.'

'Oh, my boy! my boy!' said the mother, throwing herself beside her son upon the sand.

'Haud your tongue, woman,' said the father, kneeling down slowly by the lad's head, 'whimpering that way will do 'un no good.'

Then having gazed for a minute or two upon the pale face beneath him, he looked up sternly into that of Malachi Trenglos.

The old man hardly knew how to bear this terrible inquisition.

'He would come,' said Malachi; 'he brought it all upon hisself.'

'Who was it struck him?' said the father.

'Sure he struck hisself, as he fell among the breakers.'

'Liar!' said the father, looking up at the old man.

'They have murdered him!—they have murdered him!' shrieked the mother.

'Haud your peace, woman!' said the husband again. 'They shall give us blood for blood.'

Mally, leaning against the corner of the hovel, heard it all, but did not stir. They might say what they liked. They might make it out to be murder. They might drag her and her grandfather to Camelford Gaol, and then to Bodmin, and the gallows; but they could not take from her the conscious feeling that was her own. She had done her best to save him,—her very best. And she had saved him!

She remembered her threat to him before they had gone down on the rocks together, and her evil wish. Those words had been very wicked; but since that she had risked her life to save his. They might say what they pleased of her, and do what they pleased. She knew what she knew.

Then the father raised his son's head and shoulders in his arms, and called on the others to assist him in carrying Barty towards the path. They raised him between them carefully and tenderly, and lifted their burden on towards the spot at which Mally was standing. She never moved, but watched them at their work; and the old man followed them, hobbling after them with his crutch.

When they had reached the end of the hut she looked upon Barty's face, and saw that it was very pale. There was no longer blood upon the forehead, but the great gash was to be seen there plainly, with its jagged cut, and the skin livid and blue round the orifice. His light brown hair was hanging back, as she had made it to hang when she had gathered it with her hand after the big wave had passed over them. Ah, how beautiful he was in Mally's eyes with that pale face, and the sad scar upon his brow! She turned her face away, that they might not see her tears; but she did not move, nor did she speak.

But now, when they had passed the end of the hut, shuffling along with their burden, she heard a sound which stirred her. She roused herself quickly from her leaning posture, and stretched forth her head as though to listen; then she moved to follow them. Yes, they had stopped at the bottom of the path, and had again laid the body on the rocks. She heard that sound again, as of a long, long sigh, and then, regardless of any of them, she ran to the wounded man's head.

'He is not dead,' she said. 'There; he is not dead.'

As she spoke Barty's eyes opened, and he looked about him.

'Barty, my boy, speak to me,' said the mother.

Barty turned his face upon his mother, smiled, and then stared about him wildly.

'How is it with thee, lad?' said his father. Then Barty turned his face again to the latter voice, and as he did so his eyes fell upon Mally.

'Mally!' he said, 'Mally!'

It could have wanted nothing further to any of those present to teach them that, according to Barty's own view of the case, Mally had not been his enemy; and, in truth, Mally herself wanted no further triumph. That word had vindicated her, and she withdrew back to the hut.

'Dada,' she said, 'Barty is not dead, and I'm thinking they won't say anything more about our hurting him.'

Old Glos shook his head. He was glad the lad hadn't met his death there; he didn't want the young man's blood, but he knew what folk would say. The poorer he was the more sure the world would be to trample on him. Mally said what she could to comfort him, being full of comfort herself.

She would have crept up to the farm if she dared, to ask how Barty was. But her courage failed her when she thought of that, so she went to work again, dragging back the weed she had saved to the spot at which on the morrow she would load the donkey. As she did this she saw Barty's pony still standing patiently under the rock, so she got a lock of fodder and threw it down before the beast.

It had become dark down in the cove, but she was still dragging back the sea-weed, when she saw the glimmer of a lantern coming down the pathway. It was a most unusual sight, for lanterns were not common down in Malachi's Cove. Down came the lantern rather slowly,—much more slowly than she was in the habit of descending, and then through the gloom she saw the figure of a man standing at the bottom of the path. She went up to him, and saw that it was Mr. Gunliffe, the father.

'Is that Mally?' said Gunliffe.

'Yes, it is Mally; and how is Barty, Mr. Gunliffe?'

'You must come to 'un yourself, now at once,' said the farmer. 'He won't sleep a wink till he's seed you. You must not say but you'll come.'

'Sure I'll come if I'm wanted,' said Mally.

Gunliffe waited a moment, thinking that Mally might have to prepare herself, but Mally needed no preparation. She was dripping with salt water from the weed which she had been dragging, and her elfin locks were streaming wildly from her head; but, such as she was, she was ready.

'Dada's in bed,' she said, 'and I can go now if you please.'

Then Gunliffe turned round and followed her up the path, wondering at the life which this girl led so far away from all her sex. It was now dark night, and he had found her working at the very edge of the rolling waves by herself, in the darkness, while the only human being who might seem to be her protector had already gone to his bed.

When they were at the top of the cliff Gunliffe took her by her hand, and led her along. She did not comprehend this, but she made no attempt to take her hand from his. Something he said about falling on the cliffs, but it was muttered so lowly that Mally hardly understood him. But, in truth, the man knew that she had saved his boy's life, and that he had injured her instead of thanking her. He was now taking her to his heart, and as words were wanting to him, he was showing his love after this silent fashion. He held her by the hand as though she were a child, and Mally tripped along at his side asking him no questions.

When they were at the farm-yard gate, he stopped there for a moment.

'Mally, my girl,' he said, 'he'll not be content till he sees thee, but thou must not stay long wi' him, lass. Doctor says he's weak like, and wants sleep badly.'

Mally merely nodded her head, and then they entered the house. Mally had never been within it before, and looked about with wondering eyes at the furniture of the big kitchen. Did any idea of her future destiny flash upon her then, I wonder? But she did not pause here a moment, but was led up to the bedroom above stairs, where Barty was lying on his mother's bed.

'Is it Mally herself?' said the voice of the weak youth.

'It's Mally herself,' said the mother, 'so now you can say what you please.'

'Mally,' said he, 'Mally, it's along of you that I'm alive this moment.'

'I'll not forget it on her,' said the father, with his eyes turned away from her. 'I'll never forget it on her.'

'We hadn't a one but only him,' said the mother, with her apron up to her face.

'Mally, you be friends with me now?' said Barty.

To have been made lady of the manor of the cove for ever, Mally couldn't have spoken a word now. It was not only that the words and presence of the people there cowed her and made her speechless, but the big bed, and the looking-glass, and the unheard-of wonders of the chamber, made her feel her own insignificance. But she crept up to Barty's side, and put her hand upon his.

'I'll come and get the weed, Mally; but it shall all be for you,' said Barty.

'Indeed, you won't then, Barty dear,' said the mother; 'you'll never go near the awesome place again. What would we do if you were took from us?'

'He mustn't go near the hole if he does,' said Mally, speaking at last in a solemn voice, and imparting the knowledge which she had kept to herself while Barty was her enemy; ''specially not if the wind's any way from the nor'ard.'

'She'd better go down now,' said the father.

Barty kissed the hand which he held, and Mally, looking at him as he did so, thought that he was like an angel.

9110212 H

'You'll come and see us to-morrow, Mally,' said he.

To this she made no answer, but followed Mrs. Gunliffe out of the room. When they were down in the kitchen, the mother had tea for her, and thick milk, and a hot cake,—all the delicacies which the farm could afford. I don't know that Mally cared much for the eating and drinking that night, but she began to think that the Gunliffe's were good people,—very good people. It was better thus, at any rate, than being accused of murder and carried off to Camelford prison.

'I'll never forget it on her— never,' the father had said.

Those words stuck to her from that moment, and seemed to sound in her ears all the night. How glad she was that Barty had come down to the cove,—oh, yes, how glad! There was no question of his dying now, and as for the blow on his forehead, what harm was that to a lad like him?

'But father shall go with you,' said Mrs. Gunliffe, when Mally prepared to start for the cove by herself. Mally, however, would not hear of this. She could find her way to the cove whether it was light or dark.

'Mally, thou art my child now, and I shall think of thee so,' said the mother, as the girl went off by herself.

Mally thought of this, too, as she walked home. How could she become Mrs. Gunliffe's child; ah, how?

I need not, I think, tell the tale any further. That Mally did become Mrs. Gunliffe's child, and how she became so the reader will understand; and in process of time the big kitchen and all the wonders of the farmhouse were her own. The people said that Barty Gunliffe had married a mermaid out of the sea; but when it was said in Mally's hearing I doubt whether she liked it; and when Barty himself would call her a mermaid she would frown at him, and throw about her black hair, and pretend to cuff him with her little hand.

Old Glos was brought up to the top of the cliff, and lived his few remaining days under the roof of Mr. Gunliffe's house; and as for the cove and the right of seaweed, from that time forth all that has been supposed to attach itself to Gunliffe's farm, and I do not know that any of the neighbours are prepared to dispute the right.

GEORGE MEREDITH
(1828–1909)

'The Case of General Ople and Lady Camper' is the shortest and the best of Meredith's rare finished short stories. It originally appeared in 1877 in the July issue of *The New Quarterly Magazine*. The idea of the story is reputedly based on a real retired general, named Hopkins, who brought an action against a neighbour, Lady Eleanor Cathcart, for sending caricatures of him.

The Case of General Ople and Lady Camper

CHAPTER I

An excursion beyond the immediate suburbs of London, projected long before his pony-carriage was hired to conduct him, in fact ever since his retirement from active service, led General Ople across a famous common, with which he fell in love at once, to a lofty highway along the borders of a park, for which he promptly exchanged his heart, and so gradually within a stone's-throw or so of the river-side, where he determined not solely to bestow his affections but to settle for life. It may be seen that he was of an adventurous temperament, though he had thought fit to loosen his sword-belt. The pony-carriage, however, had been hired for the very special purpose of helping him to pass in review the lines of what he called country houses, cottages, or even sites for building, not too remote from sweet London: and as when Cœlebs[1] goes forth intending to pursue and obtain, there is no doubt of his bringing home a wife, the circumstance that there stood a house to let, in an airy situation, at a certain distance in hail of the metropolis he worshipped, was enough to kindle the

[1] Latin *cœlebs*, unmarried (of a man), hence our 'celibate'. Meredith is probably thinking of Hannah More's *Cœlebs in Search of a Wife* (1809), a collection of sketches gathered round a slight plot of a young man's search for an ideal wife.

General's enthusiasm. He would have taken the first he saw, had it not been for his daughter, who accompanied him, and at the age of eighteen was about to undertake the management of his house. Fortune, under Elizabeth Ople's guiding restraint, directed him to an epitome of the comforts. The place he fell upon is only to be described in the tongue of auctioneers, and for the first week after taking it he modestly followed them by terming it bijou.[2] In time, when his own imagination, instigated by a state of something more than mere contentment, had been at work on it, he chose the happy phrase, 'a gentlemanly residence.' For it was, he declared, a small estate. There was a lodge to it, resembling two sentry-boxes forced into union, where in one half an old couple sat bent, in the other half lay compressed; there was a back-drive to discoverable stables; there was a bit of grass that would have appeared a meadow if magnified; and there was a wall round the kitchen-garden and a strip of wood round the flower-garden. The prying of the outside world was impossible. Comfort, fortification, and gentlemanliness made the place, as the General said, an ideal English home.

The compass of the estate was half an acre, and perhaps a perch or two, just the size for the hugging love General Ople was happiest in giving. He wisely decided to retain the old couple at the lodge, whose members were used to restriction, and also not to purchase a cow, that would have wanted pasture. With the old man, while the old woman attended to the bell at the handsome front entrance with its gilt-spiked gates, he undertook to do the gardening; a business he delighted in, so long as he could perform it in a gentlemanly manner, that is to say, so long as he was not overlooked. He was perfectly concealed from the road. Only one house, and curiously indeed, only one window of the house, and further to show the protection extended to Douro Lodge, that window an attic, overlooked him. And the house was empty.

The house (for who can hope, and who should desire a commodious house, with conservatories, aviaries, pond and boat-shed, and other joys of wealth, to remain unoccupied) was taken two seasons later by a lady, of whom Fame, rolling like a dust-cloud from the place she had left, reported that she was eccentric. The

[2] Small and elegant.

word is uninstructive: it does not frighten. In a lady of a certain age, it is rather a characteristic of aristocracy in retirement. And at least it implies wealth.

General Ople was very anxious to see her. He had the sentiment of humble respectfulness toward aristocracy, and there was that in riches which aroused his admiration. London, for instance, he was not afraid to say he thought the wonder of the world. He remarked, in addition, that the sacking of London would suffice to make every common soldier of the foreign army of occupation an independent gentleman for the term of his natural days. But this is a nightmare! said he, startling himself with an abhorrent dream of envy of those enriched invading officers: for Booty is the one lovely thing which the military mind can contemplate in the abstract. His habit was to go off in an explosion of heavy sighs when he had delivered himself so far, like a man at war with himself.

The lady arrived in time: she received the cards of the neighbourhood, and signalized her eccentricity by paying no attention to them, excepting the card of a Mrs. Baerens, who had audience of her at once. By express arrangement, the card of General Wilson Ople, as her nearest neighbour, followed the card of the rector, the social head of the district; and the rector was granted an interview, but Lady Camper was not at home to General Ople. She is of superior station to me, and may not wish to associate with me, the General modestly said. Nevertheless he was wounded: for in spite of himself, and without the slightest wish to obtrude his own person, as he explained the meaning that he had in him, his rank in the British army forced him to be the representative of it, in the absence of any one of a superior rank. So that he was professionally hurt, and his heart being in his profession, it may be honestly stated that he was wounded in his feelings, though he said no, and insisted on the distinction. Once a day his walk for constitutional exercise compelled him to pass before Lady Camper's windows, which were not bashfully withdrawn, as he said humorously of Douro Lodge, in the seclusion of half-pay, but bowed out imperiously, militarily, like a generalissimo on horseback, and had full command of the road and levels up to the swelling park-foliage. He went by at a smart stride, with a delicate depression of his upright bearing, as though hastening to greet a friend in view, whose hand was getting ready for the shake. This much would have been observed by a housemaid; and considering his fine figure and the peculiar shining silveriness of his hair, the acceleration of his gait was noticeable. When he drove by, the pony's right ear was flicked, to the extreme indignation of a mettlesome little animal. It ensued in consequence that the General was borne flying under the eyes of Lady Camper, and such pace displeasing him, he reduced it invariably at a step or two beyond the corner of her grounds.

But neither he nor his daughter Elizabeth attached importance to so trivial a circumstance. The General punctiliously avoided glancing at the windows during the passage past them, whether in his wild career or on foot. Elizabeth took a side-shot, as one looks at a wayside tree. Their speech concerning Lady Camper was an exchange of commonplaces over her loneliness: and this condition of hers was the more perplexing to General Ople on his hearing from his daughter that the lady was very fine-looking, and not so very old, as he had fancied eccentric ladies must be. The rector's account of her, too, excited the mind. She had informed him bluntly, that she now and then went to church to save appearances, but was not a church-goer, finding it impossible to support the length of the service; might, however, be reckoned in subscriptions for all the charities, and left her pew open to poor people, and none but the poor. She had travelled over Europe, and knew the East. Sketches in water-colours of the scenes she had visited adorned her walls, and a pair of pistols, that she had found useful, she affirmed, lay on the writing-desk in her drawing-room. General Ople gathered from the rector that she had a great contempt for men: yet it was curiously varied with lamentations over the weakness of women. 'Really she cannot possibly be an example of that,' said the General, thinking of the pistols.

Now, we learn from those who have studied women on the chess-board, and know what ebony or ivory will do along particular lines, or hopping, that men much talked about will take possession of their thoughts; and certainly the fact may be accepted for one of their moves. But the whole fabric of our knowledge of them, which we are taught to build on this originally acute perception, is shattered when we hear, that it is exactly the same, in the same degree, in proportion to the amount of work they have to do, exactly the same with men and their thoughts in the case of women much talked about. So it was with General Ople, and nothing is left for me to say except, that there is broader ground than the chess-board. I am earnest in protesting the similarity of the singular couples on common earth, because otherwise the General is in peril of the accusation that he is a feminine character; and not simply was he a gallant officer, and a veteran in gunpowder strife, he was also (and it is an extraordinary thing that a genuine humility did not prevent it, and did survive it) a lord and conqueror of the sex. He had done his pretty bit of mischief, all in the way of honour, of course, but hearts had knocked. And now, with his bright white hair, his close-brushed white whiskers on a face burnt brown, his clear-cut features, and a winning droop of his eyelids, there was powder in him still, if not shot.

There was a lamentable susceptibility to ladies' charms. On the other hand, for the protection of the sex, a remainder of shyness kept him from active enterprise and in the state of suffering, so long as indications of encouragement were wanting. He had killed the soft ones, who came to him, attracted by the softness in him, to be killed: but clever women alarmed and paralyzed him. Their aptness to question and require immediate sparkling answers; their demand for fresh wit, of a kind that is not furnished by publications which strike it into heads with a hammer, and supply it wholesale; their various reading; their power of ridicule too; made them awful in his contemplation.

Supposing (for the inflammable officer was now thinking, and deeply thinking, of a clever woman), supposing that Lady Camper's pistols were needed in her defence one night: at the first report proclaiming her extremity, valour might gain an introduction to her upon easy terms, and would not be expected to be witty. She would, perhaps, after the excitement, admit his masculine superiority, in the beautiful old fashion, by fainting in his arms. Such was the reverie he passingly indulged, and only so could he venture to hope for an acquaintance with the formidable lady who was his next neighbour. But the proud society of the burglarious denied him opportunity.

Meanwhile, he learnt that Lady Camper had a nephew, and the young gentleman was in a cavalry regiment. General Ople met him outside his gates, received and returned a polite salute, liked his appearance and manners, and talked of him to Elizabeth, asking her if by chance she had seen him. She replied that she believed she had, and praised his horsemanship. The General discovered that he was an excellent sculler. His daughter was rowing him up the river when the young gentleman shot by, with a splendid stroke, in an outrigger, backed, and floating alongside presumed to enter into conversation, during which he managed to express regrets at his aunt's turn for solitariness. As they belonged to sister branches of the same Service, the General and Mr. Reginald Rolles had a theme in common, and a passion. Elizabeth told her father that nothing afforded her so much pleasure as to hear him talk with Mr. Rolles on military matters. General Ople assured her that it pleased him likewise. He began to spy about for Mr. Rolles, and it sometimes occurred that they conversed across the wall; it could hardly be avoided. A hint or two, an undefinable flying allusion, gave the General to understand that Lady Camper had not been happy in her marriage. He was pained to think of her misfortune; but as she was not over forty, the disaster was, perhaps, not irremediable; that is to say, if she could be taught to extend her forgiveness to men, and abandon her solitude. 'If,' he said to his daughter, 'Lady Camper should by any chance be induced to contract a second alliance, she would, one might expect, be humanized, and we should have highly agreeable neighbours.' Elizabeth artlessly hoped for such an event to take place.

She rarely differed with her father, up to whom, taking example from the world around him, she looked as the pattern of a man of wise conduct.

And he was one; and though modest, he was in good humour with himself, approved himself, and could say, that without boasting of success, he was a satisfied man, until he met his touchstone in Lady Camper.

CHAPTER II

THIS is the pathetic matter of my story, and it requires pointing out, because he never could explain what it was that seemed to him so cruel in it, for he was no brilliant son of fortune, he was no great pretender, none of those who are logically displaced from the heights they have been raised to, manifestly created to show the moral in Providence. He was modest, retiring, humbly contented; a gentlemanly residence appeased his ambition. Popular, he could own that he was, but not meteorically; rather by reason of his willingness to receive light than his desire to shed it. Why, then, was the terrible test brought to bear upon him, of all men? He was one of us; no worse, and not strikingly or perilously better; and he could not but feel, in the bitterness of his reflections upon an inexplicable destiny, that the punishment befalling him, unmerited as it was, looked like absence of Design in the scheme of things Above. It looked as if the blow had been dealt him by reckless chance. And to believe that, was for the mind of General Ople the having to return to his alphabet and recommence the ascent of the laborious mountain of understanding.

To proceed, the General's introduction to Lady Camper was owing to a message she sent him by her gardener, with a request that he would cut down a branch of a wych-elm, obscuring her view across his grounds toward the river. The General consulted with his daughter, and came to the conclusion, that as he could hardly despatch a written reply to a verbal message, yet greatly wished to subscribe to the wishes of Lady Camper, the best thing for him to do was to apply for an interview. He sent word that he would wait on Lady Camper immediately, and betook himself forthwith to his toilette. She was the niece of an earl.

Elizabeth commended his appearance, 'passed him,' as he would have said; and well she might, for his hat, surtout, trousers and boots, were worthy of an introduction to Royalty. A touch of scarlet silk round the neck gave him bloom, and better than that, the blooming consciousness of it.

'You are not to be nervous, papa,' Elizabeth said.

'Not at all,' replied the General. 'I say, not at all, my dear,' he repeated, and so betrayed that he had fallen into the nervous mood. 'I was saying, I have known worse mornings than this.' He turned to her and smiled brightly, nodded, and set his face to meet the future.

He was absent an hour and a half.

He came back with his radiance a little subdued, by no means eclipsed; as, when experience has afforded us matter for thought, we cease to shine dazzlingly, yet are not clouded; the rays have merely grown serener. The sum of his impressions was conveyed in the reflective utterance—'It only shows, my dear, how different the reality is from our anticipation of it!'

Lady Camper had been charming; full of condescension, neighbourly, friendly, willing to be satisfied with the sacrifice of the smallest branch of the wych-elm, and only requiring that much for complimentary reasons.

Elizabeth wished to hear what they were, and she thought the request rather singular; but the General begged her to bear in mind, that they were dealing with a very extraordinary woman; 'highly accomplished, really exceedingly handsome,' he said to himself, aloud.

The reasons were, her liking for air and view, and desire to see into her neighbour's grounds without having to mount to the attic.

Elizabeth gave a slight exclamation, and blushed.

'So, my dear, we are objects of interest to her ladyship,' said the General.

He assured her that Lady Camper's manners were delightful. Strange to tell, she knew a great deal of his antecedent history, things he had not supposed were known; 'little matters,' he remarked, by which his daughter faintly conceived a reference to the conquests of his dashing days. Lady Camper had deigned to impart some of her own, incidentally; that she was of Welsh blood, and born among the mountains. 'She has a romantic look,' was the General's comment; and that her husband had been an insatiable traveller before he became an invalid, and had never cared for Art. 'Quite an extraordinary circumstance, with such a wife!' the General said.

He fell upon the wych-elm with his own hands, under cover of the leafage, and the next day he paid his respects to Lady Camper, to inquire if her ladyship saw any further obstruction to the view.

'None,' she replied. 'And now we shall see what the two birds will do.'

Apparently, then, she entertained an animosity to a pair of birds in the tree.

'Yes, yes; I say they chirp early in the morning,' said General Ople.

'At all hours.'

'The song of birds . . .?' he pleaded softly for nature.

'If the nest is provided for them; but I don't like vagabond chirping.'

The General perfectly acquiesced. This, in an engagement with a clever woman, is what you should do, or else you are likely to find yourself planted unawares in a high wind, your hat blown off, and your coat-tails anywhere; in other words, you will stand ridiculous in your bewilderment; and General Ople ever footed with the utmost caution to avoid that quagmire of the ridiculous. The extremer quags he had hitherto escaped; the smaller, into which he fell in his agile evasions of the big, he had hitherto been blest in finding none to notice.

He requested her ladyship's permission to present his daughter. Lady Camper sent in her card.

Elizabeth Ople beheld a tall, handsomely-mannered lady, with good features and penetrating dark eyes, an easy carriage of her person and an agreeable voice, but (the vision of her age flashed out under the compelling eyes of youth) fifty if a day. The rich colouring confessed to it. But she was very pleasing, and Elizabeth's perception dwelt on it only because her father's manly chivalry had defended the lady against one year more than forty.

The richness of the colouring, Elizabeth feared, was artificial, and it caused her ingenuous young blood a shudder. For we are so devoted to nature when the dame is flattering us with her gifts, that we loathe the substitute, omitting to think how much less it is an imposition than a form of practical adoration of the genuine.

Our young detective, however, concealed her emotion of childish horror.

Lady Camper remarked of her, 'She seems honest, and that is the most we can hope of girls.'

'She is a jewel for an honest man,' the General sighed, 'some day!'

'Let us hope it will be a distant day.'

'Yet,' said the General, 'girls expect to marry.'

Lady Camper fixed her black eyes on him, but did not speak.

He told Elizabeth that her ladyship's eyes were exceedingly searching: 'Only,' said he, 'as I have nothing to hide, I am able to submit to inspection'; and he laughed slightly up to an arresting cough, and made the mantelpiece ornaments pass muster.

General Ople was the hero to champion a lady whose airs of haughtiness caused her to be somewhat backbitten. He assured everybody, that Lady Camper was much misunderstood; she was a most remarkable woman; she was a most affable and highly intelligent lady. Building up her attributes on a splendid climax, he declared she was pious, charitable, witty, and really an extraordinary artist. He laid particular stress on her artistic qualities, describing her power with the brush, her water-colour sketches, and also some immensely clever caricatures. As he talked of no one else, his friends heard enough of Lady Camper, who was anything but a favourite. The Pollingtons, the Wilders, the Wardens, the Baerens, the Goslings, and others of his acquaintance, talked of Lady Camper and General Ople rather maliciously. They were all City people, and they admired the General, but mourned that he should so abjectly have fallen at the feet of a lady as red with rouge as a railway bill. His not seeing it showed the state he was in. The sister of Mrs. Pollington, an amiable widow, relict of a large City warehouse, named Barcop, was chilled by a falling off in his attentions. His apology for not appearing at garden parties was, that he was engaged to wait on Lady Camper.

And at one time, her not condescending to exchange visits with the obsequious General was a topic fertile in irony. But she did condescend.

Lady Camper came to his gate unexpectedly, rang the bell, and was let in like an ordinary visitor. It happened that the General was gardening—not the pretty occupation of pruning—he was digging—and of necessity his coat was off, and he was hot, dusty, unpresentable. From adoring earth as the mother of roses, you may pass into a lady's presence without purification; you cannot (or so the General thought) when you are caught in the act of adoring the mother of cabbages. And though he himself loved the cabbage equally with the rose, in his heart respected the vegetable yet more than he esteemed the flower, for he gloried in his kitchen garden, this was not a secret for the world to know, and he almost heeled over on his beam ends when word was brought of the extreme honour Lady Camper had done him. He worked his arms hurriedly into his fatigue jacket, trusting to get away to the house and spend a couple of minutes on his adornment; and with any other visitor it might have been accomplished, but Lady Camper disliked sitting alone in a room. She was on the square of lawn as the General stole along the walk. Had she kept her back to him, he might have rounded her like the shadow of a dial, undetected. She was frightfully acute of hearing. She turned while he was in the agony of hesitation, in a queer attitude, one leg on the march, projected by a frenzied tip-toe of the hinder leg, the very fatallest moment she could possibly have selected for unveiling him.

Of course there was no choice but to surrender on the spot.

He began to squander his dizzy wits in profuse apologies. Lady Camper simply spoke of the nice little nest of a garden, smelt the flowers, accepted a Niel rose and a Rohan, a Céline, a Falcot, and La France.

'A beautiful rose indeed,' she said of the latter, 'only it smells of macassar oil.'

'Really, it never struck me, I say it never struck me before,' rejoined the General, smelling it as at a pinch of snuff. 'I was saying, I always . . .' And he tacitly, with the absurdest of smiles, begged permission to leave unterminated a sentence not in itself particularly difficult.

'I have a nose,' observed Lady Camper.

Like the nobly-bred person she was, according to General Ople's version of the interview on his estate, when he stood before her in his gardening costume, she put him at his ease, or she exerted herself to do so; and if he underwent considerable anguish, it was the fault of his excessive scrupulousness regarding dress, propriety, appearance.

He conducted her at her request to the kitchen garden and the handful of paddock, the stables and coach-house, then back to the lawn.

'It is the home for a young couple,' she said.

'I am no longer young,' the General bowed, with the sigh peculiar to this confession. 'I say, I am no longer young, but I call the place a gentlemanly residence. I was saying, I . . .'

'Yes, yes!' Lady Camper tossed her head, half closing her eyes, with a contraction of the brows, as if in pain.

He perceived a similar expression whenever he spoke of his residence.

Perhaps it recalled happier days to enter such a nest. Perhaps it had been such a home for a young couple that she had entered on her marriage with Sir Scrope Camper, before he inherited his title and estates.

The General was at a loss to conceive what it was.

It recurred at another mention of his idea of the nature of the residence. It was almost a paroxysm. He determined not to vex her reminiscences again; and as this resolution directed his mind to his residence, thinking it pre-eminently gentlemanly, his tongue committed the error of repeating it, with 'gentlemanlike' for a variation.

Elizabeth was out—he knew not where. The housemaid informed him, that Miss Elizabeth was out rowing on the water.

'Is she alone?' Lady Camper inquired of him.

'I fancy so,' the General replied.

'The poor child has no mother.'

'It has been a sad loss to us both, Lady Camper.'

'No doubt. She is too pretty to go out alone.'

'I can trust her.'

'Girls!'

'She has the spirit of a man.'

'That is well. She has a spirit; it will be tried.'

The General modestly furnished an instance or two of her spiritedness.

Lady Camper seemed to like this theme; she looked graciously interested.

'Still, you should not suffer her to go out alone,' she said.

'I place implicit confidence in her,' said the General; and Lady Camper gave it up.

She proposed to walk down the lanes to the river-side, to meet Elizabeth returning.

The General manifested alacrity checked by reluctance. Lady Camper had told him she objected to sit in a strange room by herself; after that, he could hardly leave her to dash upstairs to change his clothes; yet how, attired as he was, in a fatigue jacket, that warned him not to imagine his back view, and held him constantly a little to the rear of Lady Camper, lest she should be troubled by it;—and he knew the habit of the second rank to criticise the front—how consent to face the outer world in such style side by side with the lady he admired?

'Come,' said she; and he shot forward a step, looking as if he had missed fire.

'Are you not coming, General?'

He advanced mechanically.

Not a soul met them down the lanes, except a little one, to whom Lady Camper gave a small silver-piece, because she was a picture.

The act of charity sank into the General's heart, as any pretty performance will do upon a warm waxen bed.

Lady Camper surprised him by answering his thoughts. 'No; it's for my own pleasure.'

Presently she said, 'Here they are.'

General Ople beheld his daughter by the river-side at the end of the lane, under escort of Mr. Reginald Rolles.

It was another picture, and a pleasing one. The young lady and the young gentleman wore boating hats, and were both dressed in white, and standing by or just turning from the outrigger and light skiff they were about to leave in charge of a waterman. Elizabeth stretched a finger at arm's-length, issuing directions, which Mr. Rolles took up and worded further to the man, for the sake of emphasis; and he, rather than Elizabeth, was guilty of the half-start at sight of the persons who were approaching.

'My nephew, you should know, is intended for a working soldier,' said Lady Camper; 'I like that sort of soldier best.'

General Ople drooped his shoulders at the personal compliment.

She resumed. 'His pay is a matter of importance to him. You are aware of the smallness of a subaltern's pay.'

'I,' said the General, 'I say I feel my poor half-pay, having always been a working soldier myself, very important, I was saying, very important to me.'

'Why did you retire?'

Her interest in him seemed promising. He replied conscientiously, 'Beyond the duties of General of Brigade, I could not, I say I could not, dare to aspire; I can accept and execute orders; I shrink from responsibility.'

'It is a pity,' said she, 'that you were not, like my nephew Reginald, entirely dependent on your profession.'

She laid such stress on her remark, that the General, who had just expressed a very modest estimate of his abilities, was unable to reject the flattery of her assuming him to be a man of some fortune. He coughed, and said, 'very little.' The thought came to him that he might have to make a statement to her in time, and he emphasized, 'Very little indeed. Sufficient,' he assured her, 'for a gentlemanly appearance.'

'I have given you your warning,' was her inscrutable rejoinder, uttered within earshot of the young people, to whom, especially to Elizabeth, she was gracious. The damsel's boating uniform was praised, and her sunny flush of exercise and exposure.

Lady Camper regretted that she could not abandon her parasol: 'I freckle so easily.'

The General, puzzling over her strange words about a warning, gazed at the red rose of art on her cheek with an air of profound abstraction.

'I freckle so easily,' she repeated, dropping her parasol to defend her face from the calculating scrutiny.

'I burn brown,' said Elizabeth.

Lady Camper laid the bud of a Falcot rose against the young girl's cheek, but fetched streams of colour, that overwhelmed the momentary comparison of the sun-swarthed skin with the rich dusky yellow of the rose in its deepening inward to soft brown.

Reginald stretched his hand for the privileged flower, and she let him take it; then she looked at the General; but the General was looking, with his usual air of satisfaction, nowhere.

CHAPTER III

'LADY CAMPER is no common enigma,' General Ople observed to his daughter.

Elizabeth inclined to be pleased with her, for at her suggestion the General had bought a couple of horses, that she might ride in the park, accompanied by her father or the little groom. Still, the great lady was hard to read. She tested the resources of his income by all sorts of instigation to expenditure, which his gallantry could not withstand; she encouraged him to talk of his deeds in arms; she was friendly, almost affectionate, and most bountiful in the presents of fruit, peaches, nectarines, grapes, and hot-house wonders, that she showered on his table; but she was an enigma in her evident dissatisfaction with him for something he seemed to have left unsaid. And what could that be?

At their last interview she had asked him, 'Are you sure, General, you have nothing more to tell me?'

And as he remarked, when relating it to Elizabeth, 'One might really be tempted to misapprehend her ladyship's . . . I say one might commit oneself beyond recovery. Now, my dear, what do you think she intended?'

Elizabeth was 'burning brown,' or darkly blushing, as her manner was.

She answered, 'I am certain you know of nothing that would interest her; nothing, unless . . .'

'Well?' the General urged her.

'How can I speak it, papa?'

'You really can't mean . . .'

'Papa, what could I mean?'

'If I were fool enough!' he murmured. 'No, no, I am an old man. I was saying, I am past the age of folly.'

One day Elizabeth came home from her ride in a thoughtful mood. She had not, further than has been mentioned, incited her father to think of the age of folly; but voluntarily or not, Lady

Camper had, by an excess of graciousness amounting to downright invitation; as thus, 'Will you persist in withholding your confidence from me, General?' She added, 'I am not so difficult a person.' These prompting speeches occurred on the morning of the day when Elizabeth sat at his table, after a long ride into the country, profoundly meditative.

A note was handed to General Ople, with the request that he would step in to speak with Lady Camper in the course of the evening, or next morning. Elizabeth waited till his hat was on, then said, 'Papa, on my ride to-day, I met Mr. Rolles.'

'I am glad you had an agreeable escort, my dear.'

'I could not refuse his company.'

'Certainly not. And where did you ride?'

'To a beautiful valley; and there we met . . .'

'Her ladyship?'

'Yes.'

'She always admires you on horseback.'

'So you know it, papa, if she should speak of it.'

'And I am bound to tell you, my child,' said the General, 'that this morning Lady Camper's manner to me was . . . if I were a fool . . . I say, this morning I beat a retreat, but apparently she . . . I see no way out of it, supposing she . . .'

'I am sure she esteems you, dear papa,' said Elizabeth.

'You take to her, my dear?' the General inquired anxiously; 'a little?—a little afraid of her?'

'A little,' Elizabeth replied, 'only a little.'

'Don't be agitated about me.'

'No, papa; you are sure to do right.'

'But you are trembling.'

'Oh! no. I wish you success.'

General Ople was overjoyed to be reinforced by his daughter's good wishes. He kissed her to thank her. He turned back to her to kiss her again. She had greatly lightened the difficulty at least of a delicate position.

It was just like the imperious nature of Lady Camper to summon him in the evening to terminate the conversation of the morning, from the visible pitfall of which he had beaten a rather precipitate retreat. But if his daughter cordially wished him success, and Lady Camper offered him the crown of it, why then he had only to pluck up spirit, like a good commander who has to pass a fordable river in the enemy's presence; a dash, a splash, a rattling volley or two, and you are over, established on the opposite bank. But you must be positive of victory, otherwise, with the river behind you, your new position is likely to be ticklish. So the General entered Lady Camper's drawing-room warily, watching the fair enemy. He knew he was captivating, his old conquests whispered in his ears, and her reception of him all but pointed to a footstool at her feet. He might have fallen there at once, had he not remembered a hint that Mr. Reginald Rolles had dropped concerning Lady Camper's amazing variability.

Lady Camper began.

'General, you ran away from me this morning. Let me speak. And, by the way, I must reproach you; you should not have left it to me. Things have now gone so far that I cannot pretend to be blind. I know your feelings as a father. Your daughter's happiness . . .'

'My lady,' the General interposed, 'I have her distinct assurance that it is, I say it is wrapt up in mine.'

'Let me speak. Young people will say anything. Well, they have a certain excuse for selfishness; we have not. I am in some degree bound to my nephew; he is my sister's son.'

'Assuredly, my lady. I would not stand in his light, be quite assured. If I am, I was saying if I am not mistaken, I . . . and he is, or has the making of an excellent soldier in him, and is likely to be a distinguished cavalry officer.'

'He has to carve his own way in the world, General.'

'All good soldiers have, my lady. And if my position is not, after a considerable term of service, I say if . . .'

'To continue,' said Lady Camper: 'I never have liked early marriages. I was married in my teens before I knew men. Now I do know them, and now . . .'

The General plunged forward: 'The honour you do us now:—a mature experience is worth:—my dear Lady Camper, I have admired you:—and your objection to early marriages cannot apply to . . . indeed, madam, vigour, they say . . . though youth, of course . . . yet young people, as you observe . . . and I have, though perhaps my reputation is against it, I was saying I have a natural timidity with your sex, and I am grey-headed, white-headed, but happily without a single malady.'

Lady Camper's brows showed a trifling bewilderment. 'I am speaking of these young people, General Ople.'

'I consent to everything beforehand, my dear lady. He should be, I say Mr. Rolles should be provided for.'

'So should she, General, so should Elizabeth.'

'She shall be, she will, dear madam. What I have, with your permission, if—good heaven! Lady Camper, I scarcely know where I am. She would . . . I shall not like to lose her: you would not wish it. In time she will . . . she has every quality of a good wife.'

'There, stay there, and be intelligible,' said Lady Camper. 'She has every quality. Money should be one of them. Has she money?'

'Oh! my lady,' the General exclaimed, 'we shall not come upon your purse when her time comes.'

'Has she ten thousand pounds?'

'Elizabeth? She will have, at her father's death . . . but as for my income, it is moderate, and only sufficient to maintain a gentlemanly appearance in proper self-respect. I make no show. I say I make no show. A wealthy marriage is the last thing on earth I should have aimed at. I prefer quiet and retirement. Personally, I mean. That is my personal taste. But if the lady: I say if it should happen that the lady . . . and indeed I am not one to press a suit: but if she who distinguishes and honours me should chance to be wealthy, all I can do is to leave her wealth at her disposal, and that I do: I do that unreservedly. I feel I am very confused, alarmingly confused. Your ladyship merits a superior . . . I trust I have not . . . I am entirely at your ladyship's mercy.'

'Are you prepared, if your daughter is asked in marriage, to settle ten thousand pounds on her, General Ople?'

The General collected himself. In his heart he thoroughly appreciated the moral beauty of Lady Camper's extreme solicitude on behalf of his daughter's provision; but he would have desired a postponement of that and other material questions belonging to a distant future until his own fate was decided.

So he said: 'Your ladyship's generosity is very marked. I say it is very marked.'

'How, my good General Ople! how is it marked in any degree?' cried Lady Camper. 'I am not generous. I don't pretend to be; and certainly I don't want the young people to think me so. I want to be just. I have assumed that you intend to be the same. Then will you do me the favour to reply to me?'

The General smiled winningly and intently, to show her that he prized her, and would not let her escape his eulogies.

'Marked, in this way, dear madam, that you think of my daughter's future more than I. I say, more than her father himself does. I know I ought to speak more warmly, I feel warmly. I was never an eloquent man, and if you take me as a soldier, I am, as I have ever been in the service, I was saying I am Wilson Ople, of the grade of General, to be relied on for executing orders; and, madam, you are Lady Camper, and you command me. I cannot be more precise. In fact, it is the feeling of the necessity for keeping close to the business that destroys what I would say. I am in fact lamentably incompetent to conduct my own case.'

Lady Camper left her chair.

'Dear me, this is very strange, unless I am singularly in error,' she said.

The General now faintly guessed that he might be in error, for his part.

But he had burned his ships, blown up his bridges; retreat could not be thought of.

He stood, his head bent and appealing to her side-face, like one pleadingly in pursuit, and very deferentially, with a courteous vehemence, he entreated first her ladyship's pardon for his presumption, and then the gift of her ladyship's hand.

As for his language, it was the tongue of General Ople. But his bearing was fine. If his clipped white silken hair spoke of age, his figure breathed manliness. He was a picture, and she loved pictures.

For his own sake, she begged him to cease. She dreaded to hear of something 'gentlemanly.'

'This is a new idea to me, my dear General,' she said. 'You must give me time. People at our age have to think of fitness. Of course, in a sense, we are both free to do as we like. Perhaps I may be of some aid to you. My preference is for absolute independence. And I wished to talk of a different affair. Come to me to-morrow. Do not be hurt if I decide that we had better remain as we are.'

The General bowed. His efforts, and the wavering of the fair enemy's flag, had inspired him with a positive re-awakening of masculine passion to gain this fortress. He said well: 'I have, then, the happiness, madam, of being allowed to hope until to-morrow?'

She replied, 'I would not deprive you of a moment of happiness. Bring good sense with you when you do come.'

The General asked eagerly, 'I have your ladyship's permission to come early?'

'Consult your happiness,' she answered; and if to his mind she seemed returning to the state of enigma, it was on the whole deliciously. She restored him his youth. He told Elizabeth that night, he really must begin to think of marrying her to some worthy young fellow. 'Though,' said he, with an air of frank intoxication, 'my opinion is, the young ones are not so lively as the old in these days, or I should have been besieged before now.'

The exact substance of the interview he forbore to relate to his inquisitive daughter, with a very honourable discretion.

CHAPTER IV

ELIZABETH came riding home to breakfast from a gallop round the park, and passing Lady Camper's gates, received the salutation of her parasol. Lady Camper talked with her through the bars. There was not a sign to tell of a change or twist in her neighbourly affability. She remarked simply enough, that it was her nephew's habit to take early gallops, and possibly Elizabeth might have seen him, for his quarters were proximate; but she did not demand an answer. She had passed a rather restless night, she said. 'How is the General?'

'Papa must have slept soundly, for he usually calls to me through his door when he hears I am up,' said Elizabeth.

Lady Camper nodded kindly and walked on.

Early in the morning General Ople was ready for battle. His forces were, the anticipation of victory, a carefully arranged toilet, and an unaccustomed spirit of enterprise in the realms of speech; for he was no longer in such awe of Lady Camper.

'You have slept well?' she inquired.

'Excellently, my lady.'

'Yes, your daughter tells me she heard you, as she went by your door in the morning for a ride to meet my nephew. You are, I shall assume, prepared for business.'

'Elizabeth? . . . to meet . . .?' General Ople's impression of anything extraneous to his emotion was feeble and passed instantly. 'Prepared? Oh, certainly'; and he struck in a compliment on her ladyship's fresh morning bloom.

'It can hardly be visible,' she responded; 'I have not painted yet.'

'Does your ladyship proceed to your painting in the very early morning?'

'Rouge. I rouge.'

'Dear me! I should not have supposed it.'

'You have speculated on it very openly, General. I remember your trying to see a freckle through the rouge; but the truth is, I am of a supernatural paleness if I do not rouge, so I do. You understand, therefore, I have a false complexion. Now to business.'

'If your ladyship insists on calling it business. I have little to offer—myself!'

'You have a gentlemanly residence.'

'It is, my lady, it is. It is a bijou.'

'Ah!' Lady Camper sighed dejectedly.

'It is a perfect bijou!'

'Oblige me, General, by not pronouncing the French word as if you were swearing by something in English, like a trooper.'

General Ople started, admitted that the word was French, and apologized for his pronunciation. Her variability was now visible over a corner of the battlefield like a thunder-cloud.

'The business we have to discuss concerns the young people, General.'

'Yes,' brightened by this, he assented: 'Yes, dear Lady Camper; it is a part of the business; it is a secondary part; it has to be discussed; I say I subscribe beforehand. I may say, that honouring, esteeming you as I do, and hoping ardently for your consent . . .'

'They must have a home and an income, General.'

'I presume, dearest lady, that Elizabeth will be welcome in your home. I certainly shall never chase Reginald out of mine.'

Lady Camper threw back her head. 'Then you are not yet awake, or you practice the art of sleeping with open eyes! Now listen to me. I rouge, I have told you. I like colour, and I do not like to see wrinkles or have them seen. Therefore I rouge. I do not expect to deceive the world so flagrantly as to my age, and you I would not deceive for a moment. I am seventy.'

The effect of this noble frankness on the General, was to raise him from his chair in a sitting posture as if he had been blown up.

Her countenance was inexorably imperturbable under his alternate blinking and gazing that drew her close and shot her distant, like a mysterious toy.

'But,' said she, 'I am an artist; I dislike the look of extreme age, so I conceal it as well as I can. You are very kind to fall in with the deception: an innocent and, I think, a proper one, before the world, though not to the gentleman who does me the honour to propose to me for my hand. You desire to settle our business first. You esteem me; I suppose you mean as much as young people mean when they say they love. Do you? Let us come to an understanding.'

'I can,' the melancholy General gasped, 'I say I can—I cannot—I cannot credit your ladyship's . . .'

'You are at liberty to call me Angela.'

'Ange . . .' he tried it, and in shame relapsed. 'Madam, yes. Thanks.'

'Ah,' cried Lady Camper, 'do not use these vulgar contractions of decent speech in my presence. I abhor the word "thanks." It is fit for fribbles.'

'Dear me, I have used it all my life,' groaned the General.

'Then, for the remainder, be it understood that you renounce it. To continue, my age is . . .'

'Oh, impossible, impossible,' the General almost wailed; there was really a crack in his voice.

'Advancing to seventy. But, like you, I am happy to say I have not a malady. I bring no invalid frame to a union that necessitates the leaving of the front door open day and night to the doctor. My belief is, I could follow my husband still on a campaign, if he were a warrior instead of a pensioner.'

General Ople winced.

He was about to say humbly, 'As General of Brigade . . .'

'Yes, yes, you want a commanding officer, and that I have seen, and that has caused me to meditate on your proposal,' she interrupted him; while he, studying her countenance hard, with the painful aspect of a youth who lashes a donkey memory in an examination by word of mouth, attempted to marshal her signs of younger years against her awful confession of the extremely ancient, the witheringly ancient. But for the manifest rouge, manifest in spite of her declaration that she had not yet that morning proceeded to her paintbrush, he would have thrown down his glove to challenge her on the subject of her age. She had actually charms. Her mouth had a charm; her eyes were lively; her figure, mature if you like, was at least full and good; she stood upright, she had a queenly seat. His mental ejaculation was, 'What a wonderful constitution!'

By a lapse of politeness, he repeated it to himself half aloud; he was shockingly nervous.

'Yes, I have finer health than many a younger woman,' she said. 'An ordinary calculation would give me twenty good years to come. I am a widow, as you know. And, by the way, you have a leaning for widows. Have you not? I thought I had heard of a widow Barcop in this parish. Do not protest. I assure you I am a stranger to jealousy. My income . . .'

The General raised his hands.

'Well, then,' said the cool and self-contained lady, 'before I go farther, I may ask you, knowing what you have forced me to confess, are you still of the same mind as to marriage? And one moment, General. I promise you most sincerely that your withdrawing a step shall not, as far as it touches me, affect my neighbourly and friendly sentiments; not in any degree. Shall we be as we were?'

Lady Camper extended her delicate hand to him.

He took it respectfully, inspected the aristocratic and unshrunken fingers, and kissing them, said, 'I never withdraw from a position, unless I am beaten back. Lady Camper, I . . .'

'My name is Angela.'

The General tried again: he could not utter the name.

To call a lady of seventy Angela is difficult in itself. It is, it seems, thrice difficult in the way of courtship.

'Angela!' said she.

'Yes. I say, there is not a more beautiful female name, dear Lady Camper.'

'Spare me that word "female" as long as you live. Address me by that name, if you please.'

The General smiled. The smile was meant for propitiation and sweetness. It became a brazen smile.

'Unless you wish to step back,' said she.

'Indeed, no. I am happy, Lady Camper. My life is yours. I say, my life is devoted to you, dear madam.'

'Angela!'

General Ople was blushingly delivered of the name.

'That will do,' said she. 'And as I think it possible one may be admired too much as an artist, I must request you to keep my number of years a secret.'

'To the death, madam,' said the General.

'And now we will take a turn in the garden, Wilson Ople. And beware of one thing, for a commencement, for you are full of weeds, and I mean to pluck out a few: never call any place a gentlemanly residence in my hearing, nor let it come to my ears that you have been using the phrase elsewhere. Don't express astonishment. At present it is enough that I dislike it. But this only,' Lady Camper added, 'this only if it is not your intention to withdraw from your position.'

'Madam, my lady, I was saying—hem!—Angela, I *could* not wish to withdraw.'

Lady Camper leaned with some pressure on his arm, observing, 'You have a curious attachment to antiquities.'

'My dear lady, it is your mind; I say, it is your mind: I was saying, I am in love with your mind,' the General endeavoured to assure her, and himself too.

'Or is it my powers as an artist?'

'Your mind, your extraordinary powers of mind.'

'Well,' said Lady Camper, 'a veteran General of Brigade is as good a crutch as a childless old grannam[1] can have.'

And as a crutch, General Ople, parading her grounds with the aged woman, found himself used and treated.

The accuracy of his perceptions might be questioned. He was like a man stunned by some great tropical fruit, which responds to the longing of his eyes by falling on his head; but it appeared to him, that she increased in bitterness at every step they took, as if determined to make him realize her wrinkles.

He was even so inconsequent, or so little recognized his position, as to object in his heart to hear himself called Wilson.

It is true that she uttered Wilsonople as if the names formed one word. And on a second occasion (when he inclined to feel hurt) she remarked, 'I fear me, Wilsonople, if we are to speak plainly, thou art but a fool.' He, perhaps, naturally objected to that. He was, however, giddy, and barely knew.

Yet once more the magical woman changed. All semblance of harshness, and harridan-like spike-tonguedness vanished when she said adieu.

The astronomer, looking at the crusty jag and scoria[2] of the magnified moon through his telescope, and again with naked eyes at the soft-beaming moon, when the crater-ridges are faint as eyebrow-pencillings, has a similar sharp alternation of prospect to that which mystified General Ople.

But between watching an orb that is only variable at our caprice, and contemplating a woman who shifts and quivers ever with her own, how vast the difference!

And consider that this woman is about to be one's wife!

He could have believed (if he had not known full surely that such things are not) he was in the hands of a witch.

Lady Camper's 'adieu' was perfectly beautiful—a kind, cordial, intimate, above all, to satisfy his present craving, it was a lady-like adieu—the adieu of a delicate and elegant woman, who had hardly left her anchorage by forty to sail into the fifties.

[1] Grandmother. [2] Clinker-like dross or slag left after volcanic eruption (or after metal-smelting).

Alas! he had her word for it, that she was not less than seventy. And, worse, she had betrayed most melancholy signs of sourness and agedness as soon as he had sworn himself to her fast and fixed.

'The road is open to you to retreat,' were her last words.

'My road,' he answered gallantly, 'is forward.'

He was drawing backwards as he said it, and something provoked her to smile.

CHAPTER V

It is a noble thing to say that your road is forward, and it befits a man of battles. General Ople was too loyal a gentleman to think of any other road. Still, albeit not gifted with imagination, he could not avoid the feeling that he had set his face to Winter. He found himself suddenly walking straight into the heart of Winter, and a nipping Winter. For her ladyship had proved acutely nipping. His little customary phrases, to which Lady Camper objected, he could see no harm in whatever. Conversing with her in the privacy of domestic life would never be the flowing business that it is for other men. It would demand perpetual vigilance, hop, skip, jump, flounderings, and apologies.

This was not a pleasing prospect.

On the other hand, she was the niece of an earl. She was wealthy. She might be an excellent friend to Elizabeth; and she could be, when she liked, both commandingly and bewitchingly ladylike.

Good! But he was a General Officer of not more than fifty-five, in his full vigour, and she a woman of seventy!

The prospect was bleak. It resembled an outlook on the steppes. In point of the discipline he was to expect, he might be compared to a raw recruit, and in his own home!

However, she was a woman of mind. One would be proud of her.

But did he know the worst of her? A dreadful presentiment, that he did not know the worst of her, rolled an ocean of gloom upon General Ople, striking out one solitary thought in the obscurity, namely, that he was about to receive punishment for retiring from active service to a life of ease at a comparatively early age, when still in marching trim. And the shadow of the thought was, that he deserved the punishment!

He was in his garden with the dawn. Hard exercise is the best of opiates for dismal reflections. The General discomposed his daughter by offering to accompany her on her morning ride before breakfast. She considered that it would fatigue him. 'I am not a man of eighty!' he cried. He could have wished he had been.

He led the way to the park, where they soon had sight of young Rolles, who checked his horse and spied them like a vedette,[1] but, perceiving that he had been seen, came cantering, and hailing the General with hearty wonderment.

'And what's this the world says, General?' said he. 'But we all applaud your taste. My aunt Angela was the handsomest woman of her time.'

The General murmured in confusion, 'Dear me!' and looked at the young man, thinking that he could not have known the time.

'Is all arranged, my dear General?'

'Nothing is arranged, and I beg—I say I beg . . . I came out for fresh air and pace.'

The General rode frantically.

In spite of the fresh air, he was unable to eat at breakfast. He was bound, of course, to present himself to Lady Camper, in common civility, immediately after it.

And first, what were the phrases he had to avoid uttering in her presence? He could remember only the 'gentlemanly residence.' And it was a gentlemanly residence, he thought as he took leave of it. It was one, neatly named to fit the place. Lady Camper is indeed a most eccentric person! he decided from his experience of her.

He was rather astonished that young Rolles should have spoken so coolly of his aunt's leaning to matrimony; but perhaps her exact age was unknown to the younger members of her family.

This idea refreshed him by suggesting the extremely honourable nature of Lady Camper's uncomfortable confession.

[1] Mounted sentry placed in advance of an outpost.

He himself had an uncomfortable confession to make. He would have to speak of his income. He was living up to the edges of it.

She is an upright woman, and I must be the same! he said, fortunately not in her hearing.

The subject was disagreeable to a man sensitive on the topic of money, and feeling that his prudence had recently been misled to keep up appearances.

Lady Camper was in her garden, reclining under the parasol. A chair was beside her, to which, acknowledging the salutation of her suitor, she waved him.

'You have met my nephew Reginald this morning, General?'

'Curiously, in the park, this morning, before breakfast, I did, yes. Hem! I, I say I did meet him. Has your ladyship seen him?'

'No. The park is very pretty in the early morning.'

'Sweetly pretty.'

Lady Camper raised her head, and with the mildness of assured dictatorship, pronounced: 'Never say that before me.'

'I submit, my lady,' said the poor scourged man.

'Why, naturally you do. Vulgar phrases have to be endured, except when our intimates are guilty, and then we are not merely offended, we are compromised by them. You are still of the mind in which you left me yesterday? You are one day older. But I warn you, so am I.'

'Yes, my lady, we cannot, I say we cannot check time. Decidedly of the same mind. Quite so.'

'Oblige me by never saying "Quite so." My lawyer says it. It reeks of the City of London. And do not look so miserable.'

'I, madam? my dear lady!' the General flashed out in a radiance that dulled instantly.

'Well,' said she cheerfully, 'and you're for the old woman?'

'For Lady Camper.'

'You are seductive in your flatteries, General. Well, then, we have to speak of business.'

'My affairs——' General Ople was beginning, with perturbed forehead; but Lady Camper held up her finger.

'We will touch on your affairs incidentally. Now listen to me, and do not exclaim until I have finished. You know that these two young ones have been whispering over the wall for some months. They have been meeting on the river and in the park habitually, apparently with your consent.'

'My lady!'

'I did not say with your connivance.'

'You mean my daughter Elizabeth?'

'And my nephew Reginald. We have named them, if that advances us. Now, the end of such meetings is marriage, and the sooner the better, if they are to continue. I would rather they should not; I do not hold it good for young soldiers to marry. But if they do, it is very certain that their pay will not support a family; and in a marriage of two healthy young people, we have to assume the existence of the family. You have allowed matters to go so far that the boy is hot in love; I suppose the girl is, too. She is a nice girl. I do not object to her personally. But I insist that a settlement be made on her before I give my nephew one penny. Hear me out, for I am not fond of business, and shall be glad to have done with these explanations. Reginald has nothing of his own. He is my sister's son, and I loved her, and rather like the boy. He has at present four hundred a year from me. I will double it, on the condition that you at once make over ten thousand—not less; and let it be yes or no!—to be settled on your daughter and go to her children, independent of the husband—*cela va sans dire.*[2] Now you may speak, General.'

The General spoke, with breath fetched from the deeps:

'Ten thousand pounds! Hem! Ten! Hem, frankly—ten, my lady! One's income—I am quite taken by surprise. I say Elizabeth's conduct—though, poor child! it is natural to her to seek a mate, I mean, to accept a mate and an establishment, and Reginald is a very hopeful fellow—I was saying, they jump on me out of an ambush, and I wish them every happiness. And she is an ardent soldier, and a soldier she must marry. But ten thousand!'

'It is to secure the happiness of your daughter, General.'

'Pounds! my lady. It would rather cripple me.'

'You would have my house, General; you would have the moiety, as the lawyers say, of my purse; you would have horses,

[2] That goes without saying.

carriages, servants; I do not divine what more you would wish to have.'

'But, madam—a pensioner on the Government! I can look back on past services, I say old services, and I accept my position. But, madam, a pensioner on my wife, bringing next to nothing to the common estate! I fear my self-respect would, I say would . . .'

'Well, and what would it do, General Ople?'

'I was saying, my self-respect as my wife's pensioner, my lady. I could not come to her empty-handed.'

'Do you expect that I should be the person to settle money on your daughter, to save her from mischances? A rakish husband, for example; for Reginald is young, and no one can guess what will be made of him.'

'Undoubtedly your ladyship is correct. We might try absence for the poor girl. I have no female relation, but I could send her to the sea-side to a lady-friend.'

'General Ople, I forbid you, as you value my esteem, ever—and I repeat, I forbid you ever—to afflict my ears with that phrase, "lady-friend!"'

The General blinked in a state of insurgent humility.

These incessant whippings could not but sting the humblest of men; and 'lady-friend,' he was sure, was a very common term, used, he was sure, in the very best society. He had never heard Her Majesty speak at levées of a lady-friend, but he was quite sure that she had one; and if so, what could be the objection to her subjects mentioning it as a term to suit their own circumstances?

He was harassed and perplexed by old Lady Camper's treatment of him, and he resolved not to call her Angela even upon supplication—not that day, at least.

She said, 'You will not need to bring property of any kind to the common estate; I neither look for it nor desire it. The generous thing for you to do would be to give your daughter all you have, and come to me.'

'But, Lady Camper, if I denude myself or curtail my income—a man at his wife's discretion, I was saying a man at his wife's mercy . . .!'

General Ople was really forced, by his manly dignity, to make this protest on its behalf. He did not see how he could have escaped doing so; he was more an agent than a principal. 'My wife's mercy,' he said again, but simply as a herald proclaiming superior orders.

Lady Camper's brows were wrathful. A deep blood-crimson overcame the rouge, and gave her a terrible stormy look.

'The congress now ceases to sit, and the treaty is not concluded,' was all she said.

She rose, bowed to him, 'Good morning, General,' and turned her back.

He sighed. He was a free man. But this could not be denied—whatever the lady's age, she was a grand woman in her carriage, and when looking angry, she had a queen-like aspect that raised her out of the reckoning of time.

So now he knew there was a worse behind what he had previously known. He was precipitate in calling it the worst. 'Now,' said he to himself, 'I know the worst!'

No man should ever say it. Least of all, one who has entered into relations with an eccentric lady.

CHAPTER VI

POLITENESS required that General Ople should not appear to rejoice in his dismissal as a suitor, and should at least make some show of holding himself at the beck of a reconsidering mind. He was guilty of running up to London early next day, and remaining absent until nightfall; and he did the same on the two following days. When he presented himself at Lady Camper's lodge-gates, the astonishing intelligence, that her ladyship had departed for the Continent and Egypt gave him qualms of remorse, which assumed a more definite shape in something like awe of her triumphant constitution. He forebore to mention her age, for he was the most honourable of men, but a habit of tea-table talkativeness impelled him to say and repeat an idea that had visited him, to the effect, that Lady Camper was one of those wonderful women who are comparable to brilliant generals, and defend themselves from the siege of Time by various aggressive movements.

Fearful of not being understood, owing to the rarity of the occasions when the squat plain squad of honest Saxon regulars at his command were called upon to explain an idea, he re-cast the sentence. But, as it happened that the regulars of his vocabulary were not numerous, and not accustomed to work upon thoughts and images, his repetitions rather succeeded in exposing the piece of knowledge he had recently acquired than in making his meaning plainer. So we need not marvel that his acquaintances should suppose him to be secretly aware of an extreme degree in which Lady Camper was a veteran.

General Ople entered into the gaieties of the neighbourhood once more, and passed through the Winter cheerfully. In justice to him, however, it should be said that to the intent dwelling of his mind upon Lady Camper, and not to the festive life he led, was due his entire ignorance of his daughter's unhappiness. She lived with him, and yet it was in other houses he learnt that she was unhappy. After his last interview with Lady Camper, he had informed Elizabeth of the ruinous and preposterous amount of money demanded of him for a settlement upon her: and Elizabeth, like the girl of good sense that she was, had replied immediately, 'It could not be thought of, papa.' He had spoken to Reginald likewise. The young man fell into a dramatic tearing-of-hair and long-stride fury, not ill becoming an enamoured dragoon. But he maintained that his aunt, though an eccentric, was a cordially kind woman. He seemed to feel, if he did not partly hint, that the General might have accepted Lady Camper's terms. The young officer could no longer be welcome at Douro Lodge, so the General paid him a morning call at his quarters, and was distressed to find him breakfasting very late, tapping eggs that he forgot to open—one of the surest signs of a young man downright and deep in love, as the General knew from experience—and surrounded by uncut sporting journals of past weeks, which dated from the day when his blow had struck him, as accurately as the watch of the drowned man marks his minute. Lady Camper had gone to Italy, and was in communication with her nephew: Reginald was not further explicit. His legs were very prominent in his despair, and his fingers frequently performed the part of blunt combs; consequently the General was impressed by his passion for Elizabeth. The girl who, if she was often meditative, always met his eyes with a smile, and quietly said 'Yes, papa,' and 'No, papa,' gave him little concern as to the state of her feelings. Yet everybody said now that she was unhappy. Mrs. Barcop, the widow, raised her voice above the rest. So attentive was she to Elizabeth that the General had it kindly suggested to him, that some one was courting him through his daughter. He gazed at the widow. Now she was not much past thirty; and it was really singular—he could have laughed—thinking of Mrs. Barcop set him persistently thinking of Lady Camper. That is to say, his mad fancy reverted from the lady of perhaps thirty-five to the lady of seventy! Such, thought he, is genius in a woman! Of his neighbours generally, Mrs. Baerens, the wife of a German merchant, an exquisite player on the pianoforte, was the most inclined to lead him to speak of Lady Camper. She was a kind prattling woman, and was known to have been a governess before her charms withdrew the gastronomic Gottried Baerens from his devotion to the well-served City club, where, as he exclaimed (ever turning fondly to his wife as he vocalized the compliment), he had found every necessity, every luxury, in life, 'as you cannot have dem out of London—all save de female!' Mrs. Baerens, a lady of Teutonic extraction, was distinguishable as of that sex; at least, she was not masculine. She spoke with great respect of Lady Camper and her family, and seemed to agree in the General's eulogies of Lady Camper's constitution. Still he thought she eyed him strangely.

One April morning the General received a letter with the Italian postmark. Opening it with his usual calm and happy curiosity, he perceived that it was composed of pen-and-ink drawings. And suddenly his heart sank like a scuttled ship. He saw himself the victim of a caricature.

The first sketch had merely seemed picturesque, and he supposed it a clever play of fancy by some travelling friend, or perhaps an actual scene slightly exaggerated. Even on reading, 'A distant view of the city of Wilsonople,' he was only slightly enlightened. His heart beat still with befitting regularity. But the second and the third sketches betrayed the terrible hand. The distant view of the city of Wilsonople was fair with glittering domes, which, in the succeeding near view, proved to have been soap-bubbles, for a place of extreme flatness, begirt with crazy old-fashioned fortifications, was shown; and in the third view, representing the interior, stood for sole place of habitation, a sentry-box.

Most minutely drawn, and, alas! with fearful accuracy, a military gentleman in undress occupied the box. Not a doubt could exist as to the person it was meant to be.

The General tried hard to remain incredulous. He remembered too well who had called him Wilsonople.

But here was the extraordinary thing that sent him over the neighbourhood canvassing for exclamations: on the fourth page was the outline of a lovely feminine hand, holding a pen, as in the act of shading, and under it these words: '*What I say is, I say I think it exceedingly unladylike.*'

Now consider the General's feelings when, turning to this fourth page, having these very words in his mouth, as the accurate expression of his thoughts, he discovered them written!

An enemy who anticipates the actions of our mind, has a quality of the malignant divine that may well inspire terror. The senses of General Ople were struck by the aspect of a lurid Goddess, who penetrated him, read him through, and had both power and will to expose and make him ridiculous for ever.

The loveliness of the hand, too, in a perplexing manner contested his denunciation of her conduct. It was ladylike eminently, and it involved him in a confused mixture of the moral and material, as great as young people are known to feel when they make the attempt to separate them, in one of their frenzies.

With a petty bitter laugh he folded the letter, put it in his breast-pocket, and sallied forth for a walk, chiefly to talk to himself about it. But as it absorbed him entirely, he showed it to the rector, whom he met, and what the rector said is of no consequence, for General Ople listened to no remarks, calling in succession on the Pollingtons, the Goslings, the Baerens, and others, early though it was, and the lords of those houses absent amassing hoards; and to the ladies everywhere he displayed the sketches he had received, observing, that Wilsonople meant himself; and there he was, he said, pointing at the capped fellow in the sentry-box, done unmistakably. The likeness indeed was remarkable. 'She is a woman of genius,' he ejaculated, with utter melancholy. Mrs. Baerens, by the aid of a magnifying glass, assisted him to read a line under the sentry-box, that he had taken for a mere trembling dash; it ran, *A gentlemanly residence.*

'What eyes she has!' the General exclaimed; 'I say it is miraculous what eyes she has at her time of . . . I was saying, I should never have known it was writing.'

He sighed heavily. His shuddering sensitiveness to caricature was increased by a certain evident dread of the hand which struck; the knowing that he was absolutely bare to this woman, defenceless, open to exposure in his little whims, foibles, tricks, incompetencies, in what lay in his heart, and the words that would come to his tongue. He felt like a man haunted.

So deeply did he feel the blow, that people asked how it was that he could be so foolish as to dance about assisting Lady Camper in her efforts to make him ridiculous; he acted the parts of publisher and agent for the fearful caricaturist. In truth, there was a strangely double reason for his conduct; he danced about for sympathy, he had the intensest craving for sympathy, but more than this, or quite as much, he desired to have the powers of his enemy widely appreciated; in the first place, that he might be excused to himself for wincing under them, and secondly, because an awful admiration of her, that should be deepened by a corresponding sentiment around him, helped him to enjoy luxurious recollections of an hour when he was near making her his own—his own, in the holy abstract contemplation of marriage, without realizing their probable relative conditions after the ceremony.

'I say, that is the very image of her ladyship's hand,' he was especially fond of remarking, 'I say it is a beautiful hand.'

He carried the letter in his pocket-book; and beginning to fancy that she had done her worst, for he could not imagine an inventive malignity capable of pursuing the theme, he spoke of her treatment of him with compassionate regret, not badly assumed from being partly sincere.

Two letters dated in France, the one Dijon, the other

Fontainebleau, arrived together; and as the General knew Lady Camper to be returning to England, he expected that she was anxious to excuse herself to him. His fingers were so confident, for he tore one of the letters to open it.

The City of Wilsonople was recognizable immediately. So likewise was the sole inhabitant.

General Ople's petty bitter laugh recurred, like a weakchested patient's cough in the shifting of our winds eastward.

A faceless woman's shadow kneels on the ground near the sentry-box, weeping. A faceless shadow of a young man on horseback is beheld galloping toward a gulf. The sole inhabitant contemplates his largely substantial full fleshed face and figure in a glass.

Next, we see the standard of Great Britain furled; next, unfurled and borne by a troop of shadows to the sentry-box. The officer within says, 'I say I should be very happy to carry it, but I cannot quit this gentlemanly residence.'

Next, the standard is shown assailed by popguns. Several of the shadows are prostrate. 'I was saying, I assure you that nothing but this gentlemanly residence prevents me from heading you,' says the gallant officer.

General Ople trembled with protestant indignation when he saw himself reclining in a magnified sentry-box, while detachments of shadows hurry to him to show him the standard of his country trailing in the dust; and he is maliciously made to say, 'I dislike responsibility. I say I am a fervent patriot, and very fond of my comforts, but I shun responsibility.'

The second letter contained scenes between Wilsonople and the Moon.

He addresses her as his neighbour, and tells her of his triumphs over the sex.

He requests her to inform him whether she is a 'female,' that she may be triumphed over.

He hastens past her window on foot, with his head bent, just as the General had been in the habit of walking.

He drives a mouse-pony furiously by.

He cuts down a tree, that she may peep through.

Then, from the Moon's point of view, Wilsonople, a Silenus, is discerned in an arm-chair winking at a couple too plainly pouting their lips for a doubt of their intentions to be entertained.

A fourth letter arrived, bearing date of Paris. This one illustrated Wilsonople's courtship of the Moon, and ended with his 'saying,' in his peculiar manner, '*In spite of her paint I could not have conceived her age to be so enormous.*'

How break off his engagement with the Lady Moon? Consent to none of her terms!

Little used as he was to read behind a veil, acuteness of suffering sharpened the General's intelligence to a degree that sustained him in animated dialogue with each succeeding sketch, or poisoned arrow whirring at him from the moment his eyes rested on it; and here are a few samples:—

'Wilsonople informs the Moon that she is "sweetly pretty."

'He thanks her with "thanks" for a handsome piece of lunar green cheese.

'He points to her, apparently telling some one, "my lady-friend."

'He sneezes "Bijou! bijou! bijou!"'

They were trifles, but they attacked his habits of speech; and he began to grow more and more alarmingly absurd in each fresh caricature of his person.

He looked at himself as the malicious woman's hand had shaped him. It was unjust; it was no resemblance—and yet it was! There was a corner of likeness left that leavened the lump; henceforth he must walk abroad with this distressing image of himself before his eyes, instead of the satisfactory reflex of the man who had, and was happy in thinking that he had, done mischief in his time. Such an end for a conquering man was too pathetic.

The General surprised himself talking to himself in something louder than a hum at neighbours' dinner-tables. He looked about and notice that people were silently watching him.

CHAPTER VII

Lady Camper's return was the subject of speculation in the neighbourhood, for most people thought she would cease to persecute the General with her preposterous and unwarrantable pen-and-ink sketches when living so closely proximate; and how he would behave was the question. Those who made a hero of him were sure he would treat her with disdain. Others were uncertain. He had been so severely hit that it seemed possible he would not show much spirit.

He, for his part, had come to entertain such dread of the post, that Lady Camper's return relieved him of his morning apprehensions; and he would have forgiven her, though he feared to see her, if only she had promised to leave him in peace for the future. He feared to see her, because of the too probable furnishing of fresh matter for her ladyship's hand. Of course he could not avoid being seen by her, and that was a particular misery. A gentlemanly humility, or demureness of aspect, when seen, would, he hoped, disarm his enemy. It should, he thought. He had borne unheard-of things. No one of his friends and acquaintances knew, they could not know, what he had endured. It had caused him fits of stammering. It had destroyed the composure of his gait. Elizabeth had informed him that he talked to himself incessantly, and aloud. She, poor child, looked pale too. She was evidently anxious about him.

Young Rolles, whom he had met now and then, persisted in praising his aunt's good heart. So, perhaps, having satiated her revenge, she might now be inclined for peace, on the terms of distant civility.

'Yes! poor Elizabeth!' sighed the General, in pity of the poor girl's disappointment; 'poor Elizabeth! she little guesses what her father has gone through. Poor child! I say, she hasn't an idea of my sufferings.'

General Ople delivered his card at Lady Camper's lodge-gates, and escaped to his residence in a state of prickly heat that required the brushing of his hair with hard brushes for several minutes to comfort and re-establish him.

He had fallen to working in his garden, when Lady Camper's card was brought to him an hour after the delivery of his own; a pleasing promptitude, showing signs of repentance, and suggesting to the General instantly some sharp sarcasms upon women, which he had come upon in quotations in the papers and the pulpit, his two main sources of information.

Instead of handing back the card to the maid, he stuck it in his hat and went on digging.

The first of a series of letters containing shameless realistic caricatures was handed to him the afternoon following. They came fast and thick. Not a day's interval of grace was allowed. Niobe under the shafts of Diana was hardly less violently and mortally assailed. The deadliness of the attack lay in the ridicule of the daily habits of one of the most sensitive of men, as to his personal appearance, and the opinion of the world. He might have concealed the sketches, but he could not have concealed the bruises, and people were perpetually asking the unhappy General what he was saying, for he spoke to himself as if he were repeating something to them for the tenth time.

'I say,' said he, 'I say that for a lady, really an educated lady, to sit, as she must—I was saying, she must have sat in an attic to have the right view of me. And there you see—this is what she has done. This is the last, this is the afternoon's delivery. Her ladyship has me correctly as to costume, but I could not exhibit such a sketch to ladies.'

A back view of the General was displayed in his act of digging.

'I say I could not allow ladies to see it,' he informed the gentlemen, who were suffered to inspect it freely.

'But you see, I have no means of escape; I am at her mercy from morning to night,' the General said, with a quivering tongue, 'unless I stay at home inside the house; and that is death to me, or unless I abandon the place, and my lease; and I shall—I say, I shall find nowhere in England for anything like the money or conveniences such a gent—a residence you would call fit for a gentleman. I call it a bi . . . it is, in short, a gem. But I shall have to go.'

Young Rolles offered to expostulate with his aunt Angela.

The General said, 'Tha . . . I thank you very much. I would not have her ladyship suppose I am so susceptible. I hardly know,' he confessed pitiably, 'what it is right to say, and what not—what not. I—I—I never know when I am not looking a fool. I hurry from tree to tree to shun the light. I am seriously affected in my appetite. I say, I shall have to go.'

Reginald gave him to understand that if he flew, the shafts

would follow him, for Lady Camper would never forgive his running away, and was quite equal to publishing a book of the adventures of Wilsonople.

Sunday afternoon, walking in the park with his daughter on his arm, General Ople met Mr. Rolles. He saw that the young man and Elizabeth were mortally pale, and as the very idea of wretchedness directed his attention to himself, he addressed them conjointly on the subject of his persecution, giving neither of them a chance of speaking until they were constrained to part.

A sketch was the consequence, in which a withered Cupid and a fading Psyche were seen divided by Wilsonople, who keeps them forcibly asunder with policeman's fists, while courteously and elegantly entreating them to hear him. 'Meet,' he tells them, 'as often as you like, in my company, so long as you listen to me'; and the pathos of his aspect makes hungry demand for a sympathetic audience.

Now, this, and not the series representing the martyrdom of the old couple at Douro Lodge Gates, whose rigid frames bore witness to the close packing of a gentlemanly residence, this was the sketch General Ople, in his madness from the pursuing bite of the gad-fly, handed about at Mrs. Pollington's lawn-party. Some have said, that he should not have betrayed his daughter; but it is reasonable to suppose he had no idea of his daughter's being the Psyche. Or if he had, it was indistinct, owing to the violence of his personal emotion. Assuming this to have been the very sketch; he handed it to two or three ladies in turn, and was heard to deliver himself at intervals in the following snatches: 'As you like, my lady, as you like; strike, I say strike; I bear it; I say I bear it. . . . If her ladyship is unforgiving, I say I am enduring. . . . I may go, I was saying I may go mad, but while I have my reason I walk upright, I walk upright.'

Mr. Pollington and certain City gentlemen hearing the poor General's renewed soliloquies, were seized with disgust of Lady Camper's conduct, and stoutly advised an application to the Law Courts.

He gave ear to them abstractedly, but after pulling out the whole chapter of the caricatures (which it seemed that he kept in a case of morocco leather in his breast-pocket), showing them, with comments on them, and observing, 'There will be more, there must be more, I say I am sure there are things I do that her ladyship will discover and expose,' he declined to seek redress or simple protection; and the miserable spectacle was exhibited soon after of this courtly man listening to Mrs. Barcop on the weather, and replying in acquiescence: 'It is hot.—If your ladyship will only abstain from colours. Very hot as you say madam,—I do not complain of pen and ink, but I would rather escape colours. And I dare say you find it hot too?'

Mrs. Barcop shut her eyes and sighed over the wreck of a handsome military officer.

She asked him: 'What is your objection to colours?'

His hand was at his breast-pocket immediately, as he said: 'Have you not seen?'—though but a few minutes back he had shown her the contents of the packet, including a hurried glance of the famous digging scene.

By this time the entire district was in fervid sympathy with General Ople. The ladies did not, as their lords did, proclaim astonishment that a man should suffer a woman to goad him to a state of semi-lunacy; but one or two confessed to their husbands, that it required a great admiration of General Ople not to despise him, both for his susceptibility and his patience. As for the men, they knew him to have faced the balls in bellowing battle-strife; they knew him to have endured privation, not only cold but downright want of food and drink—an almost unimaginable horror to these brave daily feasters; so they could not quite look on him in contempt; but his want of sense was offensive, and still more so his submission to a scourging by a woman. Not one of them would have deigned to feel it. Would they have allowed her to see that she could sting them? They would have laughed at her. Or they would have dragged her before a magistrate.

It was a Sunday in early Summer when General Ople walked to morning service, unaccompanied by Elizabeth, who was unwell. The church was of the considerate old-fashioned order, with deaf square pews, permitting the mind to abstract itself from the sermon, or wrestle at leisure with the difficulties presented by the preacher, as General Ople often did, feeling not a little in love with his sincere attentiveness for grappling with the knotty point and partially allowing the struggle to be seen.

The Church was, besides, a sanctuary for him. Hither his enemy did not come. He had this one place of refuge, and he almost looked a happy man again.

He had passed into his hat and out of it, which he habitually did standing, when who should walk up to within a couple of yards of him but Lady Camper. Her pew was full of poor people, who made signs of retiring. She signified to them that they were to sit, then quietly took her seat among them, fronting the General across the aisle.

During the sermon a low voice, sharp in contradistinction to the monotone of the preacher's, was heard to repeat these words: 'I say I am not sure I shall survive it.' Considerable muttering in the same quarter was heard besides.

After the customary ceremonious game, when all were free to move, of nobody liking to move first, Lady Camper and a charity boy were the persons who took the lead. But Lady Camper could not quit her pew, owing to the sticking of the door. She smiled as with her pretty hand she twice or thrice essayed to shake it open. General Ople strode to her aid. He pulled the door, gave the shadow of a respectful bow, and no doubt he would have withdrawn, had not Lady Camper, while acknowledging the civility, placed her prayer-book in his hands to carry at her heels. There was no choice for him. He made a sort of slipping dance back for his hat, and followed her ladyship. All present being eager to witness the spectacle, the passage of Lady Camper dragging the victim General behind her was observed without a stir of the well-dressed members of the congregation, until a desire overcame them to see how Lady Camper would behave to her fish when she had him outside the sacred edifice.

None could have imagined such a scene. Lady Camper was in her carriage; General Ople was holding her prayer-book, hat in hand, at the carriage step, and he looked as if he were toasting before the bars of a furnace; for while he stood there, Lady Camper was rapidly pencilling outlines in a small pocket sketch-book. There are dogs whose shyness is put to it to endure human observation and a direct address to them, even on the part of their masters; and these dear simple dogs wag tail and turn their heads aside waveringly, as though to entreat you not to eye them and talk to them so. General Ople, in the presence of the sketch-book, was much like the nervous animal. He would fain have run away. He glanced at it, and round about, and again at it, and at the heavens. Her ladyship's cruelty, and his inexplicable submission to it, were witnessed of the multitude.

The General's friends walked very slowly. Lady Camper's carriage whirled by, and the General came up with them, accosting them and himself alternately. They asked him where Elizabeth was, and he replied, 'Poor child, yes! I am told she is pale, but I cannot believe I am so perfectly, I say so perfectly ridiculous when I join the responses.' He drew forth half a dozen sheets, and showed them sketches that Lady Camper had taken in church, caricaturing him in the sitting down and the standing up. She had torn them out of the book, and presented them to him when driving off. 'I was saying, worship in the ordinary sense will be interdicted to me if her ladyship . . .,' said the General, woefully shuffling the sketch-paper sheets in which he figured.

He made the following odd confession to Mr. and Mrs. Gosling on the road:—that he had gone to his chest, and taken out his sword-belt to measure his girth, and found himself thinner than when he left the service, which had not been the case before his attendance at the last levée of the foregoing season. So the deduction was obvious, that Lady Camper had reduced him. She had reduced him as effectually as a harassing siege.

'But why do you pay attention to her? Why . . .!' exclaimed Mr. Gosling, a gentleman of the City, whose roundness would have turned a rifle-shot.

'To allow her to wound you so seriously!' exclaimed Mrs. Gosling.

'Madam, if she were my wife,' the General explained, 'I should feel it. I say it is the fact of it; I feel it, if I appear so extremely ridiculous to a human eye, to any one eye.'

'To Lady Camper's eye!'

He admitted it might be that. He had not thought of ascribing the acuteness of his pain to the miserable image he presented in this particular lady's eye. No; it really was true, curiously true:

another lady's eye might have transformed him to a pumpkin shape, exaggerated all his foibles fifty-fold, and he, though not liking it, of course not, would yet have preserved a certain manly equanimity. How was it Lady Camper had such power over him?—a lady concealing seventy years with a rouge-box or paint-pot! It was witchcraft in its worst character. He had for six months at her bidding been actually living the life of a beast, degraded in his own esteem; scorched by every laugh he heard; running, pursued, overtaken, and as it were scored or branded, and then let go for the process to be repeated.

CHAPTER VIII

OUR young barbarians have it all their own way with us when they fall into love-liking; they lead us whither they please, and interest us in their wishings, their weepings, and that fine performance, their kissings. But when we see our veterans tottering to their fall, we scarcely consent to their having a wish; as for a kiss, we halloo at them if we discover them on a byway to the sacred grove where such things are supposed to be done by the venerable. And this piece of rank injustice, not to say impoliteness, is entirely because of an unsound opinion that Nature is not in it, as though it were our esteem for Nature which caused us to disrespect them. They, in truth, show her to us discreet, civilized, in a decent moral aspect: vistas of real life, views of the mind's eye, are opened by their touching little emotions; whereas those bully youngsters who come bellowing at us and catch us by the senses plainly prove either that we are no better than they, or that we give our attention to Nature only when she makes us afraid of her. If we cared for her, we should be up and after her reverentially in her sedater steps, deeply studying her in her slower paces. She teaches them nothing when they are whirling. Our closest instructors, the true philosophers—the story-tellers, in short—will learn in time that Nature is not of necessity always roaring, and as soon as they do, the world may be said to be enlightened. Meantime, in the contemplation of a pair of white whiskers fluttering round a pair of manifestly painted cheeks, be assured that Nature is in it: not that hectoring wanton—but let the young have their fun. Let the superior interest of the passions of the aged be conceded, and not a word shall be said against the young.

If, then, Nature is in it, how has she been made active? The reason of her launch upon this last adventure is, that she has perceived the person who can supply the virtue known to her by experience to be wanting. Thus, in the broader instance, many who have journeyed far down the road, turn back to the worship of youth, which they have lost. Some are for the graceful worldliness of wit, of which they have just share enough to admire it. Some are captivated by hands that can wield the rod, which in earlier days they escaped to their cost. In the case of General Ople, it was partly her whippings of him, partly her penetration; her ability, that sat so finely on a wealthy woman, her indifference to conventional manners, that so well beseemed a nobly-born one, and more than all, her correction of his little weaknesses and incompetencies, in spite of his dislike of it, won him. He began to feel a sort of nibbling pleasure in her grotesque sketches of his person; a tendency to recur to the old ones while dreading the arrival of new. You hear old gentlemen speak fondly of the swish; and they are not attached to pain, but the instrument revives their feeling of youth; and General Ople half enjoyed, while shrinking, Lady Camper's foregone outlines of him. For in the distance, the whip's-end may look like a clinging caress instead of a stinging flick. But this craven melting in his heart was rebuked by a very worthy pride, that flew for support to the injury she had done to his devotions, and the offence to the sacred edifice. After thinking over it, he decided that he must quit his residence; and as it appeared to him in the light of duty, he, with an unspoken anguish, commissioned the house-agent of his town to sell his lease or let the house furnished, without further parley.

From the house-agent's shop he turned into the chemist's, for a tonic—a foolish proceeding, for he had received bracing enough in the blow he had just dealt himself, but he had been cogitating on tonics recently, imagining certain valiant effects of them, with visions of a former careless happiness that they were likely to restore. So he requested to have the tonic strong, and he took one glass of it over the counter.

Fifteen minutes after the draught, he came in sight of his house, and beholding it, he could have called it a gentlemanly residence aloud under Lady Camper's windows, his insurgency was of such violence. He talked of it incessantly, but forbore to tell Elizabeth, as she was looking pale, the reason why its modest merits touched him so. He longed for the hour of his next dose, and for a caricature to follow, that he might drink and defy it. A caricature was really due to him, he thought; otherwise why had he abandoned his bijou dwelling? Lady Camper, however, sent none. He had to wait a fortnight before one came, and that was rather a likeness, and a handsome likeness, except as regarded a certain disorderliness in his dress, which he knew to be very unlike him. Still it despatched him to the looking-glass, to bring that verifier of facts in evidence against the sketch. While sitting there he heard the housemaid's knock at the door, and the strange intelligence that his daughter was with Lady Camper, and had left word that she hoped he would not forget his engagement to go to Mrs. Baerens' lawn-party.

The General jumped away from the glass, shouting at the absent Elizabeth in a fit of wrath so foreign to him, that he returned hurriedly to have another look at himself, and exclaimed at the pitch of his voice, 'I say I attribute it to an indigestion of that tonic. Do you hear?' The housemaid faintly answered outside the door that she did, alarming him, for there seemed to be confusion somewhere. His hope was that no one would mention Lady Camper's name, for the mere thought of her caused a rush to his head. 'I believe I am in for a touch of apoplexy,' he said to the rector, who greeted him, in advance of the ladies, on Mrs. Baerens' lawn. He said it smilingly, but wanting some show of sympathy, instead of the whisper and meaningless hand at his clerical band, with which the rector responded, he cried, 'Apoplexy,' and his friend seemed then to understand, and disappeared among the ladies.

Several of them surrounded the General, and one inquired whether the series was being continued. He drew forth his pocket-book, handed her the latest, and remarked on the gross injustice of it; for, as he requested them to take note, her ladyship now sketched him as a person inattentive to his dress, and he begged them to observe that she had drawn him with his necktie hanging loose. 'And that, I say that has never been known of me since I first entered society.'

The ladies exchanged looks of profound concern; for the fact was, the General had come without any necktie and any collar, and he appeared to be unaware of the circumstance. The rector had told them, that in answer to a hint he had dropped on the subject of neckties, General Ople expressed a slight apprehension of apoplexy; but his careless or merely partial observance of the laws of buttonment could have nothing to do with such fears. They signified rather a disorder of the intelligence. Elizabeth was condemned for leaving him to go about alone. The situation was really most painful, for a word to so sensitive a man would drive him away in shame and for good; and still, to let him parade the ground in the state, compared with his natural self, of scarecrow, and with the dreadful habit of talking to himself quite rageing, was a horrible alternative. Mrs. Baerens at last directed her husband upon the General, trembling as though she watched for the operations of a fish torpedo; and other ladies shared her excessive anxiousness, for Mr. Baerens had the manner and the look of artillery, and on this occasion carried a surcharge of powder.

The General bent his ear to Mr. Baerens, whose German-English and repeated remark, 'I am to do it wid delicassy,' did not assist his comprehension; and when he might have been enlightened, he was petrified by seeing Lady Camper walk on the lawn with Elizabeth. The great lady stood a moment beside Mrs. Baerens; she came straight over to him, contemplating him in silence.

Then she said, 'Your arm, General Ople,' and she made one circuit of the lawn with him, barely speaking.

At her request, he conducted her to her carriage. He took a seat beside her, obediently. He felt that he was being sketched, and comported himself like a child's flat man,[1] that jumps at the pulling of a string.

'Where have you left your girl, General?'

Before he could rally his wits to answer the question, he was asked:

'And what have you done with your necktie and collar?'

[1] A Victorian articulated toy.

He touched his throat.

'I am rather nervous to-day, I forgot Elizabeth,' he said, sending his fingers in a dotting run of wonderment round his neck.

Lady Camper smiled with a triumphing humour on her close-drawn lips.

The verified absence of necktie and collar seemed to be choking him.

'Never mind, you have been abroad without them,' said Lady Camper, 'and that is a victory for me. And you thought of Elizabeth first when I drew your attention to it, and that is a victory for you. It is a very great victory. Pray, do not be dismayed, General. You have a handsome campaigning air. And no apologies, if you please; I like you well enough as you are. There is my hand.'

General Ople understood her last remark. He pressed the lady's hand in silence, very nervously.

'But do not shrug your head into your shoulders as if there were any possibility of concealing the thunderingly evident,' said Lady Camper, electrifying him, what with her cordial squeeze, her kind eyes, and her singular language. 'You have omitted the collar. Well? The collar is the fatal finishing touch in men's dress; it would make Apollo look bourgeois.'

Her hand was in his: and watching the play of her features, a spark entered General Ople's brain, causing him, in forgetfulness of collar and caricatures, to ejaculate, 'Seventy? Did your ladyship say seventy? Utterly impossible! You trifled with me.'

'We will talk when we are free of this accompaniment of carriage-wheels, General,' said Lady Camper.

'I will beg permission to go and fetch Elizabeth, madam.'

'Rightly thought of. Fetch her in my carriage. And, by the way, Mrs. Baerens was my old music mistress, and is, I think, one year older than I. She can tell you on which side of seventy I am.'

'I shall not require to ask, my lady,' he said, sighing.

'Then we will send the carriage for Elizabeth, and have it out together at once. I am impatient; yes, General, impatient: for what?—forgiveness.'

'Of me, my lady?' The General breathed profoundly.

'Of whom else? Do you know what it is?—I don't think you

do. You English have the smallest experience of humanity. I mean this: to strike so hard that, in the end, you soften your heart to the victim. Well, that is my weakness. And we of our blood put no restraint on the blows we strike when we think them wanted, so we are always overdoing it.'

General Ople assisted Lady Camper to alight from the carriage, which was forthwith despatched for Elizabeth.

He prepared to listen to her with a disconnected smile of acute attentiveness.

She had changed. She spoke of money. Ten thousand pounds must be settled on his daughter. 'And now,' said she, 'you will remember that you are wanting a collar.'

He acquiesced. He craved permission to retire for ten minutes.

'Simplest of men! what will cover you?' she exclaimed, and peremptorily bidding him sit down in the drawing-room, she took one of the famous pair of pistols in her hand, and said, 'If I put myself in a similar position, and make myself *décolletée* too, will that satisfy you? You see these murderous weapons. Well, I am a coward. I dread fire-arms. They are laid there to impose on the world, and I believe they do. They have imposed on you. Now, you would never think of pretending to a moral quality you do not possess. But, silly, simple man that you are! You can give yourself the airs of wealth, buy horses to conceal your nakedness, and when you are taken upon the standard of your apparent income, you would rather seem to be beating a miserly retreat than behave frankly and honestly. I have a little overstated it, but I am near the mark.'

'Your ladyship wanting courage!' cried the General.

'Refresh yourself by meditating on it,' said she. 'And to prove it to you, I was glad to take this house when I knew I was to have a gallant gentleman for a neighbour. No visitors will be admitted, General Ople, so you are bare-throated only to me: sit quietly. One day you speculated on the paint in my cheeks for the space of a minute and a half:—I had said that I freckled easily. Your look signified that you really could not detect a single freckle for the paint. I forgave you, or I did not. But when I found you, on closer acquaintance, as indifferent to your daughter's happiness as you had been to her reputation . . .'

'My daughter! her reputation! her happiness!' General Ople raised his eyes under a wave, half uttering the outcries.

'So indifferent to her reputation, that you allowed a young man to talk with her over the wall, and meet her by appointment: so reckless of the girl's happiness, that when I tried to bring you to a treaty, on her behalf, you could not be dragged from thinking of yourself and your own affair. When I found that, perhaps I was predisposed to give you some of what my sisters used to call my spice. You would not honestly state the proportions of your income, and you affected to be faithful to the woman of seventy. Most preposterous! Could any caricature of mine exceed in grotesqueness your sketch of yourself? You are a brave and a generous man all the same: and I suspect it is more hoodwinking than egotism—or extreme egotism—that blinds you. A certain amount you must have to be a man. You did not like my paint, still less did you like my sincerity; you were annoyed by my corrections of your habits of speech; you were horrified by the age of seventy, and you were credulous—General Ople, listen to me, and remember that you have no collar on! —you were credulous of my statement of my great age, or you chose to be so, or chose to seem so, because I had brushed your cat's coat against the fur. And then, full of yourself, not thinking of Elizabeth, but to withdraw in the chivalrous attitude of the man true to his word to the old woman, only stickling to bring a certain independence to the common stock, because—I quote you! and you have no collar on, mind—"*you could not be at your wife's mercy*," you broke from your proposal on the money question. Where was your consideration for Elizabeth then?

'Well, General, you were fond of thinking of yourself, and I thought I would assist you. I gave you plenty of subject matter. I will not say I meant to work a homœopathic cure. But if I drive you to forget your collar, is it or is it not a triumph?

'No,' added Lady Camper, 'it is no triumph for me, but it is one for you, if you like to make the most of it. Your fault has been to quit active service, General, and love your ease too well. It is the fault of your countrymen. You must get a militia regiment, or inspectorship of militia. You are ten times the man in exercise. Why, do you mean to tell me that you would have cared for those drawings of mine when marching?'

'I think so, I say I think so,' remarked the General seriously.

'I doubt it,' said she. 'But to the point; here comes Elizabeth. If you have not much money to spare for her, according to your prudent calculation, reflect how this money has enfeebled you and reduced you to the level of the people round about us here—who are, what? Inhabitants of gentlemanly residences, yes! But what kind of creature? They have no mental standard, no moral aim, no native chivalry. You were rapidly becoming one of them, only, fortunately for you, you were sensitive to ridicule.'

'Elizabeth shall have half my money settled on her,' said the General; 'though I fear it is not much. And if I can find occupation, my lady . . .'

'Something worthier than *that,*' said Lady Camper, pencilling outlines rapidly on the margin of a book, and he saw himself lashing a pony; 'or *that,*' and he was plucking at a cabbage; 'or *that,*' and he was bowing to three petticoated posts.

'The likeness is exact,' General Ople groaned.

'So you may suppose I have studied you,' said she. 'But there is no real likeness. Slight exaggerations do more harm to truth than reckless violations of it. You would not have cared one bit for a caricature, if you had not nursed the absurd idea of being one of our conquerors. It is the very tragedy of modesty for a man like you to have such notions, my poor dear good friend. The modest are the most easily intoxicated when they sip at vanity. And reflect whether you have not been intoxicated, for these young people have been wretched, and you have not observed it, though one of them was living with you, and is the child you love. There, I have done. Pray show a good face to Elizabeth.'

The General obeyed as well as he could. He felt very like a sheep that has come from a shearing, and when released he wished to run away. But hardly had he escaped before he had a desire for the renewal of the operation. 'She sees me through, she sees me through,' he was heard saying to himself, and in the end he taught himself to say it with a secret exultation, for as it was on her part an extraordinary piece of insight to see him through, it struck him that in acknowledging the truth of it, he made a discovery of new powers in human nature.

General Ople studied Lady Camper diligently for fresh proofs of her penetration of the mysteries in his bosom; by which means, as it happened that she was diligently observing the two betrothed young ones, he began to watch them likewise, and took a pleasure in the sight. Their meetings, their partings, their rides out and home furnished him themes of converse. He soon had enough to talk of, and previously, as he remembered, he had never sustained a conversation of any length with composure and the beneficent sense of fulness. Five thousand pounds, to which sum Lady Camper reduced her stipulation for Elizabeth's dowry, he signed over to his dear girl gladly, and came out with the confession to her ladyship that a well-invested twelve thousand comprised his fortune. She shrugged: she had left off pulling him this way and that, so his chains were enjoyable, and he said to himself: 'If ever she should in the dead of night want a man to defend her!' He mentioned it to Reginald, who had been the repository of Elizabeth's lamentations about her father being left alone, forsaken, and the young man conceived a scheme for causing his aunt's great bell to be rung at midnight, which would certainly have led to a dramatic issue and the happy re-establishment of our masculine ascendancy at the close of this history. But he forgot it in his bridegroom's delight, until he was making his miserable official speech at the wedding-breakfast, and set Elizabeth winking over a tear. As she stood in the hall ready to depart, a great van was observed in the road at the gates of Douro Lodge; and this, the men in custody declared to contain the goods and knick-knacks of the people who had taken the house furnished for a year, and were coming in that very afternoon.

'I remember, I say now I remember, I had a notice,' the General said cheerily to his troubled daughter.

'But where are you to go, papa?' the poor girl cried, close on sobbing.

'I shall get employment of some sort,' said he. 'I was saying I want it, I need it, I require it.'

'You are saying three times what once would have sufficed for,' said Lady Camper, and she asked him a few questions, frowned with a smile, and offered him a lodgement in his neighbour's house.

'Really, dearest Aunt Angela?' said Elizabeth.

'What else can I do, child? I have, it seems, driven him out of a gentlemanly residence, and I must give him a ladylike one. True, I would rather have had him at call, but as I have always wished for a policeman in the house, I may as well be satisfied with a soldier.'

'But if you lose your character, my lady?' said Reginald.

'Then I must look to the General to restore it.'

General Ople immediately bowed his head over Lady Camper's fingers.

'An odd thing to happen to a woman of forty-one!' she said to her great people, and they submitted with the best grace in the world, while the General's ears tingled till he felt younger than Reginald. This, his reflections ran, or it would be more correct to say waltzed, this is the result of painting!—that you can believe a woman to be any age when her cheeks are tinted!

As for Lady Camper, she had been floated accidentally over the ridicule of the brute of a marriage at a time of life as terrible to her as her fiction of seventy had been to General Ople; she resigned herself to let things go with the tide. She had not been blissful in her first marriage, she had abandoned the chase of an ideal man, and she had found one who was tuneable so as not to offend her ears, likely ever to be a fund of amusement for her humour, good, impressible, and above all, very picturesque. There is the secret of her, and of how it came to pass that a simple man and a complex woman fell to union after the strangest division.

THOMAS HARDY
(1840–1928)

'The Withered Arm' first appeared in *Blackwood's Edinburgh Magazine* in January 1888. It appeared later in the same year in *Wessex Tales*. 'On the Western Circuit' was first published in *The English Illustrated Magazine* in December 1891, but to some extent modified, Mrs. Harnham being presented as a widow not a wife. It appeared in 1894 in *Life's Little Ironies*. Many of Hardy's Wessex places may easily be recognized, even today, although few are exactly described. The following are the chief ones which appear in the chosen stories: Anglebury (Wareham); Melchester (Salisbury); Old Melchester (Old Sarum); Casterbridge (Dorchester); Wintoncester (Winchester); Knollsea (Swanage). Egdon Heath represents the large tract of heath that stretches between Dorchester and Bournemouth, considerable parts of which can still be seen between the enlarged villages and towns and the development of the twentieth century.

The Withered Arm

A LORN MILKMAID

I

It was an eighty-cow dairy, and the troop of milkers, regular and supernumerary, were all at work; for, though the time of year was as yet but early April, the feed lay entirely in water-meadows, and the cows were 'in full pail.' The hour was about six in the evening, and three-fourths of the large, red, rectangular animals having been finished off, there was opportunity for a little conversation.

'He do bring home his bride to-morrow, I hear. They've come as far as Anglebury to-day.'

The voice seemed to proceed from the belly of the cow called

Cherry, but the speaker was a milking-woman, whose face was buried in the flank of that motionless beast.

'Hav' anybody seen her?' said another.

There was a negative response from the first. 'Though they say she's a rosy-cheeked, tisty-tosty[1] little body enough,' she added; and as the milkmaid spoke she turned her face so that she could glance past her cow's tail to the other side of the barton,[2] where a thin, fading woman of thirty milked somewhat apart from the rest.

'Years younger than he, they say,' continued the second, with also a glance of reflectiveness in the same direction.

'How old do you call him, then?'

'Thirty or so.'

'More like forty,' broke in an old milkman near, in a long white pinafore or 'wropper,' and with the brim of his hat tied down, so that he looked like a woman. ''A was born before our Great Weir was builded, and I hadn't man's wages when I laved[3] water there.'

The discussion waxed so warm that the purr of the milk streams became jerky, till a voice from another cow's belly cried with authority, 'Now then, what the Turk do it matter to us about Farmer Lodge's age, or Farmer Lodge's new mis'ess? I shall have to pay him nine pound a year for the rent of every one of these milchers, whatever his age or hers. Get on with your work, or 'twill be dark afore we have done. The evening is pinking in a'ready.' This speaker was the dairyman himself, by whom the milkmaids and men were employed.

Nothing more was said publicly about Farmer Lodge's wedding, but the first woman murmured under her cow to her next neighbour. ''Tis hard for *she*,' signifying the thin worn milkmaid aforesaid.

'O no,' said the second. 'He ha'n't spoke to Rhoda Brook for years.'

When the milking was done they washed their pails and hung them on a many-forked stand made as usual of the peeled limb of an oak-tree, set upright in the earth, and resembling a colossal antlered horn. The majority then dispersed in various directions

[1] Assured. [2] Here, cow-shed. [3] Drew.

homeward. The thin woman who had not spoken was joined by a boy of twelve or thereabout, and the twain went away up the field also.

Their course lay apart from that of the others, to a lonely spot high above the water-meads, and not far from the border of Egdon Heath, whose dark countenance was visible in the distance as they drew nigh to their home.

'They've just been saying down in barton that your father brings his young wife home from Anglebury to-morrow,' the woman observed. 'I shall want to send you for a few things to market, and you'll be pretty sure to meet 'em.'

'Yes, mother,' said the boy. 'Is father married then?'

'Yes. . . . You can give her a look, and tell me what she's like, if you do see her.'

'Yes, mother.'

'If she's dark or fair, and if she's tall—as tall as I. And if she seems like a woman who has ever worked for a living, or one that has been always well off, and has never done anything, and shows marks of the lady on her, as I expect she do.'

'Yes.'

They crept up the hill in the twilight and entered the cottage. It was built of mud-walls, the surface of which had been washed by many rains into channels and depressions that left none of the original flat face visible; while here and there in the thatch above a rafter showed like a bone protruding through the skin.

She was kneeling down in the chimney-corner, before two pieces of turf laid together with the heather inwards, blowing at the red-hot ashes with her breath till the turves flamed. The radiance lit her pale cheek, and made her dark eyes, that had once been handsome, seem handsome anew. 'Yes,' she resumed, 'see if she is dark or fair, and if you can, notice if her hands be white; if not, see if they look as though she had ever done housework, or are milker's hands like mine.'

The boy again promised, inattentively this time, his mother not observing that he was cutting a notch with his pocket-knife in the beech-backed chair.

THE YOUNG WIFE

II

The road from Anglebury to Holmstoke is in general level; but there is one place where a sharp ascent breaks its monotony. Farmers homeward-bound from the former market-town, who trot all the rest of the way, walk their horses up this short incline.

The next evening while the sun was yet bright a handsome new gig, with a lemon-coloured body and red wheels, was spinning westward along the level highway at the heels of a powerful mare. The driver was a yeoman in the prime of life, cleanly shaven like an actor, his face being toned to that bluish-vermilion hue which so often graces a thriving farmer's features when returning home after successful dealings in the town. Beside him sat a woman, many years his junior—almost, indeed, a girl. Her face too was fresh in colour, but it was of a totally different quality—soft and evanescent, like the light under a heap of rose-petals.

Few people travelled this way, for it was not a main road; and the long white riband of gravel that stretched before them was empty, save of one small scarce-moving speck, which presently resolved itself into the figure of a boy, who was creeping on at a snail's pace, and continually looking behind him—the heavy bundle he carried being some excuse for, if not the reason of, his dilatoriness. When the bouncing gig-party slowed at the bottom of the incline above mentioned, the pedestrian was only a few yards in front. Supporting the large bundle by putting one hand on his hip, he turned and looked straight at the farmer's wife as though he would read her through and through, pacing along abreast of the horse.

The low sun was full in her face, rendering every feature, shade, and contour distinct, from the curve of her little nostril to the colour of her eyes. The farmer, though he seemed annoyed at the boy's persistent presence, did not order him to get out of the way; and thus the lad preceded them, his hard gaze never leaving her, till they reached the top of the ascent, when the farmer trotted on with relief in his lineaments—having taken no outward notice of the boy whatever.

'How that poor lad stared at me!' said the young wife.

'Yes, dear; I saw that he did.'

'He is one of the village, I suppose?'

'One of the neighbourhood. I think he lives with his mother a mile or two off.'

'He knows who we are, no doubt?'

'O yes. You must expect to be stared at just at first, my pretty Gertrude.'

'I do,—though I think the poor boy may have looked at us in the hope we might relieve him of his heavy load, rather than from curiosity.'

'O no,' said her husband off-handedly. 'These country lads will carry a hundredweight once they get it on their backs; besides his pack had more size than weight in it. Now, then, another mile and I shall be able to show you our house in the distance—if it is not too dark before we get there.' The wheels spun round, and particles flew from their periphery as before, till a white house of ample dimensions revealed itself, with farm-buildings and ricks at the back.

Meanwhile the boy had quickened his pace, and turning up a by-lane some mile and a half short of the white farmstead, ascended towards the leaner pastures, and so on to the cottage of his mother.

She had reached home after her day's milking at the outlying dairy, and was washing cabbage at the doorway in the declining light. 'Hold up the net a moment,' she said, without preface, as the boy came up.

He flung down his bundle, held the edge of the cabbage-net, and as she filled its meshes with the dripping leaves she went on, 'Well, did you see her?'

'Yes; quite plain.'

'Is she ladylike?'

'Yes; and more. A lady complete.'

'Is she young?'

'Well, she's growed up, and her ways be quite a woman's.'

'Of course. What colour is her hair and face?'

'Her hair is lightish, and her face as comely as a live doll's.'

'Her eyes, then, are not dark like mine?'

'No—of a bluish turn, and her mouth is very nice and red; and when she smiles, her teeth show white.'

'Is she tall?' said the woman sharply.

'I couldn't see. She was sitting down.'

'Then do you go to Holmstoke church to-morrow morning: she's sure to be there. Go early and notice her walking in, and come home and tell me if she's taller than I.'

'Very well, mother. But why don't you go and see for yourself?'

'*I* go to see her! I wouldn't look up at her if she were to pass my window this instant. She was with Mr. Lodge, of course. What did he say or do?'

'Just the same as usual.'

'Took no notice of you?'

'None.'

Next day the mother put a clean shirt on the boy, and started him off to Holmstoke church. He reached the ancient little pile when the door was just being opened, and he was the first to enter. Taking his seat by the font, he watched all the parishioners file in. The well-to-do Farmer Lodge came nearly last; and his young wife, who accompanied him, walked up the aisle with the shyness natural to a modest woman who had appeared thus for the first time. As all other eyes were fixed upon her, the youth's stare was not noticed now.

When he reached home his mother said, 'Well?' before he had entered the room.

'She is not tall. She is rather short,' he replied.

'Ah!' said his mother, with satisfaction.

'But she's very pretty—very. In fact, she's lovely.' The youthful freshness of the yeoman's wife had evidently made an impression even on the somewhat hard nature of the boy.

'That's all I want to hear,' said his mother quickly. 'Now, spread the table-cloth. The hare you wired is very tender; but mind that nobody catches you.—You've never told me what sort of hands she had.'

'I have never seen 'em. She never took off her gloves.'

'What did she wear this morning?'

'A white bonnet and a silver-coloured gownd. It whewed and whistled so loud when it rubbed against the pews that the lady coloured up more than ever for very shame at the noise, and pulled it in to keep it from touching; but when she pushed into her seat, it whewed more than ever. Mr. Lodge, he seemed pleased, and his waistcoat stuck out, and his great golden seals hung like a lord's; but she seemed to wish her noisy gownd anywhere but on her.'

'Not she! However, that will do now.'

These descriptions of the newly-married couple were continued from time to time by the boy at his mother's request, after any chance encounter he had had with them. But Rhoda Brook, though she might easily have seen young Mrs. Lodge for herself by walking a couple of miles, would never attempt an excursion towards the quarter where the farmhouse lay. Neither did she, at the daily milking in the dairyman's yard on Lodge's outlying second farm, ever speak on the subject of the recent marriage. The dairyman, who rented the cows of Lodge, and knew perfectly the tall milkmaid's history, with manly kindliness always kept the gossip in the cow-barton from annoying Rhoda. But the atmosphere thereabout was full of the subject during the first days of Mrs. Lodge's arrival; and from her boy's description and the casual words of the other milkers, Rhoda Brook could raise a mental image of the unconscious Mrs. Lodge that was realistic as a photograph.

A VISION

III

One night, two or three weeks after the bridal return, when the boy was gone to bed, Rhoda sat a long time over the turf ashes that she had raked out in front of her to extinguish them. She contemplated so intently the new wife, as presented to her in her mind's eye over the embers, that she forgot the lapse of time. At last, wearied with her day's work, she too retired.

But the figure which had occupied her so much during this and the previous days was not to be banished at night. For the first time Gertrude Lodge visited the supplanted woman in her dreams. Rhoda Brook dreamed—since her assertion that she really saw, before falling asleep, was not to be believed—that the young wife, in the pale silk dress and white bonnet, but with features shockingly distorted, and wrinkled as by age, was sitting upon her chest as she lay. The pressure of Mrs. Lodge's person grew heavier; the blue eyes peered cruelly into her face; and then the figure thrust forward its left hand mockingly, so as to make the wedding-ring it wore glitter in Rhoda's eyes. Maddened mentally, and nearly suffocated by pressure, the sleeper struggled; the incubus, still regarding her, withdrew to the foot of the bed, only, however, to come forward by degrees, resume her seat, and flash her left hand as before.

Gasping for breath, Rhoda, in a last desperate effort, swung out her right hand, seized the confronting spectre by its obtrusive left arm, and whirled it backward to the floor, starting up herself as she did so with a low cry.

'O, merciful heaven!' she cried, sitting on the edge of the bed in a cold sweat; 'that was not a dream—she was here!'

She could feel her antagonist's arm within her grasp even now—the very flesh and bone of it, as it seemed. She looked on the floor whither she had whirled the spectre, but there was nothing to be seen.

Rhoda Brook slept no more that night, and when she went milking at the next dawn they noticed how pale and haggard she looked. The milk that she drew quivered into the pail; her hand had not calmed even yet, and still retained the feel of the arm. She came home to breakfast as wearily as if it had been supper-time.

'What was that noise in your chimmer,[1] mother, last night?' said her son. 'You fell off the bed, surely?'

'Did you hear anything fall? At what time?'

'Just when the clock struck two.'

She could not explain, and when the meal was done went silently about her household work, the boy assisting her, for he hated going afield on the farms, and she indulged his reluctance. Between eleven and twelve the garden-gate clicked, and she lifted her eyes to the window. At the bottom of the garden, within the gate, stood the woman of her vision. Rhoda seemed transfixed.

[1] Room (chamber).

'Ah, she said she would come!' exclaimed the boy, also observing her.

'Said so—when? How does she know us?'

'I have seen and spoken to her. I talked to her yesterday.'

'I told you,' said the mother, flushing indignantly, 'never to speak to anybody in that house, or go near the place.'

'I did not speak to her till she spoke to me. And I did not go near the place. I met her in the road.'

'What did you tell her?'

'Nothing. She said, "Are you the poor boy who had to bring the heavy load from market?" And she looked at my boots, and said they would not keep my feet dry if it came on wet, because they were so cracked. I told her I lived with my mother, and we had enough to do to keep ourselves, and that's how it was; and she said then, "I'll come and bring you some better boots and see your mother." She gives away things to other folks in the meads besides us.'

Mrs. Lodge was by this time close to the door—not in her silk, as Rhoda had dreamt of in the bed-chamber, but in a morning hat, and gown of common light material, which became her better than silk. On her arm she carried a basket.

The impression remaining from the night's experience was still strong. Brook had almost expected to see the wrinkles, the scorn, and the cruelty on her visitor's face. She would have escaped an interview, had escape been possible. There was, however, no backdoor to the cottage, and in an instant the boy had lifted the latch to Mrs. Lodge's gentle knock.

'I see I have come to the right house,' said she, glancing at the lad, and smiling. 'But I was not sure till you opened the door.'

The figure and action were those of the phantom; but her voice was so indescribably sweet, her glance so winning, her smile so tender, so unlike that of Rhoda's midnight visitant, that the latter could hardly believe the evidence of her senses. She was truly glad that she had not hidden away in sheer aversion, as she had been inclined to do. In her basket Mrs. Lodge brought the pair of boots that she had promised to the boy, and other useful articles.

At these proofs of a kindly feeling towards her and hers

Rhoda's heart reproached her bitterly. This innocent young thing should have her blessing and not her curse. When she left them a light seemed gone from the dwelling. Two days later she came again to know if the boots fitted; and less than a fortnight after that paid Rhoda another call. On this occasion the boy was absent.

'I walk a good deal,' said Mrs. Lodge, 'and your house is the nearest outside our own parish. I hope you are well. You don't look quite well.'

Rhoda said she was well enough; and, indeed, though the paler of the two, there was more of the strength that endures in her well-defined features and large frame than in the soft-cheeked young woman before her. The conversation became quite confidential as regarded their powers and weaknesses; and when Mrs. Lodge was leaving, Rhoda said, 'I hope you will find this air agree with you, ma'am, and not suffer from the damp of the water meads.'

The younger one replied that there was not much doubt of it, her general health being usually good. 'Though, now you remind me,' she added, 'I have one little ailment which puzzles me. It is nothing serious, but I cannot make it out.'

She uncovered her left hand and arm; and their outline confronted Rhoda's gaze as the exact original of the limb she had beheld and seized in her dream. Upon the pink round surface of the arm were faint marks of an unhealthy colour, as if produced by a rough grasp. Rhoda's eyes became riveted on the discolourations; she fancied that she discerned in them the shape of her own four fingers.

'How did it happen?' she said mechanically.

'I cannot tell,' replied Mrs. Lodge, shaking her head. 'One night when I was sound asleep, dreaming I was away in some strange place, a pain suddenly shot into my arm there, and was so keen as to awaken me. I must have struck it in the daytime, I suppose, though I don't remember doing so.' She added, laughing, 'I tell my dear husband that it looks just as if he had flown into a rage and struck me there. O I daresay it will soon disappear.'

'Ha, ha! Yes. . . . On what night did it come?'

Mrs. Lodge considered, and said it would be a fortnight ago on

9110212

the morrow. 'When I awoke I could not remember where I was,' she added, 'till the clock striking two reminded me.'

She had named the night and the hour of Rhoda's spectral encounter, and Brook felt like a guilty thing. The artless disclosure startled her; she did not reason on the freaks of coincidence; and all the scenery of that ghastly night returned with double vividness to her mind.

'O, can it be,' she said to herself, when her visitor had departed, 'that I exercise a malignant power over people against my own will?' She knew that she had been slily called a witch since her fall; but never having understood why that particular stigma had been attached to her, it had passed disregarded. Could this be the explanation, and had such things as this ever happened before?

A SUGGESTION

IV

THE summer drew on, and Rhoda Brook almost dreaded to meet Mrs. Lodge again, notwithstanding that her feeling for the young wife amounted well-nigh to affection. Something in her own individuality seemed to convict Rhoda of crime. Yet a fatality sometimes would direct the steps of the latter to the outskirts of Holmstoke whenever she left her house for any other purpose than her daily work; and hence it happened that their next encounter was out of doors. Rhoda could not avoid the subject which had so mystified her, and after the first few words she stammered, 'I hope your—arm is well again, ma'am?' She had perceived with consternation that Gertrude Lodge carried her left arm stiffly.

'No; it is not quite well. Indeed it is no better at all; it is rather worse. It pains me dreadfully sometimes.'

'Perhaps you had better go to a doctor, ma'am.'

She replied that she had already seen a doctor. Her husband had insisted upon her going to one. But the surgeon had not seemed to understand the afflicted limb at all; he had told her to bathe it in hot water, and she had bathed it, but the treatment had done no good.

'Will you let me see it?' said the milkwoman.

Mrs. Lodge pushed up her sleeve and disclosed the place, which was a few inches above the wrist. As soon as Rhoda Brook saw it, she could hardly preserve her composure. There was nothing of the nature of a wound, but the arm at that point had a shrivelled look, and the outline of the four fingers appeared more distinct than at the former time. Moreover, she fancied that they were imprinted in precisely the relative position of her clutch upon the arm in the trance; the first finger towards Gertrude's wrist, and the fourth towards her elbow.

What the impress resembled seemed to have struck Gertrude herself since their last meeting. 'It looks almost like finger-marks,' she said; adding with a faint laugh, 'my husband says it is as if some witch, or the devil himself, had taken hold of me there, and blasted the flesh.'

Rhoda shivered. 'That's fancy,' she said hurriedly. 'I wouldn't mind it, if I were you.'

'I shouldn't so much mind it,' said the younger, with hesitation, 'if—if I hadn't a notion that it makes my husband—dislike me—no, love me less. Men think so much of personal appearance.'

'Some do—he for one.'

'Yes; and he was very proud of mine, at first.'

'Keep your arm covered from his sight.'

'Ah—he knows the disfigurement is there!' She tried to hide the tears that filled her eyes.

'Well, ma'am, I earnestly hope it will go away soon.'

And so the milkwoman's mind was chained anew to the subject by a horrid sort of spell as she returned home. The sense of having been guilty of an act of malignity increased, affect as she might to ridicule her superstition. In her secret heart Rhoda did not altogether object to a slight diminution of her successor's beauty, by whatever means it had come about; but she did not wish to inflict upon her physical pain. For though this pretty young woman had rendered impossible any reparation which Lodge might have made Rhoda for his past conduct, everything like resentment at the unconscious usurpation had quite passed away from the elder's mind.

If the sweet and kindly Gertrude Lodge only knew of the

dream-scene in the bed-chamber, what would she think? Not to inform her of it seemed treachery in the presence of her friendliness; but tell she could not of her own accord—neither could she devise a remedy.

She mused upon the matter the greater part of the night; and the next day, after the morning milking, set out to obtain another glimpse of Gertrude Lodge if she could, being held to her by a gruesome fascination. By watching the house from a distance the milkmaid was presently able to discern the farmer's wife in a ride she was taking alone—probably to join her husband in some distant field. Mrs. Lodge perceived her, and cantered in her direction.

'Good morning, Rhoda!' Gertrude said, when she had come up. 'I was going to call.'

Rhoda noticed that Mrs. Lodge held the reins with some difficulty.

'I hope—the bad arm,' said Rhoda.

'They tell me there is possibly one way by which I might be able to find out the cause, and so perhaps the cure, of it,' replied the other anxiously. 'It is by going to some clever man over in Egdon Heath. They did not know if he was still alive—and I cannot remember his name at this moment; but they said that you knew more of his movements than anybody else hereabout, and could tell me if he were still to be consulted. Dear me—what was his name? But you know.'

'Not Conjuror Trendle?' said her thin companion, turning pale.

'Trendle—yes. Is he alive?'

'I believe so,' said Rhoda, with reluctance.

'Why do you call him conjuror?'

'Well—they say—they used to say he was a—he had powers others folks have not.'

'O, how could my people be so superstitious as to recommend a man of that sort! I thought they meant some medical man. I shall think no more of him.'

Rhoda looked relieved, and Mrs. Lodge rode on. The milkwoman had inwardly seen, from the moment she heard of her having been mentioned as a reference for this man, that there must exist a sarcastic feeling among the women-folk that a sorceress would know the whereabouts of the exorcist. They suspected her, then. A short time ago this would have given no concern to a woman of her common-sense. But she had a haunting reason to be superstitious now; and she had been seized with sudden dread that this Conjuror Trendle might name her as the malignant influence which was blasting the fair person of Gertrude, and so lead her friend to hate her for ever, and to treat her as some fiend in human shape.

But all was not over. Two days after, a shadow intruded into the window-pattern thrown on Rhoda Brook's floor by the afternoon sun. The woman opened the door at once, almost breathlessly.

'Are you alone?' said Gertrude. She seemed to be no less harassed and anxious than Brook herself.

'Yes,' said Rhoda.

'The place on my arm seems worse, and troubles me!' the young farmer's wife went on. 'It is so mysterious! I do hope it will not be an incurable wound. I have again been thinking of what they said about Conjuror Trendle. I don't really believe in such men, but I should not mind just visiting him, from curiosity —though on no account must my husband know. Is it far to where he lives?'

'Yes—five miles,' said Rhoda backwardly. 'In the heart of Egdon.'

'Well, I should have to walk. Could not you go with me to show me the way—say to-morrow afternoon?'

'O, not I; that is——,' the milkwoman murmured, with a start of dismay. Again the dread seized her that something to do with her fierce act in the dream might be revealed, and her character in the eyes of the most useful friend she had ever had be ruined irretrievably.

Mrs. Lodge urged, and Rhoda finally assented, though with much misgiving. Sad as the journey would be to her, she could not conscientiously stand in the way of a possible remedy for her patron's strange affliction. It was agreed that, to escape suspicion of their mystic intent, they should meet at the edge of the heath at the corner of a plantation which was visible from the spot where they now stood.

CONJUROR TRENDLE

V

By the next afternoon Rhoda would have done anything to escape this inquiry. But she had promised to go. Moreover, there was a horrid fascination at times in becoming instrumental in throwing such possible light on her own character as would reveal her to be something greater in the occult world than she had ever herself suspected.

She started just before the time of day mentioned between them, and half-an-hour's brisk walking brought her to the south-eastern extension of the Egdon tract of country, where the fir plantation was. A slight figure, cloaked and veiled, was already there. Rhoda recognized, almost with a shudder, that Mrs. Lodge bore her left arm in a sling.

They hardly spoke to each other, and immediately set out on their climb into the interior of this solemn country, which stood high above the rich alluvial soil they had left half-an-hour before. It was a long walk; thick clouds made the atmosphere dark, though it was as yet early afternoon; and the wind howled dismally over the slopes of the heath—not improbably the same heath which had witnessed the agony of the Wessex King Ina, presented to after-ages as Lear. Gertrude Lodge talked most, Rhoda replying with monosyllabic preoccupation. She had a strange dislike to walking on the side of her companion where hung the afflicted arm, moving round to the other when inadvertently near it. Much heather had been brushed by their feet when they descended upon a cart-track, beside which stood the house of the man they sought.

He did not profess his remedial practices openly, or care anything about their continuance, his direct interests being those of a dealer in furze, turf, 'sharp sand',[1] and other local products. Indeed, he affected not to believe largely in his own powers, and when warts that had been shown him for cure miraculously disappeared—which it must be owned they infallibly did—he would say lightly, 'O, I only drink a glass of grog upon 'em at your

[1] Used in the sharpening of blades, knives, etc.

expense—perhaps it's all chance,' and immediately turn the subject.

He was at home when they arrived, having in fact seen them descending into his valley. He was a gray-bearded man, with a reddish face, and he looked singularly at Rhoda the first moment he beheld her. Mrs. Lodge told him her errand; and then with words of self-disparagement he examined her arm.

'Medicine can't cure it,' he said promptly. ''Tis the work of an enemy.'

Rhoda shrank into herself, and drew back.

'An enemy? What enemy?' asked Mrs. Lodge.

He shook his head. 'That's best known to yourself,' he said. 'If you like, I can show the person to you, though I shall not myself know who it is. I can do no more; and don't wish to do that.'

She pressed him; on which he told Rhoda to wait outside where she stood, and took Mrs. Lodge into the room. It opened immediately from the door; and, as the latter remained ajar, Rhoda Brook could see the proceedings without taking part in them. He brought a tumbler from the dresser, nearly filled it with water, and fetching an egg, prepared it in some private way; after which he broke it on the edge of the glass, so that the white went in and the yolk remained. As it was getting gloomy, he took the glass and its contents to the window, and told Gertrude to watch the mixture closely. They leant over the table together, and the milkwoman could see the opaline hue of the egg-fluid changing form as it sank in the water, but she was not near enough to define the shape that it assumed.

'Do you catch the likeness of any face or figure as you look?' demanded the conjuror of the young woman.

She murmured a reply, in tones so low as to be inaudible to Rhoda, and continued to gaze intently into the glass. Rhoda turned, and walked a few steps away.

When Mrs. Lodge came out, and her face was met by the light, it appeared exceedingly pale—as pale as Rhoda's—against the sad dun shades of the upland's garniture. Trendle shut the door behind her, and they at once started homeward together. But Rhoda perceived that her companion had quite changed.

'Did he charge much?' she asked tentatively.

'O no—nothing. He would not take a farthing,' said Gertrude.

'And what did you see?' inquired Rhoda.

'Nothing I—care to speak of.' The constraint in her manner was remarkable; her face was so rigid as to wear an oldened aspect, faintly suggestive of the face in Rhoda's bed-chamber.

'Was it you who first proposed coming here?' Mrs. Lodge suddenly inquired, after a long pause. 'How very odd, if you did!'

'No. But I am not sorry we have come, all things considered,' she replied. For the first time a sense of triumph possessed her, and she did not altogether deplore that the young thing at her side should learn that their lives had been antagonized by other influences than their own.

The subject was no more alluded to during the long and dreary walk home. But in some way or other a story was whispered about the many-dairied lowland that winter that Mrs. Lodge's gradual loss of the use of her left arm was owing to her being 'over-looked' by Rhoda Brook. The latter kept her own counsel about the incubus, but her face grew sadder and thinner; and in the spring she and her boy disappeared from the neighbourhood of Holmstoke.

A SECOND ATTEMPT

VI

Half a dozen years passed away, and Mr. and Mrs. Lodge's married experience sank into prosiness, and worse. The farmer was usually gloomy and silent: the woman whom he had wooed for her grace and beauty was contorted and disfigured in the left limb; moreover, she had brought him no child, which rendered it likely that he would be the last of a family who had occupied that valley for some two hundred years. He thought of Rhoda Brook and her son; and feared this might be a judgement from heaven upon him.

The once blithe-hearted and enlightened Gertrude was changing into an irritable, superstitious woman, whose whole time was given to experimenting upon her ailment with every quack remedy she came across. She was honestly attached to her husband, and was ever secretly hoping against hope to win back his heart again by regaining some at least of her personal beauty. Hence it arose that her closet was lined with bottles, packets, and ointment-pots of every description—nay, bunches of mystic herbs, charms, and books of necromancy, which in her schoolgirl time she would have ridiculed as folly.

'Damned if you won't poison yourself with these apothecary messes and witch mixtures some time or other,' said her husband, when his eye chanced to fall upon the multitudinous array.

She did not reply, but turned her sad, soft glance upon him in such heart-swollen reproach that he looked sorry for his words, and added, 'I only meant it for your good, you know, Gertrude.'

'I'll clear out the whole lot, and destroy them,' said she huskily, 'and try such remedies no more!'

'You want somebody to cheer you,' he observed. 'I once thought of adopting a boy; but he is too old now. And he is gone away I don't know where.'

She guessed to whom he alluded; for Rhoda Brook's story had in the course of years become known to her; though not a word had ever passed between her husband and herself on the subject. Neither had she ever spoken to him of her visit to Conjuror Trendle, and of what was revealed to her, or she thought was revealed to her, by that solitary heath-man.

She was now five-and-twenty; but she seemed older. 'Six years of marriage, and only a few months of love,' she sometimes whispered to herself. And then she thought of the apparent cause, and said, with a tragic glance at her withering limb, 'If I could only again be as I was when he first saw me!'

She obediently destroyed her nostrums and charms; but there remained a hankering wish to try something else—some other sort of cure altogether. She had never revisited Trendle since she had been conducted to the house of the solitary by Rhoda against her will; but it now suddenly occurred to Gertrude that she would, in a last desperate effort at deliverance from this seeming curse, again seek out the man, if he yet lived. He was entitled to a certain credence, for the indistinct form he had raised in the glass had undoubtedly resembled the only woman in the world who—

as she now knew, though not then—could have a reason for bearing her ill-will. The visit should be paid.

This time she went alone, though she nearly got lost on the heath, and roamed a considerable distance out of her way. Trendle's house was reached at last, however: he was not indoors, and instead of waiting at the cottage, she went to where his bent figure was pointed out to her at work a long way off. Trendle remembered her, and laying down the handful of furze-roots which he was gathering and throwing into a heap, he offered to accompany her in her homeward direction, as the distance was considerable and the days were short. So they walked together, his head bowed nearly to the earth, and his form of a colour with it.

'You can send away warts and other excrescences, I know,' she said; 'why can't you send away this?' And the arm was uncovered.

'You think too much of my powers!' said Trendle; 'and I am old and weak now, too. No, no; it is too much for me to attempt in my own person. What have ye tried?'

She named to him some of the hundred medicaments and counterspells which she had adopted from time to time. He shook his head.

'Some were good enough,' he said approvingly; 'but not many of them for such as this. This is of the nature of a blight, not of the nature of a wound; and if you ever do throw it off, it will be all at once.'

'If I only could!'

'There is only one chance of doing it known to me. It has never failed in kindred afflictions,—that I can declare. But it is hard to carry out, and especially for a woman.'

'Tell me!' said she.

'You must touch with the limb the neck of a man who's been hanged.'

She started a little at the image he had raised.

'Before he's cold—just after he's cut down,' continued the conjuror impassively.

'How can that do good?'

'It will turn the blood and change the constitution. But, as I say, to do it is hard. You must go to the jail when there's a hanging, and wait for him when he's brought off the gallows. Lots have done it, though perhaps not such pretty women as you. I used to send dozens for skin complaints. But that was in former times. The last I sent was in '13—near twelve years ago.'

He had no more to tell her; and, when he had put her into a straight track homeward, turned and left her, refusing all money as at first.

A RIDE

VII

THE communication sank deep into Gertrude's mind. Her nature was rather a timid one; and probably of all remedies that the white wizard could have suggested there was not one which would have filled her with so much aversion as this, not to speak of the immense obstacles in the way of its adoption.

Casterbridge, the county-town, was a dozen or fifteen miles off; and though in those days, when men were executed for horse-stealing, arson, and burglary, an assize seldom passed without a hanging, it was not likely that she could get access to the body of the criminal unaided. And the fear of her husband's anger made her reluctant to breathe a word of Trendle's suggestion to him or to anybody about him.

She did nothing for months, and patiently bore her disfigurement as before. But her woman's nature, craving for renewed love, through the medium of renewed beauty (she was but twenty-five), was ever stimulating her to try what, at any rate, could hardly do her any harm. 'What came by a spell will go by a spell surely,' she would say. Whenever her imagination pictured the act she shrank in terror from the possibility of it: then the words of the conjuror, 'It will turn your blood,' were seen to be capable of a scientific no less than a ghastly interpretation; the mastering desire returned, and urged her on again.

There was at this time but one county paper, and that her husband only occasionally borrowed. But old-fashioned days had old-fashioned means, and news was extensively conveyed by word of mouth from market to market, or from fair to fair, so that, whenever such an event as an execution was about to take place, few within a radius of twenty miles were ignorant of the coming sight; and, so far as Holmstoke was concerned, some enthusiasts had been known to walk all the way to Casterbridge and back in one day, solely to witness the spectacle. The next assizes were in March; and when Gertrude Lodge heard that they had been held, she inquired stealthily at the inn as to the result, as soon as she could find opportunity.

She was, however, too late. The time at which the sentences were to be carried out had arrived, and to make the journey and obtain admission at such short notice required at least her husband's assistance. She dared not tell him, for she had found by delicate experiment that these smouldering village beliefs made him furious if mentioned, partly because he half entertained them himself. It was therefore necessary to wait for another opportunity.

Her determination received a fillip from learning that two epileptic children had attended from this very village of Holmstoke many years before with beneficial results, though the experiment had been strongly condemned by the neighbouring clergy. April, May, June, passed; and it is no overstatement to say that by the end of the last-named month Gertrude well-nigh longed for the death of a fellow-creature. Instead of her formal prayers each night, her unconscious prayer was, 'O Lord, hang some guilty or innocent person soon!'

This time she made earlier inquiries, and was altogether more systematic in her proceedings. Moreover, the season was summer, between the haymaking and the harvest, and in the leisure thus afforded him her husband had been holiday-taking away from home.

The assizes were in July, and she went to the inn as before. There was to be one execution—only one—for arson.

Her greatest problem was not how to get to Casterbridge, but what means she should adopt for obtaining admission to the jail. Though access for such purposes had formerly never been denied, the custom had fallen into desuetude; and in contemplating her possible difficulties, she was again almost driven to fall back upon her husband. But, on sounding him about the assizes, he was so uncommunicative, so more than usually cold, that she did not proceed, and decided that whatever she did she would do alone.

Fortune, obdurate hitherto, showed her unexpected favour. On the Thursday before the Saturday fixed for the execution, Lodge remarked to her that he was going away from home for another day or two on business at a fair, and that he was sorry he could not take her with him.

She exhibited on this occasion so much readiness to stay at home that he looked at her in surprise. Time had been when she would have shown deep disappointment at the loss of such a jaunt. However, he lapsed into his usual taciturnity, and on the day named left Holmstoke.

It was now her turn. She at first had thought of driving, but on reflection held that driving would not do, since it would necessitate her keeping to the turnpike-road, and so increase by tenfold the risk of her ghastly errand being found out. She decided to ride, and avoid the beaten track, notwithstanding that in her husband's stables there was no animal just at present which by any stretch of imagination could be considered a lady's mount, in spite of his promise before marriage to always keep a mare for her. He had, however, many cart-horses, fine ones of their kind; and among the rest was a serviceable creature, an equine Amazon, with a back as broad as a sofa, on which Gertrude had occasionally taken an airing when unwell. This horse she chose.

On Friday afternoon one of the men brought it round. She was dressed, and before going down looked at her shrivelled arm. 'Ah!' she said to it, 'if it had not been for you this terrible ordeal would have been saved me!'

When strapping up the bundle in which she carried a few articles of clothing, she took occasion to say to the servant, 'I take these in case I should not get back to-night from the person I am going to visit. Don't be alarmed if I am not in by ten, and close up the house as usual. I shall be at home to-morrow for certain.' She meant then to tell her husband privately: the deed accomplished was not like the deed projected. He would almost certainly forgive her.

And then the pretty palpitating Gertrude Lodge went from her husband's homestead; but though her goal was Casterbridge she did not take the direct route thither through Stickleford. Her cunning course at first was in precisely the opposite direction. As soon as she was out of sight, however, she turned to the left, by a road which led into Egdon, and on entering the heath wheeled round, and set out in the true course, due westerly. A more private way down the county could not be imagined; and as to direction, she had merely to keep her horse's head to a point a little to the right of the sun. She knew that she would light upon a furze-cutter or cottager of some sort from time to time, from whom she might correct her bearing.

Though the date was comparatively recent, Egdon was much less fragmentary in character than now. The attempts—successful and otherwise—at cultivation on the lower slopes, which intrude and break up the original heath into small detached heaths, had not been carried far; Enclosure Acts had not taken effect, and the banks and fences which now exclude the cattle of those villagers who formerly enjoyed rights of commonage thereon, and the carts of those who had turbary privileges[1] which kept them in firing all the year round, were not erected. Gertrude, therefore, rode along with no other obstacles than the prickly furze-bushes, the mats of heather, the white water-courses, and the natural steeps and declivities of the ground.

Her horse was sure, if heavy-footed and slow, and though a draught animal, was easy-paced; had it been otherwise, she was not a woman who could have ventured to ride over such a bit of country with a half-dead arm. It was therefore nearly eight o'clock when she drew rein to breathe her bearer on the last outlying high point of heath-land towards Casterbridge, previous to leaving Egdon for the cultivated valleys.

She halted before a pool called Rushy-pond, flanked by the ends of two hedges; a railing ran through the centre of the pond, dividing it in half. Over the railing she saw the low green country; over the green trees the roofs of the town; over the roofs a white flat façade, denoting the entrance to the county jail. On the roof of this front specks were moving about; they seemed to be workmen erecting something. Her flesh crept. She descended slowly, and was soon amid corn-fields and pastures. In another half-

[1] The right to cut turf (peat).

hour, when it was almost dusk, Gertrude reached the White Hart, the first inn of the town on that side.

Little surprise was excited by her arrival; farmers' wives rode on horseback then more than they do now; though, for that matter, Mrs. Lodge was not imagined to be a wife at all; the inn-keeper supposed her some harum-skarum young woman who had come to attend 'hang-fair' next day. Neither her husband nor herself ever dealt in Casterbridge market, so that she was unknown. While dismounting she beheld a crowd of boys standing at the door of a harness-maker's shop just above the inn, looking inside it with deep interest.

'What is going on there?' she asked of the ostler.

'Making the rope for to-morrow.'

She throbbed responsively, and contracted her arm.

''Tis sold by the inch afterwards,' the man continued. 'I could get you a bit, miss, for nothing, if you'd like?'

She hastily repudiated any such wish, all the more from a curious creeping feeling that the condemned wretch's destiny was becoming interwoven with her own; and having engaged a room for the night, sat down to think.

Up to this time she had formed but the vaguest notions about her means of obtaining access to the prison. The words of the cunning-man returned to her mind. He had implied that she should use her beauty, impaired though it was, as a pass-key. In her inexperience she knew little about jail functionaries; she had heard of a high-sheriff and an under-sheriff, but dimly only. She knew, however, that there must be a hangman, and to the hangman she determined to apply.

A WATER-SIDE HERMIT

VIII

At this date, and for several years after, there was a hangman to almost every jail. Gertrude found, on inquiry, that the Casterbridge official dwelt in a lonely cottage by a deep slow river flowing under the cliff on which the prison buildings were situate —the stream being the self-same one, though she did not know it, which watered the Stickleford and Holmstoke meads lower down in its course.

Having changed her dress, and before she had eaten or drunk—for she could not take her ease till she had ascertained some particulars—Gertrude pursued her way by a path along the water-side to the cottage indicated. Passing thus the outskirts of the jail, she discerned on the level roof over the gateway three rectangular lines against the sky, where the specks had been moving in her distant view; she recognized what the erection was, and passed quickly on. Another hundred yards brought her to the executioner's house, which a boy pointed out. It stood close to the same stream, and was hard by a weir, the waters of which emitted a steady roar.

While she stood hesitating the door opened, and an old man came forth shading a candle with one hand. Locking the door on the outside, he turned to a flight of wooden steps fixed against the end of the cottage, and began to ascend them, this being evidently the staircase to his bedroom. Gertrude hastened forward, but by the time she reached the foot of the ladder he was at the top. She called to him loudly enough to be heard above the roar of the weir; he looked down and said, 'What d'ye want here?'

'To speak to you a minute.'

The candle-light, such as it was, fell upon her imploring, pale, upturned face, and Davies (as the hangman was called) backed down the ladder. 'I was just going to bed,' he said; '"Early to bed and early to rise," but I don't mind stopping a minute for such a one as you. Come into house.' He reopened the door, and preceded her to the room within.

The implements of his daily work, which was that of a jobbing gardener, stood in a corner, and seeing probably that she looked rural, he said, 'If you want me to undertake country work I can't come, for I never leave Casterbridge for gentle nor simple—not I. My real calling is officer of justice,' he added formally.

'Yes, yes! That's it. To-morrow!'

'Ah! I thought so. Well, what's the matter about that? 'Tis no use to come here about the knot—folks do come continually, but I tell 'em one knot is as merciful as another if ye keep it under the ear. Is the unfortunate man a relation; or, I should say, perhaps' (looking at her dress) 'a person who's been in your employ?'

'No. What time is the execution?'

'The same as usual—twelve o'clock, or as soon after as the London mail-coach gets in. We always wait for that, in case of a reprieve.'

'O—a reprieve—I hope not!' she said involuntarily.

'Well,—hee, hee!—as a matter of business, so do I! But still, if ever a young fellow deserved to be let off, this one does; only just turned eighteen, and only present by chance when the rick was fired. Howsomever, there's not much risk of it, as they are obliged to make an example of him, there having been so much destruction of property that way lately.'

'I mean,' she explained, 'that I want to touch him for a charm, a cure of an affliction, by the advice of a man who has proved the virtue of the remedy.'

'O yes, miss! Now I understand. I've had such people come in past years. But it didn't strike me that you looked of a sort to require blood-turning. What's the complaint? The wrong kind for this, I'll be bound.'

'My arm.' She reluctantly showed the withered skin.

'Ah!—'tis all a-scram!'[1] said the hangman, examining it.

'Yes,' said she.

'Well,' he continued, with interest, 'that *is* the class o' subject, I'm bound to admit! I like the look of the wownd; it is truly as suitable for the cure as any I ever saw. 'Twas a knowing-man that sent 'ee, whoever he was.'

'You can contrive for me all that's necessary?' she said breathlessly.

'You should really have gone to the governor of the jail, and your doctor with 'ee, and given your name and address—that's how it used to be done, if I recollect. Still, perhaps, I can manage it for a trifling fee.'

'O, thank you! I would rather do it this way, as I should like it kept private.'

'Lover not to know, eh?'

'No—husband.'

[1] Distorted.

'Aha! Very well. I'll get 'ee a touch of the corpse.'

'Where is it now?' she said, shuddering.

'It?—*he*, you mean; he's living yet. Just inside that little winder up there in the glum.'[2] He signified the jail on the cliff above.

She thought of her husband and her friends. 'Yes, of course,' she said; 'and how am I to proceed?'

He took her to the door. 'Now, do you be waiting at the little wicket in the wall, that you'll find up there in the lane, not later than one o'clock. I will open it from the inside, as I shan't come home to dinner till he's cut down. Good-night. Be punctual; and if you don't want anybody to know 'ee, wear a veil. Ah—once I had such a daughter as you!'

She went away, and climbed the path above, to assure herself that she would be able to find the wicket next day. Its outline was soon visible to her—a narrow opening in the outer wall of the prison precincts. The steep was so great that, having reached the wicket, she stopped a moment to breathe; and, looking back upon the water-side cot, saw the hangman again ascending his outdoor staircase. He entered the loft or chamber to which it led, and in a few minutes extinguished his light.

The town clock struck ten, and she returned to the White Hart as she had come.

[2] Gloomy forbidding place.

A RENCOUNTER

IX

It was one o'clock on Saturday. Gertrude Lodge, having been admitted to the jail as above described, was sitting in a waiting-room within the second gate, which stood under a classic archway of ashlar,[1] then comparatively modern, and bearing the inscription, 'COVNTY JAIL: 1793.' This had been the façade she saw from the heath the day before. Near at hand was a passage to the roof on which the gallows stood.

[1] Smooth-cut limestone blocks.

The town was thronged, and the market suspended; but Gertrude had seen scarcely a soul. Having kept her room till the hour of the appointment, she had proceeded to the spot by a way which avoided the open space below the cliff where the spectators had gathered; but she could, even now, hear the multitudinous babble of their voices, out of which rose at intervals the hoarse croak of a single voice uttering the words, 'Last dying speech and confession!' There had been no reprieve, and the execution was over; but the crowd still waited to see the body taken down.

Soon the persistent woman heard a trampling overhead, then a hand beckoned to her, and, following directions, she went out and crossed the inner paved court beyond the gatehouse, her knees trembling so that she could scarcely walk. One of her arms was out of its sleeve, and only covered by her shawl.

On the spot at which she had now arrived were two trestles, and before she could think of their purpose she heard heavy feet descending stairs somewhere at her back. Turn her head she would not, or could not, and, rigid in this position, she was conscious of a rough coffin passing her shoulder, borne by four men. It was open, and in it lay the body of a young man, wearing the smockfrock of a rustic, and fustian breeches. The corpse had been thrown into the coffin so hastily that the skirt of the smock-frock was hanging over. The burden was temporarily deposited on the trestles.

By this time the young woman's state was such that a gray mist seemed to float before her eyes, on account of which, and the veil she wore, she could scarcely discern anything: it was as though she had nearly died, but was held up by a sort of galvanism.

'Now!' said a voice close at hand, and she was just conscious that the word had been addressed to her.

By a last strenuous effort she advanced, at the same time hearing persons approaching behind her. She bared her poor curst arm; and Davies, uncovering the face of the corpse, took Gertrude's hand, and held it so that her arm lay across the dead man's neck, upon a line the colour of an unripe blackberry, which surrounded it.

Gertrude shrieked: 'the turn o' the blood,' predicted by the conjuror, had taken place. But at that moment a second shriek rent the air of the enclosure: it was not Gertrude's, and its effect upon her was to make her start round.

Immediately behind her stood Rhoda Brook, her face drawn, and her eyes red with weeping. Behind Rhoda stood Gertrude's own husband; his countenance lined, his eyes dim, but without a tear.

'D—n you! what are you doing here?' he said hoarsely.

'Hussy—to come between us and our child now!' cried Rhoda. 'This is the meaning of what Satan showed me in the vision! You are like her at last!' And clutching the bare arm of the younger woman, she pulled her unresistingly back against the wall. Immediately Brook had loosened her hold the fragile young Gertrude slid down against the feet of her husband. When he lifted her up she was unconscious.

The mere sight of the twain had been enough to suggest to her that the dead young man was Rhoda's son. At that time the relatives of an executed convict had the privilege of claiming the body for burial, if they chose to do so; and it was for this purpose that Lodge was awaiting the inquest with Rhoda. He had been summoned by her as soon as the young man was taken in the crime, and at different times since; and he had attended in court during the trial. This was the 'holiday' he had been indulging in of late. The two wretched parents had wished to avoid exposure; and hence had come themselves for the body, a waggon and sheet for its conveyance and covering being in waiting outside.

Gertrude's case was so serious that it was deemed advisable to call to her the surgeon who was at hand. She was taken out of the jail into the town; but she never reached home alive. Her delicate vitality, sapped perhaps by the paralyzed arm, collapsed under the double shock that followed the severe strain, physical and mental, to which she had subjected herself during the previous twenty-four hours. Her blood had been 'turned' indeed—too far. Her death took place in the town three days after.

Her husband was never seen in Casterbridge again; once only in the old market-place at Anglebury, which he had so much frequented, and very seldom in public anywhere. Burdened at first with moodiness and remorse, he eventually changed for the better, and appeared as a chastened and thoughtful man. Soon after attending the funeral of his poor young wife he took steps towards giving up the farms in Holmstoke and the adjoining parish, and, having sold every head of his stock, he went away to Port-Bredy, at the other end of the county, living there in solitary lodgings till his death two years later of a painless decline. It was then found that he had bequeathed the whole of his not inconsiderable property to a reformatory for boys, subject to the payment of a small annuity to Rhoda Brook, if she could be found to claim it.

For some time she could not be found; but eventually she reappeared in her old parish,—absolutely refusing, however, to have anything to do with the provision made for her. Her monotonous milking at the dairy was resumed, and followed for many long years, till her form became bent, and her once abundant dark hair white and worn away at the forehead—perhaps by long pressure against the cows. Here, sometimes, those who knew her experiences would stand and observe her, and wonder what sombre thoughts were beating inside that impassive, wrinkled brow, to the rhythm of the alternating milk-streams.

On the Western Circuit

I

THE man who played the disturbing part in the two quiet feminine lives hereunder depicted—no great man, in any sense, by the way—first had knowledge of them on an October evening, in the city of Melchester. He had been standing in the Close, vainly endeavouring to gain amid the darkness a glimpse of the most homogeneous pile of mediæval architecture in England,[1] which towered and tapered from the damp and level sward in front of him. While he stood the presence of the Cathedral walls

[1] Salisbury Cathedral, which is, unusually, almost completely in the style (Early English Gothic) of one period.

was revealed rather by the ear than by the eyes; he could not see them, but they reflected sharply a roar of sound which entered the Close by a street leading from the city square, and, falling upon the building, was flung back upon him.

He postponed till the morrow his attempt to examine the deserted edifice, and turned his attention to the noise. It was compounded of steam barrel-organs, the clanging of gongs, the ringing of hand-bells, the clack of rattles, and the undistinguishable shouts of men. A lurid light hung in the air in the direction of the tumult. Thitherward he went, passing under the arched gateway, along a straight street, and into the square.

He might have searched Europe over for a greater contrast between juxtaposed scenes. The spectacle was that of the eighth chasm of the Inferno[2] as to colour and flame, and, as to mirth, a development of the Homeric heaven. A smoky glare, of the complexion of brass-filings, ascended from the fiery tongues of innumerable naptha lamps affixed to booths, stalls, and other temporary erections which crowded the spacious market-square. In front of this irradiation scores of human figures, more or less in profile, were darting athwart and across, up, down, and around, like gnats against a sunset.

Their motions were so rhythmical that they seemed to be moved by machinery. And it presently appeared that they were moved by machinery indeed; the figures being those of the patrons of swings, see-saws, flying-leaps, above all of the three steam roundabouts which occupied the centre of the position. It was from the latter that the din of steam-organs came.

Throbbing humanity in full light was, on second thoughts, better than architecture in the dark. The young man, lighting a short pipe, and putting his hat on one side and one hand in his pocket, to throw himself into harmony with his new environment, drew near to the largest and most patronized of the steam circuses, as the roundabouts were called by their owners. This was one of brilliant finish, and it was now in full revolution. The musical instrument around which and to whose tones the riders revolved, directed its trumpet-mouths of brass upon the young man, and the long plate-glass mirrors set at angles, which revolved

[2] Dante's account of Hell in his *Divine Comedy*.

with the machine, flashed the gyrating personages and hobby-horses kaleidoscopically into his eyes.

It could now be seen that he was unlike the majority of the crowd. A gentlemanly young fellow, one of the species found in large towns only, and London particularly, built on delicate lines, well, though not fashionably dressed, he appeared to belong to the professional class; he had nothing square or practical about his look, much that was curvilinear and sensuous. Indeed, some would have called him a man not altogether typical of the middle-class male of a century wherein sordid ambition is the master-passion that seems to be taking the time-honoured place of love.

The revolving figures passed before his eyes with an unexpected and quiet grace in a throng whose natural movements did not suggest gracefulness or quietude as a rule. By some contrivance there was imparted to each of the hobby-horses a motion which was really the triumph and perfection of roundabout inventiveness—a galloping rise and fall, so timed that, of each pair of steeds, one was on the spring while the other was on the pitch. The riders were quite fascinated by these equine undulations in this most delightful holiday-game of our times. There were riders as young as six, and as old as sixty years, with every age between. At first it was difficult to catch a personality, but by and by the observer's eyes centred on the prettiest girl out of the several pretty ones revolving.

It was not that one with the light frock and light hat whom he had been at first attracted by; no, it was the one with the black cape, grey skirt, light gloves and—no, not even she, but the one behind her; she with the crimson skirt, dark jacket, brown hat and brown gloves. Unmistakably that was the prettiest girl.

Having finally selected her, this idle spectator studied her as well as he was able during each of her brief transits across his visual field. She was absolutely unconscious of everything save the act of riding: her features were rapt in an ecstatic dreaminess; for the moment she did not know her age or her history or her lineaments, much less her troubles. He himself was full of vague latter-day glooms and popular melancholies, and it was a refreshing sensation to behold this young thing then and there, absolutely as happy as if she were in a Paradise.

Dreading the moment when the inexorable stoker, grimily lurking behind the glittering rococo-work,[3] should decide that this set of riders had had their pennyworth, and bring the whole concern of steam-engine, horses, mirrors, trumpets, drums, cymbals, and such-like to pause and silence, he waited for her every reappearance, glancing indifferently over the intervening forms, including the two plainer girls, the old woman and child, the two youngsters, the newly-married couple, the old man with a clay pipe, the sparkish youth with a ring, the young ladies in the chariot, the pair of journeyman-carpenters, and others, till his select country beauty followed on again in her place. He had never seen a fairer product of nature, and at each round she made a deeper mark in his sentiments. The stoppage then came, and the sighs of the riders were audible.

He moved round to the place at which he reckoned she would alight; but she retained her seat. The empty saddles began to refill, and she plainly was deciding to have another turn. The young man drew up to the side of her steed, and pleasantly asked her if she had enjoyed her ride.

'O yes!' she said, with dancing eyes. 'It has been quite unlike anything I have ever felt in my life before!'

It was not difficult to fall into conversation with her. Unreserved—too unreserved—by nature, she was not experienced enough to be reserved by art, and after a little coaxing she answered his remarks readily. She had come to live in Melchester from a village on the Great Plain, and this was the first time that she had ever seen a steam-circus; she could not understand how such wonderful machines were made. She had come to the city on the invitation of Mrs. Harnham, who had taken her into her household to train her as a servant, if she showed any aptitude. Mrs. Harnham was a young lady who before she married had been Miss Edith White, living in the country near the speaker's cottage; she was now very kind to her through knowing her in childhood so well. She was even taking the trouble to educate her. Mrs. Harnham was the only friend she had in the world, and being without children had wished to have her near her in preference to anybody else, though she had only lately

[3] **Exuberant decoration.**

come; allowed her to do almost as she liked, and to have a holiday whenever she asked for it. The husband of this kind young lady was a rich wine-merchant of the town, but Mrs. Harnham did not care much about him. In the daytime you could see the house from where they were talking. She, the speaker, liked Melchester better than the lonely country, and she was going to have a new hat for next Sunday that was to cost fifteen and ninepence.

Then she inquired of her acquaintance where he lived, and he told her in London, that ancient and smoky city, where everybody lived who lived at all, and died because they could not live there. He came into Wessex two or three times a year for professional reasons; he had arrived from Wintoncester yesterday, and was going on into the next county in a day or two. For one thing he did like the country better than the town, and it was because it contained such girls as herself.

Then the pleasure-machine started again, and, to the light-hearted girl, the figure of the handsome young man, the market-square with its lights and crowd, the houses beyond, and the world at large, began moving round as before, countermoving in the revolving mirrors on her right hand, she being as it were the fixed point in an undulating, dazzling, lurid universe, in which loomed forward most prominently of all the form of her late interlocutor. Each time that she approached the half of her orbit that lay nearest him they gazed at each other with smiles, and with that unmistakable expression which means so little at the moment, yet so often leads up to passion, heart-ache, union, disunion, devotion, overpopulation, drudgery, content, resignation, despair.

When the horses slowed anew he stepped to her side and proposed another heat. 'Hang the expense for once,' he said. 'I'll pay!'

She laughed till the tears came.

'Why do you laugh, dear?' said he.

'Because—you are so genteel that you must have plenty of money, and only say that for fun!' she returned.

'Ha-ha!' laughed the young man in unison, and gallantly producing his money she was enabled to whirl on again.

As he stood smiling there in the motley crowd, with his pipe in his hand, and clad in the rough pea-jacket and wideawake that he had put on for his stroll, who would have supposed him to be Charles Bradford Raye, Esquire, stuff-gownsman, educated at Wintoncester, called to the Bar at Lincoln's-Inn, now going the Western Circuit, merely detained in Melchester by a small arbitration after his brethren had moved on to the next county-town?

II

THE square was overlooked from its remoter corner by the house of which the young girl had spoken, a dignified residence of considerable size, having several windows on each floor. Inside one of these, on the first floor, the apartment being a large drawing-room, sat a lady, in appearance from twenty-eight to thirty years of age. The blinds were still undrawn, and the lady was absently surveying the weird scene without, her cheek resting on her hand. The room was unlit from within, but enough of the glare from the market-place entered it to reveal the lady's face. She was what is called an interesting creature rather than a handsome woman; dark-eyed, thoughtful, and with sensitive lips.

A man sauntered into the room from behind and came forward.

'O, Edith, I didn't see you,' he said. 'Why are you sitting here in the dark?'

'I am looking at the fair,' replied the lady in a languid voice.

'Oh? Horrid nuisance every year! I wish it could be put a stop to.'

'I like it.'

'H'm. There's no accounting for taste.'

For a moment he gazed from the window with her, for politeness sake, and then went out again.

In a few minutes she rang.

'Hasn't Anna come in?' asked Mrs. Harnham.

'No m'm.'

'She ought to be in by this time. I meant her to go for ten minutes only.'

'Shall I go and look for her, m'm?' said the housemaid alertly.

'No. It is not necessary: she is a good girl and will come soon.'

However, when the servant had gone Mrs. Harnham arose, went up to her room, cloaked and bonneted herself, and proceeded downstairs, where she found her husband.

'I want to see the fair,' she said; 'and I am going to look for Anna. I have made myself responsible for her, and must see she comes to no harm. She ought to be indoors. Will you come with me?'

'Oh, she's all right. I saw her on one of those whirligig things, talking to her young man as I came in. But I'll go if you wish, though I'd rather go a hundred miles the other way.'

'Then please do so. I shall come to no harm alone.'

She left the house and entered the crowd which thronged the market-place, where she soon discovered Anna, seated on the revolving horse. As soon as it stopped Mrs. Harnham advanced and said severely, 'Anna, how can you be such a wild girl? You were only to be out for ten minutes.'

Anna looked blank, and the young man, who had dropped into the background, came to help her alight.

'Please don't blame her,' he said politely. 'It is my fault that she has stayed. She looked so graceful on the horse that I induced her to go round again. I assure you that she has been quite safe.'

'In that case I'll leave her in your hands,' said Mrs. Harnham, turning to retrace her steps.

But this for the moment it was not so easy to do. Something had attracted the crowd to a spot in their rear, and the wine-merchant's wife, caught by its sway, found herself pressed against Anna's acquaintance without power to move away. Their faces were within a few inches of each other, his breath fanned her cheek as well as Anna's. They could do no other than smile at the accident; but neither spoke, and each waited passively. Mrs. Harnham then felt a man's hand clasping her fingers, and from the look of consciousness on the young fellow's face she knew the hand to be his: she also knew that from the position of the girl he had no other thought than that the imprisoned hand was Anna's. What prompted her to refrain from undeceiving him she could hardly tell. Not content with holding the hand, he playfully slipped two of his fingers inside her glove, against her palm. Thus matters continued till the pressure lessened; but several minutes passed before the crowd thinned sufficiently to allow Mrs. Harnham to withdraw.

'How did they get to know each other, I wonder?' she mused as she retreated. 'Anna is really very forward—and he very wicked and nice.'

She was so gently stirred with the stranger's manner and voice, with the tenderness of his idle touch, that instead of re-entering the house she turned back again and observed the pair from a screened nook. Really she argued (being little less impulsive than Anna herself) it was very excusable in Anna to encourage him, however she might have contrived to make his acquaintance; he was so gentlemanly, so fascinating, had such beautiful eyes. The thought that he was several years her junior produced a reasonless sigh.

At length the couple turned from the roundabout towards the door of Mrs. Harnham's house, and the young man could be heard saying that he would accompany her home. Anna, then, had found a lover, apparently a very devoted one. Mrs. Harnham was quite interested in him. When they drew near the door of the wine-merchant's house, a comparatively deserted spot by this time, they stood invisible for a little while in the shadow of a wall, where they separated, Anna going on to the entrance, and her acquaintance returning across the square.

'Anna,' said Mrs. Harnham, coming up. 'I've been looking at you! That young man kissed you at parting, I am almost sure.'

'Well,' stammered Anna; 'he said, if I didn't mind—it would do me no harm, and, and, him a great deal of good!'

'Ah, I thought so! And he was a stranger till tonight?'

'Yes ma'am.'

'Yet I warrant you told him your name and everything about yourself?'

'He asked me.'

'But he didn't tell you his?'

'Yes ma'am, he did!' cried Anna victoriously. 'It is Charles Bradford, of London.'

'Well, if he's respectable, of course I've nothing to say against your knowing him,' remarked her mistress, prepossessed, in spite of general principles, in the young man's favour. 'But I must reconsider all that, if he attempts to renew your acquaintance. A country-bred girl like you, who has never lived in Melchester till this month, who had hardly ever seen a black-coated man till you came here, to be so sharp as to capture a young Londoner like him!'

'I didn't capture him. I didn't do anything,' said Anna, in confusion.

When she was indoors and alone Mrs. Harnham thought what a well-bred and chivalrous young man Anna's companion had seemed. There had been a magic in his wooing touch of her hand; and she wondered how he had come to be attracted by the girl.

The next morning the emotional Edith Harnham went to the usual week-day service in Melchester cathedral. In crossing the Close through the fog she again perceived him who had interested her the previous evening, gazing up thoughtfully at the high-piled architecture of the nave: and as soon as she had taken her seat he entered and sat down in a stall opposite hers.

He did not particularly heed her; but Mrs. Harnham was continually occupying her eyes with him, and wondered more than ever what had attracted him in her unfledged maid-servant. The mistress was almost as unaccustomed as the maiden herself to the end-of-the-age young man, or she might have wondered less. Raye, having looked about him awhile, left abruptly, without regard to the service that was proceeding; and Mrs. Harnham—lonely, impressionable creature that she was—took no further interest in praising the Lord. She wished she had married a London man who knew the subtleties of love-making as they were evidently known to him who had mistakenly caressed her hand.

III

THE calendar at Melchester had been light, occupying the court only a few hours; and the assizes at Casterbridge, the next county-town on the Western Circuit, having no business for Raye, he had not gone thither. At the next town after that they did not open till the following Monday, trials to begin on Tuesday morning. In the natural order of things Raye would have arrived at the latter place on Monday afternoon; but it was not till the middle of

Wednesday that his gown and grey wig, curled in tiers, in the best fashion of Assyrian bas-reliefs, were seen blowing and bobbing behind him as he hastily walked up the High Street from his lodgings. But though he entered the assize building there was nothing for him to do, and sitting at the blue baize table in the well of the court, he mended pens with a mind far away from the case in progress. Thoughts of unpremeditated conduct, of which a week earlier he would not have believed himself capable, threw him into a mood of dissatisfied depression.

He had contrived to see again the pretty rural maiden Anna, the day after the fair, had walked out of the city with her to the earthworks of Old Melchester,[1] and feeling a violent fancy for her, had remained in Melchester all Sunday, Monday, and Tuesday; by persuasion obtaining walks and meetings with the girl six or seven times during the interval; had in brief won her, body and soul.

He supposed it must have been owing to the seclusion in which he had lived of late in town that he had given way so unrestrainedly to a passion for an artless creature whose inexperience had, from the first, led her to place herself unreservedly in his hands. Much he deplored trifling with her feelings for the sake of a passing desire; and he could only hope that she might not live to suffer on his account.

She had begged him to come to her again; entreated him; wept. He had promised that he would do so, and he meant to carry out that promise. He could not desert her now. Awkward as such unintentional connections were, the interspace of a hundred miles—which to a girl of her limited capabilities was like a thousand—would effectually hinder this summer fancy from greatly encumbering his life; while thought of her simple love might do him the negative good of keeping him from idle pleasures in town when he wished to work hard. His circuit journeys would take him to Melchester three or four times a year; and then he could always see her.

The pseudonym, or rather partial name, that he had given her as his before knowing how far the acquaintance was going to

[1] Old Sarum, on a low hill a mile and a half north of Salisbury, the deserted site of a British fort and later of a Saxon and then Norman town.

carry him, had been spoken on the spur of the moment, without any ulterior intention whatever. He had not afterwards disturbed Anna's error, but on leaving her he had felt bound to give her an address at a stationer's not far from his chambers, at which she might write to him under the initials 'C. B.'

In due time Raye returned to his London abode, having called at Melchester on his way and spent a few additional hours with his fascinating child of nature. In town he lived monotonously every day. Often he and his rooms were enclosed by a tawny fog from all the world besides, and when he lighted the gas to read or write by, his situation seemed so unnatural that he would look into the fire and think of that trusting girl at Melchester again and again. Often, oppressed by absurd fondness for her, he would enter the dim religious nave of the Law Courts by the north door, elbow other juniors[2] habited like himself, and like him unretained;[3] edge himself into this or that crowded court where a sensational case was going on, just as if he were in it, though the police officers at the door knew as well as he knew himself that he had no more concern with the business in hand than the patient idlers at the gallery-door outside, who had waited to enter since eight in the morning because, like him, they belonged to the classes that live on expectation. But he would do these things to no purpose, and think how greatly the characters in such scenes contrasted with the pink and breezy Anna.

An unexpected feature in that peasant maiden's conduct was that she had not as yet written to him, though he had told her she might do so if she wished. Surely a young creature had never before been so reticent in such circumstances. At length he sent her a brief line, positively requesting her to write. There was no answer by the return post, but the day after a letter in a neat feminine hand, and bearing the Melchester post-mark, was handed to him by the stationer.

The fact alone of its arrival was sufficient to satisfy his imaginative sentiment. He was not anxious to open the epistle, and in truth did not begin to read it for nearly half-an-hour, anticipating readily its terms of passionate retrospect and tender

[2] Young 'apprentice' barristers.
[3] Not yet engaged to appear in a case.

adjuration. When at last he turned his feet to the fireplace and unfolded the sheet, he was surprised and pleased to find that neither extravagance nor vulgarity was there. It was the most charming little missive he had ever received from a woman. To be sure the language was simple and the ideas were slight; but it was so self-possessed; so purely that of a young girl who felt her womanhood to be enough for her dignity that he read it through twice. Four sides were filled, and a few lines written across, after the fashion of former days; the paper, too, was common, and not of the latest shade and surface. But what of those things? He had received letters from women who were fairly called ladies, but never so sensible, so human a letter as this. He could not single out any one sentence and say it was at all remarkable or clever; the *ensemble* of the letter[4] it was which won him; and beyond the one request that he would write or come to her again soon there was nothing to show her sense of a claim upon him.

To write again and develop a correspondence was the last thing Raye would have preconceived as his conduct in such a situation; yet he did send a short, encouraging line or two, signed with his pseudonym, in which he asked for another letter, and cheeringly promised that he would try to see her again on some near day, and would never forget how much they had been to each other during their short acquaintance.

[4] The letter as a whole, its total effect.

IV

To return now to the moment at which Anna, at Melchester, had received Raye's letter.

It had been put into her own hand by the postman on his morning rounds. She flushed down to her neck on receipt of it, and turned it over and over. 'It is mine?' she said.

'Why, yes, can't you see it is?' said the postman, smiling as he guessed the nature of the document and the cause of the confusion.

'O yes, of course!' replied Anna, looking at the letter, forcedly tittering, and blushing still more.

Her look of embarrassment did not leave her with the postman's departure. She opened the envelope, kissed its contents, put away the letter in her pocket, and remained musing till her eyes filled with tears.

A few minutes later she carried up a cup of tea to Mrs. Harnham in her bed-chamber. Anna's mistress looked at her, and said: 'How dismal you seem this morning, Anna. What's the matter?'

'I'm not dismal, I'm glad; only I——' She stopped to stifle a sob.

'Well?'

'I've got a letter—and what good is it to me, if I can't read a word in it!'

'Why, I'll read it, child, if necessary.'

'But this is from somebody—I don't want anybody to read it but myself!' Anna murmured.

'I shall not tell anybody. Is it from that young man?'

'I think so.' Anna slowly produced the letter, saying: 'Then will you read it to me, ma'am?'

This was the secret of Anna's embarrassment and flutterings. She could neither read nor write. She had grown up under the care of an aunt by marriage, at one of the lonely hamlets on the Great Mid-Wessex Plain where, even in days of national education, there had been no school within a distance of two miles. Her aunt was an ignorant woman; there had been nobody to investigate Anna's circumstances, nobody to care about her learning the rudiments; though, as often in such cases, she had been well fed and clothed and not unkindly treated. Since she had come to live at Melchester with Mrs. Harnham, the latter, who took a kindly interest in the girl, had taught her to speak correctly, in which accomplishment Anna showed considerable readiness, as is not unusual with the illiterate; and soon became quite fluent in the use of her mistress's phraseology. Mrs. Harnham also insisted upon her getting a spelling and copy book, and beginning to practise in these. Anna was slower in this branch of her education, and meanwhile here was the letter.

Edith Harnham's large dark eyes expressed some interest in the contents, though, in her character of mere interpreter, she

9110212 L

threw into her tone as much as she could of mechanical passiveness. She read the short epistle on to its concluding sentence, which idly requested Anna to send him a tender answer.

'Now—you'll do it for me, won't you, dear mistress?' said Anna eagerly. 'And you'll do it as well as ever you can, please? Because I couldn't bear him to think I am not able to do it myself. I should sink into the earth with shame if he knew that!'

From some words in the letter Mrs. Harnham was led to ask questions, and the answers she received confirmed her suspicions. Deep concern filled Edith's heart at perceiving how the girl had committed her happiness to the issue of this new-sprung attachment. She blamed herself for not interfering in a flirtation which had resulted so seriously for the poor little creature in her charge; though at the time of seeing the pair together she had a feeling that it was hardly within her province to nip young affection in the bud. However, what was done could not be undone, and it behoved her now, as Anna's only protector, to help her as much as she could. To Anna's eager request that she, Mrs. Harnham, should compose and write the answer to this young London man's letter, she felt bound to accede, to keep alive his attachment to the girl if possible; though in other circumstances she might have suggested the cook as an amanuensis.

A tender reply was thereupon concocted, and set down in Edith Harnham's hand. This letter it had been which Raye had received and delighted in. Written in the presence of Anna it certainly was, and on Anna's humble note-paper, and in a measure indited by the young girl; but the life, the spirit, the individuality, were Edith Harnham's.

'Won't you at least put your name yourself?' she said. 'You can manage to write that by this time?'

'No, no,' said Anna, shrinking back. 'I should do it so bad. He'd be ashamed of me, and never see me again!'

The note, so prettily requesting another from him, had, as we have seen, power enough in its pages to bring one. He declared it to be such a pleasure to hear from her that she must write every week. The same process of manufacture was accordingly repeated by Anna and her mistress, and continued for several weeks in succession; each letter being penned and suggested by Edith, the girl standing by; the answer read and commented on by Edith, Anna standing by and listening again.

Late on a winter evening, after the dispatch of the sixth letter, Mrs. Harnham was sitting alone by the remains of her fire. Her husband had retired to bed, and she had fallen into that fixity of musing which takes no count of hour or temperature. The state of mind had been brought about in Edith by a strange thing which she had done that day. For the first time since Raye's visit Anna had gone to stay over a night or two with her cottage friends on the Plain, and in her absence had arrived, out of its time, a letter from Raye. To this Edith had replied on her own responsibility, from the depths of her own heart, without waiting for her maid's collaboration. The luxury of writing to him what would be known to no consciousness but his was great, and she had indulged herself therein.

Why was it a luxury?

Edith Harnham led a lonely life. Influenced by the belief of the British parent that a bad marriage with its aversions is better than free womanhood with its interests, dignity, and leisure, she had consented to marry the elderly wine-merchant as a *pis aller*,[1] at the age of seven-and-twenty—some three years before this date —to find afterwards that she had made a mistake. That contract had left her still a woman whose deeper nature had never been stirred.

She was now clearly realizing that she had become possessed to the bottom of her soul with the image of a man to whom she was hardly so much as a name. From the first he had attracted her by his looks and voice; by his tender touch; and, with these as generators, the writing of letter after letter and the reading of their soft answers had insensibly developed on her side an emotion which fanned his; till there had resulted a magnetic reciprocity between the correspondents, notwithstanding that one of them wrote in a character not her own. That he had been able to seduce another woman in two days was his crowning though unrecognized fascination for her as the she-animal.

They were her own impassioned and pent-up ideas—lowered to monosyllabic phraseology in order to keep up the disguise—

[1] A last resource—when nothing better can be done or found.

that Edith put into letters signed with another name, much to the shallow Anna's delight, who, unassisted, could not for the world have conceived such pretty fancies for winning him, even had she been able to write them. Edith found that it was these, her own foisted-in sentiments, to which the young barrister mainly responded. The few sentences occasionally added from Anna's own lips made apparently no impression upon him.

The letter-writing in her absence Anna never discovered; but on her return the next morning she declared she wished to see her lover about something at once, and begged Mrs. Harnham to ask him to come.

There was a strange anxiety in her manner which did not escape Mrs. Harnham, and ultimately resolved itself into a flood of tears. Sinking down at Edith's knees, she made confession that the result of her relations with her lover it would soon become necessary to disclose.

Edith Harnham was generous enough to be very far from inclined to cast Anna adrift at this conjuncture. No true woman ever is so inclined from her own personal point of view, however prompt she may be in taking such steps to safeguard those dear to her. Although she had written to Raye so short a time previously, she instantly penned another Anna-note hinting clearly though delicately the state of affairs.

Raye replied by a hasty line to say how much he was concerned at her news: he felt that he must run down to see her almost immediately.

But a week later the girl came to her mistress's room with another note, which on being read informed her that after all he could not find time for the journey. Anna was broken with grief; but by Mrs. Harnham's counsel strictly refrained from hurling at him the reproaches and bitterness customary from young women so situated. One thing was imperative: to keep the young man's romantic interest in her alive. Rather therefore did Edith, in the name of her *protégée*,[2] request him on no account to be distressed about the looming event, and not to inconvenience himself to hasten down. She desired above everything to be no weight upon

[2] The girl she 'protected'; one whose interests a person guards and advances.

him in his career, no clog upon his high activities. She had wished him to know what had befallen: he was to dismiss it again from his mind. Only he must write tenderly as ever, and when he should come again on the spring circuit it would be soon enough to discuss what had better be done.

It may well be supposed that Anna's own feelings had not been quite in accord with these generous expressions; but the mistress's judgment had ruled, and Anna had acquiesced. 'All I want is that *niceness* you can so well put into your letters, my dear, dear mistress, and that I can't for the life o' me make up out of my own head; though I mean the same thing and feel it exactly when you've written it down!'

When the letter had been sent off, and Edith Harnham was left alone, she bowed herself on the back of her chair and wept.

'I wish his child was mine—I wish it was!' she murmured. 'Yet how can I say such a wicked thing!'

V

THE letter moved Raye considerably when it reached him. The intelligence itself had affected him less than her unexpected manner of treating him in relation to it. The absence of any word of reproach, the devotion to his interests, the self-sacrifice apparent in every line, all made up a nobility of character that he had never dreamt of finding in womankind.

'God forgive me!' he said tremulously. 'I have been a wicked wretch. I did not know she was such a treasure as this!'

He reassured her instantly; declaring that he would not of course desert her, that he would provide a home for her somewhere. Meanwhile she was to stay where she was as long as her mistress would allow her.

But a misfortune supervened in this direction. Whether an inkling of Anna's circumstances reached the knowledge of Mrs. Harnham's husband or not cannot be said, but the girl was compelled, in spite of Edith's entreaties, to leave the house. By her own choice she decided to go back for a while to the cottage on the Plain. This arrangement led to a consultation as to how the correspondence should be carried on; and in the girl's inability to continue personally what had been begun in her name, and in the difficulty of their acting in concert as heretofore, she requested Mrs. Harnham—the only well-to-do-friend she had in the world—to receive the letters and reply to them off-hand, sending them on afterwards to herself on the Plain, where she might at least get some neighbour to read them to her, if a trustworthy one could be met with. Anna and her box then departed for the Plain.

Thus it befell that Edith Harnham found herself in the strange position of having to correspond, under no supervision by the real woman, with a man not her husband, in terms which were virtually those of a wife, concerning a corporeal condition that was not Edith's at all; the man being one for whom, mainly through the sympathies involved in playing this part, she secretly cherished a predilection, subtle and imaginative truly, but strong and absorbing. She opened each letter, read it as if intended for herself, and replied from the promptings of her own heart and no other.

Throughout this correspondence, carried on in the girl's absence, the high-strung Edith Harnham lived in the ecstasy of fancy; the vicarious intimacy engendered such a flow of passionateness as was never exceeded. For conscience' sake Edith at first sent on each of his letters to Anna, and even rough copies of her replies; but later on these so-called copies were much abridged, and many letters on both sides were not sent on at all.

Though sensuous, and, superficially at least, infested with the self-indulgent vices of artificial society, there was a substratum of honesty and fairness in Raye's character. He had really a tender regard for the country girl, and it grew more tender than ever when he found her apparently capable of expressing the deepest sensibilities in the simplest words. He meditated, he wavered; and finally resolved to consult his sister, a maiden lady much older than himself, of lively sympathies and good intent. In making this confidence he showed her some of the letters.

'She seems fairly educated,' Miss Raye observed. 'And bright in ideas. She expresses herself with a taste that must be innate.'

'Yes. She writes very prettily, doesn't she, thanks to these elementary schools?'

'One is drawn out towards her, in spite of one's self, poor thing.'

The upshot of the discussion was that though he had not been directly advised to do it, Raye wrote, in his real name, what he would never have decided to write on his own responsibility; namely that he could not live without her, and would come down in the spring and shelve her looming difficulty by marrying her.

This bold acceptance of the situation was made known to Anna by Mrs. Harnham driving out immediately to the cottage on the Plain. Anna jumped for joy like a little child. And poor, crude directions for answering appropriately were given to Edith Harnham, who on her return to the city carried them out with warm intensifications.

'O!' she groaned, as she threw down the pen. 'Anna—poor good little fool—hasn't intelligence enough to appreciate him! How should she? While I—don't bear his child!'

It was now February. The correspondence had continued altogether for four months; and the next letter from Raye contained incidentally a statement of his position and prospects. He said that in offering to wed her he had, at first, contemplated the step of retiring from a profession which hitherto had brought him very slight emolument, and which, to speak plainly, he had thought might be difficult of practice after his union with her. But the unexpected mines of brightness and warmth that her letters had disclosed to be lurking in her sweet nature had led him to abandon that somewhat sad prospect. He felt sure that, with her powers of development, after a little private training in the social forms of London under his supervision, and a little help from a governess if necessary, she would make as good a professional man's wife as could be desired, even if he should rise to the woolsack. Many a Lord Chancellor's wife had been less intuitively a lady than she had shown herself to be in her lines to him.

'O—poor fellow, poor fellow!' mourned Edith Harnham.

Her distress now raged as high as her infatuation. It was she who had wrought him to this pitch—to a marriage which meant his ruin; yet she could not, in mercy to her maid, do anything to hinder his plan. Anna was coming to Melchester that week, but she could hardly show the girl this last reply from the young man;

it told too much of the second individuality that had usurped the place of the first.

Anna came, and her mistress took her into her own room for privacy. Anna began by saying with some anxiety that she was glad the wedding was so near.

'O Anna!' replied Mrs. Harnham. 'I think we must tell him all—that I have been doing your writing for you?—lest he should not know it till after you become his wife, and it might lead to dissension and recriminations—'

'O mis'ess, dear mis'ess—please don't tell him now!' cried Anna in distress. 'If you were to do it, perhaps he would not marry me; and what should I do then? It would be terrible what would come to me! And I am getting on with my writing, too. I have brought with me the copybook you were so good as to give me, and I practise every day, and though it is so, so hard, I shall do it well at last, I believe, if I keep on trying.'

Edith looked at the copybook. The copies had been set by herself, and such progress as the girl had made was in the way of grotesque facsimile of her mistress's hand. But even if Edith's flowing calligraphy were reproduced the inspiration would be another thing.

'You do it so beautifully,' continued Anna, 'and say all that I want to say so much better than I could say it, that I do hope you won't leave me in the lurch just now!'

'Very well,' replied the other. 'But I—but I thought I ought not to go on!'

'Why?'

Her strong desire to confide her sentiments led Edith to answer truly:

'Because of its effect upon me.'

'But it *can't* have any!'

'Why, child?'

'Because you are married already!' said Anna with lucid simplicity.

'Of course it can't,' said her mistress hastily; yet glad, despite her conscience, that two or three outpourings still remained to her. 'But you must concentrate your attention on writing your name as I write it here.'

VI

SOON Raye wrote about the wedding. Having decided to make the best of what he feared was a piece of romantic folly, he had acquired more zest for the grand experiment. He wished the ceremony to be in London, for greater privacy. Edith Harnham would have preferred it at Melchester; Anna was passive. His reasoning prevailed, and Mrs. Harnham threw herself with mournful zeal into the preparations for Anna's departure. In a last desperate feeling that she must at every hazard be in at the death of her dream, and see once again the man who by a species of telepathy had exercised such an influence on her, she offered to go up with Anna and be with her through the ceremony—'to see the end of her,' as her mistress put it with forced gaiety; an offer which the girl gratefully accepted; for she had no other friend capable of playing the part of companion and witness, in the presence of a gentlemanly bridegroom, in such a way as not to hasten an opinion that he had made an irremediable social blunder.

It was a muddy morning in March when Raye alighted from a four-wheel cab at the door of a registry-office in the S.W. district of London, and carefully handed down Anna and her companion Mrs. Harnham. Anna looked attractive in the somewhat fashionable clothes which Mrs. Harnham had helped her to buy, though not quite so attractive as, an innocent child, she had appeared in her country gown on the back of the wooden horse at Melchester Fair.

Mrs. Harnham had come up this morning by an early train, and a young man—a friend of Raye's—having met them at the door, all four entered the registry-office together. Till an hour before this time Raye had never known the wine-merchant's wife, except at that first casual encounter, and in the flutter of the performance before them he had little opportunity for more than a brief acquaintance. The contract of marriage at a registry is soon got through; but somehow, during its progress, Raye discovered a strange and secret gravitation between himself and Anna's friend.

The formalities of the wedding—or rather ratification of a

previous union—being concluded, the four went in one cab to Raye's lodgings, newly taken in a new suburb in preference to a house, the rent of which he could ill afford just then. Here Anna cut the little cake which Raye had bought at a pastrycook's on his way home from Lincoln's Inn the night before. But she did not do much besides. Raye's friend was obliged to depart almost immediately, and when he had left the only ones virtually present were Edith and Raye, who exchanged ideas with much animation. The conversation was indeed theirs only, Anna being as a domestic animal who humbly heard but understood not. Raye seemed startled in awakening to this fact, and began to feel dissatisfied with her inadequacy.

At last, more disappointed than he cared to own, he said, 'Mrs. Harnham, my darling is so flurried that she doesn't know what she is doing or saying. I see that after this event a little quietude will be necessary before she gives tongue to that tender philosophy which she used to treat me to in her letters.'

They had planned to start early that afternoon for Knollsea, to spend the few opening days of their married life there, and as the hour for departure was drawing near Raye asked his wife if she would go to the writing-desk in the next room and scribble a little note to his sister, who had been unable to attend through indisposition, informing her that the ceremony was over, thanking her for her little present, and hoping to know her well now that she was the writer's sister as well as Charles's.

'Say it in the pretty poetical way you know so well how to adopt,' he added, 'for I want you particularly to win her, and both of you to be dear friends.'

Anna looked uneasy, but departed to her task, Raye remaining to talk to their guest. Anna was a long while absent, and her husband suddenly rose and went to her.

He found her still bending over the writing-table, with tears brimming up in her eyes; and he looked down upon the sheet of note-paper with some interest, to discover with what tact she had expressed her goodwill in the delicate circumstances. To his surprise she had progressed but a few lines, in the characters and spelling of a child of eight, and with the ideas of a goose.

'Anna,' he said, staring; 'what's this?'

'It only means—that I can't do it any better!' she answered, through her tears.

'Eh? Nonsense!'

'I can't!' she insisted, with miserable, sobbing hardihood. 'I—I—didn't write those letters, Charles! I only told *her* what to write! And not always that! But I am learning. O so fast, my dear, dear husband! And you'll forgive me, won't you, for not telling you before?' She slid to her knees, abjectly clasped his waist and laid her face against him.

He stood a few moments, raised her, abruptly turned, and shut the door upon her, rejoining Edith in the drawing-room. She saw that something untoward had been discovered, and their eyes remained fixed on each other.

'Do I guess rightly?' he asked, with wan quietude. '*You* were her scribe through all this?'

'It was necessary,' said Edith.

'Did she dictate every word you ever wrote to me?'

'Not every word.'

'In fact, very little?'

'Very little.'

'You wrote a great part of those pages every week from your own conceptions, though in her name!'

'Yes.'

'Perhaps you wrote many of the letters when you were alone, without communication with her?

'I did.'

He turned to the bookcase, and leant with his hand over his face; and Edith, seeing his distress, became white as a sheet.

'You have deceived me—ruined me!' he murmured.

'O, don't say it!' she cried in her anguish, jumping up and putting her hand on his shoulder. 'I can't bear that!'

'Delighting me deceptively! Why did you do it—*why* did you!'

'I began doing it in kindness to her! How could I do otherwise than try to save such a simple girl from misery. But I admit that I continued it for pleasure to myself.'

Raye looked up. 'Why did it give you pleasure?' he asked.

'I must not tell,' said she.

He continued to regard her, and saw that her lips suddenly

began to quiver under his scrutiny, and her eyes to fill and droop. She started aside, and said that she must go to the station to catch the return train: could a cab be called immediately?

But Raye went up to her, and took her unresisting hand. 'Well, to think of such a thing as this!' he said. 'Why, you and I are friends—lovers—devoted lovers—by correspondence!'

'Yes; I suppose.'

'More.'

'More?'

'Plainly more. It is no use blinking that. Legally I have married her—God help us both!—in soul and spirit I have married you, and no other woman in the world!'

'Hush!'

'But I will not hush! Why should you try to disguise the full truth, when you have already owned half of it? Yes, it is between you and me that the bond is—not between me and her! Now I'll say no more. But, O my cruel one, I think I have one claim upon you!'

She did not say what, and he drew her towards him and bent over her. 'If it was all pure invention in those letters,' he said emphatically, 'give me your cheek only. If you meant what you said, let it be lips. It is for the first and last time, remember!'

She put up her mouth, and he kissed her long. 'You forgive me?' she said, crying.

'Yes.'

'But you are ruined!'

'What matter!' he said, shrugging his shoulders. 'It serves me right!'

She withdrew, wiped her eyes, entered and bade good-bye to Anna, who had not expected her to go so soon, and was still wrestling with the letter. Raye followed Edith downstairs, and in three minutes she was in a hansom driving to the Waterloo station.

He went back to his wife. 'Never mind the letter, Anna, to-day,' he said gently. 'Put on your things. We, too, must be off shortly.'

The simple girl, upheld by the sense that she was indeed married, showed her delight at finding that he was as kind as ever after the disclosure. She did not know that before his eyes he beheld as it were a galley, in which he, the fastidious urban, was chained to work for the remainder of his life, with her, the unlettered peasant, chained to his side.

Edith travelled back to Melchester that day with a face that showed the very stupor of grief, her lips still tingling from the desperate pressure of his kiss. The end of her impassioned dream had come. When at dusk she reached the Melchester station her husband was there to meet her, but in his perfunctoriness and her preoccupation they did not see each other, and she went out of the station alone.

She walked mechanically homewards without calling a fly. Entering, she could not bear the silence of the house, and went up in the dark to where Anna had slept, where she remained thinking awhile. She then returned to the drawing-room, and not knowing what she did, crouched down upon the floor.

'I have ruined him!' she kept repeating. 'I have ruined him; because I would not deal treacherously towards her!'

In the course of half an hour a figure opened the door of the apartment.

'Ah—who's that?' she said, starting up, for it was dark.

'Your husband—who should it be?' said the worthy merchant.

'Ah—my husband!—I forgot I had a husband!' she whispered to herself.

'I missed you at the station,' he continued. 'Did you see Anna safely tied up? I hope so, for 'twas time.'

'Yes—Anna is married.'

Simultaneously with Edith's journey home Anna and her husband were sitting at the opposite windows of a second-class carriage which sped along to Knollsea. In his hand was a pocket-book full of creased sheets closely written over. Unfolding them one after another he read them in silence, and sighed.

'What are you doing, dear Charles?' she said timidly from the other window, and drew nearer to him as if he were a god.

'Reading over all those sweet letters to me signed "Anna."' he replied with dreary resignation.